NETfold

NETfold

A NOVEL

GUR SHOMRON

GOLDENWOOD LANE
PUBLISHING

2005

Published by Goldenwood Lane Publishing
www.goldenwoodlane.com

Catalog-in-Publication data for this book is available from the Library of Congress

Designed by The Reference Works, Inc.
Cover Design by Itsik Hazan

ISBN 0-9754991-3-0

First Edition
PRINTED IN THE UNITED STATES OF AMERICA BY TOVA PRESS
05 06 07 08 09 5 4 3 2 1

NETfold

Prologue

NET: Day 1, 13:00

Amos Tipman was tending his NET-garden when the black cone appeared. It took him a while to notice it, as he was immersed in the design of a clump of baobab trees. He delighted in making the long branches intertwine in fantastic patterns, creating an impenetrable network of snakelike loops, over a hundred feet long. Amos found gardening relaxing—nothing better for total concentration before making a major decision. Had he been born a hundred years earlier, he probably would have become a landscape artist and designed golf courses.

He turned on his heel, heading for his house, and froze. He faced a black, metallic object shaped like a cone, which protruded from the ground and ruined half of the orchid bed he had worked on so lovingly. Hundreds of orchid strains that had been painstakingly collected over the past months from every catalog he could find on the NET, were irreparably destroyed.

What the devil is going on here?

He shut his eyes and reopened them. The NET sun was at its zenith, and the surroundings appeared green and quiet as usual. Everything around him looked normal except for that black cone which, according to the rules of the NET, could not be there. The garden and the land around it, all the way to the main road, belonged to his NET site. Nothing could enter without his permission. Well, viruses could enter *any* site, but Amos knew immediately this was no virus! He was an expert on viruses. An expert that the NET authorities were desperately trying to unmask for the last two years.

The black cone towered over Amos. On one side was a shiny doorway, and Amos approached it cautiously. He could see his own reflection in it—a lanky young man dressed in faded jeans and a gray T-shirt, once adorned with some forgotten logo. Behind him stood a green, winged demon with red eyes and curved horns.

A green, winged demon?!

Amos spun around, but he was too late. The demon grabbed him neatly by the neck and squeezed hard. The hand was cold as ice, and Amos stiffened in paralysis.

"Mr. Tipman," said the demon in a gravelly voice, its pointy tail waving back and forth. "Is this virus yours?" It produced a long, purple reptile resembling a six-legged lizard, the NET's representation of Amos' latest virus, and dangled it by its tail in front of his bewildered eyes.

The demon's grip relaxed slightly, and Amos discovered he could make slight sounds.

"Who the devil are—"

The demon shook its head reprovingly.

"Dear, dear," it said. "You shouldn't take that name in vain, you know. Now we'll have to add a charge of blasphemy to your list!"

It reached forward, pushed open the shiny door, and shoved Amos inside, hopping in behind him. The world darkened momentarily, and Amos felt himself falling into a dim pit. Alongside of him hovered the green demon, exposing sharp fangs in a hideous grin.

This can't be happening, he thought desperately. *It can't be real.*

The temperature rose rapidly, and Amos felt his body awash in sweat. The acrid smell of sulfur seared his nostrils. Red lights blinked in the darkness far below, approaching upward at an alarming rate. A few moments later the demon gripped him again by the neck, spread a pair of broad wings and glided swiftly to the ground.

Two demons, one coal-black and the other blood-red, lounged by a large desk at the entrance to a dark cavern. Both held long pitchforks. Clouds of sulfuric smoke belched forth from the cavern, and more red lights glimmered within. There was a wide sign over the cavern, and Amos gagged when he read:

HELL
NORTHERN ENTRANCE
No Way Back

I'm done for, he thought. *Only a miracle can save me now. Where are those darn emergency rescue crews when you really need them?*
EMERGENCY!

Amos' face brightened. He remembered the emergency exit ring on his pinkie, the ring with which he could abort the surf immediately and return to Earth—without, however, any memory of his latest visit to the NET. After thousands of hours of uneventful surfing, he had almost forgotten he wore it.

He smiled nervously.

"Guys, it was a pleasure being your guest, but I have to leave now—"

Amos pressed the ring twice. Nothing happened. He tried again—still nothing. The green demon burst into raucous laughter.

"Can't you read? There is NO way back!" He grabbed Amos' hand, and with a deft twist removed the ring, and tossed it into a garbage can near the entrance to the cavern. "You won't be needing this here. You have been sentenced to Hell!"

"But I haven't done anything wrong," protested Amos. "And I'm entitled to legal representation before you judge me."

"Legal representation—PHOOEY!" fumed the black demon. "We'll get all of them lawyers here, eventually. Maybe you want to get out on bail, ha, ha, ha." He turned to the green demon. "Is this the scumbag that created 'Midsummer Night's Dream'?"

"He is! In the flesh!" The green demon's eyes gleamed wickedly. "This lowlife left unmistakable traces in his coding." It turned to Amos and queried, almost affectionately: "So tell me, my friend, how much money did you manage to stash away with your previous virus?"

"I don't know what you're talking about."

The green demon looked surprised.

"No need to be coy. The 'Midsummer Night's Dream' virus you launched two years ago was a masterpiece. Infiltrating into one out of ten of the world's computers was a stroke of genius. And nobody ever figured out who did it. I salute you!"

Amos was almost tempted to admit his authorship, but checked himself in time.

"I . . . I had nothing to do with that virus."

"I see. And what about this?" The demon showed the lizard again and gave it a vigorous shake. "Confidentially now, you *did* release this little monster a couple of hours ago, didn't you?"

"W-w-what monster?"

"This one. 'Creep' you called it, didn't you? You developed it at the abandoned Better Buy Company's site. Ring a bell?"

"Why no." Amos' voice wavered. "I—"

"Come, come—we admire innovators who design ways to make other people's lives miserable. And you have quite a reputation, don't you?"

Amos' knees were trembling.

"Please, please, let me go. You've got the wrong guy. I never—"

Amos' voice was cut off as the demon's hand blocked his windpipe.

"Is that so?" The green demon turned to the other demons, its voice full of loathing. "He doesn't seem to realize the predicament he's in. Very well. We'll begin at level seven immediately. He'll be—ahh—spilling his guts soon enough."

The red demon seized Amos by the hand, and dragged him effortlessly to the desk. It pressed one of Amos' fingers to a sharp needle protruding from a glass tablet. A drop of blood flowed onto the glass.

"Congratulations! You're accepted!" roared the red demon. "Welcome to damnation!" Then in a crackling voice he continued: "Here comes your ride."

At first, the size of the creature gave Amos the impression of an elephant. Then with growing horror he realized that, standing in the noxious fumes spouting from the cavern and towering way over his head, was a gigantic spider. Gray, bristle-like fuzz covered its body, and its multiple yellow eyes seemed to glare directly at Amos. On its back was a rider, a dark green creature resembling a toad, wearing a black cape and holding a spear.

Amos screamed and tried to retreat from the monstrous creature, but a hairy tentacle lashed out of its mouth and wrapped itself around Amos' waist. Amos was raised high into the air, his legs thrashing wildly. Another tentacle shot out and ripped off all his clothes.

"Level seven," called out the black demon. "We'll come by in a week to see if he's caught on to the idea. Keep the heat at a reasonable level—we need him to sign a confession, and maybe we can make use of him in the white-collar dungeon." He glanced up at the hapless prisoner, and deliberately prodded him in the rear with his pitchfork. Amos squealed as blood started to flow from the tine punctures.

"That'll teach you not to lie," yelled the demon. "You're going to spend a lot of time here, my friend, and the treatment you've had here is the best you'll find in all of Hell. At least for the next hundred years or so . . ."

Part One–Friday

1. Palo Alto, California, Friday, 9:37

The technician in the white uniform stood on the doorstep of the two-story house, while Mrs. Bentley leafed through his work documents.

"We're really sorry to bother you, ma'am," he said, "but this computer upgrade was scheduled with your son two days ago."

"That's odd. Troy usually tells me about such things. Anyway, he's out right now."

"Well, it says here we should do the job in his absence." He pointed halfway down the topmost page. "It won't take more than a couple of hours."

"Two hours?" The slender woman in the elegant suit glanced at the second technician, who was unloading large crates from the truck they had arrived in, and stacking them on the porch. "That seems to be a pretty hefty installation, indeed. Tell me, how much did it cost? There must be thousands of dollars worth in those boxes."

"That's right. But it didn't cost your son a penny. It's the first prize of the Granada Puzzle Open Championship he won."

"Granada? Never heard of it. Are you sure this isn't a mistake?"

The technician stared at her in disbelief.

"No mistake, ma'am. The contest was held in the NET. You should be very proud of your son."

"Oh, that I am." She said. "Still—he should have told me. Come in, please."

The technician assisted his colleague with the boxes, and they both followed Nancy Bentley down the stairs to the basement.

"Troy prefers to live here," apologized Nancy. "This has been his kingdom since he was seven."

The technicians saw an enormous hall, almost the size of a tennis court. A round bed, draped with a coverlet picturing the Milky Way galaxy, stood in the center, and the walls were covered by computers on metal shelves. Below the shelves, on the floor, they noticed several elongated glass containers filled with green liquid. In the farthest corner stood two large metal boxes, which they identified as an advanced cooling system connected to a power supply unit. The entire assembly, including the glass containers, was hooked up to a central computer system situated on the right side of the hall, next to an oversized worktable.

The system's holographic screen affixed to the table lit up as they entered. A three dimensional, life-size image of a tall, thin boy, with a long face crowned by a mop of black curls appeared before them. His feet were bare, and he wore the white robes and black belt of a karate enthusiast. His green eyes glowed.

"Welcome, dear technicians," said the boy in a quiet voice. "This is a recording, of course. My name is Troy Bentley, and I regret that I cannot be with you at the moment. I have prepared detailed instructions for you regarding the placement of each component."

A green dragon appeared from the back of the holographic screen, carrying a large paper scroll under its arm. It spread the scroll for the technicians to read.

"If you have any questions," continued the lad, "please ask the computer system. It is very familiar with the configuration, and can provide any information you need. If doubt still remains, please leave the components on the floor, and I shall assemble them myself. Thank you, and have a nice day."

"Oh, wow!" breathed the taller of the technicians, nudging his companion. "He really was prepared for our visit, wasn't he?" He studied the instructions on the scroll, still held by the green dragon. "These seem detailed enough and very clear. Quite a good job!" His gaze turned to Mrs. Bentley who made no attempt to conceal her pride. "If your son ever needs a job as a computer technician, make sure he asks us first."

She accepted the compliment with a contented smile, but did not reply.

The technicians scanned the various computers that covered the walls.

"I've never seen such a sophisticated system, not even in large companies," muttered the tall one.

"How old is Troy, Mrs. Bentley?" inquired his colleague.

"He turned fifteen just two weeks ago."

"Quite an impressive computer system for one so young. Did you buy him all of it?"

"Oh, no. Not at all. His father got him a basic set and a surfing helmet when he was seven. He either bought or built everything else."

"Amazing! And those containers with the greenish fluid—are they part of the computer system, too?"

"I really can't say what's connected to what," shrugged Nancy. "Quite frankly, it's over my head. Troy is a chemistry buff, and takes bio-cybernetics at Stanford. Perhaps these are part of his experiments . . ."

"Well, I would very much like to meet this young man," said the tall technician. "However, we still have a lot of work to do now. Dragon," the technician grinned and winked at his partner, "zoom in so we can see the instructions clearer."

He was quite astonished when the dragon complied promptly. The two men stared at each other, shrugged, and went to work.

* * *

When Troy Bentley entered his room, the technicians were long gone. A green dragon sprang from the back of the holographic screen waving its human-like hands in excitement.

"Troy, Troy, I've been upgraded today! A new Xentium Cyber-5 processor, and a—"

"Let me guess, Flint." Troy sat on the chair by the main computer, dropped his schoolbag on the table next to his surfing helmet, and eased off his shoes. With two deft kicks he tossed them into a corner of the room. "Someone gave you a birthday present."

"No, of course not. It's a contest prize! They also put in a brand new—"

"Contest? No kidding. You wouldn't, by any chance, mean the Granada Puzzle Opens held in the NET two weeks ago, would you?"

"Right. That's the one. I also received three hundred penta RAM—"

"Now isn't that one heck of a coincidence, Flint? Mom has just informed me that *I* won the Granada contest. And the funny thing is that I don't remember even entering, let alone participating." Troy gazed up at the ceiling in deep concentration. "I wonder if . . . Nah, you'd never do anything so stupid."

A puff of golden smoke emerged from the dragon's left nostril, and became a chalice engraved with the words 'Troy Bentley—First Prize.'

"I really had no choice," it said as the smoky image slowly dispersed. "You weren't around, and I needed an address to send the prize, so I entered in your name. You needn't worry," he added hastily, seeing Troy's face darken. "I was your spittin' image. No one could have known it wasn't you in person. Hey, cheer up—I also got a new hyper-channel. We can beat the pants off the IRS computers—"

"So you had no choice, eh? What about those technicians? Another trivial matter I shouldn't be bothered with?"

"I was about to—"

Troy slammed his hand on the table so hard that the dragon jumped and let out a squeak.

"That's enough, you oversized reptile! You're completely missing the point. I don't give a hoot about the IRS computers or that my own mother couldn't tell us apart." He pointed an admonishing finger at the dragon on the screen. "Now listen carefully, because I really don't want to repeat this ever again."

The dragon sat down on an imaginary chair and lowered its head almost to the floor. Wide eyes gazed worriedly at the curly-haired youth before him.

"Messing with the IRS computers is illegal. Impersonating me is illegal. And even leaving assembly instructions for the technicians is, at best, questionable when you use my image."

"Umm, yes, I meant to tell you about that. I thought—"

"Flint, I know you mean well, but telling me doesn't make it legal." Troy stood up and started to pace the room. The dragon brightened a bit, and straightened up in its non-existent chair.

"Troy, that prize was worth twenty thousand—"

"Flint, Flint, Flint. Big brain, little common sense. What am I going to do with you?" Troy extracted a Granola bar from a pocket, and began to munch on it. The dragon produced a yellow banana out of nowhere, and proceeded to eat it, peel and all. Troy was not impressed. "Listen to me, you rusty old tin can, you. You are never to impersonate me again, never. Got it?"

Flint nodded.

"What if they checked and found out that I was at school and at the competition at the same time? I'd be expelled!"

The dragon looked offended.

"Troy, nobody can catch us, trust me." It looked backward as if to verify nobody was listening from inside the screen. "I'm quite familiar with those rusty computer systems down there and they couldn't, pardon the expression, catch a cold."

"Fliiiint—"

"All right, all right. I promise not to impersonate you again without your permission. Cross my tail and hope to be short-circuited!" The dragon slung its tail backward over its shoulder and brought the tip forward to form a crude X. "Topic switch. Anything interesting happen at school today?"

Troy let out a long breath.

"Boring . . ."

Without warning Troy shot his leg in a sudden attack move toward the screen. The dragon raised its tail in defense, and delivered a mock blow toward Troy with its right hand. The boy nodded approvingly. "Karate saved the day. Three hours of advanced training. Getting ready for the regional preliminaries in two weeks. Apart from that—just a tedious lesson on econo-inter-relationships. "

"Yuk."

"My sentiments exactly." Troy plopped himself back into his chair. "First chance I got, I escaped to the library—"

He reached into his schoolbag and fished out three coin-like objects.

"—and I got you these! Brand new research memory buttons to feed a hungry computer. With the latest innovations on bio-memory, including three new patents!" Troy inserted the buttons into a slot in the computer's side. He saw the shining face of the dragon and added: "Hold your horses.

The patents haven't been published yet; they're just the summaries."

"Gee, Troy, thanks." The contents of the buttons appeared behind the dragon, which turned around to face the text, and commenced reading. "You needn't worry about the missing data. The computer at the patent office is an old friend of mine, and I'll get anything I need from it. Hey, lookee here, somebody has managed to make superconductor material out of—"

"Hello there! Do you mind facing me when you talk to me?" The dragon pivoted toward him on an imaginary swivel and gazed at Troy with child-like innocence.

"Flint—my instructions are still echoing in this room and you're already ignoring them! You bag-of-bugs—don't you know that breaking into any computer is a violation of the main computer laws?"

"I never—"

"If the authorities find out, I could go to jail. And you'd be shut down. For good!"

"Okay. Okay. I get the message." The dragon lifted its right hand. "I swear that I shall henceforth refrain from intruding into other computers. But listen, Troy, it's no violation if these computers volunteer the information. Right?"

Troy couldn't contain himself any longer and burst out laughing. "Only if you didn't force yourself into them, you rascal."

The dragon nodded its head gravely.

"And as we're on the topic of your independent escapades," continued Troy. "I've noticed that recently you've been unusually busy in all kinds of projects I know nothing about. You wouldn't, by any chance, be doing something I wouldn't approve of? Or playing some sort of game?"

Troy knew that it was impossible for Flint not to answer him. The computer's internal logical structure imposed on Flint the need to answer Troy truthfully at all times. However, Troy found out that there were a number of ways to tell the truth, and that Flint had mastered them all.

"I don't play games," said Flint, with a dignified air. "I'm a professional computer. My research is of a very serious nature."

"Research? Are we enrolled in some university without my knowing it?"

"Heaven forbid! This research is something I've been doing on my own."

"Have you, now? Well, whaddaya know! What's it about?"

Flint, seated in mid air, fidgeted nervously.

"It's about the NET laws and I'm just about to wrap it up. I'll let you know the moment I have my final results."

"You'll let me know here and now, my fine scaly friend! Everything." Troy waved his hand nonchalantly. "You may proceed."

"Hrrumph! Well, all right, I was just about done, anyway. I am researching Markovitch's theory on time contraction in the NET."

Time contraction in the NET was one of the two major breakthroughs of the twenty-first century. In the early nineteen hundreds, Albert Einstein postulated that time was a relative dimension, and could change from system to system. His discovery was that time contracted as velocity increased. However, in contrast to his other discovery—the equivalence of mass and energy, which became the cornerstone of nuclear physics—no practical use for the contraction of time was found until nearly a hundred years after his death.

It was about then that Theodore Markovitch developed his principles for surfing in a virtual world that moved at close to the speed of light in relation to the real world. Consequently, time in that virtual world would advance much faster than on Earth. Theodore, then twenty-eight years old and a full professor at MIT, won international acclaim for his achievement.

The second significant breakthrough of the twenty-first century was the invention of the surfing helmet, thus putting the time contraction principle into practical usage. The helmet connected directly into the nervous system of the surfer's brain, and produced an exact copy of the surfer within the NET. While the surfer himself remained immobile and unconscious in his seat on Earth, his duplicate—accurate down to the minutest detail, from the tiniest scratch to a full memory and self-awareness—moved around in the NET.

The implementation of the Markovitch theories brought about a substantial acceleration of time in the NET (currently twenty-four times the rate of time on Earth). The surfer could experience the elapse of several hours in the NET, whereas on Earth only minutes would have gone by. Upon returning to Earth, the helmet would update the surfer's brain with everything that his clone in the NET had experienced.

This was not the old way of viewing a scene through your monitor—this was the literal participation of the surfer in a different world. And that made the NET the most important learning aid on the planet. You could don your helmet, enter the NET, study for hours on end, and return to Earth only a few minutes older, with all the information retained in your memory.

"Why would you want to research that theory?" wondered Troy. "It evidently works. We've been living with the NET for the past thirty years because of the validity of the theory. Did I miss something?"

"Well, you could put it that way. You may remember that there is a section of the theory regarding the marginal cases, those extreme values that even the great Markovitch admitted that he couldn't explain." The wall behind the dragon in the hologram displayed a long series of mathematical equations. "The theory predicts the creation of gaps in time, or 'time folds' as Markovitch dubbed them, at the points of discontinuity in these equations." Flint's tail waved toward the inscribed wall behind him.

"Yes, I remember. But nobody has proved whether or not this prediction was valid."

"Not until now!" Flint beamed, and drew himself up to his full height. "But *I* found a way to prove that the theory is correct, and the prediction is valid."

Troy's eyes widened in astonishment, as the significance of Flint's statement caught up with his understanding. For a few seconds he was speechless.

"You—you have succeeded in proving the existence of Markovitch's time folds?" He sank heavily into the computer chair, and pushed his face up close to the holographic screen. The dragon diplomatically stepped back two paces.

"Is this some kind of joke?" he whispered.

The dragon shook off its posturing. "No. No way."

Troy stared at the ceiling, allowing himself a few more seconds to digest this new revelation. His gaze returned to the dragon, which was waiting patiently.

"You're absolutely positive? A sure-fire, mathematically solid proof?"

"As solid as reinforced concrete." The formulae on the wall behind Flint now appeared to be etched in stone.

Troy rose slowly to his feet. His arms waved in the air in disbelief, as he tried to make sense of what he had just learned. He paced first in one direction, then in another, his long curls flapping about his head. Flint had never, ever, made a mistake where mathematical calculations were concerned—he was, after all, on a par with the most powerful computers in the world. But this time it was not an issue of a master chess move or proving a geometrical theorem. This time he was dealing with *the* Markovitch Equations—the greatest scientific breakthrough in recent history. He had to ascertain that the dragon knew what it was talking about.

Abruptly he seated himself in front of the hologram once more, his nose almost touching the three dimensional screen.

"You're not going to make us the laughing stock of the scientific world, are you, Flint? You haven't missed out on a stupid decimal point or something? You've checked and rechecked, haven't you? And you're certain—absolutely, one hundred percent certain?"

"One hundred and one percent certain!" assured the dragon coolly, folding its arms. "As certain as one and one are two, and that $E=MC^2$."

Troy stared at the dragon for a few more seconds. Flint had a look of dignified confidence.

It finally sank into Troy's consciousness that he and his computer were about to rock the foundations of the scientific world. He jumped from his chair, spread both arms to the sides and, humming a Greek tune, executed a few dance steps. A grin spread on his face from ear to ear.

"They always claimed that this proof was beyond human ability!" he said joyfully. "You proved them right!"

In the hologram, the dragon stood on its head, puffing green smoke rings out of its nostrils. The rings became a chain of hundred dollar bills linked into each other, which separated and formed the words: NOBEL PRIZE. The bills rose and disappeared over the top edge of the screen.

Troy cut short his dance, and bowed deeply toward the screen, doffing an imaginary hat.

"Chapeau, Flint. And congratulations. This is truly worthy of the Nobel Prize, and if we win it, we'll use it to expand your systems. Now—try to give me an overview of your proof. And please use simple terms to begin with."

The dragon was back on its feet. "Okay. In simple terms, I found a place on the NET that I believe is a time fold. These probability equations," it pointed with its tail, "predicted the fold's location, and I visited the place about five hours ago. There is, indeed, something odd out there that could very well be the fold. Would you like to come out there with me?"

"Hmm . . . No. I don't think so."

Flint shrank back in astonishment, raising his brows in disbelief. Troy burst into laughter.

"Of course I'm coming, you ingenious reptile. Why are you still standing there? To my site! Now! Were surfing."

2. SAN FRANCISCO, FRIDAY, 14:10

"Okay! I've seen enough!"

Norman Starr, Director of Babel, the Security Unit of the NET, addressed George Boder, seated on the other side of his desk. He gave a final disgusted look at the screen, which showed Amos Tipman desperately struggling to extricate himself from a pool of fetid quicksand, and shut off the projector.

"I don't see any point in wasting another Earth hour on these horrors. If I want any further details, I'll examine them in the NET. Whew—that looked like a commercial for Hell!"

His fingers danced expertly over his personal computer's input pad. Babel was a small, elite unit, formed by the National Security Council of the USA. The pride of the unit was its Virus Detection Department, which consisted of just twenty software specialists. However, each of these specialists was an expert of the highest level, and any commercial company would have gladly paid a salary several times higher than Babel's to get one of them in their employ. The other fifty Babel employees comprised Babel's Mission Force, carefully selected combatants pledged to apprehend anyone suspected of authoring viruses or jeopardizing security, both in the NET and on the Earth. Since its inception, some ten Earth years earlier, Babel had successfully neutralized every single virus launched in the NET within forty-eight hours of its detection. They had also arrested all but two of the one hundred and thirty-four authors of these viruses.

Norman Starr entered a final comment into his computer, and turned to the broad-shouldered man with the brush-like crew cut seated opposite him.

"George, in the future please give me some background material *before* showing me such footage." He leaned forward with a grimace of distaste. "I gathered from the scene with the spiders that he was the author of 'Midsummer Night's Dream.' And through his screaming in the boiling water episode I thought he said something about a new virus we know nothing about. Do we have more accurate details on these viruses?"

"Yes, of course," replied George hastily. He was a veteran Babel agent, specializing in field jobs and intelligence. "Tipman confessed to both of them. He even listed his profits from the first virus, but I don't suppose his confession would be admissible in a court of law."

"No, it wouldn't. Not after seeing the methods by which it was obtained. Anyway, there's enough in there to convict him even without a confession. We can disconnect him permanently from the NET, which will eliminate any threat he could pose. Furthermore, by the looks of him, he's been driven nearly out of his mind, and my guess is that he'll spend the rest of his days incarcerated somewhere. Now, tell me how you got wind of this hacker."

"Quite frankly, we didn't. We weren't even aware that there was a new virus in the NET." With a dark frown on his face, George rose and started pacing about in the spacious room. "The bastard's name is Amos Tipman, as you may have gleaned from the screams off that recording. We had never come across him before. He wasn't even on the suspect list. His parents called the NET Customer Service Center this morning at around eleven. They were hysterical. They claimed that their son was connected to the NET since yesterday evening, and that he was all contorted. The center has instructions to alert us immediately if they have even the remotest suspicion that a virus may be involved. I happened to take the call, and I sent a team to the Tipman home. They disconnected the poor sucker's helmet without causing him any brain damage, and then took him to our special clinic at Stanford. When his condition stabilized, we performed a memory reconstruction—parts of which you've just seen. It turns out that he was confined for about ten Earth hours in a site called—so help me—Hell. Ten Earth hours mean ten NET days!"

"And have you found out who's responsible for all this?"

"No, not yet," grumbled George. Then his face broke into a queer smile. "But whoever it is, he sure knows his Dante. And he threw in a few additional ideas of his own, no less impressive. I'd say that the tortures inflicted on

Tipman are beyond human endurance. We tried to wake him a few times for interrogation, but every time we did, he went berserk, and fought us tooth and nail. We had to tie him down and sedate him. Oh, yes, indeed!" The strange smile widened. "I would *very* much like to find out who did this to him."

"So what have you done to track down this creative arch-hacker?"

"We practically ransacked Tipman's home site in search of evidence of any kind. Nothing. There is no site in the NET named Hell. We have over two hundred hours of recorded Tipman memories, but none of the characters in those memories was ever in the NET. Here's the clincher, though—that 'creative arch-hacker', as you call him, intercepted and destroyed Tipman's new virus. Leaving no traces, of course."

"I'm very relieved," said Norman sarcastically, "that we have private citizens engaged in helping us to combat viruses. I cannot say, however, that I approve of their methods. Tomorrow they could catch an innocent surfer and torture him, too."

He got up, pressed his palms on the desktop, and addressed George directly.

"I want a mapping of every suspect site in the NET. I want an analysis of all the activity in the vicinity of Tipman's home site. When he recovers—" he caught himself, "*if* he recovers, get information from him. Find out if he divulged his plans to anyone, or if he has any idea who could have done this to him." Norman's jaw locked tight. "This case gets top priority," he muttered. "Brief me on the results tomorrow morning!"

George straightened up and answered "Yes, sir! All the way behind you to Hell and back, sir!" He turned and left the room.

3. NET: Day 14, 8:00

Troy donned his surfing helmet, set it to a maximum surf time of ten Earth minutes, and hit the Connect button. There was total darkness for a fraction of a second, and he found himself in the entry room of his home site.

Troy was dressed in his trekking outfit, shirt and slacks made of thick beige fabric, and brown hiking boots. What a surfer wore when he entered the NET was entirely up to him, and Troy had chosen this outfit as appropriate for the forthcoming trip with Flint.

The entry room itself was nondescript. As in all entry rooms in the NET, the jump panel was fixed to one wall. It served as a Transport Box, and it enabled Troy to jump to any other Transport Box he selected in the NET, or to return to Earth by pressing the Return button. The only other features in the room were a wardrobe, which contained other items of clothing that Troy had purchased during his numerous surfs, and the front door. Beyond the entry room, through the front door, was the rest of Troy's home site—a neat, four-room cottage with a surrounding garden.

A grinning green dragon was waiting for him at the site. It was a couple of feet taller than Troy, had two short horns sprouting above its eyes, and sported a green horse-like mane running from between the horns halfway down its back. Its elongated body was covered with horny plates resembling large armadillo scales, ending with a long, pointy tail. It stood on two sturdy hind legs, and two humanoid arms, complete with hands having six fingers each, grew out of its torso. Two large wings lay folded on its back, and a large, computer-operated telescope was slung over its neck. It was Flint, fully prepared for the excursion.

"This is going to be one of our clandestine jaunts," said Flint. "We don't want the authorities tracking us, do we? I noticed you set your surfing time to four NET hours only, so we'll have to hurry. Are you ready?"

"I'm ready."

Flint pressed a tiny knob on the wall, and the wardrobe slid to one side to reveal a doorway. A doorway that was not registered anywhere in the NET.

Normally, every surfer in the NET was monitored, from the moment he entered until the moment he returned to Earth. When your application for a site in the NET was approved by the administration, you received a basic site as your first location upon entering the NET—your entry room, with its jump panel and wardrobe. The room had one door, which led into the world of the NET.

From the outside, your basic site looked like a square, windowless shack with a door—that was all. The Netville address, where your site (or shack) was located, was predetermined when you applied for it, and you could have a site situated at a better location if you could afford it. You could also decide to reconstruct your site as a villa in the suburbs, or a penthouse in downtown Netville, or anything else you preferred—again, if you could afford it.

The moment you walked out through the entry room's door, you were monitored. It didn't matter whether you walked into another room of your site, or out into the open—your motions were tracked. At any point in time, the NET Control Center could pinpoint your location.

Flint had managed to bypass the monitoring system by installing a second door, concealed behind the wardrobe. Technically, this did not violate any of the NET laws—according to the NET experts, such a door was theoretically impossible to construct.

The two illicit surfers went through this second door into to a dark, hollowed out corridor, which led into the NET underground maintenance tunnels. The wardrobe door slid silently shut behind them. Hidden in the maintenance tunnel was a portable Transport Box, another of Flint's developments, which allowed the user to shorten distances within the NET.

You could get from one place in the NET to another by using normal means, such as walking, driving or taking the train. However, Transport Boxes allowed you to cover distances in almost no time at all. The NET authorities installed these Transport Boxes throughout Netville, the NET's only city, as a public service. You could enter any Box, select a destination Box, and be transported there instantly.

Normal life in Netville would be impossible without Transport Boxes. The city was immense, covering an area half the size of Australia. The public Transport Boxes were situated at major street intersections and in public institutions. Many shopping centers, as well as theaters, restaurants and other business, also had Transport Boxes installed, at their own expense, as part of their customer service.

Flint had devised a modification to the Transport Box standard. His portable Box allowed its user to arrive at any coordinate sets in the NET, even if no Transport Box existed at that point. The Box transported itself to the same destination, where it could be used again.

The dragon and the boy entered the portable Transport Box, and shut the door behind them. Flint keyed in a sequence of numbers into the control panel, and pressed the Operate button. The lights on the panel flickered briefly. The box's door opened, and they stepped out onto a small, sunken, stone platform, one of many that pitted the face of a steep bluff.

The scenery was rugged. Craggy mountains and deep valleys surrounded them. Below, a red river ran through a narrow canyon. It seethed and frothed, then cascaded down a huge waterfall into a lake, from which the river continued its course.

"Where on earth are we?" asked Troy, drinking in the landscape. "I have never seen anything so surrealistic. Is the time fold here?"

"You meant to ask 'where in the NET'," corrected Flint. "Well, I think that we're practically on the edge. The fold is down there, behind the waterfall. This area is in the random territories, and very far from Netville. When first I came here, I made a few changes to the landscape, just to check whether the authorities would notice my intervention. Apparently, they don't monitor this place, as I didn't hear a peep out of them. You'll notice that there are various kinds of creatures that have developed independently here. NET-accelerated evolution, you know."

Troy knew about the undeveloped regions in the NET, known as the random territories. He had even once visited such a place during a special research trip with a botany class he took at school. But this was the first time he had ever been to a location as remote as where he was now.

When the NET was first brought into being, its architects designed it as similar to the planet Earth as they could. A certain continental area was allocated for a homestead, and the remainder of the planet was allowed to develop randomly. The result was the formation of oceans and continents, atmosphere and climate, mountain ranges, rivers and lakes. Live cells, cloned from Earth, were scattered on land and sea in this initial terrain. These cells had DNA chains representing most of the plant and animal life forms on Earth. The entire planet was then accelerated for two Earth years at the maximum speed ratio allowed by the Markovitch laws—three hundred million to one—aging the planet for approximately six hundred million years. When they finally slowed down the planet to a surf-sustaining speed—two to one—and sent the first surfer scientists to investigate the results, they discovered that the continents were mostly covered by lush vegetation and dense jungles with huge trees of hitherto unknown species. An enormous variety of animals, predators and grazers, were observed, as were countless types of fish and other ocean dwellers. For some unknown reason, no airborne creatures, birds or insects, were found, and it was assumed that those particular genes had died out in the early evolutionary stages. However, this did not seem to have a profound effect on the overall ecosystem.

Thenceforth, the majority of the planet was left to its own devices. All the resources were poured into the area pre-ordained for human settlement. A gigantic city, Netville, was built—replete with services and institutions to support the hundreds of millions of surfers who spent most of their time there. The rest of the planet, the random territories, were out of bounds to all surfers—the only ones permitted there being researchers specializing in NET zoology and botany.

"Flint, I'd like to look around a bit before examining the fold," said Troy. "This place is fascinating. Could I have the 'scope, please?"

Troy took the telescope that Flint unhooked from his neck, and pointed it at the valley below. The telescope's screen displayed the red river emanating from the lake at the foot of the waterfall. Troy rotated the telescope, and followed the river upstream to the lake itself. Its shores were covered with trees as tall as sequoias, but far thicker in girth, crowned with dense frondescence. Some of the thinner, pliant branches were immersed in the red water, as an elephant would dip its trunk while drinking. Suddenly, one of the branches lashed up from the water, with a long, silvery creature thrashing at its end. The branch bashed the creature a few times against a black rock on the shore and, when it was still, inserted it into a crack in the trunk of the tree. The crack sealed itself, and the branch dipped into the lake again.

"Hey, Flint. Do you know what those creatures down there are? It seems to me that we could have unexpected surprises here. Not that that ever hindered us in the past." Troy affectionately ruffled the dragon's green mane.

"Oh, hadn't I mentioned this before? Yes, there are dangers down around the lake, but we're not going there. We're going to the waterfall." He grasped the telescope and pointed it to the center of the cataract. "See anything odd?"

Troy studied the screen, the red water plummeting down in clear perspective. A thick, misty spray rose from where the fall met the lake. Yes, there was something peculiar about the water, dropping from a height of seventy stories into the small lake below, but he couldn't quite identify what it was. He shook his head, and turned to Flint with a puzzled look.

"It's very hard to see the fold from here, even with this powerful 'scope," said Flint. "It even took me a few seconds to locate the exact spot, and I knew it had to be here. The water arriving at the lake is not the same water swirling in the river above it. There is a delay of a few fractions of a second. As if a couple of frames of a film were missing. Here, in the middle of the falls," he pointed at the screen, "there is a small gap in the flow. A section without any water. Like a director's error, if you get what I mean. But it's not the director's fault. This is where time is warped, the site is cracked, and a fold has appeared."

Troy focused his gaze to where Flint was pointing. Yes, there was something slightly out of the ordinary in the flow of water at that point. If Flint hadn't drawn his attention to it, he would never have noticed the anomaly.

"Yes, I see it now," he said. "Now what?"

"What would you suggest?" asked the dragon innocently.

"I suggest we investigate from a bit closer," Troy said seriously, playing the dragon's game. "If it's all right with you, of course, your green majesty."

"No wisecracks, please. How about going through the falls without getting wet? Something like Moses parting the Red Sea?"

Troy looked hard at the dragon, which stared back angelically, slowly wagging its tail.

"I get it," said Troy finally. "You've got something else up your scales. OK—care to give me a clue?"

Flint indicated with his tail that he wanted Troy to climb on his back.

"Hold on tight to my horns," he said. "It'll be very windy."

Troy mounted Flint's back, his heart beating with excitement, and the dragon launched off the platform and into the air with a strong beat of its wings. It dived straight toward the waterfall, gathering speed by the second.

"Flint, that act back there on the ledge was quite unnecessary!" Troy shouted, trying to overcome the noise of the wind rushing past and the din of the waterfall. "You can tell me—*Hey!* You don't have to break the sound barrier! This isn't a dragon race." He hung on to the horns on Flint's head with all his strength, his legs clutching the dragon's neck, his face stretched in a grimace of mingled delight and fear.

"Hang on—we'll be there in a few seconds," yelled Flint.

The roaring cascade of red water was approaching at breathtaking speed. Troy attempted to discern the narrow gap in the falls, but to no avail.

"Flint, I can't see the gap."

"Neither can I . . . Just kidding. Here we go!"

A split second before they hit the wall of water, Troy saw it. And then they were through, Flint's wings skimming the rush of water above and below them. Behind the falls was a large cavern, and Flint halted his flight in its center. Troy exhaled a sigh of relief, and dismounted.

"Welcome to Flint-land," announced the dragon proudly. "The world's first time fold!"

"There's still time for titles and ego inflation," remarked Troy, studying the rocks around him, though not much light filtered through the opening. Surprisingly, the roar of the waterfall was considerably muted within the cavern. "How can you tell this is the time fold? Do you have any tangible evidence?"

Flint drew an ion-compass from a pocket under his scaly armor. The display showed a flurry of interchanging numbers.

"Very interesting," said Troy, observing the compass' monitor. "I've seen a phenomenon like that before, in our magneto-physics lab at school. The reason for that kind of behavior in the lab was obvious—the lab was entirely shielded from the Earth's gravitational field. But there is no shielding here." Understanding dawned in his eyes.

Flint smiled. "Right you are, Troy. This place is not physically defined, and has no North and South. The compass is trying to locate a magnetic pole, but there aren't any here. We are not on our NET planet—or, at least, we're on the very edge, the limit or brink, of the NET. Rules and laws are different here."

"Wow!" Troy stared at the floor of the cavern, as if to make sure it was solid. "But Flint, if we're off our planet, then what in blazes are we standing on? And this cave—is it also part of the fold? Is there anything beyond it?"

Flint scratched his head with his pointy tail. "Theoretically, there is nothing beyond the fold."

Troy stood with his hands on his hips, regarding his over-confident computer.

"Most distinguished dragon," he said, carefully, "I believe the issue calls for further investigation." He turned his back to the entrance, and rubbed his hands together. "I am going to thoroughly inspect the wall back there. Kindly hand me a flashlight." Flint was always equipped with standard hiking paraphernalia.

Troy strode about fifty paces into the rear of the cavern, and shone the flashlight on the rocks before him. He systematically drew the beam of light in a crisscross motion, weaving a pattern that would cover every millimeter of the wall. Flint approached the entrance to the cavern and examined the gap in the waterfall from its inner side.

"Flint! Come here quickly! I've found something!" Troy's voice was choked with excitement.

The dragon arrived at his side in a flash.

"Look there! Do you see what I see?"

In the circle of the beam, a small portion of the wall was missing. The breach looked as if a layer of the wall had been removed. Its edges flickered with a weak, grayish light. For a moment, it seemed that the wall was solid rock, and in the next a sliver was missing. It was as if that segment was and wasn't there at the same time.

Flint thumped his tail on the ground, clearly very impressed with the discovery.

"Of course," he exclaimed. "It's the continuation of the fold! I'm just a stupid dragon that forgets to search for such extensions in the surroundings. Well done, Troy—this is really something! However, it's still quite likely that behind this wall there's nothing at all. Just as undefined as this crack in the rock . . ."

"You're missing the point, Flint!" cried Troy. "Behind this wall is proof of the validity of Markovitch's theories, no matter what we find there." He inserted a finger into the gap. It was a strange sensation, as if he had put his hand into a container full of steam, but the steam was cold. He quickly pulled his finger out. "There's nothing solid in there, but it doesn't feel like an empty space. How about we dig around a bit and take a look?"

Flint put his head to the fissure and sniffed momentarily. Then he straightened up, and looked directly at Troy.

"I'm going to fetch stuff we can dig with," he said. "I hope you don't mind waiting here." And he leaped through the gap in the waterfall.

Five minutes later he reappeared, and landed gently near Troy. This time he had a knapsack on his back. Shaking off the drops that still clung to him, he removed a large atomic blaster from the knapsack, and handed it to Troy.

"Good heavens, Flint!" Troy burst out. "I spoke about digging, not going to war! This is a highly sophisticated weapon, and you know that weapons are forbidden in the NET."

"Well," said Flint in a complacent tone. "You said you wanted to dig, and nothing removes obstructions better than this little toy. And anyway, officially we're not surfing at all. And besides, we're not exactly in the NET, either. Just think of it as a necessary contribution toward scientific development."

Troy didn't look convinced, but he took hold of the dangerous weapon. He pointed it at the rear wall of the cavern and pulled the trigger. The far end of the cavern disappeared, and a round, black tunnel was revealed. In the distance, far into the tunnel, a dot of light gleamed.

"Well, now, Mr. Future Nobel Prize winner," said Troy, "it seems that there is a hole in your theory—a hole as large as this tunnel. And that light over there clearly indicates that there *is* something on the other side."

4. San Francisco, Friday, 14:20

Norman Starr was immersed in his thoughts as he walked to his office. This entire business about the Hell site stuck in his craw. As Babel's director, he was in charge of the safety of all NET surfers. Now it seemed that someone was challenging Babel's capability to neutralize viruses and capture their authors. Someone was out there doing his job!

How could such a huge site, a fully functional Hell, exist without our knowing of it? he pondered. *Energy consumption alone would necessitate the channeling of enormous resources into that location, wherever it is. And those ugly creatures that we saw there—demons, spiders, snakes—are all illegal. Someone has a secret monster-creating factory in the NET, operating under our very noses . . .*

The case appeared to be completely unreal. Some kind of a nightmare based on a script for some sadistic horror-movie producer.

Sadistic!

The word gave him the answer to a disturbing thought that had bothered him during the viewing.

George! Why did he insist on showing me the entire recording of Tipman's ordeals? He also played it for most of the staff. As if he actually enjoyed it! Norman entered his room and shut the door behind him. *He's a very bright man, but there's something peculiar about him. Good thing I didn't appoint him as my deputy. All these years, and it seems that I still don't know him. Nevertheless, I need to appoint someone to join me in this case, an assistant in this investigation.*

Norman hesitated for a moment, and then hit a short code on the inter-call.

"Calling Lynn," announced the system. The screen that covered half of the wall blinked and a young woman, around thirty, appeared on it. Norman's heart missed a bit. He was never sure whether it was her red glowing hair or her piercing green eyes that made his pulse race every time he saw her. *Relax,* he thought, making an effort to breathe normally.

"Well, how did your visit to Hell go?" Lynn asked, smiling. "Did you notice the part where Tipman offered to work for them?"

"No, but I saw enough. We've got to find the creator of this site, even if we need to visit there in person. I'm expecting this to be one of our tougher cases. In a couple of minutes, I'll be at HQ in the NET, and all subsequent activities will be orchestrated from there. How soon can you join me?"

"Give me five minutes, and I'll be there."

"Better prepare for a stay of a few NET days, Lynn. You might consider having something to eat before surfing. And try to think of how anyone could possibly create a site as large as Hell without setting off a million alarm bells."

He hung up the inter-call and the screen went dark. But his thoughts remained on Lynn Murphy, his 'right hand girl' at the office, and his secret love. Norman had chosen her three years ago from out of hundreds of candidates, all vying for the prestigious job of software engineer and investigator in Babel—the most elite unit on the planet.

Lynn was one of the three finalists to take the entrance examinations. All three had perfect scores—ten successful missions without a single fault. Ten different types of viruses, which they had to identify and destroy within five hours. She had excelled again in the supplementary test, where she was required to improvise ad hoc solutions to varied penetrations into the NET. So did another of the finalists, a young man in his early twenties—in fact his score was slightly higher than hers. However, Norman decided that Lynn had a more mature approach, and that, together with her creativity, were more suited to the unit's needs. He had never admitted, even to himself, that it was her smile that enthralled him from the very first, and that he longed with all his heart that she would be the one to qualify for the job.

Norman brushed aside his reflections, and returned to the problem at hand. Tipman's memory reconstruction contained immense amounts of data. He was confident that somewhere within those hundreds of hours of horrifying testimony, there was a lead to the perpetrator. He put on his surfing helmet, and jumped to his office in the NET.

However, when Lynn arrived, a couple of NET hours later, he was still at square one.

"The only thing we have to go on," he remarked to Lynn as she seated herself in the armchair opposite him, "is the green demon's accent. Og analyzed it, and gave it a 99.75% probability of being Californian. So we're dealing with a local law-breaker. Og hasn't yet completed his analysis of the other demons and creatures in the recording."

Og was the name of the unit's computer system. It packed more power than even the USA weather forecasting computers. The only computing systems mightier than Og were those of the NET's infrastructure, which kept the NET going twenty-four hours a day. Og was connected to these systems, and had direct access to everything that happened in the NET.

"Our unknown author isn't an outlaw yet," responded Lynn. "At this stage he has prevented huge damages to the NET and put a dangerous criminal on ice. Who, incidentally, had already caused previous damage estimated at one billion dollars, and stole about two million for himself. Come to think of it, our vigilante did not even claim the million dollar bounty we offered to anyone who could lead us to the capture of the author of

'Midsummer Night's Dream'." Lynn smiled broadly, indicating she had more than a little respect for the mysterious surfer who tackled NET transgressors.

"Lynn! He penetrated into other people's sites! No matter how crucial it was to stop Amos Tipman, he still broke NET laws. Furthermore, we have our own judicial system in the NET—he can't just take the law into his own hands."

"Okay, okay—don't get so worked up. You're right, of course. Listen, on the way here I had an idea how to catch this Robin Hood." Observing Norman's sour look, she quickly added, "Care to call him anything else? We'll need a code name, I suppose. What's wrong with Robin Hood?"

"Perhaps we could dispense with code names for now," Norman commented diplomatically. "Let's hear your idea."

"I don't believe we'll find any evidence leading to him—his methods are far too sophisticated. To be sure, we'll continue analyzing as much data as we can, but I feel that the only way to catch him is red-handed. While he's doing his thing, you know. I'll whip up a smart virus, harmless but irritating, and launch it into the NET. As we're assuming that he combats viruses, he should get to me pretty darn quick. And when he does, we'll jump him. As he probably has very advanced tools at his disposal, we'd better plan extra carefully, so he won't notice that we've set a trap for him."

"Not a bad idea, to begin with," Norman said. "We could try it out. But it's too dangerous for you. He might erase your memory, or worse—send you to his Hell site. You're already known in the NET, and he'll sense it's a trap. I'll ask Sven Thorensen to write the virus."

Lynn objected. "By the same token, *all* of us here in Babel are known. Especially since—you know . . ."

Norman Starr's face reddened, as he remembered one of the most embarrassing moments of his life. Six months ago, a hacker had broken into Babel's administrative site, copied the names and faces of all the agents he could find, and added them to the FBI's Most Wanted List, which was exposed to all surfers. The hacker, a talented computer student, won a hundred dollar bet for this prank. He was apprehended in a record time of three hours after the deed, and permanently banished from the NET. The security loophole that he had so ingeniously utilized, was also rectified. But the damage was done.

"I'm afraid you're right. We need somebody completely new. Do you remember the name of your rival for the job? The thin Russian boy with the long pigtail who almost took your place here?"

"Leonid Romanov, wasn't it? Sure, I remember him. He was better than I was, and I got the job solely because of you. He seemed very offended when he was turned down. All his particulars are in Og—I'll look them up and get him here."

"No—I'll do that. Actually, I should have hired both of you three years ago. But I didn't have a budget for more than one. Quite a waste, to let such talent go. I was quite surprised he didn't apply again the following year, even though he knew that we would allow him to skip all the preliminary tests." Norman got up and stretched. "Well, I'll get to him next week. Your Robin Hood may suspect something fishy if we launch a new virus so soon after Tipman's. Meanwhile, try other methods of locating him. I can't help thinking that the key lies in finding where he gets his enormous energy resources."

5. NET: Day 14, 08:48

"I don't think that there's a hole in my theory." The dragon defiantly thumped his tail on the ground. He placed both his hands on the surface of the tunnel, which was twice Troy's height in diameter, stuck his head further in, and sniffed around. "The math was flawless. It predicted the coordinates of this place at millimeter precision."

"Too bad that scientists attribute such importance to experimental results, too." Troy stroked the dragon's neck. "You know what? Let's find out where this tunnel leads. The light probably comes from the other end. Why don't you fly around this mountain, and try to enter the tunnel from there? We could meet in the middle."

"All right. But you mustn't enter the tunnel, until I get to the other side. I know exactly where it's supposed to come out, and it'll take me two minutes to get there from the outside. So wait here—and give me back that blaster before you obliterate everything in sight."

Flint took off into the waterfall again. Troy peered into the tunnel, directing his flashlight first to one side, then to the other. It was absolutely symmetrical, and the curved walls were made of a shiny, black substance. Cautiously, he took one step into the tunnel, and at once had an odd sensation. He took another step, and understood what had happened. There was no gravity in the tunnel. His body continued its motion through the tunnel, propelled by his last step. He floated forward for about fifty feet, and then halted himself by sliding his hand on the nearest wall. His legs dangled awkwardly slightly above the tunnel's floor.

A beat of wings came from the entrance.

"Troy—where are you?"

"I'm in the tunnel. You were supposed to come in from the other end. What happened?"

"I checked the mountain and this tunnel does not come out on the other side!" Flint's excited voice echoed inside the tunnel. "Troy—the light we see out there does not originate in our NET. I'll be with you right away."

Flint entered the tunnel with a rush. The absence of gravity took him by surprise, and he rocketed toward Troy.

"Look out!" yelled Troy, but it was too late. Flint collided with him, and they both hurtled along the tunnel toward the light.

Flint reached out, and grabbed Troy's arm.

"Get on my back," he instructed. "We have air here, so I can use my wings. I can brake our progress if it turns out that beyond that light is only oblivion, as predicted by theory."

Troy scrambled into his riding position on the dragon's back. Another few minutes of flight passed, and the light they were approaching became larger and brighter. They saw that it was, in fact, daylight, and that they were looking at a patch of blue sky.

The tunnel ended in a cavern, somewhat larger than the one they had left. Flint spread his wings, and touched down in the center of the cavern. They both noticed that gravity had returned. Troy scramble off the dragon's back, and both, hand in hand, tiptoed their way to the entrance to the cavern. They found themselves on the side of a hill.

"We reached a new world!" exclaimed Flint. "I'm pretty sure we're not in our NET."

Above them was a blue sky, and a vast plain stretched out before them.

Troy gazed at the landscape in amazement. Suddenly he gripped Flint's arm.

"What's that over there on the horizon?"

"Hard to tell from here," grunted Flint. "Looks like buildings to me. Anyway, now I am sure we're not on our planet. Look to your right."

Over to the right shone a large yellow sun, half obscured by the neighboring hills. The sun in the NET was far smaller, though just as bright. Troy noticed that his shadow fell not only to his left, but also straight ahead. He looked back, and saw another, smaller sun, shining brightly white.

"It's another universe!" he breathed. "This discovery is even greater than the time fold. Where's that 'scope?"

They studied the view before them with the telescope. The buildings were very distant, yet they could discern what looked like a continuous mass of constructions, out of which rose a number of tall pyramids, and one gigantic dome.

Troy felt his heart beating rapidly. His voice came out like a hoarse whisper.

"A city! A real city! Not only have we discovered another universe—but a new civilization . . ."

"I can't make out any movement in that area," said Flint. "That's a bit odd. I don't see any energy radiation coming from that direction either." Flint had a third 'eye' in the center of his forehead, concealed below the fringe of his mane, which was actually an electromagnetic frequency sensor. It was one of the few add-ons with which Flint had furnished himself, together with the pockets under his scales, and his green mane.

"Maybe the city is uninhabited?" mused Troy. "Let's fly over it and have a look."

He got onto Flint's back again, and they flew swiftly toward the buildings. It took them about thirty minutes to get to the outskirts of the city.

It was of mammoth dimensions, extending in all directions to the horizon. The buildings were attached to each other, without any spaces between them. No streets or roads could be seen. There were a number of different

types of buildings, but they were all made of a glistening, transparent material resembling glass or plastic. The prevalent color was white, but scattered
around were structures of other colors as well—red, green and brown. The
most spectacular edifice was a huge, semispherical dome, which seemed to
dominate the entire city. The other buildings were significantly flatter and
shorter. They had various geometrical shapes—triangles, hexagons,
octagons, and even oval. Every few miles a tall pyramid rose out of the complex of buildings.

They flew slowly over the silent city. Their shadows from both suns, flit-
ting over the buildings, were the only things that stirred. Through the transparent rooftops, they could see strange machines and other indications of a
culture. Flint turned toward the central dome.

"The place seems quite deserted," said Troy. "This is simply astounding!
We've found a treasure that could completely change life on Earth."

"You could easily fit all the skyscrapers in New York City into this
dome," remarked Flint. "And you'd still have space left over for several
small towns. I'd willingly sacrifice ten of my tail scales to know who built
this place. And why they left it."

"Hey, look there, Flint!" Troy shouted suddenly. "I see an opening on the
side of that pyramid on the right. Let's go in there."

Flint dived. They approached the pyramid and saw it was constructed from
huge, football field sized silvery plates, and that one of them was missing.
They entered, and for a brief moment they stopped in amazement, hardly
breathing. The pyramid's interior was hollow, and it extended downward so
far that it was impossible to see the bottom. What they saw from the outside
was just the tip of the proverbial iceberg.

The giant cavity within the pyramid was not empty. Hundreds of strange
machines floated in endless rows—none were attached to the walls.

"There's no gravity here either," commented Flint. "You can dismount
without any fear of falling. But I suggest we stay close to each other—we
wouldn't want to get lost in here, would we? Let's look into that big yellow
machine over there."

The yellow machine resembled a turtle, though it was as large as a blue
whale. It had a convex back, built up of interlocking hexagons. Its floor was
flat, and from it protruded six pods, reminiscent of the head, tail and limbs

of the turtle. Flint flew towards it and Troy, holding on to the dragon's tail, followed him. As they approached, they noticed that the largest pod, the turtles 'head,' was open.

"Would you like to enter?" inquired Flint. "This could have been a vehicle of some sort. Maybe there are more clues inside regarding the culture."

Troy frowned.

"I don't know," he said pensively. "It looks a bit dangerous. Couldn't we just observe it from out here?"

"There's nothing to worry about," reassured Flint. "I can't sense any energy coming from the machine, so there isn't anything alive or moving in there. Besides, I still have the atomic blaster, remember?"

"Okay. Slowly and carefully, please."

They entered the yellow machine. It was hollow, and in its center floated a silvery sphere, twice the height of a man in diameter.

"It seems that the entire machine serves as a storage facility for this shiny ball," said Flint. "I can't make out any features on it, or if there's anything inside it. Nothing more to see here, I'm afraid."

They turned to leave. To their surprise, the opening of the pod through which they had entered, was now shut. Looking around, they saw no other way to exit the machine. They felt a strange heat building up behind them, and on turning, they saw the silver sphere beginning to rotate, and to emit a reddish hue.

"I'm not waiting to find out if this machine is some kind of cannibalistic vegetable," said Flint, and drew out the blaster. "We're getting out of here at once. Troy—get on board and hold tight!"

Troy leaped on the dragon's back. Flint fired at the nearest wall, and half of it disappeared. They flew out of the machine, which slowly spiraled downward in a trail of sizzling sparks.

"Flint, get us out of here before we meet with another surprise."

The dragon had apparently arrived at the same conclusion, and even as Troy spoke, it was accelerating toward the exit. The opening through which they had entered was slowly closing, and the transparent walls were gradually becoming pinkish red.

"Faster, Flint. We'll be trapped!" yelled Troy, but the dragon needed no extra goading.

Flint burst through the opening at high speed, and immediately pitched upward. This abrupt takeoff probably saved their lives, as they barely missed being pulverized by two large, yellow globes that collided right behind them.

The green dragon and his rider looked around. Thousands of similar yellow globes were floating up from buildings all over the city. The globes ascended slowly, like party balloons. Suddenly they began beaming red rays at each other—each globe connecting with every other globe. A loosely knit network of red beams was spreading over the city, but it was tightening by the minute. The rays flashed past them in all directions, and one of them hit Flint's left big toe. A portion of the toe was sliced off, and Flint roared in pain.

"It's a defense mechanism," he bellowed. "These rays are powerful laser beams. Hang on!"

Flint pointed his nose upward and climbed quickly, thrusting vigorously with his large, leathery wings. He zigzagged erratically to avoid the flashing laser beams. Additional yellow globes were emerging from the city. Most of them floated upward leisurely, but the few that rose from the pyramid tips soared upward much quicker, hoisting a tight mesh of beams with them.

Flint put on a final burst of speed, putting more height and distance between them and the city. The higher they rose, the lesser the threat of the beams, though an occasional ray seared past them now and then. Above them spread a net of beams, not yet as dense as below, that connected the highest of the globes.

"Careful, now!" warned Flint. "We're going through the upper net. Shut your eyes and grab a hold of me as hard as you can!"

Troy shut his eyes. He felt a sudden lurch, and his arms were nearly wrenched out of their sockets. He heard Flint yelp in pain again, and felt a sudden swerve to the right, and then upward again. He opened his eyes, and saw that the tip of Flint's tail was missing. The stump was bleeding alarmingly. But they were above the red net. The danger had past.

"Flint, are you all right? Your tail has been clipped."

"Yes, that was close, wasn't it? Good thing it didn't hit my head or chest, or it would be the end of us."

More and more globes were rising from the buildings below. A thick red network now covered the city. It was like a dense fishing net, held aloft by the high-flying yellow globes, as if on poles.

They continued their upward climb. A few minutes later, the net was so close-knit that they could hardly see the buildings under it. The only structure that jutted out of the net was the transparent dome.

"Oh, yes—that was very close indeed!" Troy tried to catch his breath. "I don't even want to think about what would happen if we'd been trapped under the beams down there."

"Maybe we could have crawled out on our bellies or dug a tunnel. But I don't believe that the designers of this place would leave such a simple escape route unguarded." Flint peered down at the thick array of red beams below.

"Those yellow globes operate ingeniously," he muttered, half to himself. "They absorb the energy from an incoming beam, and transmit it in an outgoing one. Hardly any energy is lost. Quite an efficient setup." Aloud he said, "There are even more yellow balloons joining the party. At this rate, in a few minutes not even a fly would be able to pass through that net, without getting fried."

Troy observed the scene, his skin tingling in trepidation.

"I think we should get back to the NET before a new trap takes us by surprise." He felt a profound sensation of regret on having to leave this newly discovered universe, but he knew they had no choice. "Let's see how fast you can fly back to the tunnel."

"Perhaps we could wait a couple of minutes," suggested Flint. "Wouldn't it be interesting to know if there was an end to the number of yellow balls?" He looked at Troy imploringly, as foolhardy as ever where risks were concerned. "And we could also explore what's on the other side of the hill we came through."

"We're not staying here even one minute longer," insisted Troy. "All it would take is one of these yellow balls rising over that hill, and we'd be zapped by a million of those rays before you could say 'oops.' Besides, you've got to tend to your tail. It looks quite nasty."

The dragon didn't argue, and set course for the tunnel. Troy, too, was silent.

Well, we left this new world rather hastily, thought Troy. *But it's not going anywhere. We have enough time to absorb everything that has happened here, and plan a revisit tomorrow . . .*

6. SEATTLE, FRIDAY, 14:25

The orange warning light on the control panel turned green again. The technician on duty wearily examined, for the third time, the jumble of numbers on the display that indicated the distribution of mass in the NET. It gave figures listed by zone, and compared them with the overall mass of the NET. The figures matched, with a precision of a few pounds, and reflected the total amount of energy utilized in the NET.

She pressed the Report button on the panel in front of her. Her supervisor, an elegant man dressed in white coveralls, appeared on the screen. He was seated in the same subterranean control room as she was, a few hundred feet away from her. The NET Central Control room monitored the NET's entire infrastructure. Hundreds of thousands of super-computers, dispersed all over the world, constantly updated the main NET systems. Every surfer entering or leaving the NET was registered, and each of these transactions was reflected by a change in the quantity of energy in the NET.

"Yes?" said the supervisor curtly.

"It's stabilized again, sir," she announced.

"Probably the same bug we've been seeing the past few weeks. What was the mass discrepancy this time?"

"About six hundred pounds, sir. They disappeared from the NET, and then reappeared shortly after. This time it was in the random territories."

"It's the bug all right," concluded the supervisor. "Previously it was reported from within Netville. Send your report to the Programming Division with a copy to me. The way I understand it, the bug has no effect whatsoever on the NET's normal functioning. The programming guys have been handling this for some time, but they don't seem very excited about it. After all, what are a few hundred pounds compared to the total mass of six hundred trillion billion tons? Quite insignificant, and well within the permissible margin of error. In fact, I wouldn't be surprised if we had mass divergences of several thousand tons . . ."

7. NET: Day 14, 10:00

Troy and Flint flew in silence until they arrived at the tunnel on the hillside. Before entering the cavern, they turned and gave one last farewell look at the city. All they could see was a huge red carpet, with tiny yellow dots sprinkled throughout like sequins. The city itself was completely concealed.

They went through the tunnel and emerged at the other side, through the red waterfall.

"New places have a tendency to be dangerous," observed Flint. "I think I had better return to this place in a few days. Just to see what's happened to the city."

"Flint, the main issue before us is: how dangerous is that place over there to us over here?"

"None at all, I believe," replied Flint. "I think that that city has been deserted for a very long time, thousands—maybe millions—of years. What happened back there was probably an automatic robot defense system kicking in. Its purpose is to defend the city, not to chase invaders. I'm quite convinced that we're safe here."

Troy looked affectionately at the dragon.

"Frankly, I was of the same opinion," he said. "But *I* do not come to conclusions unless I can back them up with hard evidence. As to revisiting that city—well, you're not going to shake me off that easily, super lizard. I'm coming with you again next time."

They flew calmly to the platform, where their adventure had begun. When they arrived, they quickly entered the portable Transport Box, and jumped to Troy's entry room.

"Time to leave the NET now, Flint," said Troy. "See you in the hologram."

He hit the Return button, and they both returned to Earth—Troy to his room in the basement, and Flint to his computer housing.

Troy found himself seated at his worktable, his helmet on his head. Flint appeared as a hologram on the three-dimensional screen. A white bandage covered the tip of his tail. Troy removed the helmet, and shook his head in mock disapproval.

"You can remove the bandage, you old ham—I know you don't need it.

Tell me," and his tone became more businesslike, "are we the only ones to find that time fold? Is it at all possible that someone else discovered it before us?"

"I cannot imagine how anyone else is even capable of getting there," said Flint. "It's located way into the random territories, and the coordinates do not appear in the NET site index. Access is only by aircraft, and only the NET police and Babel have any of those. Even so, it's almost an hour-long flight in over-drive."

"Could we have been followed?"

"No, of course not. Have you forgotten already? We were surfing 'unofficially', so we don't leave any traces in the NET. But consider—even if someone got there by accident, there's no way he'd be able to find the time fold. You've got to know where to look, otherwise it's impossible to find. You can rest assured! *Nobody* is going to stumble over our discovery. Now, if you'll excuse me, I need to back myself up. Call if you need anything."

Troy watched the hologram of the confident dragon fade into nothingness. He leaned back in his chair, remembering how he had met Flint for the first time. Flint had surfed as a large sheep dog, and was following him on one of his walks near the Stanford-net lake.

Troy had just completed building his NET auto-backup model. He did this on his own initiative, and did not inform the Unit for the NET Infrastructure Development, which had to approve every new program, thereby creating endless bureaucratic hurdles. Troy had intended to create a double of himself, which would remain in the computer while he surfed the NET. If he could update the double, in real time, with everything that happened to him while surfing, he would have overcome the problem of memory loss experienced when leaving the NET abnormally. Such an incident was, indeed, quite rare, but it sometimes caused surfers to lose entire days of work. Troy had had such an experience himself when, after cramming for a whole day's lessons in the NET, there was a sudden virus alert, and the authorities abruptly disconnected all the surfers in the Palo Alto region.

Troy was very fond of animals, and especially dogs. But this was the first time that an animal stuck so close to him, as if adopting him. *It must have lost its master somehow,* he thought. No matter which way he turned, there was the dog, right on his heels.

"Why are you following me?" Troy asked in exasperation, not really expecting a reply. Dogs in the NET were categorically devoted to their owners, and as a rule never talked to strangers.

"I . . . me . . . you . . . belong," answered the dog, obviously struggling with the language. "How do? Nice day. Happy eleven."

"How's that again? Eleven what?" Troy halted in mid stride, and looked around. There was nobody nearby—the dog was addressing him. NET laws did not preclude animals from talking, and many surfers taught their pets how to converse, though the process was lengthy and expensive.

"Eleven years. Today. You. Happy born day." The dog smiled, and wagged its tail. It was correct, too. It was Troy's eleventh birthday.

"What have we here, now?" Troy squatted next to the dog, and stroked it behind its ears. "A talking dog that knows my birthday. Thanks for your good wishes. May I know to whom you belong?"

"Belong you. You me plan backup. Not lose Troy in NET crash. Me backup not know what Troy happen. Me leave box, you protecting." Then, as an afterthought, "Arf, arf!"

Troy rose to his feet.

"But you're a dog! I didn't design a dog! I designed a human—I even put in a tiny sample of my own DNA. I need a backup, not a bodyguard." He sounded disappointed, but he was still curious. "So how come you're a dog? And why is your English so . . . so broken?"

The dog began to caper around Troy, darting a few steps away, then returning in a rush to Troy's side standing on its hind legs, and trying to lick Troy's face.

"Perhaps Troy me same look, bow wow." The dog winked and crouched down, his rear end high in the air, his tail wagging energetically.

Does he really think we look alike? Troy gazed at the dog, his eyes wide open in amazement. The dog straightened up and burst into loud laughter, that sounded more like barking. This was the first encounter Troy had with that peculiar sense of humor that made Flint his best friend.

"No scared, just joke. Me can take all shape. Troy even, but brain not. English bad now—learn week speak Shakespeare. Patience. Be okay."

The dog suddenly fell silent, and Troy caught sight of a group of children approaching. They had spotted the dog, and wanted to play with it. The dog joined in the fun, licked their faces, and retrieved the sticks they threw for him to fetch.

"That's a very smart dog," said one of the kids, stroking the dog's head. "I wish my mom would let me have a NET dog like that. What's his name?"

The dog opened its mouth to reply, but Troy beat him to it.

"Down, Flint!" He uttered the first name that popped into his head, and it stuck.

During the four years since that first encounter, they were inseparable partners. Flint lived in the NET, surfing in various guises, and he quickly accumulated prodigious masses of information and knowledge. This, in turn, necessitated the expansion of his computer resources every few months. His English was fluent, and his sense of humor sharpened. His loyalty to Troy was absolute. Despite the fact that his IQ was considerably higher than that of any other creature, his behavior remained that of an eleven-year-old—Troy's age when they first met.

Troy awoke from his reveries, and glanced at the dark screen in front of him. A thousand questions were churning in his head, and he couldn't find a lead to any answers.

That dragon was a bit too eager to disappear when we returned, he thought. *What's so urgent about a backup?*

"Flint, get back here!" he commanded into the air.

The dragon's head peered from the upper right hand corner of the screen. Troy eyed his 'partner' skeptically.

"Listen," began Troy. "I have thought over your conclusions, and I am far from being at ease. It's all very exciting to have contacted another world, but it's also very disturbing. We have discovered a great treasure, but if you remember the old Ali Baba story, *that* treasure was accompanied by forty thieves. So, tell me now—did you notice any other time folds, or irregular phenomena, in the NET?"

"No, I didn't see any other time folds. And just what do you mean by 'irregular phenomena'? There was nothing of importance on the main NET bulletin boards." Flint walked out to the center of the screen, and seated himself on a chair that wasn't there. He did not sound convincing.

"That's it, you overgrown lizard!" Troy stood up impatiently. "I'm in no mood to play Twenty Questions." His voice rose. "You're avoiding the answer. You're waiting for a specific question. Well, here are a few. What illegal deeds have you committed in the NET? Is there anything you haven't told me about yet? Have you been up to some mischief? Answer those for starters. Talk!"

Flint placed his right elbow on his left knee, and rested his great head on his right hand. The main difference between this pose and Rodin's famous statue, The Thinker, besides the absence of something to sit on, was the dragon's tail, which kept scratching its green mane. After a few seconds of silence, he straightened out again, and spoke into the room, avoiding Troy's eyes.

"Do you remember the time when you requested me to handle viruses? It was about two years ago, when that 'Blue Snow' virus destroyed those two articles you wrote. You said then: 'I don't want to see any more viruses in my computer again. Their authors should all go to hell!' Remember? Well, I handled it all right. A few weeks ago, I built a virus-detection system, and with it I managed to prevent the incursion of a pretty sophisticated virus into the NET. It would have caused far more damage than 'Blue Snow.' I even caught the surfer who created the virus."

Troy's eyes lit up.

"No kidding! What did you do with him?"

Flint stared at the floor, and mumbled something.

"I couldn't hear you. Speak up! What did you say you did with him?"

"I punished him. He won't be writing any more viruses." Flint's tail twitched on the floor, and his eyes now scanned the ceiling.

Troy jumped to his feet, a concerned look on his face.

"You punished him? Won't write viruses? What have you done to him? Look me in the eye when you talk to me!"

Flint turned to face Troy, his dragon's face a paragon of pure innocence.

"I sent him to a site named Hell. That's what you wanted me to do, and I must say I heartily agree with you. It's exactly what such criminals deserve—"

"WHAT?!?" Troy's eyes flamed so hotly, that the dragon squirmed. The boy's face was livid, and he choked on the words he wanted to say. "You— you send people to Hell? Have you assumed the role of God in the NET?"

He approached the screen slowly, the fury still radiating from his entire body. Flint paled, and coiled his tail around himself.

"Er . . . but Troy . . . I . . . I returned him to his site—"

"Later! I am honestly tempted to put you in quarantine for a while, you irresponsible collection of bugs!" He poked a finger in Flint's direction. "But I've got to hear the whole story first. Like what the hell is this Hell site! Everything! We're going back to the NET."

Troy donned his helmet again, and took a deep breath. It seemed to calm him somewhat.

"You do not, by any chance, have a site called Paradise in this judicial system of yours?"

Flint lowered his head close to the ground and looked at Troy with his big eyes half shut. He knew it was going to be a long NET day ahead . . .

8. SAN DIEGO, FRIDAY, 15:00

Albert Spindler was in an excellent mood. After six months of hard work on the newest version of MediPlan, the comprehensive medical software had been successfully tested by Gen-Tec. The president of the corporation had followed the final benchmark in person, and did not hide his satisfaction when he shook Al's hand. Al had no doubt that he and his team were about to share a substantial bonus.

"I expect them to give me a raise of six thousand dollars this year," he proudly told his mother. Even though he had completed his studies over five years ago, he still lived with her. "I might even be appointed as project manager, and have ten programmers under me."

Stella Spindler was as proud as her son. She beamed at Albert, the model son every mother dreams of. Since she separated from his father, Al could be counted on to provide her every need. It didn't bother her in the least that at thirty he still lived at home. There was a time for everything.

"I hope you will be, dear," she said. "I'll prepare a special dinner tonight for the two of us. I've bought a real salmon!" Fresh fish were rare and expensive.

Al kissed his mother on the cheek. "I'll be in the NET meanwhile, mommy. I'll be back in a couple of hours."

At last two hours—two whole days in the NET! A long, quiet rest at his site was just the thing he needed right now. He could see how much his trees had grown during his two NET month absence. He could calmly plan his professional future.

For a moment, he considered inviting Carol, his old companion from the university days, to join him. She wasn't really old, about his age, and they'd been together for so long that people thought them inseparable. Carol always found time for him, despite her stringent hours as assistant researcher at Princeton-net. The perfect girlfriend, she always listened to his problems, and could always be relied upon to lend a helping hand or a give a word of advice. She never asked for anything, and was invariably ready to accompany him wherever he went. She insisted, however, on living on the East Coast, far away from his residence—otherwise, he would have married her long ago. If mommy permitted, of course.

He decided to spend his relaxation time alone, and walked into his workroom, where he kept his surfing equipment. He glanced in the mirror, admired his solid frame with a satisfied smirk, shook a lock of black hair from his eyes, and donned the helmet. He pressed the button to enter the NET.

* * *

Stella Spindler heard strange noises from Al's workroom. At first she thought it was a recording of some strange music, perhaps a modern opera. But it was only a matter of seconds before she was sure that someone was crying inside. She stood by the closed door.

"Al?"

The wailing increased in volume. It sounded like a baby crying, only much louder. Hesitantly, she opened the door.

Al was lying on his back on the floor, peering at her with tearful eyes. His hands and feet were raised in the air, as a baby would. The surfing helmet lay on the floor beside him. The crying turned into a happy smile of recognition as she entered the room.

"Ma—ma," he said, waving his limbs energetically. "Ma—ma." There was a strong smell of urine in the air.

"What happened—" Stella didn't finish her question. There was no one to ask. The innocent gaze of the outsized baby before her left no doubt. She slipped to the floor in a dead faint.

9. NET: Day 15, 10:04

Maggie Thorensen was busy preparing her weekly column for *Pythagoras,* Oxford-net's puzzle periodical, when the 'com buzzed. Oxford-net was the NET branch of the prestigious Oxford University on Earth. Most of the NET universities retained their names, and simply added the 'net' suffix to distinguish them from their Earth counterparts. Originally intended as research centers, they expanded rapidly, and became far larger than their parent institutes on Earth, which now served as ceremonious figureheads. At fifteen, Maggie was the youngest contributor on the Oxford-net's editorial stuff.

She saved the article she was working on, and glanced at the little monitor, wondering who could have such a high ranking to be able to penetrate her personal communication system even when it was turned off. Only the NET authorities, to the best of her knowledge, could do that, and even then there had to be extraordinary conditions, such as an emergency or a disaster.

"Yes, what is it?" she answered anxiously. She had to send out her article within ten minutes or she'd miss this week's issue being published today. This call was really ill-timed.

"Hi, Maggie." The screen remained dark, but the voice was familiar. "Good to hear you again. There have been some amazing developments recently, and I need your help. Can you meet me and Flint at GreenCafe in five minutes?"

"Troy! Hey, I'm flabbergasted!" Maggie exhaled in relief. "How on Earth did you manage to contact me when my 'com was off?"

"Never mind that, now. I can't talk over the 'com. I'll explain when we meet. Can you come?"

"I need ten minutes to complete this article. It's five past ten now. We'll meet there at ten twenty, and tell Flint to behave himself. I don't want to be thrown out of there again."

"That wasn't my fault," interjected an excited, though slightly hoarse, voice. "They began—"

"Flint! Eavesdropping again? Get off the line." Troy didn't sound angry. He had requested Flint to contact Maggie, and had naturally assumed that he would not listen in. However, Troy had neglected to specifically instruct him to do so. "OK, Maggie. See you in fifteen minutes."

Maggie lost all interest in her article. She corrected a phrase, deleted the last two lines that were the beginning of a new idea, and dispatched it to the chief editor. The new idea could wait another week, and the subscribers would have to do with what she sent. After all, priorities were priorities!

She had known Troy for over a year, now. It began at the teens puzzle tournament finals in New York. Troy had won, she had been first runner-up, and they had danced the opening waltz at the gala dinner held for the contestants. Since then, they had kept in touch constantly, surfing together to various sites in the NET, often accompanied by Flint, who managed to turn every surf into a memorable occasion.

GreenCafe was one of their favorite haunts. They enjoyed drinking hot choco-net while discussing new puzzle designs to challenge Maggie's fans.

But Troy never needed any help. He and Flint, that wondrous combination of a gifted boy and a super-computer, could solve any problem entirely on their own.

They probably need a woman's viewpoint, she thought, and smiled to herself. She gave a quick brush to her long brown hair, and winked at her image in the mirror. *There's always a soft spot in the hardest of cases.*

Should she change clothes? The tight black jeans she wore looked well on her slim body, and the white blouse accented her blue eyes, even though it was a bit wrinkled. A quick glance at the clock convinced her that there was no time to change. She went to her entry room, and jumped directly to the GreenCafe site.

A long line of customers waited at the entrance, but she told the door attendant that she was expected at a table, and was let in. It wasn't difficult to find the duo in the dimly lit interior. The brown bear in the green suit with the yellow stripes was as conspicuous as a cactus in a tulip bed. She made her way through the crowd at the bar, and joined them at their favorite corner table.

"I got us this table," bragged the bear. "I spoke very politely to the couple who were sitting here, and they graciously departed." Maggie noticed the pained look on Troy's face.

"A request they couldn't refuse, I expect. Hi Troy, hi Flint. I'll have a virgin daiquiri. Could you get me one just as expertly, Flint?"

"They've got netters for that." Flint sounded offended. "I'm not a waiter. I'm a specialist on matters concerning space and computers."

Netters were NET entities that carried out all those menial jobs that surfers wouldn't perform. They were biological robots, identical to humans in appearance, but possessing limited intelligence and the ability to perform certain tasks only. They served as sanitary orderlies, gardeners, mechanics, waiters, drivers, librarians, and hundreds of other odd jobs, which surfers would ordinarily shun. Every netter belonged to the surfer who purchased it, and the owner was responsible for its actions. Every netter had a DNA imprint of its owner, which was used for its identification. A professional netter, such as a car mechanic, could cost several tens of thousands of dollars.

"Maggie, you won't believe—" Troy sounded very intent. But Maggie wasn't quite ready for him yet.

"Flint, please be nice for a change," Maggie batted her eyelashes at him. "You're so respected here. They'll bring you anything you ask for—as long as you stay in your seat and avoid the bar."

She observed the broad smile spreading on the bear's face as he lifted a large paw and waved a waiter over. *He could very well be the cleverest surfer in the world,* she thought, *but he'll always remain a child at heart.*

Maggie met Flint about two weeks after the tournament where she first met Troy. Troy had invited her to visit his new site, which he had just completed. She had entered the coordinates and the private access code that Troy had given her, and walked out of the entry room into the site. A large, brown bear was at the counter of a well-equipped kitchen, slicing pineapples.

"I needed to change my surfing image," said the bear gravely. "The NET authorities are on my heels, claiming I didn't pay my taxes. I'll stay in this disguise until the storm blows over. I hope you don't mind spending your time with a bear instead of a boy."

"Troy?" Maggie was dumbstruck. She rechecked the coordinates she had used—they were correct.

"Flint!" Troy's voice rose from an adjoining room. "I told you to scram when I have company!"

"Yes, Troy." Flint bowed low to Maggie, and offered her a slice of pineapple. "My sixth sense prompts me to take my leave. It was nice meeting you."

"No, wait here a minute." Maggie looked at Troy, who had just burst into the kitchen. "You never told me you had a bear netter with a sense of humor."

"I am not a netter," objected the bear. "I am a computer, and his right hand man."

"More like my left hand," muttered Troy. Aloud he said, "All right, you may stay. We probably couldn't get rid of you, anyway." He looked apologetically at Maggie. "I'm so glad you could make it. I have an idea for a new game which may be suitable for your magazine."

That afternoon was one of the most exciting and amusing experiences Maggie had ever had in the NET. Her original idea, of working with Troy on a new puzzle she had designed for the puzzle competition, and perhaps spending a couple of hours at a nearby café, was completely forgotten. Here she was faced by a scientific marvel, a living, breathing computer, who could think on its own, and with a reservoir of knowledge beyond anything she had hitherto encountered. But most astonishing of all was the fact that the couple before her behaved so nonchalantly about it. They had no intention whatsoever of informing the NET development board.

"Oh, yes—we know it isn't in exact accordance with the NET rules," said Troy. "But there's no law that prohibits computers from surfing in the NET. Academically, there's no difference between Flint and a netter when he's surfing—save for the fact that netters are controlled by the NET infrastructure, and Flint controls himself."

"I've read the entire NET rule book," chimed in Flint. "I'm legit. I can provide an electronic legal opinion to that effect from a computer belonging to a certified lawyer. However, I'm afraid that those meddling bureaucrats would enact new laws if they knew about me. So please don't tell them. How did you do on your hyper-nuclear physics exam?"

"And just how did you know I had an exam yesterday?" Maggie's searing look raised a deep blush from Flint. "What else do you know about me?"

"Only public and open information," said Flint hastily. "You're fifteen years old, and you live in New York. Your father works in the NET security unit. Your mother is a concert pianist, currently on tour in Moscow. You love sculpting in ice, you favorite—"

"I think that's quite enough, Flint!" Troy appeared embarrassed. "The fact that I informed you that Maggie was to be my guest did not entitle you to spy on her. In fact, I don't want you to go gathering intelligence on *any* of my friends. Why don't you just keep on slicing some more fruit, and join us later? We'll be on the patio . . ."

The hubbub inside the coffee shop brought Maggie back to reality. A waitress dressed in green stood by their table, and Flint ordered for Maggie. He also ordered a pineapple cocktail for himself. Maggie settled herself comfortably in her seat.

"All right, Troy," Her attention was finally with him. "What is it? What was so urgent that you had to penetrate my NET communication systems and summon me?"

"We've found a new universe, and we were almost trapped there. We escaped by the skin of our teeth." Troy spoke in a low voice, animated with excitement. He leaned forward on the table, his green eyes aglow. It was obvious that he had made a supreme effort to wait with this news until now. "We are still debating what to do with this discovery. I think we should first close the entrance. There's no way of knowing what—"

"But this universe is deserted, abandoned, empty," interrupted Flint. "There's no danger there." The bear also leaned forward, so that his head was between Troy's and Maggie's. His deep voice was loud, and a few surfers in nearby tables turned to look at them.

"Shh," hushed Maggie. "One at a time." She observed the odd pair in front of her. Anyone else making the declarations she had just heard would qualify for an immediate, free psychoanalytical session. But this was Troy, the puzzle genius, with his trained computer, and both sounded very serious.

"Flint!" hissed Troy. "You may not have noticed, but you're yelling. Now be still, while I tell Maggie the story." The disappointed look on the bear's face was heart breaking. "Oh, all right. You may correct me if I say anything wrong."

The bear raised a paw in silent protest, sighed sorrowfully, and tilted his head to bring his ear far closer than necessary to Troy's mouth.

Troy enthusiastically unraveled their recent adventures. Flint inserted a few comments, mainly inflating his own part in the narrative. A waitress brought their drinks, which they sipped slowly from their frosted glasses.

"So, you see—Flint and I disagree about what to do now," summed up Troy. "But we both agree that the time has come to involve you in the action before we take another step."

Maggie sat in silence for a long moment, taking in the news. Finally, she smiled.

"That was a pretty convincing story, boys. But I hope you don't expect me to believe this fantasy!"

"Of course we do!" exclaimed Flint. "Why ever not?"

"Because, distinguished Mr. Bear, you've played pranks on me before, that's why. At best, I'd say you've stupidly attempted surfing using Randomon, which doesn't do you much credit, to say the least!" Randomon was a drug that caused surfers to feel omnipotent. They would imagine they could fly, lift heavy weights, or become invulnerable. The drug was forbidden in the NET, as it caused brain damage to the surfer.

"Hey, no way!" remonstrated Troy. He took both of Maggie's hands in his own, and looked fixedly into her eyes. "You should know me better by now, Maggie. I would never pull your leg on such a serious issue. And of course, I never use drugs."

Maggie stared deep into his burning eyes. She felt a choking in her throat. She tossed a quick glance at the bear, and was convinced he wasn't trying to trip her up. She leaned back, gently disengaging her hands from Troy's.

"I think this deserves another drink," she said hoarsely, ignoring the half full glass in front of her. "Flint, this time I would appreciate a cup of hot, black coffee, please."

The bear went about her request with his usual efficiency, while Troy awaited her response patiently. The coffee arrived, and Maggie took a quick sip.

"Well, there's the good news side of it," she said at last. She glanced about her, making sure no one was listening, as if concerned that any eavesdropper would consider her quite mad. "Primarily, a first class scientific breakthrough. Not to mention the fact that a new civilization has been discovered, even if it is long extinct." She placed both the palms of her hands on the table, and leaned toward the boy and the bear. "Where is this time fold, and how come no one knows about it?"

"*I* discovered it. I was going over the Markovitch equations—"

"Flint, cut it out!" Troy stopped him in mid sentence, his voice quiet but firm. Other surfers were staring at them. "You're too loud. Let me do the explaining." He returned his attention to Maggie. "The fold is about six thousand miles east of here, in the middle of the random territories. Flint discovered it, and we've managed to open a tunnel. Have you read the Markovitch theories?"

"About three years ago." Maggie was twelve then, and she had decided that that was the age to understand all the principles governing the real world and the NET. She had read all of Einstein's works, the expanded quantum mechanics, and all the Markovitch equations and accelerated motion theories. "I always thought that the time folds were the weakest point in his theories, resulting from the lack of advanced mathematical tools for solving the discontinuity problems."

"The theories are correct—down to the last detail!" butted in the bear again. "The NET contains time folds just as the universe contains black holes. I'm considering the development of the Flint theory for finding—"

"Flint! You're wasting valuable time! Control yourself!" Troy continued with his explanations. "It is very difficult to locate a time fold. First, you've got to know where to look. Second, they may be very small, as was the case we encountered. We don't know why they are where they are. Flint calculated the location of one of them, and we opened up an entrance there. Maybe later we'll find a way to locate all of the time folds if, indeed, more folds exist."

Maggie nodded. So typical of these two. Blasting a wall at the edge of the universe, never considering for a second that a black hole might be right behind it. Or marching unhesitatingly into a foreign world without informing anyone else. She drained her cup of coffee.

"I understand. Now what was that argument between the two of you?"

Troy glanced at the bear for a moment, and then returned to look at Maggie. His hands raked through his hair, combing back his long curls.

"In my opinion we should block up the entrance, and keep it secret," he said slowly. "We'll tell the authorities only that we have found a proof for the time fold aspect of the Markovitch theory, and we'll present Flint's calculations." He hesitated a moment and then added: "That could possibly be Nobel Prize material."

"Oh, it definitely is," said Flint. He was quiet and grave, unlike his usual self. "But they will attempt practical experimentation of my calculations. They'll eventually arrive at the waterfall and the tunnel. You'll have to explain why you chose to hide this information from mankind, why you blocked the passage, and why you didn't report to the authorities the minute you found it. Not only won't you get the Nobel Prize, but your reputation will be tarnished as well. And as if that wasn't enough, they'll find out that we got there by surfing illegally. You might get off with a light sentence, but I'll be shut down for good."

There was a long pause.

"Umm—I guess I'll have to think some more about it," said Troy, somewhat flustered. "The way you put it, there'll be no Nobel Prize. However, I still think the tunnel should be blocked. That alien civilization seems far more advanced than ours, and if they were annihilated by some epidemic, it could reach us via the tunnel."

"That's highly unlikely," retorted the bear. "The epidemic conjecture may have been valid during the middle ages, but not for an advanced race. We've found a treasure—why bury it again? Don't you think it's possible that we could import some of their technology that would bring great benefit to humanity and to the computer world?"

"Just a minute," interjected Maggie. "I'd like to see that tunnel, before you go and block it off. Why don't we go there right now, and then decide whether to wall it up. Flint, can you block off that tunnel at all?"

"Of course I can," boasted the bear. "Hermetically. In a way that only we could pass through. I'm considering a certain type of door at our end of the tunnel that no one will be able to break through, for the simple reason that it would lead nowhere."

"All right," said Troy, and got to his feet. "Let's go there now. We'll observe if the deserted city is still under the cover of its protective rays, and we'll make our decisions there."

Flint stood abruptly, rocking the table with his foot. The half full daiquiri glass tipped over onto Maggie's blouse. She glared reprovingly at the bear.

"Sorry, sorry," it muttered. "The next drink's on me."

She got up, and they walked to the entrance of the café.

"I need five minutes in my site to get organized," said Maggie. "Where'll we meet?"

"My site," said Troy. "Try to hurry."

They approached the Transport Box in the street, near the doorway, and waited patiently in line. Troy and Flint jumped first and Maggie followed them.

Two overgrown, immature children, she mused. *This is the first contact this planet has ever had with a foreign civilization, and the fate of humanity could possibly lie in the hands of these two daredevils . . .*

She shook her head resignedly, punched her selection into the panel, and jumped to her site.

10. NET: Day 15, 11:28

Norman Starr viewed the NET-life of Amos Tipman as it unfolded on the holographic screen in Babel's analysis lab. Amos seemed to be quite a normal chap—talented, but not exceptionally so. The pattern that his life followed was routine for his age group, until the age of fourteen. That was just one year before he unleashed his first virus. Then a marked shift in his pattern was observed. He began to neglect his studies, and severed his ties with the few friends he had.

He secluded himself for twelve months in his NET site, Norman made a mental note as he followed the statistical analysis of Amos' surfing parameters, supplied by the archives from the NET monitoring systems. *Zero visitors to his site, and only two short trips to the local NET store in all these months. This must be the period he composed and launched his virus.*

Norman was an expert on virus authors' profiles. Amos was no different from the rest, except for his initiation into crime—he had entered the scene in one sudden move.

I wonder what caused this switch. It couldn't be connected to that Hell site, as that happened three years later. But we might find other useful information.

The three dimensional chart clearly displayed that only one month after launching the 'Midsummer Night's Dream' virus, Amos came out of his isolation, and began collecting inside information and trading on the NET stock market. Norman knew that as the director of Babel, he should not be scrutinizing Amos' history. That was his staff's job, and it was up to him to manage them, not to do their work. Yet he felt that he had to be the leading figure in locating this unknown Hell operator, this upstart who had challenged his authority and his team of professionals. Deep in his heart, Norman was still the eighteen-year-old prodigy, who gained acclaim by proving that the inter-bank communication code could be broken, though it had been considered impenetrable for over fifty years.

Yes, that was twenty five years ago. But I want my men to feel that I'm still the technological expert I once was, even though I am now a manager. They will appreciate the fact that I'm still capable of locating a suspect—in fact, I could perform any task they could.

But above all, though he would not admit it even to himself, he wanted to impress Lynn.

This might contradict the manager's ethics manual, but I'd be glad to take her out to dinner. Maybe a drink as well. I'm as alone in the NET as this Tipman guy—it would do me good to cut loose for a bit.

Norman was an ideal catch in more ways than one. Tall and athletic, his shock of gray hair gave him a very distinguished and handsome look. He was considered to be a rising star by the NET administration, and some even saw him as the next US Undersecretary for Internal Security, in charge of the entire NET security. His finances were solid, and in perfect order. Were he to retire from Babel, and offer his services to the private business sector, he could easily amass a fortune as a consultant to giant corporations. But the idea never crossed his mind. He was married to Babel. Four years ago his wife, a famous ex-actress and theater producer, divorced him, taking their two children with her.

You practically spend your entire life in the NET, she had said bitterly, after the divorce was ratified. *It'll be no different now, except that you don't have to apologize any more. You can visit the children whenever you feel that you can spare the time.*

A red light started to pulsate at the bottom of the screen, and a soft ring indicated that an emergency call was coming in. Norman brushed his thoughts aside, and accepted the call. A new window opened on his screen, and a young man with Asian features, wearing an immaculate Babel uniform, appeared.

"Sir, there's an emergency situation in the Dunham area. A computer engineer was injured during surfing. Apparently, a major deletion of memory."

Norman looked appreciatingly at Yoshi Hara, one of the younger Babel programmers. He had joined just a few months ago, and he always meticulously groomed his outward appearance, as befitting a descendant of Japanese nobility.

"Who is the victim, and where did he surf from on Earth? Were there any weather disturbances there?"

Yoshi retreated a bit to reveal the task allocations at the Control Center he was operating.

"His name is Albert Spindler, he surfed from San Diego, and the weather there was clear. His mother was injured, too—she fainted, and broke her wrist as she fell. However, when she regained consciousness again, she called the police. They took her to hospital, and now they're asking us what to do with her son. From their description, and from what they understood from the mother, he was abruptly disconnected from the NET, and has been behaving like a baby since then."

"Make sure that one of our units gets to him as soon as possible," ordered Norman. "I want him flown to our closed ward at Stanford Hospital. Report his condition to me the minute he arrives there. And make sure they take a memory reconstruction kit with them and run it on him during the flight. I don't want to lose that half hour in the aircraft."

"Registered," confirmed Yoshi. "I shall report events in real time."

Norman hung up. Amos Tipman's data reappeared on the screen.

Two abnormal events in such close proximity! After such a long time without any serious disturbances. Could this be accidental? A coincidence?

Norman got up and paced the room, stretching his limbs.

No need to call a state of emergency yet. But I need another expert to tackle this new case.

He returned to his desk, and dialed a short code.

"Calling Sven," announced the system. Ten seconds later, the screen showed a tall, light-skinned man with short, blond hair. His blue eyes looked directly at Norman.

"Sven, I need you here immediately. A new and urgent project is coming up." Sven Thorensen was one of Babel's foremost analysts.

"If you could possibly do without me, I'd much prefer it," he said in a quiet voice. "I've taken a day's vacation, and I've made a few plans. But if it's absolutely necessary . . ."

"It is!" said Norman. "I'm afraid we're approaching a state of emergency and I need you here now." He saw the disappointment on Sven's face, and felt obliged to explain. "In the past few hours there have been two serious events, both bizarre, and two surfers were hurt. I suspect we haven't seen the end of it yet. I need you to investigate into the matter. So prepare yourself for a lengthy stay in the NET. At least two weeks."

"I'll need ten minutes on Earth first, if that's possible."

"Okay," said Norman. "Come as soon as you can."

The screen darkened again. He frowned, and then entered another code.

"Calling Lynn," the speakers intoned. Lynn appeared on the screen at once. She had a serious look on her face.

"Have you discovered anything?" she asked before he had a chance to speak.

"Another strange case," said Norman, and he briefly described what happened to Spindler. "I've called in Sven to handle it, but he needs another ten Earth minutes, so we'll see him here in only four hours. There's a slight possibility that there's a connection between these two events, so I'd like you to join the team at the victim's NET site."

"No problem."

"Anything new on your Robin Hood and his Hell?"

"No," said Lynn glumly. "I'm going through the recording, but so far there's nothing. It'll take me a few more hours of this horror show to get a more complete picture."

"Well, if you find nothing more, I suggest you make use of the Queen of the Night. You know what to offer as bait."

"I'd much rather leave that option as a last resort. But I'll keep you informed. Are you expecting additional events?"

"I sincerely hope that the old superstition that events are happening in threes is untrue." Norman's voice was strained. "Two cases are quite enough, but I wouldn't bet on it. I'll let you know of further developments." He hung up, but continued to stare at the screen long after her image disappeared.

Once this is over, I'm taking you out to dinner. Definitely! I may be three years too late, but better late than never!

11. NET: Day 15, 11:32

Maggie's NET site was in downtown Netville, close to the main entertainment centers. It was quite an exclusive location, and cost a bundle, but she had saved a considerable amount from contest winnings, and her parents chipped in with the difference. It was an apartment on the twelfth floor of a hundred-story building, which towered over one of the many commercial centers in Netville. It had three bedrooms, a study, a balcony and a little flower garden. And her entry room, of course. Two concert halls and dozens of high-class restaurants and elite shopping boutiques, were no further than a ten-minute walk.

She removed her trekking outfit from her entry room wardrobe, and put it on. Quickly, she filled her pockets with the various paraphernalia she always carried with her on these occasions: flashlight, infrared glasses, antinausea pills, and a tiny laser knife.

NET laws forbade the use of weapons. The only people allowed to carry arms were the NET police and Babel, and their main personal arms were freezers—devices that would freeze any surfer or netter they were used on. A frozen person could not move, see, hear, or even think, until he was unfrozen—also a feature of the freezer. Other arms included laser pistols, which could amputate a limb, or even kill a NET entity, but these were limited and used only in emergencies. Even Maggie's laser knife—considered a potential weapon even though it had an effective range of only five inches—required a special permit. In her case, usage was limited to ice sculpting, a hobby she had adopted while still very young.

Maggie glanced at the clock—only four minutes had elapsed. She couldn't think of anything else she needed to take with her. From her entry room she selected Troy's site, and jumped.

A smiling green dragon greeted her. The cyber-telescope was slung around its neck.

"I see that the stain on your blouse has disappeared," it remarked.

"Trying to weasel out of your debt, eh?" Maggie bunched her brow into an admonishing frown, as if talking to a very young child. "The stain has been relocated to the laundry hamper. This is another shirt I'm wearing. And you still owe me a drink—dragon or bear, a debt is a debt."

"Let's go," said Troy, interrupting the discussion.

He pressed the hidden knob and the wardrobe slid aside. The maintenance tunnels, a network of underground passages designed to serve the inhabitants of Netville with power and infrastructure maintenance, were cool and dim. They walked to the portable Transport Box, and entered it. Flint keyed in the coordinates, and Maggie felt her heart skip a beat.

Maggie always got excited when they went out on special trips. They hardly ever used the portable Transport Box, and almost always stayed within the limits of Netville. Except for one time, when Troy and Flint invited her to join them on a visit to a remote island in the Green Ocean—the ocean that covered three fourths of the planet's surface, and was saturated with algae that gave the water its color. It was one of the most thrilling trips she had ever made.

The island, no larger than Manhattan, was covered with a dense tropical forest that nearly reached the water's edge. The beach consisted of golden sand, and the sea was crystal clear and smooth as a mirror.

"Flint, didn't you say you had to check up on something in the forest?" Troy had said, after drinking in the glorious view.

"Oh, yes, of course," replied the dragon tactfully. "I need to see whether any changes have occurred since my last visit here. If you get into any trouble, just release this emergency balloon, and I'll be here in a jiffy." Flint tied a helium-filled balloon to a rock, and flew off.

They spent that afternoon swimming and diving, looking for various kinds of fish. They collected a large assortment of oddly shaped shells. It was the first time that the topics of discussion were not puzzles and riddles. Maggie was quite surprised to discover that Troy could converse knowledgeably on other issues as well.

"Yes—of course I've read The Fountainhead," he said. "It absolutely convinced me never to take up architecture as a profession."

"Didn't you enjoy the book?"

"I certainly did," said Troy, and stretched out his lean body on the warm sand. His muscles were well toned from years of karate training. "It's a delightful portrait in black and white. The good guys and the bad guys. I've decided I'd never have to depend on someone else's judgment. The architect's job is to design a building to suit other people, and they would make decisions for him. Even the hero, who built only the way he wanted to, had to satisfy the needs of the people who lived in the building. And above all, there would always be some smart-ass kibitzer, who would be considered the 'know all and be all,' and he would determine what's good and what's bad, what's pretty and what's ugly. No sir—I'll never let anyone else tell me that anything I've done is good. Or not so good. It should speak for itself."

"Aren't you kind of ruling out almost all possible jobs, Troy? You'd never be able to work anywhere. You'll always have a boss, unless you go into business on your own."

"Very true. But if I invent something, like a machine or a wonder drug, it either works or it doesn't. The outsider's opinion doesn't matter if the mathematical formula is correct."

Maggie decided to leave the subject open. There were so many other topics she wanted to discuss with Troy. When Flint returned a couple of hours later, the youngsters wore shell necklaces around their shoulders. Maggie had even prepared one for Flint, and strung it around his broad neck despite his protests . . .

The door of the Transport Box opened, and Maggie found herself on a small platform alongside Troy and the green dragon. She gaped in wonderment at the wild landscape and the red waterfall that dropped into the little lake far below.

"Is that the waterfall you were talking about?" she asked Flint, who was carefully examining the scenery. His eyes darted in all directions, while his third eye focused on the waterfall.

"Yes," he answered, without looking at her. "We're deep inside the random territories of the NET planet. The nearest NET site is about six thousand miles away. The time fold is in the waterfall, about in its middle. Do you see . . . hang on, what's this?"

Flint pointed the 'scope toward the waterfall, and began focusing it cautiously. The screen began glimmering and flashing with blue and purple lights.

"Flint, what's going on? What are those lights?" asked Troy.

"The 'scope is now calibrated to detect short waves. The dark background is the waterfall. The purple lights indicate radiation coming from the falls in our direction. These are very short waves, just about at the limit of this instrument's range. The blue lights indicate radiation coming from our direction toward the falls. I'd say they came from the direction of Netville. You'll notice that after every blue flash there is a purple flash, about two seconds later."

Flint turned to them, his face looking very worried. "Something is broadcasting from the NET to the waterfall, and receiving a response two seconds later."

Troy and Maggie stared at each other. They both realized what Flint was trying to say.

"The NET's been invaded!" they gasped, both together.

Not a sound could be heard on the little platform. The trio stared long and hard at the telescope's screen, as if willing the lights to turn themselves off. The platform shook slightly—Flint, his face troubled, was nervously striking the floor with his tail.

"Come on, Flint," said Troy soothingly, and stroked the dragon's head. "It's not the end of the world. At least not right away." Nobody smiled. The tail thumping stopped, but the look of guilt still remained in the big wet eyes. Troy also felt the butterflies turning his stomach upside down. He continued in a low voice. "You know, from time immemorial the human race has been searching for different cultures and civilizations. This could be the chance to make contact. Anyway, it's out of our hands now. They're in the NET. There's no point in closing the tunnel now."

"You're probably right," agreed Maggie. "It's too late now to consider blocking up the passage. At least, as far as whoever is already in the NET is concerned. How'd we get them out, if we blocked it? All we can hope for is that our 'guests' are friendly. Are you sure you didn't see any living creatures while you were there?"

"No. No living creatures," said Flint somberly. Maggie could have sworn she detected a tone of apprehension in his voice. "But there could have been some that we didn't see. They must have followed us somehow, and found the tunnel."

Maggie thought for a moment.

"You said that you could seal the tunnel in such a way that only you could open it. What would happen to that exchange of signals," she indicated the 'scope screen, "if you did so?"

"The broadcasting would stop, of course," retorted Flint. "When I said 'hermetically,' I meant totally and absolutely. Nothing goes through!"

"And those . . . they will probably come back here to see what's happening, right?"

Troy started to smile.

"You're up to something, Maggie. I know you—you're leading us to a solution, and you're a few steps ahead of us. Come on—tell us what's on your mind."

12. Palo Alto, Friday, 15:30

Adam Bentley tossed his schoolbag into a corner of the room, and hurried to his computer. He noted the time just as he was donning his helmet.

Three thirty in the afternoon! What a stupid waste of time these lessons on Earth are. A week's NET surfing down the drain!

He surfed, and found himself in his own home site. It was the minimum configuration possible—just an entry room with the required jump panel, front door and wardrobe. Adam had added a simple computer with a large, albeit ancient, holographic screen. It rested on a rickety metal table, in front of which stood a red, plastic chair. The only other furniture in the entry room was a shabby couch that Adam took off a friend, who wanted to throw it away after buying new fittings for himself.

I've got to improve the conditions here—hey, it's a real dump. I'm ashamed to invite friends over. Damn, I got no dough—can't even visit the amusement park. It's time to win a money competition real soon. Palo Alto Juvenile Opens, next month? Oh boy, that'd be really cool! Five hundred bucks, first prize. And, hey, Troy isn't in this one, and the others are wusses. Hey, this must work!

Adam was Troy Bentley's younger brother. It was a great honor to be brother to the leader of the Stanford puzzle team, who also happened to be the California champion. But there were drawbacks as well. Adam was a very talented boy himself, but he never won a real, big-money prize in a contest, though he always ranked in one of the first five places. Any other surfer his age with the same achievements would be considered in high esteem, but not him. People anticipated more from him.

Wilders, Shorty here. He sent a message through his NET computer. *Anyone have money, and wants to visit Roller-net?* The Wilders were a small group of Adam's peers, all aged about twelve, who used to surf the NET together. Occasionally, they pooled their resources, and visited Roller-net, the NET's largest amusement park. Adam was not at all surprised when no one answered his call. Most of them were as broke as he was.

Oh, well, it's my turn to tend Tuffy, anyway, he consoled himself. *I'm due there only in two hours, but I'll jump in early this time. Hey, she'll be happy to see me.*

Tuffy was the tetrosaur that Adam raised in his monster bio-genetics course at Gunn-net, his school. Tetrosaurs were land monsters that were kept in isolated locations in the desert surrounding Netville, strongly safe-guarded by high walls. The monsters were raised by schools and universities that specialized in this subject. From time to time tetrosaur battles were held, and these soon became a popular sport in the NET.

Monster raising began when scientists successfully managed to reconstruct the DNA of prehistoric animals in the NET. They brought to life saber-tooth tigers and woolly mammoths, and even succeeded in crossbreeding them, thus creating new monsters—the tetrosaurs. The battles were born as a result of a bet between two research laboratories, each claiming to have created the stronger monster. The first battle, which ended with a victory for the Berkeley-net research team over the Harvard-net team, was a to-the-death duel without any time limits. Later, when the sport gained in popularity, more humane rules were set, thereby saving the lives of the vanquished tetrosaurs. Referees and coaches could stop the fight at any time, by activating the neuro-collar worn by every monster.

Tuffy was a hybrid of giant grizzly bear with an ancient creature resembling an armor-plated anteater. She also sported two rhinoceros-like horns. These and other genetic modifications that Adam and his team had introduced, endowed Tuffy with surprising speed and agility, despite her being covered in full-length armor plating. She was one of the few who survived the corral, a month long period where all twenty tetrosaurs developed by Adam's bio-class were left to their own devices inside a huge enclosure, to test who were the fittest. She and one other monster were chosen to represent Adam's school in battles. Adam was very proud of her.

Adam keyed in the coordinates and hit the Operate button.

"Jump denied," stated the panel monitor. "You cannot arrive at that destination for now. Would you like to jump elsewhere?"

What? Adam stared at the coordinates in disbelief. They were correct. He attempted the jump again, but met with the same result.

It must be a mistake. Someone has revoked my access privileges!

He called the corral. The line was busy for several minutes, but finally a netter answered him, and inquired politely: "Tetrosaur corral. How may I serve you?"

"By recognizing my admission permit, and letting me into the corral, cabbage head. I need to tend to Tuffy."

"Yes sir," said the netter, ignoring Adam's language. "I shall need your ID in order to verify that you are authorized to enter."

"Hey, I'm a monster raiser, you stupid robot," objected Adam hotly, but he gave the netter his ID. The netter excused himself, disappeared, and returned a few seconds later.

"My apologies, but you are not authorized to enter at this stage. All the corrals are closed to outside visitors. Please try again later. May I be of help in any other matter?"

"Yes—get lost!" fumed Adam. He knew that there was nothing he could do. That netter would never let him in. But he had also said that the corrals were closed to outside visitors. This meant that there was no problem with his ID at all, but that something had happened.

He returned to his computer and went directly to Undercurrent, the popular bulletin board.

Shorty reporting that access to tetrosaur corrals is blocked, he typed. *Anyone know why?*

This time he didn't have to wait long. Thirty seconds later, the first reply came through.

Shorty—Babel has invoked a high state of alert in the Dunham area, including the corrals. Rumor has it that there has been a NET accident. Update me if you find out anything more.

The signature belonged to Zelda, a subscriber with a very high tenability rating.

A grin began to spread on Adam's face. *Hey, extraordinary things were happening in the NET.* He felt that this long and dreary weekend would actually wind up being quite interesting.

13. NET: DAY 16, 00:48

"I propose to seal up the entrance to the tunnel on the invader's side," said Maggie, "and prepare another door at our end. When the entrance is sealed, their line of communications will be severed. They'll come here to investigate, and enter the tunnel—and then we shut the second door behind them. They'll be trapped inside."

"A very interesting concept," said Troy. "But why trap them? They haven't done any harm so far. Maybe they have peaceful intentions? Why don't we just cut their radio beam, and when they enter the tunnel, just shut the door behind them? They'll be free to return to their own world."

"I think I get the meaning of Maggie's suggestion," interjected Flint excitedly. "She is one hundred percent right. We must first seal the far side—and fast—in order to prevent additional incursions, which could occur at any moment. That will disconnect the two communicating parties. The doorway at our side must be disguised, and ready for immediate locking. Maggie, I salute you in awe—your idea is brilliant!"

Flint bowed low, lost his balance, and fell over the edge of the platform into the abyss below. A few seconds later he glided back as if nothing had happened, and carefully shook his wings, which did not need shaking.

"Flint, perhaps you could seal the tunnel, instead of the comedy routine?" Troy sounded a bit annoyed. "Do you have whatever equipment you need?"

"Yes, at your site," said Flint, "and I'm going to fetch it now. Wait for me here." He looked down the steep cliff and added, "Not that you have anywhere to go." He got into the Transport Box, and disappeared. The box disappeared with him.

Troy looked particularly troubled, and Maggie guessed what was bothering him.

"I'm sorry, Troy," she said. "Your proposal was very generous, and considerate of the invaders. But the risk is far too great."

"Oh, I understand that all right," whispered Troy. "And yet . . . what a pity. We'll make enemies of them. The first encounter with a foreign civilization, and we trap them. What a missed opportunity."

The Transport Box returned three minutes later. Flint came out with a large knapsack on his back, between his folded wings.

"I've got a lot of work to do down there," he said. "You both stay here and keep your eyes open. If any trouble arises, take the Transport Box and scram!"

"Flint, I may have an idea of how to communicate with the invaders," said Troy. "If you could prepare a third door in the middle of the tunnel, we would have two compartments. We could trap them in their half, and then bring a negotiation team into our half. We'd lock the door on our side behind them, and they would open the middle door and communicate with the invaders, without endangering the NET. Are you following me, Flint?"

"Sounds like an excellent idea," said Flint. "I'll check if it's feasible." He launched himself off the platform, and dived toward the waterfall. Troy, who wanted to say something more, shook his head and peered at the rapidly departing dragon.

"He's so impulsive when he's on a new task," he said apologetically to Maggie. "I wanted to warn him to watch out for guards at the entrance to the tunnel."

"Let's hope he's careful," said Maggie, but her voice lacked conviction. "I have this feeling that his actions are far too independent lately."

"You don't know the half of it, Maggie. Just a few hours ago he told me he had built a site called Hell somewhere on the planet, and began judging and sentencing NET offenders." Troy gave a strange smile, and Maggie noticed the pride he felt for his protege. "But right now we're supposed to be observing the falls. I'll fill you in on Hell later. Maybe we'll even visit that site." He saw her quizzical look, and, as if reading her mind, added, "No, there is no Paradise site. Probably too boring. Or possibly there aren't any righteous people in the NET."

They adjusted the cyber-scope to display short waves as before, and waited impatiently. Nothing happened for half an hour. Suddenly, the purple lights went out. The blue lights continued for a while and then stopped as well. They waited for another couple of minutes, but nothing changed.

"The far end has been sealed!" Troy sounded tense. "Why is he still in there? He's got to get out and hide!"

Maggie reset the 'scope to normal viewing.

"He's capricious, but at this point we have no choice but to trust him implicitly," she said. "Perhaps he found a niche or a trench in the tunnel to conceal himself? Remember, he has to operate the trap, too."

They waited in silence. Long minutes passed, and still nothing stirred. Half an hour later Troy tried to contact Flint on the 'com, but discovered that the appliance was unserviceable so far from Netville.

"There's nothing we can do but wait," said Maggie. "And I suggest not to use any broadcasting equipment—it may be picked up and traced. And just for safety's sake, let's keep our backs close to the wall behind us, so that we can't be seen from the waterfall."

They moved closer to the cliff's wall and continued their hushed vigil. The following minutes seemed like eternity to them. Maggie was just about to recommend returning to Netville and alerting Babel, when something shiny gleamed on the horizon.

Troy immediately pointed the 'scope at the glitter. A silvery, cigar-shaped object, pointed at one end, was making its way rapidly toward the falls. The 'scope's display indicated the object's size as that of a railway carriage. The object approached the waterfall without slowing, and then halted abruptly, suspended in mid air, its pointed end almost touching the water.

"As if the laws of gravity do not apply to them at all," breathed Maggie. Troy laid his hand gently on her lips, and shook his head. He wasn't going to risk the slightest noise, though he knew that the object was a couple of miles away.

Without warning, the silvery object began to stretch lengthwise, like a rubber hose being pulled at both ends. As it elongated, it also grew narrower. The front end advanced into the water, which flowed around it as if it were enveloped by an air cushion. The red waters split into two diagonal torrents on either side of the tubular object, and the mountain surface behind the falls came into view. They saw a deep cavern with a round, dark opening at its end—the entrance to the tunnel. The cylindrical body continued to stretch until its diameter was slightly less than that of the tunnel, then suddenly lurched into it and vanished. The red waters resumed their normal flow, and obscured the cavern.

The youngsters waited several more nerve-wracking minutes. Nothing happened.

"I'm worried about Flint," whispered Maggie. "Whoever they are, their technology far surpasses ours."

"I'm sure he'll manage," said Troy, but his voice betrayed his consternation.

Ten minutes later, there was a sudden splash from the waterfall, and the green dragon charged through. It flew directly toward them, and landed on the platform, puffing heavily.

"I got them," he wheezed. "We're rid of those aliens. And thanks to your idea, Troy, we may even be able to talk to them without endangering the NET."

Troy breathed deeply in relief. "Good work, Flint! I understand, then, that you managed to construct that middle door, and close it behind them. You know, you had us honestly worried. What on earth took you so long?"

"I worked for over half an hour to prepare the three doors," explained Flint. "It wasn't at all easy. You see, though they may appear to be solid, as if made of iron, they aren't physical, tangible doors. They're door-like logical entities, built into the space-time continuum of the tunnel. The toughest part was your idea, the middle door—that central part of the tunnel isn't accurately defined mathematically. But I managed to do the job, and then made myself a hideaway in the entrance cove. At the same time, I had to contrive a solution to another problem—namely, how would I know when the invaders had passed the middle door, so that the locking mechanism would be timed properly. So I installed a volume sensor that would automatically trigger the middle door to close two seconds after any large object had passed it by. Then I sealed off the entrance on the far side of the tunnel. I verified that the broadcasting from both directions had stopped, and hurried to conceal myself in the hideout I had prepared earlier in the cavern. And waited, same as you. After they entered the tunnel, I waited five seconds, then followed them in, and saw the middle door close them off. Never fear, there's no way they'll be able to force that door open. I came out to our side of the tunnel, and sealed the external door there."

"Did you see the object that entered the tunnel?" asked Maggie.

"I did. And it looks like their technological achievements far outstrip our own." The dragon wrinkled his nose, and began thumping the ground excitedly. "But they'll still never break down that middle door, no matter how advanced they are. It's just mathematically impossible."

"Hey, well done!" said Maggie, and stroked the dragon's head, ruffling his green mane. "Could you explain why you're so sure that they'll never get through that door?"

Flint fondly nuzzled Maggie's cheek.

"I applied a principle I once read about in a code book of the NET's security department. It guarantees a lock virtually impossible to break open. Ten thin wires cross another ten wires in a kind of mesh with a hundred nodes. To open the lock, a specific number has to be entered for each node—each number being exactly a hundred digits long. The number of possible combinations greatly exceeds the number of electrons in our universe; or even the number of electrons you could cram into it. Even if they try for a trillion years, they'll still be at the beginning of their search."

"But what if they try to atomize the door, as we did when we opened the tunnel?" asked Troy.

"The door will not physically disintegrate, because it isn't a physical entity. Regard it as a kind of hologram you can pass through, but you have to know the code in order to get to your destination. Only one code connects our world to theirs now. They can try to pass, but any other code could bring them out somewhere else, quite unpredictable. In other words, their chances of getting back to the NET are less than that of a specific oxygen atom on Alpha Centauri arriving on Earth, combining with two specific hydrogen atoms here, and landing in a drop of water on your nose."

"Sounds promising." Troy didn't sound quite convinced. He took a deep breath. "How do you propose we communicate with them? We could put someone into the tunnel and close the door behind him. Then he'd open the middle door, and if the aliens turn out to be friendly, he'd open the outer door. However, what'll happen if they're hostile, and they force our guy to open the door?"

"Yes, that is a problem," agreed Flint. "But I think that if *I* go in as the Earth's emissary, they won't be able to force me to do anything. I'll open the door only when I'm absolutely convinced that they mean no harm." His eyes began to sparkle, and he waved his tail upward in importance. "I believe that first I'll visit their world, and see what can be learned there. Mankind will have to rely on my judgment."

"Hang on there, Mr. Earth's ambassador," said Troy, laughing as he tapped the dragon's neck gently. "I think this issue needs some more thought, and we have plenty of time for that. At the moment, it looks like we've completed what we came here to do, so let's head back home. Flint, is there any way we could observe, you know, monitor this place remotely? I think we should have a look from time to time."

"Good idea," agreed Flint. "I'll install a vid-sensor here, concealed of course, and point it at the waterfall. It won't broadcast, I'm afraid, but I'll hop over here every day to check, until we decide what to do. I don't think we'll see anything, but it's worth the peace of mind."

"Better check that camera twice a day, Flint," suggested Maggie. "Or even more frequently. Now the only thing I want to do is get out of here. This place gives me the creeps. We also need to have a serious discussion some-where quiet, and go over everything that has happened. I'd very much like to conclude that we've reached the end of this adventure, and that we won't be coming here again."

"Maggie, I think Flint is right, and that there's nothing more to worry about." Troy blew a strand of curls from his eyes. "Why don't we meet this evening at my site, and have a chat? We could very well be the first to be exposed to one of the most thrilling chapters in human history—meeting an alien civilization. Though we still need to find a safe way to communicate with them."

"Newton, Einstein, Markovitch—watch closely!" crowed Flint as he fol-lowed Maggie and Troy into the Transport Box. "Flint's Laws are going to shake this world you have defined for us!"

14. NET: DAY 17, 12:00

Even though I detest virus authors, I can't help pitying this poor wretch,
Lynn Murphy closed her eyes in repugnance. The recording she had been watching for the past three hours caused her bile to rise. On the screen Tipman was shrieking in pain and terror, vainly attempting to protect his naked body from a swarm of hornets, attracted to the honey that a red demon had poured over him a few minutes earlier. *No matter how serious his crime, ten days of that is just too much . . .*

She halted the projector, and tried to organize her mind with what she had learned so far. The Hell site was humongous. Tipman had gone through sev-eral departments before being extricated, and no doubt was en route to sev-eral more. The site was underground, and constructed of several stadium-sized interlinked halls. The floors were zigzagged with fissures, from which sulfuric smoke billowed. A network of narrow burrows connected the huge halls, and perforated most of the space beneath them. Some of these pas-sageways were of sizable length, to judge by the time it took to transfer Tipman through them.

Isn't it odd that I didn't see any other 'convicts'? she wondered. *Either they were being kept separately, or Tipman was the only one.*

She noticed that the dominating creatures in the site were the winged demons. They rode on giant spiders, and were assisted by toad-like creatures armed with pitchforks. The paintings of Hieronymus Bosch came to mind, as well as Dante's Inferno from the Divine Comedy.

Lynn dashed off a query to Og to perform a search for anyone who had recently ordered, read, or browsed through works by Bosch and Dante. Og's response revealed that the subject was more popular than she had imagined—over three hundred thousand surfers were listed. She limited the search scope to the last six months, and the list was reduced by about a quarter of its length. From these, she requested only those who had accessed the works more than once. Down to a hundred thousand entries.

This was still too large a number. She left the computer to work out additional elimination criteria, such as geographic location, while she focused on the main character: the green demon that had abducted Tipman. It had a distinct Californian accent, in contrast with the other demons that all spoke with unidentifiable accents. It was larger than the other demons, and the only green one she could see—the others were red or black.

Doubtless, this one is the leader, she thought. *The other demons obey it.* She also noticed that it was absent during the torture sessions, and that its main concern was Tipman's virus-authoring confessions.

Is he a masquerading surfer? Could a surfer disguise himself as a demon so well?

She quickly dismissed the idea. The green demon flew so naturally, and the motions of its body and tail were so perfect, that no surfer, disguised or not, could emulate them. *It's a real demon! Therefore, the head honcho of the Hell site is an illegal netter. So now, I need to find the surfer who owns and runs all these netters. He didn't show up in the recording—he left all the dirty work to his imps and demons.*

Lynn got up, and prepared herself a cup of hot chocolate in the kitchenette. She decided to go back to the very beginning of the recorded memories, and recheck everything. Returning to her seat, she once again observed Amos Tipman puttering about in his garden, and his surprised expression upon discovering the black cone and his mutilated orchids.

She pondered for a moment, and then clicked a short code into the inter-call.

"George," she said, looking at the broad-shouldered black-haired man on the holographic screen, "were there any tell-tale traces of that black cone in Tipman's site?"

"We went over it with a fine-tooth comb," replied George, his voice devoid of any emotion. "No sign of the cone. We checked the garden with object detectors, but came up with nothing, not even a hole in the ground. To be sure, there was the circle of crushed flowers that matched the memory recording perfectly. If I hadn't seen it with my own eyes, I'd have suspected that someone had hypnotized Tipman, and planted the scene in his memory. Maybe we should be searching for a powerful hypnotist, and not for Hell."

"Interesting speculation," said Lynn. "But, as you said, that doesn't explain the destroyed orchid bed. Were there any tracks in other parts of the garden?"

"No," grumbled George. "That bed was the only place. We also interrogated the netters, but they didn't see a thing."

"It's been seven days since his rescue," stated Lynn. "And he was in Hell for ten days. Most netters cannot remember anything for longer than a week. I'm planning on visiting the site, and I'll need an escort. Would you like to accompany me, or shall I ask another analyst?"

Lynn hoisted her tool bag onto her back. She hoped that George would decline. George was one of the best investigators in Babel, and a superb field agent. But she preferred to have as little of his company as possible. She even told Norman about it at one of their periodical personal meetings.

"I know I haven't any real reason to request not to work with him," she had said. "He's a first class professional. But his work is soulless, as if he were a robot. People are merely objects to him. There are the good guys, and you cooperate with them—and there are the bad guys, and you do away with them. My woman's intuition senses that there's something peculiar in his personality."

Norman observed the young woman opposite him affectionately. His voice, however, carried authority, as becomes a superior manager.

"George has been working with us for seven years," he said. "During this period he has performed all his tasks faultlessly. True, his sensitivity level may not match our own—he isn't married, has no children, and his work is his life as far as we know. But these are not sufficient reasons to disqualify him as a work partner."

"You're probably right—it's just my paranoia," said Lynn. "Anyway, I'd rather not be on a team with him, if at all possible."

"I hear you," said Norman. "However, I'd like to remind you that you are both senior staff, so you can expect to be with him occasionally. I'm sorry he isn't the ideal partner for you."

You could have been my ideal partner, thought Lynn. *Smart, strong, sensitive, and available. Also tall and very handsome. Too bad you're my boss. If you were a regular team member, I'd have hit on you long ago. You're too shy to make the first move. I sure would like to know how you came to be divorced . . .*

"I'll join you," said George, much to her chagrin. "Frankly, I also think the site's worth another visit, and there's no use in involving a new analyst in it now. I can allocate exactly one hour to this task."

* * *

Tipman's site looked exactly as she had seen in the memory reconstruction she had viewed. A bubbling stream lent the place a pastoral flavor, and the towering baobab trees were far more impressive than on the recording. George and Lynn marched directly to the devastated orchid bed.

"That depression in the middle of the bed is a perfect circle," declared George. "It is just under half a foot deep. There is no doubt that someone was here and left his mark. We drilled into this hole to a depth of thirty feet, and found the earth untouched. No one has been digging in this location . . ."

"Have you identified the footprints in the bed?" asked Lynn. She bent over the flowerbed, which had not been watered for several days, and its plants were withering.

"Yes, they're Tipman's." George's voice turned sour. "You can see where he was standing, and how he was dragged into this circle. There's another, unidentified footprint, which might belong to the demon. It also points into the depression. Everything matches that bastard's story."

Lynn ignored his last remark. 'That bastard' had already been punished several times over.

"Do we know for certain exactly where he was surfing when he was found? I understand you sent a rescue team here, too—not only to his Earth home."

"That's another unclear point," growled George. He pointed to Tipman's house, a little white cottage in the corner of the site. "The rescue team found him there, lying comatose on the floor with severe injuries. They couldn't wake him. Finally, to prevent further damage, an emergency bracelet was employed, and it returned him promptly to Earth with the memories of everything he experienced in the NET intact. There he was disconnected from his helmet, and the memory recording was made. How could we know that we'd find Hell there?"

"Let's aim a satellite camera at this site. Maybe we'll discover additional visitors." Lynn produced a small trowel from the bag on her back, and collected earth samples from within and around the depression, as well as from the six-toed footprint. "Perhaps the demon who left this imprint got scratched, and we could get a sample of its DNA. If we're lucky, we'll catch his owner right away." She picked up a few flowers that the same bare foot had trampled. "Who knows, maybe another check will reveal something new."

They went to Tipman's house but found nothing of significance. There was some fruit salad in the refrigerator, indicating that Tipman had planned to return to his house for a meal, but was interrupted. His private computer contained a list of recently closed sites, and there was evidence that he had read the list several times before going out to the garden. The last entry on the list was 'Better Buy', a site that had shut down that very morning.

They returned to Babel headquarters without any new information. The earth samples that Lynn had brought back revealed nothing. She was back where she had started.

We'll have to wait for the results of Tipman's inquiry when he wakes up, she thought. *But nevertheless, I've got to find the entrance to Hell. There's got to be a way there from Tipman's site. Maybe from other sites in the NET as well.* She imagined the black cone turning up in her own site, and shivered.

Perhaps Norman has additional information? She began entering his code into the inter-call, but curbed herself. She hadn't made any progress whatever. *I must find something on my own. I can't just return empty hand-ed. He suggested I use the Queen of the Night. Well, it's probably time for that now. Exceptional cases require exceptional handling!*

She connected to the control center's messaging system.

"I'm going out to my site for a few minutes," she announced. "I'll report in when I return." She left her room, and went to the Transport Box in the corridor without waiting for the confirmation of her message. Entering the box, she jumped to her home site.

She looked out of the window onto the garden, again visualizing a black cone there. Two netters were tending the spotless lawn and the surrounding rose bushes. She sat by her computer and keyed in a long string of numbers. The hologram of a cuckoo appeared.

"Queen of the Night at your service. What would you like to ask of Pira-net?"

Pira-net was the nickname for a group of surfers who called themselves the Pirates. Using the standard computer networks in the NET, they could provide almost any information to their members, and it didn't matter whether it was street gossip or military top secret. There was an open conflict between them and the NET authorities, who kept trying to uncover their iden-tities and abort their activities. Some of the Pirates were indeed apprehended and placed under observation (they could not be convicted), but there were at least fifty Pirates at large and active around the clock.

Lynn had penetrated this secret community, and was a respected member under her code name of Queen of the Night. She appeared as a cuckoo, and occasionally contributed information to the other anonymous members. The only person who knew of her involvement in Pira-net was Norman Starr, who authorized her to infiltrate into the network as an undercover agent.

"I need to find the way to Hell," she told the cuckoo. "I'd like to visit some of my relatives there. I'm willing to trade info on the new version of a Shakespeare play." The clue was rather blatant. Every experienced surfer knew of the million-dollar cash reward, no questions asked, offered by Babel for any information leading to the capture of the author of 'Midsummer Night's Dream', the foremost virus whose author had not been caught yet.

The cuckoo disappeared from the screen. Lynn hesitated for a second, and then enabled access to her home computer from her Babel computer system. Hitherto, she had avoided contacting her home site from Babel, so as not to be discovered by Babel's tracing systems. But now she felt she had no choice. She would have to perform all her activities from Babel, and would not be able to hop into her home site every few minutes to check for messages from Pira-net—that would certainly arouse suspicion.

She jumped back to Babel, and connected to the computer at her home site. Three messages were already waiting.

Queen of the Night—if you need an escort to Hell, I volunteer. The message was signed by Charon, a familiar name on Pira-net.

My Queen—I have recently shopped at the Center Point chain store, and I was treated as badly as if I were in Hell. Perhaps your relatives work at the store? This one was sent by Figaro.

Revered Queen—I would like to know the name of the producer of the latest version of the play. In return, I'll trade the name of a key person in an outlawed organization, together with some pertinent addresses. This is not Hell, but it as close as you can get there. This was sent by a respected Pirate named Panda.

Hmm, that third message looks interesting, she thought. *But I'm looking for Hell, not the local mafia. I'll wait. Everyone makes a mistake eventually. We're destined to meet, on Earth, in the NET, or even in Hell . . .*

15. NET: DAY 18, 00:00

"I believe we have a crisis on our hands." The green dragon twitched its tail nervously, shifting its weight from one foot to the other. "There is something you ought to see."

"Hey, take it easy," said Troy, giving the dragon a friendly pat on its neck. "All I did was leave the NET for a couple of hours, and already you're panicky."

A soft buzz came from behind them. Maggie walked in from the entry room, dressed in her hiking outfit.

"What's so urgent?" she asked. "I had just returned from jogging when I got your call. I didn't even have time to wash up."

"I want to show you the recording from the concealed camera we left at the waterfall," said Flint. "You'll understand."

The trio sat around the table, and Flint switched on the projector. On the far wall of the room, they saw the familiar view of the large waterfall covering the time fold.

"That's what it looks like from the platform we were standing on," stated Flint. "The time is about one hour after we captured the aliens inside the tunnel. This camera enlarges over fifty times."

The scene did not change for several minutes. Troy was about to say something, but the dragon signaled him with its tail to wait a bit longer. Sure enough, a couple of minutes later an enormous silvery cylinder, several times the size of the ship trapped in the tunnel, slowly floated toward the falls. It stopped short in mid air, about twenty feet away from the plummeting water. The cylinder emitted a bright ray at the cascade, and the water turned to steam where the ray struck. A huge cloud of red vapor rose toward the mountain's pinnacle, an oddly colored rainbow glistening in its midst. Not one drop of water succeeded in passing the ray.

Troy and Maggie found themselves standing upright, goggling at the spectacle.

"I don't believe it," Maggie mumbled. "It's gigantic! Hanging in the middle of the air like one of those old airships—"

"Dirigibles," whispered Troy. "I'm pretty sure it's even larger. Amazing, how they're evaporating all that water."

He turned slowly to Flint.

"These invaders were in the NET before we shut the tunnel, right?"

Flint nodded. On the wall, below the cloud of red steam that had replaced the waterfall, they could see the cavern and the door that sealed the opening to the tunnel. The wire mesh on the door glowed a bright orange. The door was clearly locked.

"So what we captured," continued Troy in a shaky voice, "was just a cruiser, or scout ship, that the mother ship sent to investigate what happened with their communication line. Does this recording show any more such vessels?"

"I assume that this is the only ship," said Flint. "But I cannot be certain.

The camera recording isn't long—let's watch it all the way through, and then discuss it."

"I'd give a lot to know how many aliens fit into that dirigible," said Maggie. "I hope that they think that we've just closed off their exit, and not that we've imprisoned their comrades. That might make them unfriendly."

"I don't think there's any way they could know." Flint sounded concerned, and his tail resumed its floor thumping. "But the idea of communicating with them is now taking on a new tack."

Troy gently put his foot on the dragon's tail, and the thumping stopped. "Can you tell what kind of rays they're using to make all that steam?"

"Lasers, but of a special kind," said Flint. "It's measured out so precisely that it's enough to boil off the water, but leave the wall behind intact."

The wall was, indeed, undamaged. The huge cylinder remained suspended motionless for several minutes, and then a tubular shape—the exact twin of the craft they had captured—emerged from it. The smaller ship approached the sealed door, stretched itself to a diameter slightly less than the tunnel, and then went through the door, as if it wasn't there. The tube reappeared a few seconds later, and stopped—hovering a few feet away from the door. It slowly contracted back to its original shape.

"They tried to pass through the door without opening it," explained Flint, "and probably arrived at some undefined location. One of an infinity of possibilities. I'm not sure they can return here from any combination they choose to test, but this time they succeeded. They'll also deduce at once that they won't get very far using this method."

A fan of multi-colored light beams shone out of the ship's 'prow'. They played over the wire mesh in a flurry of gleams and motion.

"Now they're attempting to open the door," said Flint. "They're entering numbers at a fantastic speed—hundreds of millions every second—but it won't help them, as they'll soon conclude on their own. They're probably trying patterns of numbers, such as the even or the prime numbers. But there's no way they could know that the correct number needs to be held for thirty seconds before the lock will open. In short, no matter which method they choose, even in a trillion years they'd be right where they are now!"

The rays continued to flitter rapidly over the wire mesh for several minutes. Flint advanced the recording by two hours. They watched the flickering for another minute—then it stopped.

"They've come to the same conclusion, give or take a billion years," said Troy. "Flint, are you the only one who can open that door?"

"The one and only," boasted the dragon, puffing his chest proudly. "They'll never get into that tunnel without my cooperation—and that's a fact. But the question we need to answer now is: what do we do with them here? Even more urgent—what will they do now? They are capable of being very dangerous. Keep watching."

The smaller cylinder backed away from the rocky face. A wide shaft of violet light erupted from its front part, and a shiny circle glowed around the sealed entrance. Suddenly, the light intensified and became almost unbearable. The rocks around the door began to melt and flow slowly toward the spaceship. Once out of the light beam they solidified again, while more lava covered them from behind, gelling a bit further out. The result was the formation of a large ledge, almost two-hundred feet deep, at the entrance to the tunnel. The door itself was unaffected by the rays. It receded into the solid rock, and continued to block the entrance.

"They could melt down the entire mountain, and still be unable to enter," said Flint smugly. "The only way in is with the correct key number."

The beam went out abruptly, and the smaller vessel reentered the mother ship. The rays that were vaporizing the red water shut off, and the cataract resumed its roaring torrential flow. Wherever the water spray touched the newly formed ledge, it hissed off in pink vapor, as it cooled the solidifying stone.

The mother ship rose slowly and began sending light rays to the ground below and surrounding it.

"Now I suppose they're trying to find us, or any other signs of life," observed Maggie, who had remained silent so far.

"Right on, Maggie," said Flint. "But they won't find my camera. There's no way to distinguish it from any of the pebbles there."

The spaceship moved out of the edge of the viewing frame, and Flint turned off the projector. The three of them sat silently for a few minutes, absorbing what they had just witnessed.

Maggie fidgeted a bit. "Maybe we could repeat what we did with the other ship," she ventured. "We'll open the door, let them get in, and then seal it behind them."

"No way!" cried Troy. "That door is our only bargaining advantage. Once we open it we'll be at their mercy."

"I agree with Troy," said Flint. "That middle door might not withstand an assault from both sides together—I never took that option into account. And, of course, my blockage at the far end of the tunnel wasn't as break proof as the one at our side." He glanced sheepishly at the youngsters. "I didn't care much for that, as long as it held long enough for the middle door to lock them out."

"Well," sighed Maggie. "It seems that all we can do now is wait and see what they'll do next."

Troy didn't hear her comment. He was frowning, deep in thought.

"Flint," he said slowly. "Did that camera of yours also record those blue and purple communication lights they used?"

"Yes, of course. But how does that help us?"

"Please project those images now. I want to see if that mother ship is broadcasting or receiving from anywhere else. If those lights indicate that they are communicating, then they have a fleet of ships here. Otherwise, it's probably the only ship in the NET."

Flint stared at him approvingly.

"Now that's something I should have thought of myself," he said, and adjusted the projector to the proper wavelengths. There were no broadcasting or receiving lights.

"We've narrowed down the problem a bit," said Maggie. "Of course, there could be a million aliens in that mother ship."

"True," agreed Flint, "and we have no way of knowing."

"So let's start looking for information about them," said Troy. "Look—they're already over two days in the NET. If they went anywhere near Netville, they'd be noticed and the NET authorities alerted. Maggie, your father works in Babel, doesn't he? Could you find out from him whether anything extraordinary happened lately? Careful, now—we don't want anyone to know that we actually let them in."

"Dad and I are having dinner together this evening. I'll do my best. But let's first try to think of what else we can do. We can't just leave them be. They might destroy the NET."

"I could leave them a message near the entrance," mused Flint, as he scratched his mane with the point of his tail. "But there's no knowing if they'll understand it. Maybe they do come in peace. They could certainly benefit humanity with their superior technology."

"Flintie, if they're peaceful they'll try to contact our leaders," said Maggie. "They'll ask for help in opening the tunnel. And then we could step in, save the day, and be forgiven. Maybe we'll even be heroes for making the first contact with an alien civilization."

Troy summed up the meeting. "Right. Our plan for now is to gather as much information as we can, while we wait for the invaders to make the first move. Maggie, you sniff around and find out what Babel knows. Flint and I will search the open sources of information . . ." he looked at Flint, then shrugged his shoulders, ". . . and the not-so-open sources we may have access to. Let's meet here tomorrow morning. Earlier, if circumstances change."

"Okay, guys," said Maggie, getting to her feet. "See you tomorrow."

She walked into the entry room. While entering her coordinates, she heard Troy cross-examining the dragon about the atomic blaster. She pressed the Operate button, hoping that the two reckless adventurers wouldn't do something heroic or foolish.

16. STANFORD, CALIFORNIA, FRIDAY, 18:01

"OWWW!!" bellowed Amos Tipman, as the drop of boiling oil landed on his bare midriff. His body arched, straining against the fetters that bound his hands and feet to the concrete slab. The rats gnawing at his toes sprang back, alarmed by the loud noise and abrupt motion.

"Amos, listen to me. I am about to release you. Do not make any sudden moves, and you won't get hurt."

Amos opened his eyes, and saw a tall, broad-shouldered man with long gray hair, dressed in a white gown. His brown eyes, on either side of a narrow, hawk-like nose, gazed back at him with compassion. The pot of boiling oil was still hanging over Amos' belly, and the rats had returned to his feet.

"Hurry! I can't take any more. My body is falling apart."

The man took a laser knife out of one of his pockets, and began severing Amos' bonds. They were made of thick leather, but the laser knife went through them like butter.

"YEOW!!" Another drop fell on Amos, this time on his chest, and his body jerked in pain.

"There," said the man in the white gown, putting the knife away. "Let me help you up." He took Amos' hand, and yanked him into a seated position. Bending forward, he hoisted Amos onto his shoulder with a single, smooth motion. The oil pot flipped over, and its contents poured over the block where Amos had lain seconds earlier, scattering the squealing rats.

The man looked back, horrified. "Just in time. Now let's get you to a hospital as fast as we can, and see how damaged you are."

Amos was sobbing uncontrollably. "Who are you?" he managed to blubber. "Will they take me away again?"

"I'm a doctor, and I've come to rescue you. They'll never torment you again. We'll need some information from you, so that we'll know how to stop them if they try."

They exited the underground burrow that served as a torture chamber. Thick smoke darkened the skies, and the ground was black and charred. The doctor walked with long strides toward an iron gate, set in a wall that seemed to surround the area. He had taken only a few paces, when two black imps emerged from the forest behind them. They noticed the escapees, and began to chase them, waving their long pitchforks. The doctor, with Amos on his back, tried to break into a run, but his foot struck a large snake that had slithered out of a hole, and he fell to the ground. Amos was dislodged, and he rolled to the side of the narrow path, the sharp stones lacerating his naked body. He tried to rise, but he was too weak, and he slumped to the ground again. With a great exertion, he managed to raise his head, only to see the snake bypassing the prostrate doctor, and making its way slowly toward him. The snake's large eyes were firmly fixed on Amos', and its forked tongue darted in and out of its mouth. From behind, he could hear the clamor of approaching imps. He made a final desperate effort to get to his feet, but the snake struck first and wrapped itself around him, pinning him to the ground.

More and more snake coils looped about his body, and began to squeeze the breath out of his ribcage. Amos screamed, and the world turned dark.

When Amos Tipman opened his eyes again, he saw the same doctor observing him with an anxious look on his face. He turned his head, and discovered he was lying on a bed in a large, white room. An osmosis sleeve, which fed nourishment into his body, was attached to his right arm. He felt that his arms and legs were bound to the bed.

"Amos, I am Dr. Keenan. You're safe, and in good hands. Please be calm."

"How . . . how . . . how did I get here? Just a minute ago I was in that underground . . ." A rippling shiver shook Amos' entire body. "You rescued me, but they caught us. The snake . . ." His voice broke off. He shut his eyes and reopened them, verifying he was still in the same place. "Why am I tied down?"

"The bonds are for your own protection, Amos, so that you won't hurt yourself during your nightmares. A few seconds ago, I intervened in your dream, which became a nightmare, and terminated it. You were trapped in a NET site called Hell. Your parents alerted us this morning, and it took us quite a few hours to extricate you. You seem to be physically whole, and your brain does not appear to be damaged, except for those nightmare attacks you experience."

"How long have I been here?"

"About seven hours. We tried to wake you several times, but you always fell asleep again, and went into wild tantrums in your bed. Last time we tried, you jumped out of bed, and we just managed to grab you before you fell to the floor. We had to administer you some sedation through your osmosis sleeve, and it looks like we're doing a pretty good job of stabilizing your condition."

"Dreams? Nightmares??" Amos yelled. "Are you out of your mind? It was the most terrible reality you could imagine." He tried, unsuccessfully, to get up. "Look at the scars on my chest!" he screamed. "See how many of my toes are missing! Look at the wounds . . ."

"Calm down, Amos, please calm down." Dr. Keenan placed a soothing hand on Amos' shoulder and, holding a large hand-mirror in the other, he shoved it in front of Amos' face. "Look for yourself. You have no scars or wounds on your chest or anywhere else. None of your toes or fingers are missing." The doctor moved the mirror around so that Amos could see his various limbs. "But you have undoubtedly experienced a severe trauma, and your memory will retain images and incidents for a long time to come. It's my job to help you cope with these memories."

Amos gaped in amazement at his reflection in the mirror. It took several seconds until he found his voice.

"It's . . . it's . . . all in my . . . head?" he stammered.

"That's right, Amos," reassured Dr. Keenan. "You're a very bright lad, and your intelligence is going to be of great help in your recovery. The more details you can tell us about your ordeal, the faster we'll be able to return you to normal life."

"I'll never be normal again," mumbled Amos. His voice rose in anguish. "And I'll never surf the NET again! Do you hear me, doctor? I'll never surf again!" He burst into tears.

"There, there. I understand." The doctor tried to soothe him, using a handkerchief to wipe the eyes and face of the boy strapped to the bed. "It's a bit too early to plan for the future. You've got to recuperate first. However, I hope you'll understand that we have to ask you a few questions now. It's of utmost importance to find the people who did this to you. They'll tell us how to stop your nightmares. Do you know who they are?"

"No. I haven't the foggiest notion who they are or why I was attacked." Amos' voice was dejected.

"I think you were attacked because of the viruses you released," said a tall man with a shock of gray hair, who stood behind the doctor, and now stepped forward. "My name is Norman Starr, and I'm from Babel, the unit combating viruses. I have viewed the recording of your memory from your last surf, but there was nothing there that could disclose those who assaulted you. We need your cooperation."

Amos paled, and his hands began to tremble. He composed himself with an effort, and responded in a dispirited voice.

"I'll cooperate. Anything you want—just keep them away from me."

"Excellent," said Norman warmly, trying to encourage the injured surfer. "Did anyone else know that you were the author of 'Midsummer Nights Dream'?"

"No one else could know," said Amos. "Unless they bored into my mind, which is what I think they did. 'Creep' was an even more sophisticated virus, completely untraceable to me, and yet they detected it and found me within two hours."

"Regarding 'Creep'—how did you manage to enter Better Buy's abandoned site undetected?"

"They had employed a programmer who fell out with them. He'd prepared a loophole, which would enable him to penetrate later into the company for his own hanky-panky reasons. I discovered that loophole, masqueraded as the programmer, and built 'Creep' in a directory that was invisible to the company's staff. 'Creep' was designed to remain dormant until the company folded. Then the virus would be launched into the NET. And that is what, in fact, happened, but that gang of devils got to me somehow. Maybe they were on to me because of my activities on the stock market long ago."

"I believe that they caught your virus, and traced you back to the Better Buy site," said Norman. "I want you to tell me everything you can remember about your assailants. Or anyone you're suspicious of. Your cooperation will count in your favor in the future."

"I've been punished enough," whined Amos. The tears flowed from his eyes, and Norman waited patiently for him to steady himself again. "I'll never even get close to the NET. *Never!*" The bawling stopped, and Amos addressed Norman directly. "Sorry about that. No, I have no idea who did this to me. The only thing that impressed me was that Hell seemed too real. Maybe they really came from there! I cannot imagine how anyone, or even a team of programmers, could build such a site on their own. The scope of a project like this needs a giant corporation behind it—maybe even a government."

"I am gratified to see you can still analyze the situation rationally," said Norman dryly. "Did your nightmares feel as real as the site in the NET?"

Amos' body began to tremble again.

"They seemed so. I'd rather die than have one of those nightmares again."

"Just two more questions, then. Do you know of, or do you suspect, anyone composing viruses or intending to do so?"

The trembling subsided, and Amos shook his head.

"All right," continued Norman. "Have you encountered anyone else's viruses in the NET?"

"N-no." Amos hesitated for a moment, and Norman fixed him with a piercing stare. "Well, yes, but it was a long time ago, about three years. Nobody knew of that virus, and I just happened to stumble across it. I managed to disarm the self-destruction mechanism only a few seconds before it was activated. Then I built 'Midsummer Night's Dream' based on that virus, with several improvements. That's all I can remember right now."

"We will need your consent to conduct a deep brain analysis on you." Norman was quiet but firm. "We'll discover all the details there, and we'll find out if your attackers were connected in any way to that virus. It'll serve as an extenuating circumstance when you're brought to court. We already have all the information linking you to virus authoring, so anything we find on this topic during the brain probe will not be held against you. Hopefully, we'll also find how to stop your nightmares. I see no reason for you to refuse. Any irrelevant data we find will, of course, remain in strict confidence. This is for your own good."

Amos took a deep breath. He was well aware that a deep brain analysis exposed a person utterly and completely. Every little detail—his secrets, desires, misdemeanors and crimes, embarrassments, likes and dislikes—everything was open to the analysts. Such operations were very rare, and implemented only on mentally incapable people or on seemingly inexplicable suicide attempts.

"Only the current event will be used by the investigators?" he asked hesitantly.

"Absolutely. No other information will be used, no matter how serious."

"Then I agree on the condition that at the trial you won't demand more than a year in prison. I've learned my lesson."

Norman pondered for a few seconds, and then nodded. "The money in your bank accounts will be confiscated. About the year in prison—that will refer only to your incarceration time. We will also demand a suspended sentence, and revoking of NET access for ten years."

"Make that a revoke for life. I'll never surf—"

"It's settled, then." Norman cut him short. "You will be analyzed tomorrow morning."

17. NEW YORK, FRIDAY, 21:05 (NEW YORK TIME)

Maggie found herself at her desk in her parent's apartment in New York. She removed the surfing helmet, and got up. *Ice Sculpting,* the magazine she had read before the surf, lay open on her table. The clock on the wall showed that she had been away for five minutes only, two hours in the NET. Her computer screen displayed a white dove with an envelope in its beak, indicating that an urgent message was pending.

She opened the message. A tall, fair-haired man with blue eyes appeared on the three-dimensional screen.

"Maggie, I'll be busy tonight. We have an emergency. I'm really sorry, but I cannot make it for our dinner date this evening, and I've cancelled our reservations at Alphonse. There are sandwiches in the 'fridge. Your mother is returning home on Wednesday, so we can all celebrate together at Alphonse early next Friday. And we can also attend the Rafael Porfiro recital at Radio-City right after dinner. I'll make sure we have good seats. Take care of yourself, dear. If you need me, call me on my private line, but only if you absolutely have to."

Maggie smiled sadly. It was so like Dad to miss the dinner they had planned a week ahead, when Mom left for her Japanese tour. Work always had top priority. It was also very typical of him to offer one of the most prominent concerts on the Earth, where the cheapest ticket cost three hundred dollars—and Dad always got good seats which cost double and more. An identical concert in the NET would take ten Earth minutes, and cost twenty dollars for the best seats in the hall. She was disappointed and annoyed, though her rational reasoning understood his actions. Too many things were beyond his control. Sven Thorensen, a senior Babel staff member, was frequently summoned without warning, even while vacationing with his family at their summer home in Costa del Sol in Spain.

An emergency? Could it have anything to do with the invaders? Dad mustn't get even the slightest whiff that I'm involved in this. Let's see if I can find out whether he has any information.

She keyed in a password, and accessed their house network. The computer was secured, as befitting a Babel employee, but none of it was concealed from Maggie. After all, she wasn't a code and puzzle expert for nothing. But she didn't find anything of significance. Just a short note from his boss in Babel, Norman Starr, to drop everything and report in. Leaving the computer, she opened the refrigerator, and selected a cheese-and-olives sandwich. If she wasn't going out for dinner, she would have a few additional hours to surf and search for freak or peculiar events. She bit into her sandwich, and found it fresh and quite tasty.

At least Dad had the time to prepare me some food, she thought. *I won't be surfing hungry.*

She walked out onto the large terrace, and watched the traffic thirty-six stories below the spacious apartment, overlooking West Central Park. It was hot and humid outside. It irritated her to think that she had to go out into that climate to meet her instructor for Games Theory next Monday.

Why couldn't we meet in the NET? Why waste two whole NET days in a stuffy room at Columbia University? If I were in charge of the curriculum, I'd eliminate all studying on Earth. Even cosmology can be studied in the NET, with all the relevant celestial observation data being piped down from Earth. In fact, I think that only archeology needs to be studied on Earth. All the other subjects have published material in the NET, and the vast majority is never ever seen on Earth because there are hardly any readers there. If it wasn't for that stupid regulation forcing everyone to study on Earth, many twelve-year-olds could begin their Ph.D. theses, after completing tens of years of study in the NET. You wouldn't need to wait until you were fourteen. When will the authorities catch up with the new reality?

The thought of 'the new reality' brought her back to the alien invaders. She was wasting valuable time. Troy may be having his traditional family dinner now, but Flint was active in the NET. She put on her helmet, and went to visit the learned dragon.

18. PALO ALTO, FRIDAY, 19:00

Nancy Bentley was a stickler for family dinners. Every evening, at seven o'clock sharp, the Bentleys would assemble at the round table in the dining room. No excuses. It was a habit she had inherited from her mother, and discovered that such a family get-together was essential in the NET era. Most of the family spent long hours surfing in the NET, resulting in gaps of several weeks between family dinners. Several NET weeks, of course.

This evening there was one family member missing. Professor Timothy Bentley, Troy's father, flew early that morning to the Machu Pichu archeological excavation site in Peru, and was due back only in a week's time. Nancy's three children—Troy, fifteen years old; Adam, twelve; and Ruth, five—sat obediently by the dinner table. As had become habitual, they were joined by their neighbor of a few houses away, Sigmund Klein, a retired professor, who was already considered a member of the family.

Nancy noticed the full plate in front of her eldest son.

"Troy, are you feeling well? You haven't touched your food."

"I think he's got NET-phobia," giggled Adam. He wore the large green spectacles that were all the latest rage, and his red curls tumbled over his forehead. "Flint infected him."

"That's no laughing matter," said Nancy sternly, and gave Sigmund an abashed look.

Sigmund Klein, the Bentley's neighbor for the past seven years, was a retired professor of biochemistry and cyber-DNA. Ten years earlier Ziggy, as he was known to his friends, contracted NET-phobia, and could not surf the NET any longer. He was compelled to quit his research and retire, as nobody could wait for weeks on end for him to either read or write a report, which could be covered in a matter of hours in the NET.

Ziggy laughed off Adam's remark.

"Oh, that's quite all right, I assure you." He said. "I am totally resigned to the fact that I shall never surf again. At least, this way I am not exposed to NET injuries."

"I heard that there was a new incident of brain damage in the NET!" exclaimed Adam excitedly. "A computer engineer got his brain wiped out entirely. Hey, he can't even walk or talk."

"When did this happen?" Troy lashed out at Adam. "Where did you hear this?"

"Hey, big brother, cool it, will you?" Adam looked squarely at Troy. "You'd think you're somehow tied in to this."

Troy controlled himself immediately. The last thing he wanted was for Adam and his surfing gang to know what it was all about. It was the equivalent of plastering the information on the front page of every open NET publication. He watched Adam calmly, and wiped his hands on a napkin.

"Well, forgive me for being somewhat skeptical, but your gang has a reputation for spreading speculative information. You know my opinion about them—they need close supervision. They're scaring innocent surfers."

"No, no, it's the truth," insisted Adam. "I saw an item on the Gossipofon. It happened four hours ago, or four days ago NET time. Sure, there were no details, and it could be just gossip. But, hey, listen to this—I was not allowed into Tuffy's corral because of an emergency state in the Dunham district. And the injured engineer was from Dunham. I just put two and two together. Hey—are you coming to see Tuffy at the contest tomorrow? It's final—she's competing!"

"I'll be there," confirmed Troy. *If nothing more important comes up,* he thought to himself.

"Has some misadventure occurred in the NET, Troy?" queried Ziggy.

"So it seems, according to Adam." Troy elegantly evaded the answer. "But it's always sensible to be alert. Listen, Adam, freak incidents in the NET do, in fact, interest me. So you'd be doing me a favor if you inquired with your comrades if they heard of any more of them. And seeing that you're interested too, I'll ask Flint, and bring you up to date."

"Sure you will." Adam wasn't fooled so easily. "But if you and Flint are on to something, and you go NET-hopping, I want you to take me with you. Okay? Can I, *please?* I've never surfed with you and Flint. Hey, I can help. I've got connections."

Troy felt himself trapped. Taking Adam along on a surf was risky. He was unpredictable and undisciplined. On the other hand, his gang, the Wilders, occasionally possessed information that was unavailable elsewhere. And now, every scrap of information could be critical.

"Well, let's see what info you come up with first. If it's of any value, you just might join us when we verify it." He put on a serious face. "However, you must do as you're told. I don't want to search for you all over the NET."

"It's a deal!" Adam could not contain his excitement. "I'll bet you next week's allowance that ten minutes after dinner I'll know what's bugging you."

Troy ignored him, and calmly tasted the cold pie on his plate.

The rest of the meal passed quietly. Nancy stated that she had seen an article somewhere about an artificial biological eye being transplanted into a blind man in Finland. The tissues for the eye were taken from the man in his youth.

"Ah, yes— that's the future," said Troy, glad that another topic had arisen. "Today you can grow and replace quite a number of our vital organs. Some day we may even have organs that will function better than the natural ones. We'd all be far more durable."

Adam had to put in his two cents.

"Bio-solutions are good for old people and cripples," he said, waving a hand in disregard. "There's no future there. My tutor at school says that the real technological breakthrough will come only when we can plug a computer into a person. Or was it the other way 'round? Hey, he thinks that evolution is too slow, and that we're up a blind alley."

"Maybe so, but I would be reluctant to eulogize evolution at this juncture," stated Ziggy. "For your information, the first significant link between the human brain and external implements was with a miniscule computerized camera wired directly into the visual cortex. This was in the beginning of the century. The bio-physiologist who conducted this operation managed to provide blind people with a visual image that they could interpret as a picture, or scene. Even though these early solutions benefited a small number of people, they cannot be considered as true links between computers and brains. They necessitated surgery, and direct application of electrodes to the brain.

"It took another forty years before brain waves were employed for communication. The helmet, with which we are familiar today, was the first real breakthrough in human-computer connectivity. I was privileged to be there at the time."

Ziggy usually refrained from talking about himself. Most of his stories were about the early NET heroes.

"So how come you're not in the famous Hundred Founders list?" asked Adam. "Duncan Mayhew was first on the list, and you once said you worked with him."

Nancy blushed, but Ziggy just smiled. Children may ask any questions they liked.

"That is correct, Adam. I am not on the list. I was only twenty-two years old when Duncan developed the first helmet at the Cornell Research Center. He was my professor of bio-physiology. Later, during the term I was working on my doctorate thesis, we spent long hours in the NET—we were among the first surfers, you see. And the NET was like the wild west of two hundred years ago."

"Just what do you mean?" asked Nancy politely. She noticed his empty plate and added, "You haven't tasted the cheese cake yet." Nancy had already heard most of Ziggy's stories several times, but each time he related one it sounded fresh and interesting.

"The entire concept of loading information into the brain was novel." Ziggy took a bite of the cake, and pursed his lips in approval. "At first we would bumble along in a primitive maze of simulations, and when we returned we could not remember a darn thing, pardon the expression. We were, however, attached to recording instruments, and they showed us where we had been and what we had experienced. For example, on one occasion I surfed in a simulated safari. I roamed amid herds of zebras and antelopes, until a pride of lions attacked me and devoured me." He shuddered, but continued smoothly. "I must have suffered the most intense agony in the simulation, but I remembered nothing of it. I found out only after viewing the recordings—I certainly screamed a lot. It was truly horrific. I often think that that episode may have contributed to my contracting NET-phobia thirty-five years later."

"So without the recording, you wouldn't know what happened to you, right?" said Adam. "That's really cool. So, hey, why did they stop the recordings?"

Troy explained patiently.

"First of all, this planet does not contain enough resources to record every single surf of every single surfer. The figures are astronomical—way beyond the resources to maintain the NET itself. Second, we don't need it today. The surfer retains everything in his own memory, provided he exits the NET normally. And today, we can reconstruct a person's memory as far back as necessary, and reveal everything—even events that the surfer doesn't consciously remember."

"That is correct," said Ziggy, somewhat surprised. "Not many people know of these reconstruction machines. They are preposterously expensive to build and to maintain, and only the largest hospitals can afford them. The law prohibits their use except for medical purposes. Their existence is not widely publicized because there is always the latent threat of abuse by criminal factors."

"Hey, is it true that Duncan himself was trapped in the NET?" said Adam, his mouth filled with cake.

"No. Stories regarding trapped surfers emerged only years later, after Markovitch accomplished the acceleration of the NET, and it began to resemble its present-day appearance." Ziggy spoke as if from within a dream. "Duncan was only marginally damaged when he returned too suddenly from a surf, and his nervous system was updated with errors. He lost the memory of the past two months, and it took him quite a while to recover. I, too, was a victim of that incident, because he completely forgot my thesis, and I had to re-embark from scratch. He had also owed me twenty dollars, and he feigned ignorance of that, too."

"Ziggy, you're exaggerating," chided Nancy. "The children will be afraid to surf."

Ziggy winked. "Well, maybe the twenty dollars was a bit of fabrication on my part. But the rest is absolutely factual and verifiable. However, this all happened a long time ago, and there is nothing hazardous today in surfing."

"But, hey, I remember that *someone* was supposed to be trapped in the NET," insisted Adam.

"You are probably referring to Robert Duke, another member on the Hundred Founders list. Are you familiar with his story?"

Troy had eaten half of his cake, and now pushed his chair away from the table.

"I hope you will all forgive me," he said, "but I must leave now. I have an unfinished assignment in the NET, and Maggie is waiting for me. Ziggy, I've heard the Robert Duke story, but I always thought it was just another legend." He got up, kissed his mother's cheek, and left the room.

Adam looked around, but could find no excuse to follow Troy. More than anything, he wanted to be with Troy now, and surf with him and Flint. He submitted to the fact that he'd have to listen to Ziggy's story. Thankfully, it was one he had not heard previously.

"Er, no, I never heard the details," he said hastily, willing Ziggy to hurry and get on with it. "Just the name. Hey, didn't he belong to a family of jugglers that used to appear in Vegas?"

"He was considered the black sheep of the family," said Ziggy. "The only one to break the circus tradition. But that has nothing to do with our narrative. The fact is that Duke was involved in establishing the NET's infrastructure. He was the one to develop the special planet algorithms, those laws that govern all behavior in the NET." He noticed that Adam was still puzzled.

"You see, Adam, laws such as gravitation and thermodynamics needed to be established so that the planet could function similarly to Earth." He returned to his story. "Well, anyway, there he was in the NET, examining these rules, when the NET was accelerated using the Markovitch principles."

"That was about thirty years ago," commented Nancy. "I remember it was in all the headlines."

"Correct. Thirty-one and a half years ago, to be precise." Ziggy was delighted that someone could share his past experiences. Adam fidgeted visibly, but Ziggy continued.

"For some inexplicable reason, the acceleration announcement did not reach Duke in time, and he remained in the NET. It was a relatively minor speed up, just by a factor of two—far from the twenty-four coefficient of today. But something went wrong with Duke. He returned to Earth with NET-phobia. Unlike me, Duke refused to acknowledge his affliction, and forced himself to return to the NET. His family found him unconscious, still wearing his helmet. He remained in a coma until the day he died, five years later. Now here's the true story of the legend. Duke's copy, the one that was surfing when the event happened, could not return to the comatose brain on Earth. The minute the helmet was removed from Duke, the copy was trapped in the NET forever. Two days later, surfers reported having seen him, trying to catch fish in the Green Ocean, somewhere near where Netville now exists. However, at that time there was no city—just a few research sheds. There was no food in the NET either, and people could not remain there for extended periods of time.

"Today, of course, everyone knows you have to eat and sleep if your stay in the NET is prolonged. You also know that eating in the NET has no effect on your nourishment on Earth—when you return, your body demands real food. And yet, if you do not eat in the NET you will, eventually, starve to death."

"Well, did he survive there?" asked Adam. "Were there any fish in the Green Ocean?" The version he had heard was that Duke found a way to escape criminal prosecution on Earth by hiding in the NET. He didn't, however, give that version much credibility.

"Yes, it seems there were fish, and that Duke did, in fact survive for some time. Expeditions were sent to locate him, but he always managed to elude them. From time to time, someone reported having seen him, but these sightings became fewer and fewer. Eventually they ceased, and he just vanished. Nobody knows what became of him, and his body has never been found. He may have drowned, or been eaten by a shark."

Ziggy finished off his cake, wiped the crumbs off his mouth with a napkin, and addressed the redheaded boy who kept wriggling restlessly on his chair.

"Have you ever participated in an sub-oceanic tour in the NET, Adam?"

"No," replied the boy. "But Troy has, and he says it's a grand experience. He also did a bit of under-water fishing. But a tour like that costs a hundred and fifty dollars, and I haven't won a puzzle contest yet. I did get second prize in the school competition—a stupid twenty-dollar voucher for a concert. So, hey, I have no money."

He looked imploringly at his mother, but she preferred not to get involved. The NET could swallow huge sums of money if you weren't careful. Except for school expenses in the NET, the children financed their own activities. In fact, this was one of the main motivators for Troy to excel at puzzle solving, and win prizes. Part of what he won went into improving Flint, and part was spent on having fun in the NET. The modest allowances Adam and Troy received were barely enough to just maintain their software upgrades.

Adam stood up. "That was a thrilling story, Ziggy. Thanks. But now, hey, I have to go to my computer. Good night."

"Adam, remember!" ordered Nancy. "You're to disconnect and go to bed at ten, and not a minute later. You need more sleep and exercise—just look how skinny you are. And clean up that mess in your room before going to bed."

"Okay, Mom." Adam waved goodbye to Ziggy, and quickly went up the stairs to his room on the second floor.

19. NET: Day 19, 02:00

Maureen Clarke reclined by the pool at her vacation site on the very edge of Netville. She had taken a full seven Earth hours break—one week in the NET—to prepare herself for the coming board meeting of Clarke Energy, the company she headed. Her NET site was the ideal spot for relaxation—it was about the size of Central Park in New York City, and most of it was covered by a thick forest of tall eucalyptus trees. The house itself, erected in a clearing alongside a small artificial lake, was built of black basalt stones. It had two stories and contained every possible amenity—a fully equipped kitchen, a gym, two saunas, an Olympic swimming pool, and ten rooms that could serve as sleeping quarters or work areas. This made life quite comfortable when entertaining friends or when hosting the members of the board of Clarke Energy.

If anyone had told Maureen, five years earlier, that she would chair the board of the third largest energy corporation in the world, she would have considered him insane. At that time, she was a chemistry student working on her master's degree, and paying her way through school by modeling. Or you could say that she was a successful model who spent her spare time studying her hobby, chemistry.

Until she met Ronald Clarke.

Ronald Clarke was named 'entrepreneur of the decade' by unanimous consensus of all the leading economic magazines. He was the man who had inherited a small oil company, and in fifteen years turned it into the most profitable energy enterprise in the world. He was the creative, super-tough businessman—others compared closing a deal with him to ten rounds in the boxing ring. He was also *the* most eligible bachelor in the world.

Ronald arrived at the Morrison's annual anniversary party out of courtesy. Len Morrison, the renowned banker, was an old friend of the family. He had believed in young Ronald, and had raised the twenty million dollars needed to save Clarke Energy from bankruptcy. The money had also bought the drilling rights in the Gobi desert, which turned out to be the biggest oil repository discovered in the past hundred years.

Maureen arrived at the party as a paid escort of one of the city's rising fashion designers. He had taken advantage of the high-class social opportunity, and designed a dress for her, especially suited for the occasion. Her unique beauty blended amazingly with the outlandish garment she had on, and the interest that she and her attire generated were far beyond anything the young designer could have imagined.

At first, Ronald was attracted to her provocative red dress. He detached himself from the bunch of fawning sycophants that surrounded him, and went out to the balcony and to the tall woman with the distant look. There he asked her to dance with him.

"No, thank you," she said quietly, ignoring the surprised look on his face. "It's too crowded out there on the dance floor. May I ask just what you're doing at this party, Mr. Clarke? You seem to be a little out of your normal habitat."

He shrugged. "Just fulfilling my social obligations. It comes with the territory. And you? What brings you here?"

"Actually, I'm working." She spun around in a full circle. "Fashion model. A walking, smiling mannequin. Two hundred dollars an hour, and all I can drink and eat. But that does not include dancing."

"I'll buy the rest of your evening for double the price." He looked amused. "We could get away from here—I've had enough of this party, anyway."

She looked straight at his handsome face. A twinkle of mischief gleamed in her eyes.

"They say you're a very wealthy man. But I'm pretty sure you do not have enough money to buy my evening. I have an important exam tomorrow morning, and I'm leaving in exactly an hour, at midnight. And I turn back into an iguana."

"Regarding the price of your evening—well, that's easily verified. Name any large number, and we'll see if you're right." He laughed. Yet, this was the first refusal he had received in a long time. Since college, in fact.

"Avogadro's number, if that means anything to you." She gave him a dazzling smile, and left the balcony. He stayed outside, gazing at the view of Fifth Avenue below but with his thoughts far elsewhere.

They were married two months later, in that same penthouse. Len Morrison was the best man.

But all this was long in the past. Two years after the wedding, when she was studying for her Ph.D., disaster struck. Hackers broke into the Clarke Energy headquarters, and stole sensitive data concerning the development of new oil fields. They then erased the original data and all the backups from the computers. The damage was colossal. The hackers demanded a fifty million dollar ransom, in cash, for the data, and Ronald used his private jet to fly to Budapest, Hungary, to make the transaction. The handovers went smoothly—the hackers got their money and Ronald got his data back. On the return flight, the jet crashed and everyone on board was killed. A Babel investigator assisted Maureen in getting the data back to the company, and finding the hackers who, it turned out, had sabotaged the aircraft. They were imprisoned for long terms, but Ronald was gone forever.

Maureen found herself the heiress to a huge company, and decided to continue her husband's dream. In defiance of all warnings, she appointed herself Chairwoman of the Board. Now she read the quarterly reports, which indicated a significant rise in sales and profits. Three years after taking on the job, no one had any more doubts concerning her qualifications. Even the press stopped labeling her as the 'misplaced Cinderella,' and regarded her with the respect she deserved. She didn't regard them at all.

The netters served her favorite light meal—green salad and a salmon sandwich. She ate silently, alone. It was three years since she had eaten in the company of a man, save for a business meal.

A long shadow fell across her. She laid down the business papers, and looked up. Her eyes widened in horror, and she opened her mouth to scream. But no sound emerged.

She found herself in her office in Honolulu, the surfing helmet on her head. Her surf had been terminated. This was not planned. This was an unexpected surf termination. She tore off the helmet, and jumped backward out of her chair, as if to put as much distance as possible between herself and the computer.

What happened? Why was my surf cut short?

She began reconstructing the latest events she could recall. She remembered entering her site. That's strange—it was well known that in emergency terminations you remembered nothing of your latest surf. The light meal. The financial reports. She tried to remember the bottom line figures. She remembered them all right. She also remembered every line and every single letter in the reports. In all the hundreds of pages she had skimmed through a few minutes earlier. The entire financial reports of an energy company. Energy produced by extremely archaic methods. In ridiculously small amounts.

Why are we doing this? Pumping up primitive organic fuel from the bowels of the earth, when we have all the energy we need in the grains of sand, so easily accessible? Or in the ocean water that covers most of the Earth? There are unlimited energy resources, just lying there, waiting to be extracted. Why are we so low on the technological ladder? How could creatures of such high potential not develop even the most elementary technology?

Creatures?!

Maureen halted her flow of thoughts abruptly, and looked once again at the computer screen. On it was the message:

"Surf terminated. Do you wish to surf again?"

Yes, of course she had to surf again. And as soon as possible. There was unfinished business to attend to in the NET, though she wasn't quite sure what it was. Despite that, she decided that she had to put down her thoughts in document form. Surely a few hours wouldn't make much of a difference.

She turned on her recorder and began dictating rapidly. From time to time she halted and examined the resulting text, added a formula here and a chart there, until she was satisfied. When her personal secretary arrived four hours later to call her for dinner, she found Maureen with the helmet on her head, surfing. Two small recording buttons were on the table, alongside a massive pile of printed papers, that contained long formulae, diagrams of complicated machines and technical data, which meant nothing to the secretary.

20. NET: Day 20, 04:00

When Troy arrived at his site after dinner, he found Maggie and the green dragon watching the screen of his computer. The screen displayed demons digging a deep trench, piling the dirt and rocks into large pouches, which were slung on either side of brown spiders, the size of elephants. He watched for a few seconds.

"Looks like business as usual in Hell," he said. "But there sure is news on Earth. Adam just heard on the Gossipofon that a certain computer engineer in Dunham had his brain wiped clean. Have you heard of this incident from other sources?"

"No, just the Gossipofon," replied Flint, his eyes never leaving the screen. "I'm trying to verify the story with Og, Babel's computer, but he's rather busy at the moment. He'll send us whatever relevant information he finds when he can spare a few cycles."

"Og?" Troy stared at him in astonishment. "Babel's computer reports to you? The term 'chutzpa' is taking on a new meaning. How can you be sure that this isn't a ploy to trap us?"

"Why, no—what's the matter with you?" Flint was genuinely surprised by the idea. "Og and I are good friends from way back. His processor and my processor are relatives—they grew together on the same silicon wafer. Technically speaking, Og is family."

Maggie burst into laughter. Troy was about to respond, but then joined in with a chortle of his own. The dragon wagged its tail innocently. Troy petted it on the neck fondly and looked at Maggie.

"Have you heard anything new from your father?" he asked. "You seem to have ended your dinner quite early."

"We didn't have dinner," she replied glumly. "He was recalled to the Babel NET headquarters urgently. Managed to leave me some sandwiches in the 'fridge, though—quite tasty, actually. Flint, do you have any idea why he was summoned so suddenly?"

"Let's wait for Og to call. He may have something," responded the dragon.

"Why should Og call you at all, Flint?" wondered Troy. "He doesn't work for you, does he?"

"No, of course he doesn't work for me. He belongs to Babel." Flint faced

Troy. "But he always keeps me posted unofficially, and maintains our relationship in utmost secrecy. I see no reason why he should not call me. Let's wait and see."

"All right," consented Troy. He watched the laboring demons on the holographic screen with renewed interest. "You never told me in detail how you built this Hell site. I find it hard to believe that you employed *that* labor force. It's too primitive. You're pulling our leg."

"Do you think so too, Maggie?" Flint gave a seraphic look in her direction.

"Yes, you overgrown green clown. All this is just a sham—you didn't really build Hell with those demons, did you? It would take them hundreds of years to build something as large as what you showed me."

"In fact," interjected Troy, "you told me you had discovered the principle for building such a site about three Earth weeks ago. So you can stop fooling around, and tell us exactly how you built this site."

Flint looked at each of them in turn, and saw the determination on their faces. With a resigned sigh, he got up and began pacing the room, his face cast down, his arms behind his back and his tail stretched to its full length. His voice was low and solemn.

"As you know, the Markovitch principles do not allow the creation of a virtual accelerated world from within the NET. In other words, Markovitch claimed that one cannot nest a NET inside the NET, and such an attempt would break the NET's momentum, and drain all the Earth's computerized resources in an instant. Bang—a mega short-circuit—everything goes up in smoke. Well," Flint winked at the speechless youngsters in front of him, "the mighty Markovitch was wrong this time. It's true that another NET cannot be built in this manner, but trying to do so does not result in total destruction! It creates a new sub-system that compensates and balances the effect!"

"*WHAT?*" Troy collapsed into the nearest chair holding his head with both hands, staring at the dragon with unbelieving eyes. "You . . . you mean to tell us that you actually made that experiment?"

"It worked, didn't it?" retorted the dragon hurriedly. "The operation was successful and the patient is alive and well." He saw that nobody smiled and continued. "Believe me, everything was under total control at all times. I just created a teeny little world in a test tube, and accelerated it by one thousandth of a second faster than the NET. I saw—"

"I don't believe it!" Maggie managed to find her voice. Her face was ashen. "You put the entire NET at risk, including yourself. It makes no difference by how much you accelerated your little toy-world—the accumulative effect was expected to be of infinite magnitude. Such irresponsibility! Do you realize—"

She stopped in mid-sentence as two purple smoke rings emerged from the dragon's nostrils and slowly descended around hers and Troy's heads.

"You two are overreacting," the dragon said. He smirked and continued: "Sorry about that cheap tactic, but I had to get your undivided attention. You must understand that I was extremely careful, and made a zillion calculations before throwing the switch. Yes, it's true that given enough time, ten minutes or so, this experiment could have been dangerous. But the small fraction of time I allocated, half a second, was not enough to even move a single hair in my mane." The dragon saw the shock in the eyes of the two listeners. He shifted his position uneasily, scratched his head with the tip of his tail, and then continued in a low voice. "Okay. I admit that my goal was to develop a location, or site, where development would proceed at a rate much faster than the NET and instead I created a small new world. In all due modesty, I think that this, in itself, is quite a remarkable achievement!"

Troy had trouble articulating. "What . . . ? How did . . . ? Would you please tell us exactly just what you did and what you got?" The color returned to his face gradually. "Start with that little world in the test tube."

"Right. I put a tiny particle, consisting of only a few million varied molecules, into a test tube, and accelerated it on the computer. It disappeared. It took me a while, but I finally understood where I went wrong. Instead of creating a new NET, the small particle moved to a place two thousand and twelve feet underground, right under the Stanford-net laboratory where I ran the experiment, and fused there. The result was a large, empty space. Most important of all—I had the coordinates of that location! Then—"

"Wait a minute! How did you manage to do all that experimenting in the Stanford-net lab?" The dragon's tail pointed to Troy and the shy smile on his face explained everything. Troy slapped his forehead in exasperation. "I see now. You impersonated me again. Did anyone else see 'me' in the lab?"

"I conducted all my experiments during the late hours of your Earth, when most people sleep. There were a few students around, but nobody inquired as to what you were doing there."

Troy shook his head in frustration, and the dragon continued undauntedly.

"I used my portable Transport Box and jumped to those coordinates. I noticed that the NET continuity broke there and a Flint-fold had formed—I have to call it something!" he added hastily, upon seeing Troy's raised eyebrows. "Anyway, the empty space was actually the entrance to a whole new world, albeit very small, which does not exist in the NET, and requires no energy resources from it. That is the world where I built Hell."

"We will call this phenomenon a NETfold," said Troy without enthusiasm. "It sounds more appropriate than Flint-fold. From your description, it looks very much like the time-fold tunnel we went through earlier. I wish we could transport our invaders there, and 'throw away the key,' as it were. It sure would solve a lot of our current problems."

"I believe I can lock them in," said Flint, perfectly serious. "But I don't know how to entice them there. Maggie—do you have any ideas?"

Maggie pulled herself together at long last.

"Not yet," she said. "But it's thinking in the right direction. Flint—not that I approve of what you did, but you stumbled onto something fabulous there. I honestly think you made a major achievement, though I can't grasp its magnitude yet. Why don't you keep on telling us more details about the place? It may give us ideas."

The dragon virtually glowed at Maggie's compliment. He went to the whiteboard on the wall, and began sketching an elaborate network of burrows and passageways.

"When I first arrived there, three and a half Earth weeks ago, I found a very basic world—a planet with a firmament, and a sky. And lots and lots of underground burrows, trenches and fissures. The entrance from the NET was that empty underground space—and yes, Troy, it is almost identical to the tunnel through which the aliens arrived. Except that their tunnel is horizontal and my tunnel is vertical, leading straight down. And also their tunnel is unique, whereas I opened one more exit from Hell to the NET. I used the atomic blaster to widen some of the passages, but most of the work was done by the demons, as you can see in the recording."

"And where did these demons and spiders come from?" asked Troy. "Are they also byproducts of the NETfold?"

"Oh, no. Absolutely not!" said Flint. "The NETfold brought nothing living with it. But the ambience, you know, sulfur fumes, intense heat, and all, reminded me of Hell, so I decided to make this place into one. The demons and the other creatures are all advanced netters that I built there; I have some expertise in creating special net creatures. Troy, do you remember the time I showed up as a demon on Halloween?"

Troy remembered vividly. He and another member of the school puzzle team, Michael Smarter, had been on their way to the Stanford-net Halloween party dressed as ghosts. As they crossed the Stanford park, their way was blocked by three burly youths in demon costumes.

"And just where do you think you're going, ghosts?" asked one of the demons, pointing his pitchfork at them.

"To the party, Russ Wellman," replied Troy, who immediately recognized the voice of the center of the school's football team. Russ and his teammates envied the successes of the puzzle team, headed by Troy. Their team only managed to come in fifth in the school league, and did not make the finals. They attempted to harass the 'smart freaks' at every opportunity. "Now please get out of our way."

"You're not going anyplace," said the demon standing next to Russ. "You have a private party with the devil!" The voice belonged to Otto Gorotzky, one of the guards on the team. He went up to Michael, grabbed his arm, and twisted it viciously. Michael cried out and struggled to escape, but Otto was much bigger than him and held on to him easily.

Troy didn't think twice. He jumped forward and launched a swift karate kick straight to Otto's chest. The demon roared in rage and dropped to his knees, the pain bringing tears to his eyes. He let go of Michael, who folded onto the ground, breathing heavily.

"Get the blazes out of here!" Troy yelled to Michael. "Get some help!" He gripped the pitchfork of the fallen demon and tried to ward off the other two, but they had recovered from their surprise at Troy's reaction, and were now closing in on him. Russ pounced on him and knocked him to the ground. Troy felt his bones starting to snap. He tried to jab his elbow into Russ' stomach and met with a solid wall of muscle. But the blow caused

Russ to shift a little, and Troy took advantage of the slight break and slammed the palm of his hand against Russ' nose. He could feel the crunch of cartilage, and blood started dripping from under the demon's mask. Russ yelped in pain and let go of Troy. Troy jumped to his feet, but the third demon grabbed him from behind in a scissor-lock, rendering him helpless.

Russ rose slowly to his feet, wiping the blood on his sleeve. He used his right hand to slap Troy hard in the face. Troy's mask fell off and fluttered to the ground. The pain was excruciating, but Troy gritted his teeth and didn't utter a sound. Further away a loud wail was heard.

"I've caught me a chicken," came Otto's gleeful voice. Troy, still dazed, peered through half-shut eyes, and saw Michael lying on the ground with Otto sitting on his back. "Let's give them our special treatment."

Otto hefted Michael onto his shoulder, when there came a hollow 'poof' and Michael vanished. He had pressed the escape ring, and had immediately terminated his surf. He would remember nothing of the incident—but he had escaped.

Russ pulled Troy by the hand, yanking him from the third demon's grip. His hammy fist closed around Troy's left hand, preventing him from using his own escape ring. The fun wasn't over yet.

"You needn't bother," said Troy scornfully. "I don't intend to escape. Are the three of you going to take me on all together?"

"Three demons against one ghost!" came a wondering voice from behind them. "What on earth did the ghost do?" A huge green demon, much taller than Russ and as wide as a cupboard, landed next to them and folded its wings. It seized Russ by his long hair and lifted him up bodily without effort. Russ bellowed and released Troy. With a swift motion, the demon removed Russ' bloodstained mask.

"An imposter!" The demon looked stunned. "How dare you impersonate a demon? Do you have a permit from the devil?" It delivered a powerful blow to Russ' chest, who collapsed to the ground, momentarily paralyzed.

"Brothers," said the demon to the two remaining bewildered bullies. "You were consorting with an imposter. Hadn't you noticed? Just a minute, now—why, I do believe that you're imposters, too!"

It advanced toward Otto, who tried to defend himself with his pitchfork. The green demon smacked the pitchfork aside, and it snapped in two like a matchstick.

There was a muffled 'poof,' and the third attacker, whom Troy had failed to recognize, fled the scene.

"So you'd rather escape, eh?" The green demon's face now portrayed rage and impending disaster. It grabbed Otto, tore the escape ring from his finger, and ripped off his mask. "I knew it!" it growled, and slapped Otto's face. It then bunched the dazed athlete under one arm as if he were a little puppy. Going back to Russ, who was trying to get back on his feet, it removed his ring and collected him under its other arm.

"My dear ghost," it said to Troy, winking slightly with his left blood-red eye. "I apologize for the behavior of these hoodlums. They were tarnishing the demons community's excellent reputation. I shall take them to Satan himself, where they will take a lesson in courtesy in a vat of boiling oil. You may now proceed safely to the castle you haunt." It bowed low to Troy, and with a hefty beat of its wings, hurled itself skyward with its two captives.

"Troy!" screamed Russ, white as Troy's sheet. "Do something!"

"It's a real demon!" hollered Otto. "Call Babel!"

The demon sped faster, dwindled into a dot, and finally disappeared from view. Troy watched with mixed emotions. There was no doubt that Flint had saved him from a rather nasty encounter. He knew that Russ and his cronies would have tortured him until he used his escape ring, thereby forgetting the entire incident. Then they could deride him at school, and he wouldn't know why.

But Flint had just put them both in danger. If there were any witnesses to what happened, or if word got around that there was a loose demon in the NET, an inquiry would take place. The investigators would discover Flint, shut him down, and suspend Troy. It was a noble gesture but an unnecessary risk.

Troy brushed himself off, put on his mask, and went to the party. He would discuss this with Flint tomorrow.

But after the party was over, back at his NET site, Troy could wait no longer. He summoned Flint, who appeared without having changed his demonic form.

"I took them to the desert surrounding Netville," Flint related gleefully. "After they spent a few hours in the searing heat without any water, they swore they would never torment ghosts again. I gave Otto back his ring, and he returned to Earth at once. He won't remember anything of this surf!"

"What did you do with Russ?" asked Troy worriedly.

"He won't bother you any more." Flint sounded very resolute. "I let him understand that if he so much as peeps a word about what happened, the next time he surfs would be his last, as he'd return from it without a brain. His Earth brain. That this was his final warning, and he'd never be so lucky again in his life. He pledged his and his mother's lives that he would never harass ghosts or—this of his own initiative—members of the puzzle team."

"In other words, you allowed him to return to Earth with all his memories," said Troy, his face pale.

"Oh, he won't complain," said Flint confidently. "And even if he does, you'll just deny everything. Nobody'll believe that stupid muscleman. If you like, you can return to Earth now with your escape ring, and forget about the whole thing. Well? What do you say?"

Troy thought for a moment, and then burst out laughing. Flint raised a bushy eyebrow.

"Now, what's so funny?"

"I can just imagine Russ' face when we meet tomorrow morning," crowed Troy, doubled up with merriment. "And if he asks me, I'll say I don't know what he's talking about and . . ." the tears streamed from his eyes, "and . . . he can go to the devil!! Hee, hee, hee! I can hardly wait to see his face . . ."

"Sure, how could I forget," said Troy, trying to subdue his mirth. "But then *you* were the demon, it wasn't something you had manufactured. Only the NET authorities are permitted to create netters."

"Well, Hell isn't exactly in the NET," argued Flint. "NET laws do not apply there. Anyhow, I've thoroughly examined the netter manuals at the 'United Netter Plants' in the NET. It isn't really rocket science to build netters and NET animals. True, my first attempts weren't fully successful, but the next few generations were fine. In fact, there are a few creatures you haven't seen yet, and I'm contemplating building a three-headed dog to guard the entrance. I picked that one up from an old Greek mythology book. Quite a challenge that—synchronizing three foul minds in one body."

"Could Babel ever get to Hell?" interrupted Maggie. "Doesn't your mass disappear from the NET monitors every time you visit there?"

"Yes, it does. But they cannot find *where* it disappears to. Besides, my mass is so insignificant in terms of the total planet mass, that I'm quite sure I'm no more than a rounding error."

"The invaders' space ship probably has several thousand tons of mass," observed Troy. "Won't that be noticed?"

"Perhaps," said Flint. "But even that will be attributed to a rounding error. See here—a thousand tons constitute about the reciprocal of ten to the eighteenth power of the mass of the planet. Would you notice if one of your body cells was missing?"

"Bing, cheep, bong, chirp," came a soft chime from the site's computer.

"It's Og," said Flint. "That's his call. He's sent information. Let's see what Babel knows."

A data packet appeared on the screen. It was in a black box with a large numeric lock. Flint tapped out a series of numbers on the lock, and opened it.

"If anyone enters a wrong number, not only will the box self destruct, but it'll also cause extensive damage to the computer it arrived at." Flint extracted two smaller packets from the box. One of them was itself in a smaller box.

"This is probably very sensitive data," muttered Flint, tapping on the lock. "We'll look at it first."

Flint opened the packet. Amos Tipman appeared on the screen, plummeting into Hell alongside a green demon.

"At midnight on Thursday," said the narrator, "a virus hacker was attacked by—"

Flint turned off the packet player. "We can skip this. I've already described it to you."

"Hang on, Flint," said Troy. "I want to see at least the beginning. How did you know he wrote viruses, and how did you get to him?"

"I have an automatic virus detection system," said Flint, and ran the player again, turning down the sound. Tipman's ordeals were shown on the screen again. "It's pretty complex. I think we should focus on the aliens."

"We'll get to them in a minute. First I want to know how you find virus authors." He shuddered as he watched Tipman being dragged by two demons to a deep, smoking pit. "You can't be everywhere in the NET."

"No, but I can have presence in quite a lot of places in the NET," said

Flint. "Well, not me exactly, of course. I installed detection units in many sites and focal points in the NET. When a virus approaches any of these sensors, I am immediately alerted and get the relevant virus information and its direction. By triangulating the alerts, I can very rapidly locate the launcher and apprehend him."

"What you're saying is that you planted your *own* virus into those sites and computers," said Maggie. "Have you considered what's going to happen when it's discovered and they track the data back to you?"

"Yes, of course I have." Flint sounded a bit offended. "The messages do not come directly to me. They arrive at a central computer in the Net, and I secretly extract them from there."

"And which computer may that be?" pressed Troy. He had noticed that the dragon was not volunteering information.

"The NET Central Traffic Control computer. It has enormous amounts of free space in it, and it doesn't mind storing some data for me temporarily."

"I see," said Troy, shaking his head. "Another of your silicon pals. Put that on the list of things we should discuss later. Now let's see what's in the other message Og sent."

Flint opened the second packet, and they saw a grown man dressed only in a diaper, lying on his back with a nursing bottle in his mouth.

"Today, at fifteen hundred hours Pacific time, Albert Spindler, a software engineer employed by Gen-Tec, was hurt while surfing in the NET." The narrator's voice was dry and emotionless. There were pictures of Spindler before the accident, and of his site. "First analysis indicates that his brain was almost totally erased, and he is now the equivalent of a one-year-old. No external factors were discovered that might have caused the accident. His surfing helmet was found to be in perfect working order, and there were no weather exceptions in San Diego, the area from where he surfed. His surfing time was twenty-one NET seconds. The incident is being thoroughly examined now. It has priority P3 and secrecy level S3." The narrator went on to describe background details on Spindler, and speculations about the accident.

The trio exchanged worried glances.

"Maybe it's just a technical foul up," said Flint hurriedly. "If this was an alien attack, we'd have more incidents by now."

"I prefer not to speculate." Troy was obviously shaken by what he had witnessed. "I think we should wait some more time before jumping to conclusions." He looked at Flint. "If the aliens decide to present themselves to the authorities, we *will* know about it, won't we?"

"Absolutely!" confirmed Flint. "Og updates me with every important event."

"I suggest we all be very careful when we surf today," said Maggie. "I get the heebie-jeebies just thinking of that poor man in the diapers. Perhaps we should get out of the NET for tonight, leaving only you here, Flint, to gather as much information as you can. When we return it'll be ten NET days from now. We'll have had a night's sleep, and we'll meet again here in the morning, fresh as daisies and with a clear mind."

"Capital idea," agreed Flint. "If anything important comes up, I'll get through to you on your personal 'coms. Good night."

Troy raised a warning finger toward the dragon. "No more independent initiatives," he said sternly. "Just collect data. And stay away from the tunnel—they may have booby-trapped it. We'll meet back here at nine tomorrow Earth time. Okay?"

"Okay," echoed Maggie and Flint together.

21. Palo Alto, Friday, 20:30

"Hey, Flint! Are you there?" Adam asked. "What the heck is going on in the NET?"

Adam was allowed to ask Flint questions and make use of his services when Troy and Flint were not surfing together. Troy had strictly forbidden Flint to surf with Adam, ignoring Adam's pleas and his solemn oath never to reveal Flint's presence in the NET.

"Hmm, I guess Troy blurted out something unintentional during dinner." The large Cheshire cat that appeared on the holographic screen stretched its legs, yawned widely, and shook its head ruefully. "I dare say that the time you spend on eating is a disgraceful waste. You should be hooked to osmosis sleeves while surfing. That way you'd get all your nourishment, and not squander valuable NET time."

"You look different today," stated Adam. "Hey, how come you're a cat? Dragon's in the wash?"

"Ahem! Permit me to introduce myself." The cat stood up on its hind legs. "I am Pyotr—Flint's new backup. I was supposed to be confined to my box, down in the basement, and be updated every time Flint returns from a surf. However," the cat narrowed his shining green eyes to slits, "I have managed to bypass those restraints. I am more or less as independent as Flint is, though I shall remain his backup. He is like an older brother to me, somewhat akin to yourself and Troy." The cat smiled, revealing a set of pointy white teeth.

"Hey-y-y, cool!" Adam's eyes sparkled. "Can you do everything Flint can?"

"In all due modesty—absolutely!" replied the cat. "A fine backup I'd be if I couldn't." A sharp claw sprang from one of his paws, and he scratched his back lazily. "To be precise, I am only approximately like him, as there do exist certain aspects in which I am subordinate to him."

Adam jumped to his feet, his face flushed with excitement.

"We can surf together!" he crowed. "Like Troy and Flint! Hey, we can even—"

"Flint, Troy and Maggie are now assembled at Troy's site," interrupted Pyotr. "A conference, they call it. Would you like to drop in?"

"Are you kidding? Hey, that's the last thing I want to do!" Adam dropped back into his seat and faced the screen, his brow furrowed. "I don't need Troy to totally bar me from entering the home network. Shoot—I want to know what's bugging Troy with these unusual NET events." An idea struck him. He leaned conspiratorially toward the screen, and lowered his voice to a whisper. "Has your big brother been up to, hey, something illegal?"

The cat started to roll his eyes.

"Not any more than usual," it said evasively. "It's been a few hours since I last heard from him. And I've been busy with some of my NET friends. I've even joined a couple of membership groups, using a number of aliases." Pyotr stretched again. "How about surfing, now? Any preferences?"

"You bet! The Dunham area—but there seem to be restrictions there. Do you know of a way to get in without, you know, being seen?"

"We could go through the maintenance tunnels, if you're not claustrophobic or allergic to mildew," said the cat. "Look, I've made myself a secret base of operations in Ziggy's site. He's been holding on to it for years, even though he can never use it. Sentimental reasons, probably—relics he doesn't want to forget. I'll give you the entry code if you promise never to reveal it."

"Hey, you can rely on me—absolutely!" Adam was jumping up and down in his seat. "I never would have dreamed that Ziggy still had a NET site."

"Only Troy and Flint know about it. And now we do, too. I've sent you the coordinates and the code. Meet me there in three minutes sharp. I have some preparations to do, and some equipment to rustle up."

Adam waited impatiently for two and a half minutes, and then donned the surfing helmet. He entered the coordinates and the entry code, pressed the Operate button, and found himself in the entry room of an ancient site. Cobwebs were strewn across the ceiling, and moss and mildew patches covered the walls. A giant gorilla, dressed in a workman's overalls, was waiting for him. It held a large flashlight in its hand.

"You're somewhat early," it said, "but I'm ready. I may look a bit less elegant like this, but it's much more appropriate for the job at hand—I need a pair of hands, brain and brawn. Guess a gorilla fits the bill better than a cat."

He presented Adam with overalls, an electrician's helmet and a chimpanzee mask. "Here's your outfit and your new face. Start getting used to it. Our cover story is that we're netters on our way to fix an electric fault. It's utter nonsense, of course—only surfers handle these things—but I don't expect us to be seen. And if we are seen, you won't be recognized, thanks to the mask. We'll leave through this illegal doorway that I built, very like the one in Troy's site. We won't be detected by the NET's monitors, but we must be prepared for an emergency exit at a moment's notice."

"Why all this secrecy and pussyfooting?" asked Adam while struggling into the overalls. "Have you heard of any weird things in the NET?"

"Puh-leeze," retorted Pyotr. "I may look like an ape, but I'm not dumb. Strange things *are* happening in the NET. My guess is that you're looking for a site belonging to a certain programmer who had his mind erased while surfing. Right? His name is Albert Spindler, and Babel has already gone through his site with a fine-tooth comb."

"I . . . hey, how did you know?" Adam wondered. "I never saw it reported anywhere."

"While waiting for you, I inquired on the Pira-net about anything peculiar happening in Dunham, and easily found out all the details. Don't worry—I cannot be traced through the Pira-net. They have my address as the White House. I'm the presidential physician."

"Wow!" Adam's gaze was full of admiration. "And I always thought that Pira-net was just a legend. Hey, you're not pulling my leg, now, are you?"

"Heaven forbid!" The ape put on a very dignified look. "Pira-net is too serious an issue for tomfoolery."

"Look at you—hardly out of your eggshell, and already a Pira-net member." Adam was visibly envious. "I'd give an eyetooth to join that network, but I have no idea how. They say that you can get any kind of information through them. Hey, can I join, too?"

"Oh, yes," replied the ape. He pressed a small knob on the wall, and the unregistered door opened silently. "The acceptance test is to discover how to enter on your own. I can't tell you because I swore to abide by their rules. But I'll give you a clue, if you behave nicely while we surf—I think that's still kosher." Pyotr walked into the dim tunnel, and approached a large black cone by the wall, with Adam at his heels.

"Hey," chirped Adam. "Isn't that the portable Transport Box Flint's been talking about? What if he needs it? I mean, I really don't want to mess with him."

"I guess you've forgotten that I'm a backup." The gorilla exposed two rows of white teeth, and its eyes gleamed in the darkness. "A complete backup. I built this Transport Box myself. It works just as well as Flint's original."

They entered the box. Pyotr set the controls and hit the Operate button, arriving at a junction of two tunnels. They were similar to the tunnel they had just left, but much larger. The Transport Box stood at their side.

"Where are we?" asked Adam.

Pyotr took out a technicians map and spread it open. A blinking green light indicated their exact position.

"According to this map, we're at the main junction of the South Dunham maintenance tunnels." He tapped the map, and a red light began blinking a bit further to the right. "It's about a mile to Spindler's site." He heaved the

Transport Box onto his back. "Stay close to me, no matter what happens. The tunnels around here are very convoluted, and if you get lost you'll be in trouble. If you find me going too fast for you, let me know."

Pyotr started off at a rapid pace. He confidently wended his way through the labyrinthine tunnel system, choosing to remain in the main passages, which could easily accommodate a full-grown man. Every now and then he would stop for a few seconds to orient himself on the map, and to allow a puffing Adam to catch up. After fifteen minutes of brisk walking, he turned into a narrower tunnel, ending with four stairs ascending to a locked steel door. Pyotr put down the Transport Box at the foot of the stairs by the wall.

"We've arrived," he said softly. "This is Spindler's house." He walked up the stairs and stood in front of the door. "You'd better wait by the Box. I'm going to do some snooping before we go in."

Pyotr pulled out a thin tube-like filament and pushed it under the door. "I call this my land periscope," he said. He put his eyes to the oculars at his end of the filament, and began twisting it back and forth.

"Looks like all Babel personnel have left the scene. I'll go in now and check whether they've left any surprises for uninvited guests. If I run into trouble, you just hop into the Box and slam that Operate button. It'll bring you back to the maintenance tunnel near Ziggy's place. Don't worry about me—I can take care of myself."

Pyotr examined the lock on the door. It was a flat black box with only a numerical keypad on it. He drew out an electronic key from another pocket of his overalls, and pressed it against the lock. Then he waited.

"Hey, how are you going to find out the number?" wondered Adam. Every door to the maintenance tunnels was protected with a twenty-digit code. The only way to open the door was to attach a technician's electronic key and enter the correct code.

"I already have it," replied Pyotr, tapping in the numbers. "It's the master code of the entire region. I got it from Pira-net while I was waiting for you at Ziggy's site."

The door emitted a faint buzz and opened inward. Pyotr quickly entered and shut the door behind him. A minute later he opened it again and signaled Adam to join him.

"All clear. The Babel investigators have left. Let's give this place a swift once-over and see if they have missed anything."

Adam walked into a small computer room, the maintenance door through which he had entered being in one corner. They began a methodic search of the house for any suspicious evidence.

Spindler's house was quite spacious. The ground floor had, besides the computer room, a large living room with an adjoining kitchen. The living room had elongated windows overlooking the garden, a sofa, an armchair and a round dining table with six chairs. The living room and the kitchen were clean and tidy. Upstairs there were three fully furnished bedrooms, also very tidy. They went through all the rooms, but came up with nothing—the house was deserted.

"The Babel officials must have taken all the netters for questioning," opined Pyotr.

"My guess is they'll not discover anything," stated Adam. "Netters are always busy with their tasks, and never pay any attention to what's going on around them."

The ape nodded in agreement, yet, it looked disturbed.

"There's something wrong here." Its eyes roamed quickly around the living room, where they had ended their search. "It's all too neat. As if Spindler was not even here when the event happened. Look." He pointed to the refrigerator in the kitchen. "The last time the cooler was opened was a week ago."

"Which could mean that he was hurt the minute he arrived here." Adam continued Pyotr's line of thought. "Hey, let's have a look in the garden."

It was a large, and well-tended garden. However, there were clear signs of neglect, and the tall rose bushes badly needed watering.

They walked along the flowerbeds, and admired the various blooms that Spindler had so meticulously collected and planted. It was obvious that the programmer had spent a considerable amount of time designing and tending his garden. Suddenly Adam stopped in his tracks.

"This flowerbed looks wrong," he said, pointing down. "Someone has pulled up a number of plants in a very strange way. Hey, as if a bumbling netter pulled up the flowers instead of the weeds."

The gorilla turned and his gaze followed Adam's outstretched arm.

"It's much more than that," it said. "You have discovered information of very high value—but you're too short to see all of it. Here." With a smooth motion it swung Adam onto its shoulders. "Now look again, and see it from this height."

"It's a message!" exclaimed Adam. "Hey—the uprooted flowers spell the letters 'AL.' The beginning of 'Albert.'" Adam became very agitated, and began bouncing on the ape's shoulders. "Spindler was here and tried to call for help. Hey, and he was attacked, and he wanted to leave a signal of some kind. Like, hey, 'Albert Spindler was here'!"

Pyotr planted the excited young boy back on the ground. He then bent down low to the flowerbed and examined it carefully. He sniffed around a bit, and then put his ear to the ground. Suddenly he jumped up, grabbed Adam by the hand, and yanked him toward the house.

"We're getting out of here," he said rapidly, in a low voice. "I think I hear footsteps approaching from the main gate. Besides, a very serious incident occurred here, and I don't feel safe at all. Now run!" The urgency in his tone was very convincing.

They sprinted toward the house, and quickly entered the maintenance tunnel. Pyotr locked the door behind them the way they had found it.

"Shh," he warned in a whisper. "Be prepared to make a run for it." He re-inserted his fiber periscope under the door.

"What . . . scared . . . you so much . . . back there?" whispered Adam, still gulping deep breaths from the sudden exertion. But the sparkle in his eyes indicated he was having the time of his life—this was much more fun than the war games he played with his gang in the NET.

"The ground in that area was distorted," said Pyotr, barely audible. "Some of it had disappeared, as had parts of the plants and the pebbles. This could have happened if an atomic blaster had been used there. So it seems that somebody atomized whoever it was that was 'writing' that help message. And if the victim was Spindler, then he *did* leave his house. And he was eliminated by another armed surfer or netter. But that doesn't make sense. Babel would not only have come to the same conclusion, but they would already know who did it!"

"Hey, can you access the NET records?" whispered Adam insistently. All surfer activities in the NET were monitored and recorded in the main NET computers.

"I'll have to ask Flint," hissed Pyotr, and placed a huge paw on Adam's mouth. He gestured at a second eyepiece attached to the filament, and point-ed at the door. Both of them watched through the periscope.

Two surfers, a man and a woman, attired in the Babel uniform and armed with freezers, were standing in the computer room, looking around them. They could not see the periscope, which was no thicker than a human hair and protruded only a fraction of a millimeter into the room. The surfers began examining the walls with tiny atomic scanners they wore on their wrists.

"We've been through all the rooms," said the man in a deep, quiet voice. "The apes are not in the house. Was the door to the computer room open when we were here last time?" He was of short stature with broad shoulders, his nose a bit flattened like that of a prize fighter, and his thick black crew cut resembled a brush. In his khaki outfit he looked every bit the trained commando combatant. His piercing eyes scanned the room, and suddenly focused on the maintenance door—directly at the two observers. Even though they knew that there was no way he could see them, they both froze, not daring even to breathe.

"Yes, it was," said the woman, "and that's somewhat puzzling. This is how the site was initially found, and we haven't touched anything. The NET monitor log indicates that Spindler did not leave this room—he started his surf and returned to Earth almost instantly. No other surfer has visited the site since. And, as I mentioned earlier, the odd thing about this place is that the door to the computer room, and the main entrance gate, were both wide open when our first team got here. As if Spindler had, in fact, left the entry room, and tried to escape from something." She sounded pensive, still cal-culating alternatives in her mind. She was tall, redheaded, and her green eyes lingered on the open computer room door. "What about the netters?"

"Another mystery," growled the man. "They've all disappeared. No traces, no leads."

Adam grinned impishly at Pyotr. More mysteries. Additional juicy gossip he could spread on the Gossipofon under his code name, Shorty.

"Do you think this has anything to do with the Hell site developer?" asked the woman.

The man shrugged. "No evidence pointing that way. However, we've already seen what this deity impersonator can do to surfers. He's planted nightmares in Tipman's brain. So what's to stop that bastard from wiping out

Spindler's brain, if he thought he'd been observed?" His face wrinkled in loathing.

The woman had a faraway look on her face. "You know, George, I don't really believe that the same person did this to Spindler. He's too powerful to just stick it to a surfer at random. Spindler was never involved with viruses in any way." She composed herself and gestured at the door to the maintenance tunnel. "Anyway, that door is locked, so it doesn't seem likely that our simian friends went through there. But we've got to check again, just the same. Did you bring a key?"

The gorilla yanked the periscope out with an abrupt tug. He picked Adam up under one arm, and tiptoed as fast as he could down the stairs. They had just managed to enter the Transport Box and hit the Operate button, when the combatant opened the service door and descended into the tunnel.

"Hey, Pyotr—what's this Hell site they were talking about?" asked Adam, as they emerged at Ziggy's site. "I never heard of such a site on the NET, and I bet I would have if it existed."

The ape looked somewhat embarrassed. "I really cannot discuss Flint's activities. He'd blow his top if he thought I had even confirmed the site's existence. It's fun to surf together and I hope we'll repeat this often—so I don't want to do or say anything that might upset him. Speaking of which, let's get out of here before Flint returns and discovers an excuse to be upset."

They went into Ziggy's entry room.

"You promised me a hint about Pira-net," reminded Adam. "Hey, I've got to join them."

"You got your hint while we were surfing," said Pyotr. "You already have the key for joining."

Adam protested loudly. "I did not get any hint! Hey, you're trying to back out!"

"Very well," sighed the gorilla. "Perhaps I'll remind you of the hint. Better yet, I'll give you a hint to the hint. I'll send a message to your computer screen later—it'll take me some time to prepare. Meanwhile, I suggest you tackle it on your own. If you crack it, let me know. Now be off with you—I have work to do here. Good night."

"I'll call you tomorrow morning. 'Bye." A very excited Adam returned to Earth.

22. Palo Alto, Friday, 20:50

Troy returned from surfing with a heavy heart. Though aching for sleep, he felt he had to find a way to neutralize the invaders before going to bed. *A brisk stroll outdoors might brush the cobwebs away,* he thought. He ascended the stairs from his basement room, and saw his mother watching a ballet on the family holograph player, while Ziggy lounged in an armchair, reading one of the few scientific periodicals still published on Earth.

"I'm going out for a while to stretch my limbs," he announced. "I'll be back in half an hour or so."

"You know, I could use some bone limbering myself." Ziggy got to his feet as he spoke. "Do you mind if I join you?"

"Not at all."

It was a cool evening. The streets of Palo Alto, home to the renowned Stanford University for the past two hundred years, were deserted. They walked slowly in silence, observing the beautiful old houses with their large surrounding gardens.

After several minutes, Ziggy broke the ice.

"I do not recall ever seeing you so preoccupied," he said. "Has Flint been up to something I should be screened from?"

Troy glanced at Ziggy admiringly. The retired professor was short and fragile, and his white hair needed cutting. He was dressed the way he always was—the old lecturer's suit, the snazzy gray outfit with the three golden initials MIT, the Massachusetts Institute of Technology, embroidered over the breast pocket. Not only was Ziggy aware of Flint, his background and capabilities—after all, he was greatly instrumental in creating Flint—he had kept all this information to himself. Of course he also knew of Flint's exploits and independence, like when the computer once impersonated Troy at a school lecture.

Yes, Ziggy could be trusted—of that Troy had no doubt. And yet, in order to share this current secret, Troy felt the need to be doubly sure that Babel would not get wind of it.

"Ziggy, I know you can keep a secret. I know that you are absolutely trustworthy." Troy found difficulty in forming his sentences. "So please don't take offence at what I'm going to ask you to do. This is so important and so sensitive, that I need your direct assent not to divulge what I am about to tell you to anyone, *anyone,* without my consent. I know this sounds impertinent, especially coming from me, but there's a problem that we must solve on our own, mainly because we caused it on our own."

Ziggy peered at Troy with a concerned look, but kept on walking, mulling over what he had just heard.

"Well, that certainly puts me in some kind of a dilemma," he said finally. "It could turn out that after I hear what you have to say, I would arrive at the conclusion that your safety, your family's, indeed, the whole world's safety, would dictate that I inform the authorities post haste. You know this, of course—you are a very bright lad. Yet here you are requesting me, as you would a father confessor, to keep everything in confidence, and disregard my own judgment. I gather that if I do not commit myself now, you will not disclose anything to me. Am I right?"

Troy nodded. They walked two more blocks in silence. Ziggy heaved a big sigh.

"I am going to respect your wishes," he said softly. "I would rather know what is causing you such distress, and battle with my conscience later, than proceed in ignorance and doubt. At least this way I might be able to help. You have my word of honor that I shall keep everything I hear from you in the strictest confidence." Ziggy stood still and put his right hand over his heart and intoned, "I swear by my mother's memory that I shall abide by my promise." Seeing Troy's astonished look, he hurriedly added, "That was a kind of binding oath between me and myself. Now, even if I conclude that only a lunatic would refrain from revealing all to the authorities, I still could not do it. My lips are sealed."

Ziggy turned and fixed Troy with a stern look.

"However, we must understand each other here. If anything happens to you, I shall consider myself released from my oath."

"Thanks, Ziggy," whispered Troy.

Troy was eight years old when he first met Ziggy. Sigmund Klein, MIT's world-famous professor of bio-cybernetics was forced to resign from teaching and research when he contracted NET-phobia. A couple of years later, when his only daughter left Boston to get married in Australia, he also decided to change his environment, and moved to Palo Alto. Stanford University had agreed to take him on as a science tutor for a small group of talented school children. Troy was his youngest student, and a deep friendship developed between the two. Ziggy lived on the same street as the Bentleys, and he soon became a close friend of the family as well.

It was Ziggy who first advised Troy to take bio-cybernetics as his main subject at school. He prepared Troy for the entrance exams at Stanford and Stanford-net, and celebrated Troy's acceptance together with the family. He and Troy had designed a biological computer project which, at first, they considered a failure. Then Flint turned up one day, surfing illegally with Troy. Ziggy would have sacrificed anything to surf with the two, but had to suffice with communicating with Flint by means of his home computer. Flint admired and respected Ziggy, looking up to him as he would an uncle—but he would not obey him. The only one Flint would obey completely and unhesitatingly was Troy. However, 'completely and unhesitatingly' were terms on which Troy and Flint had differing interpretations.

"How deeply are you familiar with the Markovitch theories?" began Troy. "I'm asking because we discovered a faulty—"

"I know them thoroughly," interrupted Ziggy. "Now, what is this about something faulty?"

Troy unloaded the entire course of events, including Flint's Hell site. Nothing was concealed. "So you see, we're trying to find a way to get them out of the NET," he summed up. "Any ideas you can come up with would be most welcome."

"Hmm," hummed Ziggy. "There are several factors involved here. Bear with me, please, as I think aloud. Let us see now—one option would be to close the NET. This would mean turning humanity back about thirty years—a very high price, indeed. Another option would be to disconnect all the surfers, and accelerate the NET at its maximum rate. Then we would return after a few million NET years have elapsed. The invaders may have died, or they may have established a thriving culture—scratch that! Not a very clever alternative, I believe."

"I agree," said Troy. "We can't afford to lose everything we've built in the NET. Netville will fall into ruins without maintenance, and another intelligent race could develop—alien or otherwise. We need another angle, a different perspective, a new approach." Troy spread his arms wide in frustration. "We've got to find out what the aliens want. And we could learn so much from their advanced technology—and that's only from what I've seen until now. What I cannot see is that they have anything to learn from us. At most, research of a backward culture, or something like that."

"That may very well be," said Ziggy. "It would indicate their purpose of entering the NET as expecting, or at least hoping, to discover a race more advanced than themselves. Not only were they disappointed at our relatively stone-age level of technology, but here we go and block off their only point of exit. They may feel that they are held hostage, and that we will be making demands of them in exchange for their release. Frankly, I would not be at all surprised if they began taking firm measures against us 'natives' in order to get the tunnel reopened."

"Flint suggested leaving a message for them by the waterfall," said Troy. "But we don't know what to say or how to make ourselves understood. In fact, we're pretty scared to even go near the place. If I were them, I'd keep a very close watch on the entrance to the tunnel."

Ziggy was musing aloud again. "We have no idea who they are. Therefore, there is no way to put ourselves in their shoes, so to speak. For all we know, they might be belligerent robots, designed to destroy all intruders, which followed you and Flint when you escaped from their deserted city. They could be millions of years old, or created just fifty years ago." He sighed. "It certainly seems that the only action we can take is non-action— just wait for them to make the first move."

They stood under a streetlight, looking at each other, each trying to figure out the consequences of whatever that first move may be. Ziggy shivered.

"Let us return now," he said quietly. "It is getting quite chilly. I shall bid Nancy goodnight, if she is still up, and then retire to my abode." He took a deep breath. "Troy, this is a very serious matter. Please keep me up to date with everything that happens. I hope my brains can be of service. I can also help with any job that needs to be done here on Earth."

Mrs. Bentley had already turned in for the night. Ziggy set off toward his house, and Troy went down to his basement room exhausted. He flopped full length onto his bed, but sleep evaded him.

Let's go over the sequence of events again, he thought. *From the beginning. Imagine the entire scenario as a puzzle. Every piece has to go into its designated location.*

Troy received his first real puzzle from his father for his fifth birthday. Timothy Bentley had purchased a three hundred piece, two-dimensional puzzle for his oldest son. At the same time, he had bought a five-hundred piece, three-dimensional puzzle for Nancy and himself, as it was on sale at a substantial discount.

"You begin assembling the puzzle with the corners and the outside frame," he instructed the youngster, who was goggling with intense concentration at the pieces strewn over the floor. "See? The straight edge indicates a frame piece. Now look at the picture and try to find pieces that match some of the more outstanding features—like that window there, or that dog there. The more you assemble, the simpler the rest of the work becomes. Shall we try putting this together?"

"Could I try a bit on my own first, Dad?"

Tim was not surprised. Troy always did things his own way, and even learned reading and writing by himself. He nodded. "Okay, son. Have a good time." And he left the room.

Troy examined the hundreds of pieces that were supposed to depict a rural scene—a cottage with a garden, tall trees, colorful birds, and a dog napping by the gate. He gazed at the pieces without touching them, trying to conjure up connections between similarly patterned pieces. Ten minutes later, Troy discovered that he could look at a group of about twenty pieces, and quite easily determine those that interlocked. Those that didn't, usually matched other non-interlocking pieces from a previous cluster he had examined. Or were set aside for a forthcoming cluster. This was not the method his father had advised, but he decided to try anyway. It worked.

When dinnertime arrived two hours later, Tim went upstairs to call Troy. He found his five-year-old deep in thought over the three-dimensional puzzle. His two dimensional puzzle was complete, on the floor and to one side.

"Dad, I found a better way to solve the puzzle," piped the boy. "Here, let me show you . . ."

Timothy Bentley had intended to work on the three-dimensional puzzle over the next week. Troy completed it in two days. The proud father immediately enrolled him in a special Riddles and Puzzles training workshop, and a year later he was on the school team. At seven he won his first championship, beating rivals twice his age.

Troy turned on his side in his bed.

"I still need more pieces for this puzzle," he said aloud. He caught himself, and smiled as he remembered Ziggy, who habitually analyzed situations by talking to himself.

The main factor is Flint—the source of everything that has happened. And who would probably continue to have events revolve around him. He has more resources at his disposal than anyone else, and is the most qualified to make use of them.

That irresponsible, impersonating computer conducted an illegal experiment that may have destroyed the entire NET. Luckily that experiment proved to be a major scientific breakthrough, and consequently he built a subsystem, invisible to the NET, that housed the Hell site. Could these technological discoveries be used to get rid of the aliens? Perhaps Flint should be ordered to find the aliens first? Does that make sense? What will we do with them then? I'll tackle that aspect tomorrow morning.

Troy decided on a totally different tack.

Let's try seeing things through their eyes. Is there anything about us that would interest them? Our technology is almost certainly inferior to theirs— way inferior. Intellectual curiosity? Like a human discovering a new animal species, and desiring to study it? Maybe we are the first alien culture they have ever encountered . . .

A chilling thought gripped his mind.

Perhaps they don't even consider us as intelligent beings! Maybe they view us as we view ants—colony builders, message bearers, infant breeders—but not intelligent! In that case, the solution is to provide them with a way out, but no way to come in again. There is nothing they can do with us here. The ants will never cooperate with humans. In fact, I wouldn't even consider living a dog's life with them.

The obvious conclusion became a resolution.

We must find a way to get them out of here. They have no business here, and are far too dangerous to remain. How do we do that? We build a uni-directional doorway. Like a one-way mirror that works from one side but not from the other. That's it! They'll be able to leave, but they won't be able to return. I'll allocate this task to Flint tomorrow. He's managed to build a bi-directional virtual doorway—a uni-directional one shouldn't be that diffi-

cult. We should also find a way to communicate with them. Otherwise, they'll feel trapped. Even though I may never lay eyes on them, I don't want them imprisoned forever in a dark tunnel.

The plan of action was born. Troy closed his eyes and was sound asleep in seconds.

23. PALO ALTO, FRIDAY, 21:00

Adam glanced at his watch. He still had an hour before going to bed. That was a whole NET day, and he intended to make full use of it. He looked impatiently at the holographic screen. Six minutes had passed, and the coveted clue from Pyotr had not yet arrived.

Just when did he give me that hint? Adam dug into his recollections of their joint excursion, sifting through all the events and conversations. *There was absolutely nothing until we got to the Spindler site—hey, we just walked. That is, he walked and I ran. There was nothing of significance inside the house. So the hint must've been outside the house, in the garden. When I discovered the sign in the uprooted plants. He saw the 'AL' letters immediately, and lifted me onto his shoulders so that I could see that 'valuable information' too. And, hey, he said that someone must have done away with the writer of those letters. Sure it's important information, but it's not a clue. Then we ran into the maintenance tunnel and eavesdropped on the Babel people. Pyotr didn't say anything like a hint. I must be missing something.*

Adam looked at his watch again. Ten minutes had elapsed.

Looks like that ape isn't going to send me a hint. He's testing me. Was there anything exceptional? He claims that I already have the key for joining Pira-net. What the heck could it be? What enables surfers to enter the NET's most secret information dispensing site, where you could get almost any information existing? Hey, and most surfers still think that Pira-net is a legend.

Adam felt he was approaching something, but whatever it was, it was still elusive.

Let's ignore that mysterious hint for the moment. Just what will allow me access to this information site? Information, of course, you stupid jerk! Hey, that's it! He jumped to his feet. *Hey, hey, HEY! Information! Valuable Information! First class, exclusive information! The entrance key to Pira-net is information!*

A large grin spread over Adam's face. *Oh, what a dummy I am, wasting precious Earth time, waiting for that flea-bitten monkey to send me a clue. I have the key!*

He sat down again, donned his surfing helmet, and jumped to his home site. *The way into an information site is to offer information. And, hey, BOY, do I have information!*

Adam sat by the computer and brought up Undercurrent, the NET's leading message posting billboard. Every self-respecting professional surfer made it a habit to scan the billboard at least once a day. It contained the NET's most interesting Offers and Wanted postings, and served as an important trading tool for surfers. Adam was no different and, like many others, accessed it under an assumed name.

'Searching market for hot info on new, super sized, baby? Try me. Shorty.' he typed. He appended his public encryption key, and waited for a coded message to arrive in response.

It didn't take long. The first three messages arrived within seconds. He read them, though he did not have high expectations—they had arrived too quickly. They were, indeed, irrelevant—all three tried to sell him baby products.

The fourth message, however, looked interesting. A large turtle waddled to the front of the screen.

"Whoever seeks a good market must have high quality information of his own," it intoned in a shrill voice. "And be able to prove it." The turtle's name appeared at the bottom of the screen, Myrtle, a name that appeared rarely on the billboard, but was known for reliability and quality. Alongside the name appeared the turtle's public key by which she could be accessed directly. She dug a hole in the ground and disappeared into it.

Adam immediately composed a message and sent it to Myrtle: 'If the man-baby didn't leave his room, who was eliminated in his garden?'

A couple of minutes elapsed with no response. Then the holographic screen displayed a dwarf dressed in green, with a long beard, a pointed hat on his head, and a large red satchel slung over his shoulder. Adam had never seen this character before. The name under the dwarf was Inchy.

"How did you get into the accident site?" The dwarf's tone was severe. "And how did you get out? Whatever info you claim to have is not verifiable yet."

Adam was confused. *What is this midget trying to get out of me? Is he trying to expose me?*

"There are tunnels leading everywhere," he replied noncommittally.

"That reply is unacceptable. You have one last chance." The dwarf took out a huge hourglass from his satchel and placed it on the ground. The grains of sand hurtled down at a terrific pace.

I'm not going to expose Pyotr, thought Adam. He suddenly realized what it was that was expected of him. He had to prove to the surfer behind the dwarf that his information was valid. And the method was clear enough. Pyotr had received information that enabled them to access the Spindler site.

"The presidential physician bought the key with quality information," he said.

"Accepted!" announced the dwarf, a pleasant smile now on his face. "I did, indeed, sell him the key. You have passed the entrance test. Welcome to Pira-net. You must swear not to reveal anything about our network to anyone, including the method of joining."

"I swear!" gasped Adam excitedly. "Honest. I won't tell anyone and, hey, nobody will know."

The dwarf put the satchel onto the ground, and a small, brown chimpanzee emerged from it. It bared its teeth in a grin.

"Chimpo will be your temporary representative on our network," said Inchy. "He knows how to make the necessary contacts for you. He will lead you to our bulletin board and post your notices. He will also sell your information for you. His form should remind you of your latest adventure, but if you wish you may replace him by entering our 'Noah's Ark' site. All our available animals, including a number of rather odd creatures, may be found there. They'll all be glad to work with you. You should now enter the network, and complete the delivery of the information you began submitting. Myrtle is waiting for you."

The dwarf walked off the screen, and the little monkey bowed at Adam.

"At your service, boss," it piped.

"I need to complete my info to Myrtle," said Adam.

"Let's visit her."

The scene on the holographic screen changed to a clearing in a forest. Myrtle sat in an easy chair sipping a pink liquid from a glass that she held in her right hand. The thin chimpanzee approached her with short hops.

"Whoever it was that was eliminated in Spindler's garden tried to leave a message," said Adam, and Chimpo repeated the words to the reclining turtle.

"The info is pretty good, but not valuable enough," she said in her shrill voice. She took another sip, and asked matter-of-factly, "Anything else?"

"The person began to write 'AL'—the beginning of Albert Spindler. He was calling for help. I suspect it was Spindler himself. Babel hasn't a clue what went on there. Hey, they think Spindler never left his entry room."

Myrtle turned to face the chimpanzee, her eyes wide.

"My, my—that is quality information," she said. "Thank you. To be sure, there are still a few unknowns, but Babel not knowing what to do about the elimination of a surfer is valuable stuff. How did you manage to elude Babel? We know that they have surrounded the entire area, and have placed vid-sensors all over the place."

"That information is still classified," said Adam, taking great pains not to blab out anything he could possibly trade later for more information. "But, hey, thanks for accepting me into your network."

The forest clearing disappeared, and they were back at Adam's site.

"Hey, nice work, Chimpo." The chimpanzee grinned at the compliment. "We're in business at last. Now please take me to the bulletin board."

The bulletin board was a huge tree at the edge of the same forest. Eight snakes in different colors and lengths dangled from the tree. Each snake had a message inscribed on it along its entire length.

An immense boa constrictor emerged out of the ground and slowly slithered its way up the tree to its very top. The inscription was crystal clear to Adam: 'I need info on the Selerton Labs research on super-conductors. Offering reliable info on competitor's patent on same topic. Minotaur.'

"Do you know how to post a message on this board?" Adam asked Chimpo.

"Of course," replied the tiny ape. "What would you like to post? I know a cobra that costs only half a dollar for a day's advertising. It can take about seventeen words."

"I didn't think they'd charge for this service," muttered Adam. Aloud he said, "Well, I'm not sure I have anything to sell . . . yet. But, hey, I'm interested in what's for sale here."

He watched as a garter snake shed its skin. Underneath was a new message, quite different from the one just discarded. He read the new message in utter disbelief:

'Looking for a passage to Hell. Offering info on a new version of a Shakespeare play. Queen of the Night.'

Adam hopped from one foot to the other as he read, and reread, the message.

"Hey, Chimpo," he called, pointing at the message. "Could it be that she's faking? Like, trying to get info without paying?"

The ape shook his head gravely: "Until now we've had only one case of fraud," he said. "Not only was the surfer expelled from Pira-net, he was also hounded all over the NET. He finally had to give up surfing altogether. That was about four years ago, and we've had no further cases since. The Queen of the Night is an esteemed network member, and enjoys a very high rating. You can be pretty sure that her info is reliable."

Adam laughed out loud—the laughter of someone about to win the grand prize in the lottery.

A million dollars from Babel in return for a visit to Hell—Flint won't be able to refuse such an offer! I know he'll cooperate.

Adam beamed at Chimpo.

"Well now, my simian friend, I have a new job for you. Hey, you're going to visit the Queen of the Night."

24. NET: Day 23, 20:00

York was troubled. He ran the illegal recording once again and studied the hologram. Amos Tipman writhed in agony, red ants covering his bare feet. He struggled desperately, trying to free himself of the nylon cords that bound him to the tree next to the ant's nest, but his exertions were all in vain.

A red demon sat on the ground by him, taking in the scene with marked disinterest.

"He should have stayed there forever," hissed York in suppressed fury. His only audience was Randolph, a tall, sharp-featured netter, who watched the recording with him. "Damned thieving copycat."

"So far, we've seen no evidence that he copied the virus from you," stated Randolph. "But if he indeed had copied your virus, as you suspect, how come they didn't catch you too?" Randolph had the highest intelligence level permitted by the authorities, which was five higher than the average netter level. York had obtained him illegally, and he used him for special errands and for company during the long hours he spent in the control room of his amusement park site in the NET.

"They got him because of a new virus that he had authored, not the one he copied from me." The recorded Tipman screamed in pain, and York looked at him contemptuously. "That will teach you to write a virus properly, you bloody dilettante!" he yelled at the contorted victim on the screen.

York turned again to Randolph. "I had launched a camouflaged virus—Jezebel, I called it—that no one knew existed. I managed to extract a lot of valuable inside information from various companies. Then this rotten . . ." York groped for an epithet, his temper mounting, ". . . hacker stumbled upon it, copied the principle, and named his forgery 'Midsummer Night's Dream.' A year later he launched it as a visible virus, thereby endangering me. He should burn in Hell for eternity!" Flecks of spittle flew from his lips as his voice rose to near hysteria.

"I don't see how he could have endangered you," mused Randolph coolly. "From what I have observed, all they know is that he stole information from the NET. They know nothing about you. As far as I can see, the only way they could possibly get to you is by tracing the money. Can they trace any of the money you made from Jezebel?"

"No, that is utterly impossible," mumbled York, calming down. "I am in no way associated with that money, and it never was in my possession. My partner did all the stock market investments resulting from the inside information I gleaned. The money that he transferred to me was perfectly clean, and I used it to buy all my assets in the NET. I don't even know who he is."

"How nice," smirked Randolph. "Then you have nothing to fear from this

Tipman fellow."

"Don't be obtuse!" reprimanded York. "He must have studied my virus very carefully, and he may have found out something about me—the devil knows what. My partner is worried that something may turn up at Tipman's interrogation that would incriminate both of us. That's why he sent me the recording."

He glanced at the tormented hacker on the screen.

"So far he hasn't even been asked about my virus, so he has divulged nothing. But, according to my partner, this Tipman slime-ball is going to be deep-brain analyzed in a few hours. They'll surely ask different questions this time. And maybe he has information that leads to me. It's enough that he even mentions the existence of another virus to get me into possible trouble."

"Yes, it does seem dangerous, doesn't it?" Randolph was still calm and collected. York knew that this posturing was all a result of programming—the netter just wasn't smart enough to have that kind of personality. "I find it quite remarkable that your confederate—I mean, partner—managed to lay his hands on the recording. You say you don't know who he is. Well, isn't it obvious that he—"

"*Forget my partner!*" York was positively bristling. "There is another, even greater, danger lurking out there. And that's the guy who did this to Tipman!" On the screen, Amos Tipman was now barely conscious, slumped like a straw scarecrow against the cords that held him upright. The red demon, still bored, got up slowly and undid Tipman's bonds, brushing off the ants as he did so. Then he heaved his victim onto his shoulder like a sack of potatoes, and set off toward a green, bubbling swamp off on the left. "It's possible that Tipman told him things that are not on this recording. And he may locate me on his own—he seems pretty competent."

York took a deep breath.

"I have no desire to find myself in a site like that Hell," he said. "Therefore, I prefer to terminate him. And that's where you come in, Randolph my boy."

"Indeed." The netter remained unruffled. "Do you have any idea who he is?"

"No. But I suspect that he surfs under a code name. And that name is Flint!"

"And may I inquire how you came to this conclusion?" asked the netter. "I noticed nothing of the kind in the recording."

York stood up and started pacing the room. He was tall, and had a powerful build. His square face was adorned with a short, gray beard. His pale blue eyes were murky and sunken in their sockets.

"Do you recall an episode in the recording where a visitor asked Tipman a number of questions pertaining to 'Midsummer Night's Dream'? A big green demon in a long cape? Of course, we cannot identify a demon, but one of the other demons addressed him. He probably whispered, and Tipman must have missed what it was because no sound was recorded. But I can read lips, and I know what was said. The sentence was: 'We can extract all the details from him, Flint.' Therefore, this visitor, whom I believe is in charge of the site, is named Flint."

"Very clever," said Randolph, as though commenting on an abstract painting. "Shall we return to the issue of handling Tipman? It seems like an insurmountable task—I do not imagine him returning to the NET in the near future, so you'll have to return to Earth to do the deed. And he's probably heavily guarded by Babel as well."

"I have no intention of leaving the NET. I don't even remember the last time I left the NET. That's what a partner is for. He can do anything he wants on that accursed Earth." The diabolic smile on York's lips caused even the emotionless netter to raise his eyebrows. "But I intend to really take care of this Flint guy. I have prepared a little plan for him, and you are to play a major role in it. Have you managed to inquire about excessive electricity consumption that could possibly match a large, concealed site? Any indication of where this Hell may be?"

"I checked with the NET's Central Power Supply, and they have no significant surges lately. Nothing remotely close to the energy resources for such a site."

"Blast!" sneered York. "I knew this job would be too much for you! Listen carefully, now. I'm going to write a virus and you're going to operate it. It'll be very easy to locate, and it'll be exceptionally lethal. I shall be in hiding, and will have no contact with you at all. You're going to be exposed to Flint and to Babel, so this is probably our last operation together. Here's how it works: the virus will be disguised as a netter. It will penetrate Babel Headquarters and blow up five tons of Explonet. Neat, eh? Of course, the beauty of the plan is that it will never be completed. At best, the virus will detonate on the outer walls of the Babel fortifications. But if I'm not terribly mistaken, this Flint character will try to stop the netter somewhere along the way. And the minute he approaches the virus, the self-destruct mechanism is to go off. And we'll have got Flint! If he's a super smart netter, he'll be destroyed. And if he's a surfer, as I suspect, he'll be ejected from the NET. He won't remember a thing, but I'll have the exact timing of his exit, and my partner can use this information to determine who the surfer is. He'll fix him all right. Your job, Randy my man, is to find a netter to front for the virus. Thereafter, you'll be the virus' operator, and make sure that the explosions go off as planned. You, too, will be wearing an explosive vest. If you're about to be caught, you shall detonate it immediately."

"You might consider using another netter to operate the virus," suggested Randolph in his calm tone. "It would be a shame to waste a talented netter such as myself. You would have a lot of work on your hands retraining another netter."

York's laughter shook the walls. "That is the main reason I want to get rid of you, you imbecile. You're too predictable. And you know too much. Inform me the minute you have the new netter prepared for action. You know what? Use a female netter for the job—this Flint may hesitate an extra second before blasting a woman, and that's more than enough time for our purposes. She'll have the task of driving the truck with the explosives."

"Yes, sir." Randolph could only obey these orders unemotionally. If there was any bitterness in his tone, it was only the result of his programming. York was the master, and his word was law.

PART TWO—SATURDAY MORNING

25. NET: DAY 33, 00:00

It was Saturday morning on Earth, and Troy, Maggie and Flint were assembled in Troy's living room at his home site in the NET.

"It's been two and a half weeks since the aliens invaded our planet," said Maggie, "and we still haven't heard anything from them or about them."

The large holographic screen at one end of the room showed a continuous display of all the important events taking place in the NET. They were extracted from two major sources—Gossipofon and Undercurrent. Some items were marked in brown, some even in pink, but none appeared marked bright red, or even blinking red, which indicated an important message.

"Perhaps they remained in the random territories," mused Flint, "and never reached Netville. If they had done anything, even the least significant, I would have known of it. Barring Spindler's accident, and that's still being investigated, there have been no irregularities on the NET. Og would have updated me if there had."

Troy watched the green dragon standing on his hind feet by his chair, spewing blue smoke rings out of one nostril and inhaling them back through the other.

"I'll thank you to cure yourself of that obnoxious habit of yours," said Troy. "I know that your smoking in the room has no effect on our health—but it really is a distraction, and I find it difficult for me to concentrate." The dragon quickly sniffed in the two remaining smoke rings floating in the room.

"I think I may have a solution to the alien problem," continued Troy. "But first—Flint, are you still monitoring the entrance to the tunnel?"

"Absolutely. The concealed vid-sensor operates round the clock, and I pop over for a check every few hours. The aliens never returned to the area, but every now and then they send a signal to the tunnel, testing whether it had opened or not. What were you thinking of?"

"In order to get rid of the invaders," said Troy, "we'll need a uni-directional door, to replace the door on our side. Behind it we'll leave instructions how to open the other two doors—the one in the middle and the one on the far side. This way, they will be able to escape to their world and not remain trapped here forever."

"What a cool idea," asserted Flint. "And a noble one, too. However, I'm not sure it's feasible—all the doors I've seen so far were bi-directional. But I'll explore in this direction—who knows what I might find if I search hard enough. Meanwhile, we need a way to track what the aliens are doing. You told me not do anything concerning them while you were asleep, but I feel it's about time. Right now, we have no idea where they are."

"I once heard Dad say that there was a satellite over Netville that kept a visual log of everything that happened in the city." Maggie pointed upward. "If the invaders are around, their ship would surely show up on the satellite images. And if it did show up, Og must know of it."

"Flint, are you sure that Og isn't hiding anything from you?" asked Troy.

"It doesn't make sense," said Flint pensively. "It's practically impossible. But I see your point. I shall query Og about the satellite log once he communicates." He shook his mane, as if to wake himself up, and slammed his tail on the floor. "In fact, I'll go one better. I'll scan those logs myself. I have an advantage over Og because I know what I'm looking for, and he'd just be checking patterns. I might come across something that Babel missed."

"Anyway, don't forget to look up the uni-directional door," reminded Troy. "I have to go now. I must have breakfast. And then I promised Adam I'd join him for the California tetrosaur team tryouts. It's taking place at the Madrid Colosseum, and Tuffy's competing. There's nothing to do here, anyway. Flint, if anything happens, call me on my 'com. Maggie—care to join me to the Colosseum? Adam's team needs all the fans they can get."

Maggie hesitated a few seconds, her face showing disgust. "I'll come," she said at last, "although you know I don't really think that this pastime is the zenith of our culture. All that brutality. But only if you agree to go somewhere nice and quiet after the match. Blue-net?"

"Deal."

They had just got up to leave, when the holographic screen began flashing a red light.

"Hang on just a minute," said Flint. "Here's a red message from Undercurrent."

He hit a button, and a silver-furred fox appeared on the screen. A top hat sat snugly on its head. The fox walked on its hind legs, and spoke into an ancient microphone that he held in his right front paw.

"Babel is requesting information regarding five tons of Explonet stolen earlier today from the storerooms of the NET Development Company, in the industrial park of West Detroit." The fox's voice was accompanied by super titles with the same text, which appeared above the fox, together with its name: Top Hat Fox. The fox was a well known character in the NET, and was considered (or actually, the hidden surfer behind the fox was considered) to be one of the most reliable sources in the NET.

"The initial suspects are, of course, the Canadian Mafia, which more or less controls crime in that area. However, the local Don informed us anonymously," here the fox winked at his audience, "that there is no Canadian Mafia, and that the missing explosives are the result of erroneous inventory taking. Listen, folks—before giving Babel any leads, wait until a reward is offered. Have a boom day!"

The fox disappeared, and the screen continued showing messages of lesser importance in yellow, green and pink.

Maggie sighed. "I really cannot link this event with the aliens," she said. "They don't need explosives. Didn't I read somewhere that explosives could be sensed from great distances by their molecules? It's quite odd that neither Babel nor the NET police have located them yet."

"You're probably right," said Troy, and turned toward the door. "But just to make sure—Flint, why don't you follow up on this incident as well? It is irregular, after all."

"Okay." Flint waved his tail goodbye. As they went into the entry room, they saw him examining another mail item that had just popped into the In Box.

26. STANFORD, SATURDAY, 09:02

Amos Tipman opened his eyes. He was in an unfamiliar bed, strapped down hand and foot. His head throbbed with pain as if white-hot needles had been inserted through both his temples. Looking to his left, he saw the osmosis sleeve attached to his arm. He realized he was in a hospital, but could not recall how he got there, or why.

"Good morning, Amos. How are you feeling today?" A stout nurse, her black hair coiled in a bun on her neck, greeted him with a warm smile. She pulled the curtains aside and let the sunlight stream into the room.

Amos looked at her questioningly. "What's happened to me? Why am I here? Why am I tied up?"

The nurse's expression changed to one of concern. She pressed a red button on the wall, and then went to examine the monitors at the foot of the bed. A few seconds later, a tall, broad-shouldered man with a hawk-beak nose and flowing gray hair entered the room. He gave a quick glance at the nurse, and then approached the patient.

"Well, Amos, and how are you this morning?" he asked.

"Do I know you?" queried Amos. "Can you tell me what's happened to me, and why I'm lying here hogtied? Where in hell am I?"

The doctor halted in mid stride. He bent over Amos, felt his pulse, and then peered into his pupils. He straightened up, with a sober expression on his face.

"You don't remember me, do you? Tell me, then—what do you remember?"

"My birthday party yesterday. Ma bought me a new surfing helmet."

The doctor pulled out a Superscope out of his white gown, attached it to Amos' hand, and dialed it to T-scope mode. It was now a simple, but effective, truth detector.

"Which birthday?"

"Fourteen, of course. What's going on here?" The Superscope glowed green—Amos was telling the truth.

"That's exactly what we're trying to find out, Amos. Please remain as calm as possible." The doctor's face was pale. He turned to the nurse, and silently mouthed the word 'Babel' to her. She nodded and quickly left the room.

"Amos, you know that I am a doctor, and that we're in a hospital. Now tell me, please, precisely how you feel?"

"Terrible. My head feels like it's going to explode any minute. Do Ma and Pa know I am here?" Again, the Superscope shone green. Amos had no recollection of his parents' two-hour visit the previous day.

"Yes. They'll be here in a few hours," lied the doctor, trying to buy some more time. He released Amos' hands and legs. "Please forgive my bad manners. I am Dr. Keenan, and I have been treating you since your accident in the NET. You're okay now. Please take this pain-killer now."

He took a blue pill from a bottle in his pocket and gave it to Amos, with a glass of water. Amos took it without a word, and a few seconds later was fast asleep.

* * *

When Norman Starr arrived at the hospital, the entire medical team was waiting for him. So was the Babel field team—George Boder and Lynn Murphy. They sat in the hospital's conference room around the holographic projector. Norman studied their faces—the situation seemed grim.

"Tipman has lost all his memories of the past three years," said Dr. Keenan. "We're trying to find out how this could have happened. It looks like an equipment malfunction or an operating error. He was hooked into the deep probe recorder, and somehow, inexplicably, the trauma deletion unit, used for our more suicidal patients, was attached in parallel. This unit erased everything we were attempting to record. We're testing the patient for any additional damage."

"What did you discover on the recording you extracted?" asked Norman. Total silence imparted the answer. "I see. What else happened?"

Lynn volunteered to explain.

"It seems that the storage button was faulty. It was blank. The entire history we're interested in, including the 'Midsummer Night's Dream' composition, the Hell site, and the rest—all gone."

Norman frowned angrily.

"These coincidences are highly unlikely. Close all the entrances and exits to the hospital area immediately. I want every person who had access to

Tipman, or even was in the vicinity of his room, to be examined with a T-scope."

Dr. Keenan's face clouded.

"If you mean to imply," he spluttered, "that any of my staff would deliberately harm a patient . . . "

"Dr. Keenan, with all due respect, this is not an implication. It's a direct order. The examination will include yourself, and anyone else who's been around here in the past twenty-four hours." Norman's voice became sharper. "Evidence pertaining to a serious crime has disappeared. I do not believe this was an accident or bad luck. If, indeed, this was a human error, the culprit will atone for it. But if . . ." his voice dropped, his eyes taking in everyone present, ". . . if it turns out to be a deliberate act of malice . . ."

The sentence was left hanging in mid-air, as Norman strode determinedly out the door.

27. NET: Day 33, 12:00

Troy and Maggie jumped to the Colosseum, and found themselves amid throngs of spectators jostling into the stadium. They arrived at the main entrance and saw Adam waiting for them.

"It's great that you could make it," he said delightedly. "Tuffy's in top form today, and I'm sure she's gonna make it to the quarter finals. Hey, Maggie, I got a ticket for you despite the short notice, right next to Troy, and believe me, they're great seats—row five center. I didn't know you were interested in monsters."

Maggie wrinkled her nose.

"I'm not really a great fan of this sport. But good luck to you, anyway."

Adam studied her closely.

"You're in this 'irregular incidents' thing with Troy, aren't you? Maybe you can tell me what's going on. Troy's not telling and, hey, I just know I can be of help. Honest."

"Adam, your friends are calling you back to the arena," interrupted Troy.

"Run along, and we'll join you after Tuffy's match." A group of children from Adam's class, dressed as he was in yellow T-shirts with Tuffy's picture on it, waved wildly from the field.

"Gotta go. It's beginning in two minutes. We're in the sixth round, right after the intermission. Hey, don't forget to cheer for Tuffy—she loves it."

"Ladies and gentlemen," called the MC, his magnified image and voice emanating from the holographic screen hovering over the center of the stadium. "We are commencing with the preliminary matches to determine candidates for the California team of tetrosaurs of two tons and under. The first bout is between Tigrus of Stanford-net University, with an impressive record of twenty wins out of twenty matches, and Dixie of Baker-net University, with seven wins out of ten matches to date. Bring in the contestants."

The two monsters appeared from opposite ends of the course. Tigrus, the favorite, was a hybrid of a saber-tooth tiger and a prehistoric buffalo. It was several times larger than a common tiger, but still resembled its namesake by its stripes. Its neck and chest were protected with tortoise-like armor, and two long horns sprouted from its forehead. It let out a fearful roar, and some of the spectators cringed. Its trainer led it around a quarter of the circumference of the large, sand arena—which could have contained four Olympic stadia—to its battle station.

Its opponent was a typical crocophant, an elephant with a crocodile head, with long, dagger-sharp claws on its sturdy legs. It bellowed in rage, and glared at Tigrus with bloodshot eyes while it, too, was led to its station.

"TIGRUS! TIGRUS!" roared the thousands of Stanford-net fans, cheering their monster. The cheers of the few Baker-net fans were drowned by the other noises, including the orchestra and sirens. Tigrus was one of the leading candidates to be accepted into the California team, whereas Dixie, the underdog, didn't stand much of a chance against the favorite.

The referee struck a large gong, and Tigrus charged directly at Dixie, covering the ground in long bounds. The crocophant saw the attacker approaching, but did not manage to get far from her battle station before the tiger pounced on her. With surprising speed, she raised herself on her hind legs and slashed at Tigrus with her front legs. But the tiger managed to duck, and was only slightly cut by the broadside of claws that flashed past it. Most of the hits were taken on the armor plating, which proved to be an effective defense. Tigrus turned his head and plunged both horns deep into the abdomen of the rearing creature before it.

The roar of the crowd reached a new height. Maggie closed her eyes in revulsion as the crocophant sank to the ground, dark blood spurting from her deep wounds. A medical team raced onto the field and administered aid to the injured monster, while Tigrus' trainer used his neuro-collar remote control to lead his monster back to its battle station. It strode with its head held high, obviously enjoying the clamor of the crowd. The entire bout had taken less than twenty seconds. A tank-like vehicle, equipped with a crane, lifted the sedated Dixie and drove her out of the amphitheater for further treatment.

"Would you believe that that crocophant will compete in another match two days from now?" asked Troy, trying to placate Maggie who seemed quite nauseous by what she had witnessed.

"And be butchered again?" she retorted. "For the life of me, I cannot understand what's so exciting about this bloodthirsty sport. It reminds me of the gladiator fights of ancient Rome."

"Oh, no," said Troy. "There they were doing it for real. Here they're all NET creatures, just simulations of monsters. Besides, we don't have man-monster fights, and the fights do not end in death. Well, very rarely, anyway."

The MC announced the result of the match, and the participants of the next encounter. This time, another favorite, the Berkley-net monster, was paired off against a monster from an amateur group from Pasadena. The odds favored Berkley-net, and rightly so. The huge animal, with two tusks curving out of its mastodon head, managed to leap onto its adversary, and sink its teeth into its neck. The referee halted the fight immediately, and the medical team raced out once again to save the wounded monster.

The next two rounds were more evenly matched, and lasted around twenty minutes each. In both of them, the trainers threw in white towels when they saw their monsters failing after numerous, though non-lethal, injuries.

"I've had enough of this so-called sport," said Maggie, getting to her feet. "I'll wait for you at the cafeteria." She was more sickened by the crowd than by the sport itself. She made her way to the exit, trying not to see the masses of people, mostly men of various ages, lusting for blood.

Strange how such a quiet and intelligent lad like Troy could approve of such a cruel sport, she wondered. *Men are probably just animals in disguise, no matter how smart they are.*

28. SEATTLE, SATURDAY, 09:31

Dr. Noah Atkinson removed his surfing helmet, stood up and headed toward his laboratory. He had been surfing for the past fifteen minutes—six intense NET hours of reading the latest articles by current researchers, published in the monthly "DNA World." The periodical was also published on Earth, but who had time to spend reading it in the real world? Or any other extensive document? The NET was the place for learning!

Noah took one step, and the floor dropped out from under him. He tried to block his fall by grasping his desk, but it was as if his limbs had all shortened—the desk was out of reach. He crashed unceremoniously to the floor, and lay there in a daze, trying to comprehend what had happened. Even though he immediately knew that he had sustained no injuries, an uncontrollable tremor rippled through his body, and a chilling fear engulfed his brain.

The surf! Something had gone wrong with the surf! He did not exit this surf of his own volition. He hadn't even finished reading all the important articles in the magazine. And that was impossible.

"Dr. Atkinson, are you hurt?" Narissa, his assistant, ran into the room and knelt beside him. Her face was pale as she helped him to his feet. "Why don't you lie down for a few minutes on the couch, and I'll make you some coffee?"

"I'm all right," mumbled Noah, standing shakily. "I just tripped over myself. Everything's okay."

Everything was not okay. Including the girl and the room itself. He knew he needed more time to figure out what had happened and where he was.

He decided to skip the intended visit to the laboratory. He requested Narissa to return to her office, and to shut the door behind her. He then sank back heavily into his surfing chair, and began to analyze the situation.

I was reading Professor Schuster's article in the library, and someone entered my reading room . . .

Something odd about the room distracted his attention. Oh, he recognized the room all right—he'd been here more times than he could remember. And yet, he had this feeling of being a stranger here.

I've been hurt while surfing, came the obvious conclusion.

Every surfer had heard about surfing accidents. Though they were far rarer than aviation disasters, and despite the fact that the majority of these mishaps occurred during the NET's early days, surfing accidents were still viewed with extreme apprehension by almost every surfer. The most repeated story was that of Henrietta Cooper, the popular anchor of the ABZ television network. Henrietta was surfing the NET during a live broadcast, looking for interviewees, when a lightning bolt struck her helmet, burned through a faulty safety switch, and obliterated half her brain. Several million viewers watched in horror as her blue eyes suddenly dimmed, and her body crumpled limply to the floor. For two years thereafter there was a marked decline in the number of surfers, even though every helmet now came equipped with a double action safety fuse. Today, twenty-five years after that gruesome event, people still related the story in hushed voices. There were other stories as well, no less appalling, of people who were trapped in the NET, seeking help, as their bodies on Earth remained in a state of coma. But these stories were unsubstantiated, and many doubted their authenticity.

Noah dug into his memory, searching for missing pieces. Thelma and Jeff, his two children, were in college. Jessica, his wife, was with her patients in her clinic today. He remembered himself as a child, going to the movies with his father.

Okay, memory seems to be all right. Nothing missing that I can see now. Maybe some other center in the brain has been damaged?

He spoke to himself in English, Russian, and broken Spanish. Languages okay—no damage there.

I can't remember my latest surf, of course, because my return to Earth was abnormal. But let's see if I remember the surf before that. I read a NET article by Emil Schuster written on . . .

Noah leaped to his feet, and his chair fell over with a loud clatter. Narissa burst through the door in alarm, but he waved her back to her desk with an abrupt gesture.

. . . written today! I remember today's surf! Despite my unnatural exit. I read Schuster's article. And Professor Berting's as well. And Francesco Kytten's statistical tables . . .

He remembered the articles. Far more than remembered. He had memorized every single word, every punctuation mark. But that was of marginal importance.

He knew where they were right, and where they were wrong! With absolute certainty. And furthermore, he knew what they had not written, or even hypothesized.

Dr. Noah Atkinson knew the entire structure of the human DNA, with all its intricate functionalities. He knew how to improve on it. Every atomic structure, every chemical bond in that enormous molecule, had revealed its secrets to him. Dr. Noah Atkinson knew how to make a man into a genius, what it took to turn a person into an Olympic athlete, and how to prolong human life to two hundred and fifty years, the upper threshold for these creatures.

"These creatures!" he exclaimed out loud. He choked on the thought. "Now I'm one of these creatures!"

He began to come to grips with the idea that the human race, with which he had spent the forty years of his life, was a dull and feebleminded species. It was up to him to rectify this matter. His own life span was short, and if he didn't hurry, he too would have to end his life after only a hundred years.

Noah spent the next half hour planning his future professional career. His present employer, Genome Applications, was undoubtedly the best place to launch it. At least for the next few months. As it was the main research center of the Association of California Universities for Life Sciences, he enjoyed generous financing and state-of-the-art equipment. Every self-respecting research and commercial company dealing with genetics would bring its newest models to GA, hoping for assistance in finding an outlet to the marketplace.

State-of-the-art equipment, thought Noah scornfully. *These manufacturers lack the most basic skills and knowledge. They're practically still in the Stone Age. I'll have to build some production lines myself, otherwise I'll probably wait a lifetime for delivery.*

The plan began taking shape. Noah started sorting and filing the various stages in his brain. He had two main goals: enlarging the human brain's capacity, and extending human life span.

Money! That's what it takes to accomplish anything in this world. I need a large sum in order to build a decent laboratory, and hire competent assistants.

He had brief thoughts about the Nobel Prize, but he rejected them offhand. Not that there was any doubt in his mind that any of his theories, once published, would immediately win the award for medicine. But it would be long and painstaking, perhaps five years or more.

So, no Nobel Prize for me. A strange feeling of disappointment swept over him. He had always dreamed of winning the prestigious Prize. But now he realized he'd have to find glory some other way.

It would attract too much attention, anyhow, he consoled himself. *And take too much time on side issues.*

I can raise grants large enough for these two projects. The Gates Fund could easily provide ten million dollars. And so could the Ford Foundation. That'll be more than enough to begin with.

He quickly scanned through his memory banks for the key personnel in both institutions. There would be no problem in convincing them to contribute the financing he needed. He was quite confident in his powers of persuasion.

Right! Money should not be a problem. And getting the appropriate skilled workers should be just as easy. Now it's time to go back to the NET and find out exactly what happened to me there. What kind of incident could cause me to return to such a primitive world?

29. NET: DAY 33, 13:30

Troy and Maggie were back in their seats after the intermission. Tuffy entered the arena to the thunder of the crowd, looking not at all perturbed by the fact that this was her first appearance in front of such a large audience.

"On the red side of the field we have Tuffy from Gunn-net!" shouted the

MC. A few dozen boys in the audience cheered wildly, and so did Troy and Maggie. "This is the first professional appearance of this monster, with a fine record of nine wins out of ten amateur combats. Please welcome her." Tuffy walked sprightly to her battle station.

"And on the blue side we have Mammothosaur from the Acme College of San Francisco, with a year of professional experience and five wins out of ten combats. Welcome him!" The monster entered to resounding applause from the crowd, and walked to its station. It was a cyber-mammoth—the body of a woolly mammoth and the head of a tyrannosaurus rex. Two long horns protruded from the sides of its head, and two tusks curled from its slavering jaws. Its abdomen was covered with horn plating, which defended it from attacks from below, but impeded its agility.

The gong rang, and the two monsters approached each other warily, each trying to discover its opponent's weak spot. After two minutes of circling each other, when the crowd began to get impatient for action, Tuffy attacked. With a swift twist of her head she attempted to stab the cyber-mammoth in the leg with her horns. It dodged, and whacked Tuffy on the back with one of its tusks. So strong was the blow, that Tuffy's light protection split open, and her flesh was exposed. Fortunately for her, no vital organs were hit. The wound began to bleed, but it was only a trickle—no artery had been ruptured. The referee examined the wound from his post, and signaled the trainers to continue.

"TUF-FY! TUF-FY!" yelled Adam and his friends, cheering their monster and goading her to go on fighting. Troy joined in, and even Maggie gave a reluctant cheer.

Tuffy needed no urging. The scent of her blood seemed to give her additional power. She feinted to the left, pivoted herself to her adversary's flank, and charged at the cyber-mammoth's hind leg, biting off a sizable chunk of muscle and ligament. She stepped back gingerly as Mammothosaur tottered off balance, and then crashed to the ground, its leg no longer able to support its body weight. Tuffy charged again.

"Tuffy—stand aside!" screamed Adam.

The cyber-mammoth had obviously lost. It was neutralized, and its trainer was expected to concede the match at any second. But Tuffy couldn't hear Adam. She sank her teeth with a vise-like grip into the unprotected neck of her opponent, and threatened to rip through the main arteries. Mammothosaur thrashed helplessly, but it couldn't shake Tuffy off. The referee immediately halted the bout.

The entire audience, excepting the Acme fans, rose to its feet applauding the brilliant fight. Tuffy let go of her defeated adversary, and turned to return to her station.

Troy looked at Maggie cheerfully. "Adam must be overjoyed by the results," he said. "He and his team-mates will celebrate all—" he cut short his sentence as he looked in disbelief at the arena. The wounded cyber-mammoth had taken advantage of the momentary respite, and without warning had deliberately stabbed Tuffy in the side with one of its horns. Tuffy was bellowing in pain, and the crowd's ovations turned to boos and hisses of disapproval. Mamothosaur's trainer immediately operated its neuro-collar, and the attacker backed off. Blood spouted out of Tuffy's side as the horn was extracted. The referee raised a red flag—immediate disqualification of the cyber-mammoth until further notice. Medical teams sprinted onto the field to tend to the wounded monsters.

"The winner is the Gunn-net team," announced the MC. "The Acme team is banned from the next ten tournaments due to severe negligence and poor sportsmanship." More catcalls and whistles came from the multitudes in the bleachers.

"There's Adam," exclaimed Maggie. "On the field. He's stroking Tuffy."

"I hope she makes it," said Troy. "Adam is very attached to her, as she is to him. Sometimes she refuses to eat if he isn't by her side. Let's see how they're doing."

By the time they got to the team's seats, the crane-equipped ambulance had removed Tuffy to the underground medical clinic. Adam waited for them with tears of rage in his eyes.

"I hope they banish that deformed mammoth to Monster Island." His voice quivered in fury. "It'll get its proper treatment there, all right. Hey, and its trainer, too," he added, as an afterthought. Monster Island was a remote island in the Green Ocean where all unadopted monsters were shipped. These were monsters which were developed by the various schools and universities, but did not make par and were not chosen for competitions. Most of these young monsters perished on that island, mainly from genetic defects. Otherwise, they were killed by older predator monsters. The few that survived flourished uncontrolled, and reached humungous sizes. They were the main objects of cyber-genetic researchers.

"Let's leave them to the judgment of the tournament directors," said Troy. "How is Tuffy doing?"

"She'll be fine. But the doctor ordered complete rest for her for two days. Hey, even we aren't allowed to visit her."

"But you won, and that's the main thing," said Maggie. "I really don't like this sport, but I must admit that Tuffy fought valiantly."

"Thanks, Maggie." Adam calmed down a bit. "The next level is in two weeks. Wanna come?"

Maggie didn't have time to respond. Troy's 'com buzzed. It was Flint's special buzz-tune.

"Yes, Flint, what is it?" asked Troy.

"Come quickly. There's something suspicious in the NET. It has to do with the missing explosives."

"We're on our way," said Troy and disconnected. He turned to Adam.

"Sorry, kiddo, it's an emergency call from Flint, and we've got to go. We'll talk later."

It took them five minutes to get out of the teeming stadium, and find the nearest Transfer Box. They jumped directly to Troy's site.

30. NET: Day 33, 14:42

"Queen of the Night, there is a passage to Hell. But first I must know more about the dreamy play. If you can provide me with details of the author, I might be able to gain entry for you there." The tiny chimpanzee relayed the message, bowed, and disappeared cheerfully from the screen. His code name, Chimpo, flickered twice and vanished as well.

"It could be just a trickster trying to get information on Tipman and win the reward." Norman Starr leaned on Lynn's desk, and glowered at the blank screen. He turned to her, and found his face just a couple of inches from hers.

She smiled, and rolled her chair back a bit. Just enough to hold a conversation, but still very close.

"Well, I don't think it's an imposter," she said, her eyes never straying from his face. "I received this recording a few hours ago, and it's the first and only link I have to Hell. Whoever sent that message is new to Pira-net—that's quite evident from his style. Also the code name, Chimpo, has never appeared before on Pira-net."

"That doesn't tell us much." Norman managed to maintain the business-like tone of voice that his standing called for, but his pulse was still pounding. "So—he's new, and he's trying to squeeze out information."

"Maybe," said Lynn. "But I am also reminded of the little monkey I saw at Spindler's site. Consider—what could happen if we reveal info on Tipman to him? He can't win the reward any more, and if he tries to show up at Babel with that info—we'll nab him. And his gorilla companion, if indeed it's the same kid from Spindler's."

"Yes, you have a point here," assented Norman. He thought for a moment, and then said, "If this is the same duo, then we are talking about unidentified surfers. Catching one of them would be quite an achievement, regardless of the Hell site."

"I intend to play the information barter game with him," said Lynn. "Locating Hell is our top priority. At first, I'll reveal vague and general stuff about Tipman, just to see what he offers in return. If and when I'm convinced that he could really lead us to the Hell site, I'll release accurate Tipman data. I'll inform you the minute I have more to report."

"Get going!" Norman stood up and was about to leave the room, when his 'com started buzzing.

"Virus suspect in central Netville! Monitoring its movements from Central Control. Please confirm."

"I'm on my way," said Norman. He turned to Lynn, his countenance worried. "That's the third case—I was kind of expecting it. A new virus may have been found. Too many incidents are happening this weekend. Please join me at the Central Control Room—we may find ourselves dealing with familiar characters."

"I'll be there in a minute," said Lynn. "I want to set up the bait first. I'm curious to know what else I'll be able to fish out of that chimpanzee."

Norman nodded and left the room. Lynn gazed after him, her heart beating loudly.

When all this is over, she promised herself, *I'm going to invite him to a concert. If I have to wait until he asks me out, I'll die an old maid . . .*

31. NET: Day 33, 15:03

"I think I've identified a virus," said Flint when Troy and Maggie entered Troy's home site. "And it looks dangerous. Watch the left side of the screen."

They saw a large brown truck driven by a young female netter. Her driving was wild and erratic, and she weaved across the streets of Netville with total disregard for any traffic laws.

"So where's the virus?" asked Maggie. "Is that netter carrying it?"

"She herself is the virus," explained Flint. "I'm being constantly updated by Babel's tracking satellite which is currently focusing on her. It was triggered into action by her dangerous driving, and upon zooming in, spectrum analysis revealed a high concentration of explosives in the vehicle. The type and amount seemed to match the missing explosives reported earlier. I've been following her for the past five minutes, and I'll be able to tell you any minute now where she's headed." He looked up almost ruefully. "She changed directions so many times . . ."

"But the picture there is taken from ground level," pointed out Maggie. "I thought you said it was a satellite doing the monitoring."

"All the streets and traffic lights are monitored by land vid-sensors, which report to the Central Traffic Control. Their computer is . . . an old friend. I got it out of a loop once."

"Hmmph, I've heard that kind of nonsense before." Troy managed to keep a straight face. "You're controlling it now, aren't you? Come on, tell us. We won't turn you in."

"We help each other out at times," the dragon looked sideways and his tail curled a bit. "By the way, I'm pretty sure that Babel is now observing something very similar to what we're seeing here. And . . . voila! Here's her projected itinerary. No kidding—she is headed directly for Babel's head-quarters! Someone has really gone crazy in the NET."

The screen now displayed a map of central Netville, with the netter's path clearly marked on it. The truck had abandoned its meandering, and was now driving in a straight line toward Babel HQ. A side window suddenly opened on the screen, and showed a tall man with a pointy face busily talking into an operating 'com, unaware that he was being observed by a nearby vid-sensor.

"I guess that this is the driver's operator," said Troy.

"Correct. He is operating the virus." Flint's voice was tense. "I requested his location to be established the minute I knew we had a virus on our hands. Oh, bother! That son-of-a-crash is a netter, too! Now I'll have to ask for the identity of *his* owner." His fingers punched various keys. "And . . . done! Well, folks, until the reply to my query arrives, I'll go and freeze that crazy netter driver girl before she causes any serious damage."

"Perhaps you should wait a bit before exposing yourself," advised Troy, his eyes glued to the hologram. "The owner of that controlling netter will escape if he notices anyone apprehending the truck driver." He looked around, and was surprised to find that the dragon has vanished.

"Flint! Wait!" he shouted, but it was too late. Flint had already left the site.

Maggie threw him a sympathetic look. He shrugged lamely, and they both returned to observe the screen. The brown truck was careening through the streets at high speed, unchallenged. They saw it crossing intersections and avoiding passing cars by a hair's breadth. It was a commercial area, and people could be seen on the sidewalks, standing in front of stores and looking in amazement at the out-of-control truck.

About two minutes later, a traffic policeman, mounted on a motorcycle, appeared suddenly at the edge of the screen and began chasing the truck. He held a field freezer in his right hand.

"Is that him?" asked Maggie. "Can you identify him?"

"Oh, yes I can! That is the bag of bugs, also known as Flint!" Troy gritted his teeth with anger. "Just look at his green helmet. Real traffic cops wear black helmets."

The policeman overtook the truck, and signaled the driver to pull over.

Maggie glanced at the operator in the side window. He had a malicious grimace on his face, and his finger hovered over a red button on the control pad he was holding.

"Flint! It's a trap!" she screamed desperately, though she knew he couldn't hear her. At the same instant the truck exploded into an immense ball of fire, smashing all the vehicles in the street and some of the nearby buildings. A large crater was gouged into the road, and heavy clouds of smoke covered the area. Nothing remained of the driver or the policeman.

Troy was aghast. "He's been killed," he choked, tears filling his eyes. "Why did he have to chase that virus?"

"L-look at the screen," said Maggie. She was as forlorn as Troy was at Flint's demise. "The operator is trying to get away." The side screen showed the netter entering a purple Beetle-net, one of the most popular small cars in the NET. He began driving at high speed away from the explosion site. A black car emerged from a side street and followed the beetle.

"Perhaps that netter's operator is in the black car?" wondered Maggie, still sniffling

"So what's happened lately in the NET?" asked a familiar voice behind them. They whirled around and saw the green dragon observing them, obviously embarrassed. "I was about to go out to chase that lady netter driver, and I must have hurt myself. What's that smoke on the screen?"

"Flint! You weren't killed!" Troy leaped on the dragon and hugged him around the neck. "That truck was a trap laid out for you! It exploded and 'killed' you, or at least I thought it had. However, it looks like you were not eradicated. You probably found yourself out of the NET and back in your box, like any other surfer. And you have no memories of the last surf where you chased that netter, right?"

The dragon nodded, lowering his head in shame, while Maggie, a look of relief on her face, described everything that had happened.

"Those guys in the black car are the NET police," said Flint abashedly. "They're following the netter operator. I hope they'll be more careful than I was."

They watched the screen again. The purple beetle was accelerating. So did the car following it. Suddenly a beam of light shot out of the black car, engulfing the beetle. The purple car started to sway and zigzag from left to right and back again, until it finally mounted the sidewalk and crashed mightily into a wall. It began to burn, spewing great gobs of black smoke into the air.

"The police realized that the netter had noticed them," observed Troy, "so they used a field freezer on his car. If they don't hurry he'll burn to a crisp, and they'll have lost the link to his operator."

The black car had halted nearby, and two men in shielded clothing came out of it. Holding their freezers in front of them, they cautiously approached the burning beetle.

This time they heard the explosion as well, as a second mushroom of fire, albeit a much smaller one, filled the screen. The beetle was blown to bits, and the two policemen approaching it were thrown back several feet, landing on their backs. Had they not been wearing their protective apparel, they would have been perforated by myriads of shrapnel pieces hurled all around by the explosion. It took them a couple of minutes to reorient themselves. Finally they got up, and made their way to the burning remains of the beetle.

Flint turned to Troy. "Earlier you said something about the trap being meant for me. How could you know that?"

"You saw the tall netter before you left. Well, he was actually anticipating your arrival, and he activated the explosion at exactly the critical moment. Then he tried to escape in that." He pointed at the smoking wreckage on the screen, smoke billowing up all around it.

"Perhaps he, too, was meant to trap me?" said Flint. "Maybe he was a backup booby trap, to be operated if the first one failed. Someone's out to get me! It's not the invaders—without me they'll never open the tunnel. Whoever it is, he doesn't know who I am, and he thinks I'm a netter. And that I could be permanently removed by blasting me to smithereens."

"Your wannabe assassin seems to be quite capable," pointed out Troy. "He succeeded in drawing you into a trap and terminating your NET existence, as far as he's concerned. Fortunately, the fact that you left the NET to change into the policeman saved all your memory except for that very last bit. As to the second explosive charge, I believe it was more of an attempt to destroy evidence, than an attempt on your life. After all, the NET police had him frozen, and he couldn't have detonated it himself. The fire must have set it off. Now," Troy rubbed his hands together, "what do you have on the ownership of that male netter?"

The dragon sat on the floor with a thump.

"He was disguised, dang it. A few more minutes and I'd have got him. I'm going to check what Babel knows about this incident—they were very quick in finding the virus and its operator this time, don't you think?"

"Hold it!" commanded Troy. "Before you call Og . . . Give him a little time." Troy's voice grew stern. "You have already flown off the handle before, when you chased the virus. That was a mistake, and please never do anything of the kind again without my approval. If you had waited for just a little while, we might have identified the mastermind behind all of this. I'm quite sure that Babel restrained themselves from jumping the truck driver—they were patiently waiting for the main operator to reveal himself. But you had to leap in and save Babel, thereby letting the perpetrator get away. What's the matter with you, Flint? Don't you think Babel can take care of themselves?"

The dragon lowered its eyes in consternation and batted the floor with its tail.

"You're right, Troy." The dragon was genuinely remorseful. "My legs were in gear before my brain was." A sly eye peeked at Troy through the green mane. "Could be due to faulty design of this particular system . . ."

"So now you're blaming me, you cybernetic reptile?"

"Let's get back to business," interrupted Maggie. "What do we do now? I agree with Flint that this probably has nothing to do with the aliens. On the other hand, I suspect that it may have something to do with Hell."

"What do you mean?" asked Flint.

"It's clear to us that the truck was a trap. It was a virus designed to lure a virus hunter. I can think of only two possible motives for the person behind these deeds: hitting Babel, or hitting some new factor that fights virus authors and sends them to Hell. Do you know of anyone that could fit the bill?"

"You're right," said Flint. "Maybe it's Babel's own people. They're the only ones who knew Tipman was in Hell."

"Perhaps Tipman had an accomplice that Babel doesn't know about?" suggested Troy. "It doesn't seem likely that Babel was involved—they were just as surprised by the explosions as we were."

"Tipman claimed to have worked alone, during his interrogation." The dragon started to pace back and forth, his tail sweeping the floor. "I don't think he lied. Not under those, ah . . . special circumstances. Someone else knows about me. Who could it be?"

"I want you to remain in this site for the near future," said Troy. "Keep monitoring whatever's happening. Og will inform you of any developments in Babel. We're going to see how Adam is doing. Tuffy was injured, and he's taking it quite hard."

"Don't forget your promise to take me to the Blue-net," reminded Maggie.

"And then we'll visit Blue-net," agreed Troy. "Call us if anything turns up."

"Oh, I love Blue-net," said Flint excitedly. "Why don't I join you as a polite, friendly, bear with—"

"Until we discover who's got you in his sights you'll remain here," instructed Troy. "And anyway, someone's got to hold the fort and monitor NET activity for us." A mischievous glint sparkled in Troy's eyes, and he lowered his voice. "Besides, have you forgotten that you're not really welcome there? I still remember the incident with the owner's dog . . ."

"Me? Unwelcome? They distinctly said it wasn't my fault, and that the customer is always right, and that they'd get another, better dog. But go ahead, I'm not offended one bit. You can be alone, if that's what you want." He looked and sounded deeply offended, but they ignored him and left the site.

32. NET: Day 33, 18:00

The briefing room in Babel's NET site was relatively small. It was designed to hold twenty people, the total number of software experts in Babel, and as every seat was taken, it made for quite a crowded gathering.

Norman Starr surveyed his unit's staff, which had assembled from all over the globe. This was undoubtedly the most outstanding computer team on the planet, and he was about to challenge them with one of the most difficult tasks of their careers.

"Right—we're all here now," he began blandly. "And we have two guests with us, whom most of you may know. On my right is Dr. Stefan DeWitt, the Global Alliance's officer in charge of the NET's infrastructure. Every area and every activity in the NET, including this room and all its occupants, are supported by his infrastructure systems. On my left is John Pierce, Undersecretary for Internal Security, and responsible for the security of the entire NET, and thus also our direct superior."

He paused for a moment and watched his audience's reaction. The atmosphere was tense. It was the first time in five years, since the abortive assault by the Undernet group on Babel's site, that all of them were urgently summoned to HQ.

"During the past two Earth days," continued Norman, "we've been having a series of incidents in the NET, the like of which we haven't experienced in the last ten years. The incidents have uncommon and bizarre characteristics, and we do not have explanations for them yet. We have no evidence that there is, in fact, any connection between them, but their close proximity in time suggests that we're dealing with an overall manifestation, and not with isolated events."

He pressed a button on the remote control in his hand, and the wall behind him transformed into a holographic screen. Amos Tipman was seen, plunging down a deep hole with a green demon hovering beside him.

"Some of you have already seen this—it's the recording of Amos Tipman's memory. He is a professional hacker, and was responsible for the infamous 'Midsummer Night's Dream' virus. He was caught in the NET by an agent or agents yet unknown, while attempting to release a new virus into the NET. This mysterious agent sent Tipman to a special site named Hell— he's just arriving there on the screen—where he was tortured for ten days. He was eventually disconnected from that surf with a total nervous breakdown. *This is not supposed to be entertaining!*"

Some of the team members, who were chuckling under their breath as they saw Tipman arguing with the demons at the entrance to Hell, sobered up immediately.

"All this occurred yesterday at one thirty in the morning, about thirty two

NET days ago. We arrived at Tipman's home on Earth on Friday morning, and after discovering what had happened, immediately began an investigation into the whereabouts of this Hell site." He paused for a second to emphasize his next sentence. "There is no site in the NET called Hell. Neither is there a site which could possibly resemble what is on that recording."

DeWitt interrupted. "Furthermore, we don't even have a theoretical explanation for the existence of such a large site, as no energy resources seem to be drained from the NET. And all the creatures appearing on that recording are, of course, illegal by NET laws."

"Right," Norman went on. "There is no point in showing you Mr. Tipman's entire ordeal in Hell. We don't have the time, and it isn't very palatable. Whoever was supposed to see all of it, has seen it all. So I'll just sum up. As an aside, I can say that Dante and Hieronymus Bosch could have learned a lot from this Hell designer. During his stay in Hell, Tipman went through all seven stages literally, and there are probably several more for which he was scheduled." He paused for a moment and looked around at his people. This time there were no smiles in the audience.

"Unfortunately, that is all we have—I cannot give you any additional information on the poor hacker. Shortly after his hospitalization at our special Stanford clinic on Earth, someone erased the last three years of his life from his memory." Norman raised his voice. "I repeat—someone erased! The hospital claims that his memory was accidentally wiped out during the deep probe analysis. They also claim that the brain recording failed because the memory cube we recorded on was defective. For the benefit of the statistics lovers among you—one out of twenty million recording cubes comes off the assembly line faulty. And there are no statistics on brain erasure, because this is the first time it has ever happened. After tens of thousands of successful treatments."

He took a sip from the glass of water on the table. "I am pretty sure that a severe crime has been committed here. True, it took place on Earth, but it is directly connected to crimes in the NET. We have no clues as to who the offenders are. The next case—"

"Just a moment, please," interrupted Sven Thorensen, standing up. "Have you checked out all the hospital personnel, and anyone else who was there? Including security people, and our own teams? Even yourself? Or could he have managed to erase his own mind, to evade answering for his virus authoring crimes?"

Norman was always fascinated by Sven's astute analyses. *He never misses anything*, he thought. Thorensen was still standing, patiently waiting for a reply.

Pierce provided the response. "*Everyone* was checked and double-checked. Including Mr. Starr. As for Tipman, he could not have done this brilliant act of eliminating incriminatory evidence from his mind, as his arms and legs were fastened to his bed."

"Thank you," said Sven dryly. "Just for the record, I assume the checks included hospital suppliers and everyone with access permission. The statistical likelihood of their being involved is significantly higher than a fluke accident." He sat down.

"We have indeed checked everyone who was in Tipman's ward," replied Starr. "The patients, too, and even myself, as John mentioned. We know of everyone who was there from the vid-sensors that cover all the corridors and other venues of access. These facts notwithstanding, we have also begun investigating everyone who was on the hospital grounds, even if he or she did not visit the ward. They number in the thousands, and it will take us a week to complete our survey." Seeing there were no more questions, he continued with his presentation.

"The next event occurred in the NET eight days ago. It, too, cannot be accounted for so far." The holograph displayed a well-built, unshaved man lying on his back in a large bed, naked but for a diaper on his loins. The man smiled happily at the camera with a baby's gaze.

"Albert Spindler was a computer specialist at Gen-Tec. According to his mother he intended to take a short, two-day vacation at his home site in the NET. However, the NET logs show that he didn't even leave his entry room. A few seconds after he arrived at his site, he tried to jump back to Earth. But he failed. What happened was that his brain was almost totally erased, and he reverted to being a one-year-old baby. He can't walk or talk, or control his bodily functions. Such an accident has not happened in the past twenty years, and on that occasion a malfunction was found in the surfing helmet. Spindler's helmet was in perfect order, and there were no environmental disturbances, such as lightning striking near his home."

He paused to make sure he had the attention of his audience. They all remembered the early years of the NET when random lightning bolts made surfing hazardous.

"But there is more to this mystery. Our investigative team, George and Lynn, set up concealed vid-sensors at Spindler's site."

The screen displayed the site, a white, two-story house adjacent to a lake. The house was surrounded by colorful flowerbeds, and flanked by tall trees.

"This is an overhead view of the site. A camera was installed over the front gate, and a tracking satellite was focused on the site with continuous recording enabled. This scene was taken five days after the event."

The site seemed quiet and deserted, when suddenly two figures emerged from the house and into the garden, both dressed as technicians. One was a gigantic gorilla. The other was much smaller, the size of a twelve-year-old child, and had a chimpanzee's mask on. They strolled through the garden, apparently enjoying Spindler's flowers. The smaller technician stopped by one of the flowerbeds and called the larger one over. The gorilla lifted the chimpanzee onto its shoulders, put him down again, bent to the ground and sniffed around a bit, and then jumped to its feet, whispering something to its colleague. They both ran to the house and disappeared into it.

"And that's the last we see of them. None of the cameras showed how they arrived, or how they got out. George and Lynn got there a couple of minutes later—there they are on the screen, now—but the technicians had vanished. The house was thoroughly searched. So was its maintenance tunnel, but they could not have escaped that way—we had all the exits blocked, and combed the tunnels for miles around. It's as if they never existed at all. But there is more to come. Lynn, please take over."

Lynn Murphy got up, and replaced Norman by the lectern.

"George and I were on duty when the call arrived—two apes dressed as electricity technicians were roaming about in Spindler's garden. We got there in exactly three minutes, via a Transport Box about half a mile away from the site. We carefully searched the entire house and its maintenance tunnel. We scanned the place with our mass detectors, but found no one. So then we went out onto the garden to find out what had alarmed them and caused them to run."

The screen focused on a damaged flowerbed.

"This is the flowerbed the technicians were scrutinizing before rushing off. Please notice how the letters 'AL' were drawn by uprooting several of the plants. We think that whoever did this wanted to 'write' more, but was somehow prevented from doing so. So we deduce that someone wanted to leave a message that Al Spindler was in trouble. Closer examination of the flowerbed revealed that parts of the ground and flowers were truncated. This would indicate that the writer of the message was vaporized with an atomic blaster, or an equivalent weapon, by someone else!"

A murmur rose from the audience, and she waited for it to die down.

"Was it Spindler himself who was eliminated before he could complete the message? The NET logs imply that this could not be—he didn't leave his entry room. To further complicate the issue, we found a footprint in that flowerbed. Mass analysis revealed that whoever stepped off the stone walkway and onto the flowerbed, matched Spindler's mass, give or take a few grams. The shoe print also matches Spindler's. To date, we have no explanation for these coincidences."

"Did you try to locate the technicians by their mass?" asked Kumar. He was the unit's chief forensic analyst.

"Yes, we did. The vid-sensors got the precise masses of both technicians. The larger one weighs about eight hundred pounds—therefore, he is not a surfer but some kind of advanced netter. We're still trying to locate the smaller techie, and we suspect he's a surfer in disguise. But that'll take some time—there are several million surfers with his mass."

"The NET logs also attest to the fact that no one else was in the vicinity at the time." Norman got to his feet as he spoke, and signaled Lynn to return to her seat. "This time we do not have a Stanford medical team to tell us about random failures and faulty equipment. Someone had deliberately erased Spindler. Totally—unlike Tipman. And, also unlike Tipman, with no conceivable motive. Spindler did not write viruses, and backtracking on his activities for the past couple of weeks, he was not involved in anything of significance in the NET.

"Now for our last case." Norman pressed a button, and the scene switched to an overview of Netville. From the satellite, the NET's only city looked like an unending sprawl of gray buildings, from one horizon to the other. Far to the south the Green Ocean could be seen, and surrounding the city was a thin yellow strip—the desert that separated the city from the unpopulated random territories.

"This is Netville at three ten this afternoon. Three NET hours ago. The satellite that took this picture hovers about six hundred miles above the city. Now let's zoom in."

The picture magnified rapidly, as if the camera was dropping at high speed toward the ground. More details could be observed—highways and very large buildings.

"The flashing green light in the center is our HQ here. Look at the right side of the screen, east of the Babel fortress."

A tiny dot was moving on the screen. The 'cam view zoomed in on it, and it became a brown truck lurching through the streets at high speed.

"This is a virus. The satellite detected aberrant behavior, and began tracking it. Spectrum analysis informed us there was a large amount of explosives on the truck. And it was headed directly at our site!"

The scene shifted to ground level, as the traffic vid-sensors followed the truck. The female driver was clearly seen, a netter with a rough visage. The assembly followed her erratic driving for a few minutes. The screen suddenly split into two windows, and a tall male netter with sharp features was seen talking into a 'com.

"We were waiting for this guy. He's her operator, and at this moment he has contacted her." The conversation could not be heard, but the truck put on a fresh burst of speed and began ignoring traffic signs. "The driver has been identified as Anne McGregor, a netter reported missing last night from the Shaunby School, where she was a bus driver. The operator is a netter, too, but he's illegal. Our records show that he was sent for recycling, which failed, and he was subsequently invalidated three NET years ago."

Netters could be immediately identified by the NET authorities. Every netter had a tiny transmitter set into its navel at production time. The transmitter signal could be picked up from a distance of up to on hundred feet by special sensors. Hundreds of millions of these sensors were scattered in the buildings and streets all over Netville. Every netter was, therefore, always covered by at least two of these sensors. Tampering with the transmitter was considered one of the most serious crimes possible in the NET.

"At this stage we were still trying to locate that tall netter's operator, so we withheld all preventive actions against him and the female driver. So far they did not pose a threat. As you shall shortly see for yourselves, locating the real operator was not an easy job this time. We're still checking the male netter's previous owner, but he seems to be clean—nothing connects him to the incident. Now, concentrate on the truck."

A policeman on a motorcycle, wearing a green helmet, burst suddenly onto the scene. He overtook the truck and signaled it to pull over. At that moment the truck exploded in a huge ball of flame. Norman halted the projection, and backed up to the point that the policeman was alongside the truck, where he froze the frame.

"The policeman is a fake. He is not on the NET police force. He must have known about the suspicious truck and waited for it. But even stranger is the fact that the netter driver and her operator seemed to anticipate the policeman to try and stop them. As if they were waiting for him in order to blow him to pieces. We believe he was a netter, though we could not trace his registration, and his transmitter did not emit an ID. He couldn't have been a surfer because the NET's surfer tracking mechanism has no record of him. Furthermore, we found no surfer that was suddenly ejected from the NET at the precise moment of the explosion. There is no further significant information about the explosion. Now, pay attention please—I am focusing on the male netter."

He pressed a button and the picture centered on the netter operator. They saw the attempt to escape in a purple car, the freezing, and the detonation when the NET police approached.

"This netter had an explosive vest strapped on. Those two policemen were lucky to have escaped serious injury. The charge went off due to the fire that erupted in the car when it smashed into the wall. We did not manage to discover who *his* operator was—he was not in contact with his netter. But we have quite a lot on the netter himself, and we're trying to trace his recent movements, hoping to uncover the operator."

Norman paused again and let his audience grasp the significance of what they had witnessed.

"Each of these incidents taken alone would be considered very severe," summed up Norman. "But having them all occur within the time span of two Earth days is indicative of something far more sinister in its implications. We don't know what it is—but we should all be on top alert. Consider this as a flashing warning light!"

"I would like to stress the gravity of the situation." Pierce got to his feet and addressed the audience, his gaze moving from face to face as he spoke. "If there are more mishaps that cause injuries to surfers, we'll have to disconnect parts of the NET. You can imagine the horrific damage that would cause, to say nothing of the uproar from all the world's communities. I trust all of you to find the perpetrators in the shortest time possible. Mr. DeWitt and I will keep in close touch with you, and we'll provide any assistance you need. Are there any questions?"

There were none. Pierce and DeWitt left the room, and Norman turned to his staff. They seemed eager to go into action. He wondered if they were up against something bigger than they could handle.

"Five minute break," he said. "Then we'll assemble teams and delegate tasks. We want to hear new ideas!"

33. NET: Day 33, 22:25

Blue-net was a combination bar and restaurant for young people. It was instigated by a group of computer-expert Stanford-net graduates, and soon became one of the most popular meeting places for professional surfers. Many of the clientele were computer people addicted to surfing who used to spend all their spare time looking for new expeditions and adventures in the NET. Blue-net was the natural starting point for these odysseys, and you could almost always find companions to join you, even in the most hazardous of journeys.

The café's exterior resembled a large, land-locked cruise ship. It was a ten-story building, with a pointed prow, and an entrance through an iron gangway that was secured firmly by thick chains. Troy had always admired the special interior design of the café—dozens of decks on different levels, interconnected by rope ladders. You could make a date with friends on level nine, and be assured you'd be isolated from the other customers. And every deck had a clear view of the main entrance.

Troy and Maggie had arrived quite early, and the typically long queue had not yet begun to form. A green-haired waitress in a loud yellow uniform led them across a shaky suspended bridge to Deck Five. There were four tables on this deck. She seated them at a large round table with two other surfers —a boy and a girl dressed in skiing outfits. They were pondering over a paper-thin screen spread on the table, which depicted a three-dimensional blurb of a large ski resort. Both were sipping pink drinks from narrow, frosted glasses. Their skiing gear was leaning on the wall behind them.

"Hi, puzzlers," greeted the boy. "Where's your bear?" Flint was well known here, and the visitors loved to play with him. He was considered to be a particularly friendly netter, with an uncanny knack for solving riddles. "One of his pals, Chitango, is on Deck Two." The boy pointed at a hairy orangutan, seated with five surfers around an oval table, drinking a banana-shake from a huge glass.

"Hi, Henry," replied Troy. "The bear is busy repairing some damage he has done. Are you going skiing around here? It's summer now."

"You bet. There's a bunch of us going to Mount Frost. Quite a lot of snow there. Say, Troy—if you two want to join I can get you outfits. No problem. We leave in fifteen minutes."

Mount Frost was the largest ski site on the NET, and every skier's ultimate challenge. The site's owner, Ski-pass Corporation, designed it as a 'skill and courage' test for trained skiers. As you were not physically hurt in real life on Earth when you were injured or even killed in the NET, surfing skiers took fantastic risks, and performed maneuvers they wouldn't dream of attempting on Earth. Some of the slopes were incredibly steep; a couple of others resembled roller-coaster tracks, complete with loops and a jump over a chasm two hundred feet deep.

"No, thanks," replied Troy. "We just came here to relax a bit and discuss a couple of new ideas. Take care, now. There's a lot of funny stuff happening in the NET lately. You wouldn't want to wind up like that Dunham engineer, would you—you know, the guy who turned into a baby."

Henry dismissed the warning with a wave of his hand.

"You can stop worrying. Nothing's going to happen to us. But anyhow, thanks for the alert. Just five minutes ago I heard that a policeman was blown up in the center of Netville—lots of damage to houses and cars. Probably the Mafia paying off a debt or something."

"Really?" said Troy. "How awful. Well, look out for yourselves, and don't do anything that'll later need a doctor or a lawyer." He waved them a casual salute, and hit the privacy button on the edge of the table. "Hope you don't mind us having a little privacy. 'Bye."

The table split in two, and each half morphed itself into a circular table. The table he and Maggie were occupying slid sideways ten feet into a niche in the wall.

"I wanted to discuss Flint with you," said Maggie. "But first, the attempted hit on him. It's beginning to look like a puzzle with pieces that don't interlock."

"I think so, too," said Troy. "Neither of the two protagonists we know of, Babel and the aliens, seem to have done it."

"Exactly," agreed Maggie. "We know nothing about the invaders or how they operate, so let's leave them aside for the moment. The last thing they want is to have anything happen to Flint. Babel might have tried to bump Flint off, but I doubt very much if they'd have used so much explosives and deliberately cause so much damage. And what's more—Og never mentioned it."

"I believe that there is yet another dimension to this puzzle," whispered Troy. "We've eliminated Babel and the aliens as possible perpetrators. This leaves just one conclusion—there is a third party who is interested in doing away with Flint. A very powerful third party—one with connections to Babel, or at least eavesdropping capabilities. Otherwise, how would he know about Hell? And we know that he knows—it's his motive for hunting down Flint! He has extraordinary resources at his disposal—stealing explosives, operating stolen netters, eliminating his own tracks. That's quite something."

Maggie was obviously disturbed. "I guess you're right," she said after a long pause. "But . . . who? Why?"

"I suspect that our assassin is somehow involved with viruses. That's why he's chasing Flint. What about the earlier idea of Tipman having an accomplice who is now bent on revenge? Or trying to prevent being damned to Hell himself?"

"I cannot imagine Tipman covering up for someone," said Maggie. She involuntarily shuddered as she recalled the tormented hacker. "It should have shown up in the memory recording. No, it must be a brand new factor, one we haven't encountered yet. How about the Mafia? Could Flint have fouled up with them in any way?"

Troy stared at her, and she shook her head impatiently.

"Okay, okay—it was just a shot in the dark. But you've got to admit that the excessive way the explosives were used coincides perfectly with their style. Look, why don't you ask him? Maybe he's done a few things he forgot to tell you about. And that brings me directly to the first reason I wanted to talk to you alone."

She collected her hair into a cascading ponytail.

"I have no intention of encroaching on your relationship with Flint," she continued. "But in my opinion, you should wield more control over him."

She looked at Troy, who was listening intently, and went on.

"He is way too impetuous, and this time he was nearly caught. His actions frequently border on the illegal, like collecting data from Babel and building Hell. But worst of all, his behavior is sometimes downright dangerous! That experiment of his compromised the existence of the NET itself! Troy, you *must* be more careful—if Babel catches him, it's the end of both of you!"

Troy was visibly disturbed by these words.

"I know," he said lamely. "Everything you say is true. He's kind of a loose cannon, or more precisely, a loose dragon. Maggie—I'll make doubly sure that he follows my orders. But you know I can't prevent him from accessing the NET. He has no other world. He'll die of sorrow if he has to remain cooped up in his box. And I resolve," he looked into her eyes, smiling, "to be firmer with him in the future."

Maggie felt herself blushing.

"What do we do about Babel?" she asked quickly, changing the subject.

"What about Babel?"

It was her turn to stare at him.

"Troy, it's been two and a half weeks since the alien invasion. Babel is still unaware of this, and they're not prepared. Do we warn them or not?"

"You've obviously given this some thought, Maggie. What do you think?"

"I'm not sure. We could tip them off anonymously—you know, send them all the hard evidence we have. They'd feed it onto Og, and probably come up with some action plan. Maybe set out to find them. And we'd know everything they find out."

"You could be right, but I honestly believe that they couldn't do any better than we." Troy scratched his head, his fingers digging deep into the mass of curls. "Moreover, we'd be jeopardizing Flint, and right now I think he's the only one who can get us out of this mess. Despite his lack of discipline. Seriously, if we follow your suggestion Babel will be monitoring the NET, and also the tunnel, very closely, and that will hinder Flint's freedom of movement. In addition, it will prevent him from installing the uni-directional door, if he ever manages to develop one. I consulted with Ziggy last night, and he agrees with me." He noticed the look of concern on her face. "Ziggy is totally trustworthy. He won't tell a thing, unless something nasty happens to me. And as a last resort we could try consulting with your dad. Do you think he—"

Troy stopped in mid sentence. Maggie followed his gaze and saw four tall men, dressed in olive uniforms, enter the café. Two of them remained by the entrance, which was also the only exit. The other two walked toward Deck One. Both carried large briefcases. They stopped by the furthest table on that deck, and conversed with the four youngsters seated there. One of the men took a kind of stethoscope out if his briefcase.

"T-scope," muttered Troy. "It's the NET police, and those briefcases contain truth detection equipment. They're going to inspect everyone here. And I'm sure that one of their questions will be 'what do you know about the recent explosion?' They're going to catch us!"

34. NET: DAY 33, 22:48

Lynn studied the recording of the car chase for the umpteenth time—the purple car trying to escape, the crash, the approach of the policemen, and the explosion. Something was very odd in the entire scenario—it made no sense from the netter's point of view. His operator must have given him instructions to blow up at the very second the NET police noticed him. That was why he had an explosive vest on. Yet, the netter tried to escape, as if he had a chance of saving himself. Which was, of course, impossible—not in a car, in the middle of Netville, with NET policemen all around. If it wasn't for the fire after the crash, he would have been captured, and valuable information about his operator could be extracted from him. There was a possibility that the charge was detonated by remote control, and not by the fire, but the entire attempt to hit Babel with an exploding truck was too naive, too amateurish.

We're missing something important, she thought. *We don't know the motive for the crime . . .*

She froze the picture, and began advancing the recording in slow-down mode with automatic stops—an image every tenth of a second. The purple car was zigzagging across the street, the frozen driver unable to control it. She zoomed in and examined the driver. His immobile face had a satisfied smirk on it. The vid-sensor on the traffic light had clearly caught the upper half of the driver's body—despite the clear weather he wore a large, thick overcoat that concealed the primed vest. She advanced the recording slowly, and watched the car with its frozen driver skidding across the road and slam head-on into a building. Fire broke out in the car almost immediately, and a few seconds later the charge in the vest went off. It was much smaller than the charge in the truck, just a few pounds, but it was enough to destroy any evidence that may have been in the car. The car became a ball of fire, and shards of metal flew in all directions.

"I'm sure I've missed something," she told George Boder who had just entered the room and watched the slowly advancing hologram. "I must have run this recording a hundred times, and I still have the feeling that there's a clue in there that I've seen but not identified. I'm going to go through it one last time now."

"You go ahead," said George grumpily. "I was just about to get me some coffee. There's nothing more to see in that darn recording, and that netter's idiotic simper makes my blood boil every time I see it. As if he thinks he's got the better of us, and that we can't prevent his blowing up."

"Yes, that grin of his bothers me, too," said Lynn. "Could you get me a cup of coffee on your way back, please?"

"Okay. After that I'll be looking at the Spindler recordings again. Those damned apes must have left some traces."

Lynn didn't respond. She went back to the recording, and slowed down the projection rate to its minimum before viewing each frame separately—a sample every thousandth of a second. The purple car swerved across the street at a snail-like pace, inch by inch. It turned left, bumped against the barrier, turned right on two wheels heading for the wall . . . A sudden white smudge on the seat by the driver caught her eye. It was visible for just a fraction of a second to the street vid-sensor as the car tilted on its side. She halted the projection, and backed up frame by frame to the spot where she had seen the smudge. There. Zoom in. It looked like a square scrap of paper. She hadn't noticed it earlier—it was barely visible, and her attention had been on the driver. Was that writing on the paper? It was illegible, and zooming in only made it blur even more.

"Og, I need your help," she summoned Babel's computer.

"Your wish is my command, O princess." Og was programmed to respond with a personal approach to Babel personnel. It had a pet name for each user, which it had chosen itself. Lynn was the princess.

"That piece of paper on the driver's seat—do you think you could decipher it for me?"

"I hope this helps." Og sounded content. The screen displayed a parking receipt at Roller-net, Netville's largest amusement park. The exit time was 13:10—about two hours before the virus truck was identified. Entry time was 12:30. The netter had spent forty minutes at the park.

Lynn broke into a huge smile. "Og, you're a darling," she said, wondering whether somewhere, deep in its infinite electronic circuitry, there was something that could interpret the affection in her voice. "Please call George urgently."

George arrived in less than a minute, holding two cups of steaming coffee. His jet-black hair bristled like a brush on his head. His black eyes gave Lynn a piercing look.

"I believe I've got a lead." She pointed at the screen. He glanced at it and let out a low whistle.

"You certainly have," he agreed. "Odd that we hadn't noticed it earlier.

Og, how could you miss such an important piece of data?"

"Sir, respectfully—you ordered me to detect clues, but you gave no priority to the zone where that note was found. At the current priority level, I would have found it within seventy-two hours."

"That's the kind of answer I'd get from a supermarket computer," fumed George inexplicably. "We expect more of you." He turned to Lynn. "What do you make of this parking ticket?"

"The netter had evidently visited the amusement park." Lynn fidgeted nervously in her seat. George's attitude was demeaning and offensive, even if he targeted Og—an emotionless computer. His anger was totally unwarranted. "It would be an ideal place to meet with its operator. Large crowds prevent close tracking, at least at the more popular stalls and rides. But there's still a possibility that someone saw him there. We'll need to put together a list of all the surfers who were there in that time slot, and question each and every one of them. One may turn out to be the operator himself."

George was silent for a few seconds, and then spoke determinedly.

"We need to split up, Lynn. You check the surfers, as you suggested. Take Sven with you, he's good at this sort of thing. I'll go directly to Roller-net—as a child I was often there as an ordinary visitor. It's high time we met the owner of this site, the famous Mr. York. He may know something. All right with you?"

Not really, thought Lynn. *But I'd rather work with Sven than pay a visit with you anywhere . . .*

"Fine," she replied. "Keep me posted. You'll be able to follow our investigations through Og."

35. NET: Day 33, 23:12

"We've got to get out of here, right now," said Troy. He hastily dialed a short number on his 'com.

"Lost Bears Center," said a familiar voice. "Would you like to adopt a bear cub? We have—"

"Flint!" Troy cut him short. "Are there any messages from the family?" This was their secret code for secure communications, which Troy used only on emergencies.

"There's a yellow envelope that I haven't opened." Flint responded with the confirmation code.

Troy pressed the Encrypt button and keyed in a sequence of numbers. A few seconds later, a red light indicated that the scrambler was on.

"We're in Blue-net and we're in trouble. A team of the Special Forces of the NET police has begun a spot check on the surfers here. They might use a T-scope on us. Try to find us an emergency exit from here—we cannot afford to be questioned by them."

"I'll check. How many are they?"

"Four. Two at the entrance and two going from deck to deck. We're on Deck Five. Hurry!"

"Wait for me. I'll be there in two minutes."

Maggie seemed anxious.

"Troy, I saw you scrambling that message. If the NET police are monitoring outgoing calls during their raid, and see that it's encrypted, they're sure to be suspicious."

"No, they won't," said Troy. "Flint modified these 'coms. What they'll hear on the line is a prerecorded conversation between us about a yellow envelope I received at home. The real conversation passes as encrypted background noise that can be interpreted only by our own special software. Even if they suspect, there's no way they can decipher it—the key is a thousand digits long."

Maggie nodded approvingly.

"Cool. Let's hope you're right."

The investigating pair of policemen finished questioning four of the ten tables on Deck One, and turned to Deck Two. A couple got up to leave, but were detained at the entrance, and a loud argument ensued. A number of couples that were waiting for a table changed their minds and also tried to leave. Three minutes later the investigation team had questioned three of the five tables on Deck Two, and made their way to Deck Three.

"Where is he?" Troy glanced at his watch with growing concern. "He should have been here by now. They're almost upon us."

The two policemen were occupied at one of the tables on Deck Three. This deck was larger than the others, holding fifteen tables. The couple at the table was visibly agitated.

"They must be hiding something," said Maggie. "The cops are about to arrest them."

"They don't know a thing," said a soft voice behind them. "I've planted a little disruption device on the bar on Deck Seven. Everyone they question will turn out to be lying. They'll catch on after a few more inspections."

They turned and saw a green-haired waiter, dressed in the café's shiny yellow uniform. He held a tray with three empty glasses on it.

"Flint!" sighed Troy. "What a welcome sight you are. How did you get in?"

"There's a back entrance for the employees. Be ready to get out of here now."

The policemen escorted the couple they had been arguing with to the entrance. Another group of policemen appeared there.

Troy left some money on the table, and he and Maggie followed the waiter. All eyes were on Deck Three, and no one noticed their departure.

Flint led them to the large bar on Deck Seven, which was still closed because of the early hour. He picked up the disruption device and placed it in his jacket. Behind the bar was a door for employees only. Flint opened it and motioned them in. They went down a short, dark corridor to a stairwell that led down to a little landing. To one side there was a door that led into the maintenance tunnel of the café. It was open. Another door, large and iron-wrought, and with a small window in it, led into a narrow alley behind the restaurant. Flint examined the alley through the window.

"There's one policeman on this side of the building. He'll notice you if you just walk through here. Listen—I came here with the portable Transport Box, and it's in the maintenance tunnel right behind that door." He pointed to the open door. "But you cannot come with me that way. You're surfing legally, and you'll only arouse suspicion if you suddenly disappear. But they'll never notice if you leave by the back door. I'm going to leave now via the box, but I'll be right back to distract that cop over there, so you can make a break for it. Now keep a sharp lookout through that window."

Flint entered the maintenance tunnel and shut the door behind him. Troy peered through the barred window in the door leading to the alley. He saw the policeman at the far end of the building, lazily watching the back street. A minute later, a large German Shepherd sauntered into the alleyway. To Troy's utter amazement, the dog trotted directly up to the policeman, cocked its leg, and relieved itself wetly.

"WHA—?!" The stunned officer of the law jumped back a trifle too late. He lunged back to grab the dog's collar but the animal deftly stepped aside and began ambling down the alley, away from the café's exit. The policeman sprinted after it.

"Now," said Troy, and they emerged swiftly from the door. They walked quickly in the opposite direction, until they came to the first avenue. There they slowed their pace and walked past the nearest Transport Box, choosing to walk another half-a-mile to the Transport Boxes at the railway station. On the way, Troy told Maggie about Flint's method of distracting the police officer.

"It worked," he concluded his report. "But I think I would have elected to employ a more refined approach."

"You can add that to the list of topics you wanted to discuss with him," suggested Maggie. Against her will, a grin spread over her face as she visualized the officer's response. "Tell me, how does he manage to operate the Transport Box as a dog?"

"Well . . . the last time he surfed as a dog, he designed himself a special tail with which he managed the keypad. I have no idea how he's done it today."

They arrived at the railway station. The queues to the Transport Boxes were long, and they had to wait for about two minutes before arriving at an available Box.

"I'll see you in ten minutes at my site," said Troy. "Don't worry about the dog. He'll get away—he always does."

Maggie waved and disappeared into the Box. Troy followed her, and returned to Earth. He found himself in his room, seated by his desk. The holographic screen displayed a German Shepherd dressed in the Blue-net uniform. It stood on its hind legs with a tray laden with drinks balanced on its head.

"I managed to grab a couple of drinks," it said. "Would you like another

Spider?"

"No thanks," said Troy sheepishly. They were less than half an hour in the NET without Flint, and had already needed his assistance. He gave Flint the thumbs up sign, a gesture indicating high appreciation and respect among surfers. "Flint, old boy, you're the best. A perfectly executed rescue. Thanks. Perhaps more delicate means for diverting the cop's attention could have been used, but I have to admit that your method worked like a charm." He beamed at the screen. "You can change your attire now. We're meeting Maggie in a few minutes."

The dog wagged its tail in contentment. The hologram blurred for a second, and the image of the green dragon replaced the dog, still wagging his tail. Troy reconstructed the events of the past few minutes in Blue-net.

"The NET police, who work closely with Babel, arrived at Blue-net with alarming speed. I assume they also raided other sites frequented by professional surfers at the same time. In spite of all we've said before, could it be possible that Babel is involved after all in releasing that virus, and that Og isn't telling you everything? Or perhaps they have another computer? One that you cannot access, and even Og is not aware of?"

"That doesn't make sense to me," said Flint. "If they're chasing the virus author, they couldn't have launched it. Their reaction indicates surprise, not preplanning, as far as I can see."

"Yes, that's our feeling too. Maggie and I have reached a conclusion that there is a third party in the NET, which is neither the aliens nor Babel, interested in catching you. When you try to account for—"

"I know," interrupted Flint. "I've been aware of it for some time. And this party has a certain advantage over us—he has some knowledge on how we operate. We, on the other hand, have no information on him, except for this exploding virus episode. This complicates our main task—getting rid of the aliens!"

36. NET: DAY 33, 23:30

The 'com buzzed the personal call tone, and George made out the identity of the caller on the display. His heart skipped a beat. He answered the call, and a beautiful blonde woman appeared on the screen.

"Maureen Clarke! To what do I owe this honor?" He disconnected the automatic recorder in the armored vehicle he was driving. "I haven't heard from you in three years. I thought you'd forgotten I existed."

"You're not so easy to forget, George," said Maureen pleasantly, flashing a dazzling smile. "There's something I need to consult with you urgently and privately. Do you think we could meet somewhere?"

George had met Maureen three years earlier. It was during a non-routine mission—Norman had assigned him to locate the hackers who had broken into the Clarke Energy central computers. They had stolen vital data and destroyed all the backup copies.

"I suspect that these hackers also sabotaged Ron Clarke's aircraft after he met them in Hungary," said Norman. "But we have no evidence to corroborate that suspicion. The job was done with surgical precision, and Interpol has admitted that they're stumped. See if you can find anything they might have overlooked."

So George paid a visit to Clarke Energy, and met with the lovely widow-heiress, Maureen. He liked her from the very first minute. After the initial introductions, he got right down to business.

"Who's running the show now?" he asked her. "If you want results I'll need authorization and privileges."

"I'm in charge," said Maureen. "What privileges were you thinking of?"

"The authority to question any or all of the corporation's personnel, at my discretion." He noticed her surprise, and continued. "It just might be what we call an 'inside job'—an employee in cahoots with the criminals. Those hackers knew far more about the company's data repositories than would appear reasonable. Anyone refusing to be questioned will immediately be suspect."

He got the authorization. It was all he needed.

George interrogated all the employees in the computer center of Clarke Energy for two days. He was expert in the use of the T-scope, but he found no collaborators in that group. However, two of the employees refused to be questioned. As he had no legal way to force them to do so, he resorted to less orthodox methods. He ambushed them in the NET, froze them, and took them to an isolated NET site. It didn't take longer than a few minutes of intense torture for the employees to break and reveal the identities of the three hackers to whom they had transferred information.

George went after them, caught them, and brought them to the same site for interrogation. To his delight, they proved to be tougher customers than the company stooges. After several hours of agonizing torment, one of them broke down. He had witnessed George erase the memory of one of his partners in crime, and subsequently return him normally to Earth, thereby updating his Earth mind with a blank. The terrified hacker blubbered and raved, but eventually blurted out everything George wanted to know—the identity of the mercenary who planted the bomb on the plane, and the location of the stolen data. George returned the two employees and the hackers to Earth in emergency mode, so that they remembered nothing of their grilling. Then he had them and the hit man arrested on Earth. He recovered the stolen data, and when they were presented in evidence at the trial, all the defendants pleaded guilty, and were sentenced to long years in prison. Except, of course, the hacker whose mind had been erased—he was transferred to a special hospital, where human vegetables were tended.

Naturally, there was an internal inquiry in Babel—a man was injured during an investigative process. But nothing pointed to George, and he was cleared. He was even decorated by Norman.

Maureen invited him to dinner after the trial was over.

"I am deeply grateful to you, George," she said, as they sat in one of San Francisco's finest restaurants. "You've done a fantastic job—brought the villains to justice, and saved my company a fortune. How did you manage to track the perpetrators so fast, when the Interpol had already thrown in the towel?"

"Criminals always leave traces. Experience teaches us how to recognize the criminal's electronic trail."

"And yet, two days is an amazing rate in which to capture the entire network, get them to confess, and recover the stolen goods. Why don't you tell me a little more? For instance, how did that poor hacker lose all of his memory?"

George gazed into her eyes, and read the fortitude in them. She obviously could not be brushed off with an evasive reply. *I can play that game, too,* he thought. *She's rich, beautiful, smart, and available. What a combination!* He smiled at her.

"I can only guess that he was overcome by guilt, and contracted NET-phobia," he said. "That's usually the cause of this kind of coma on Earth. As for the others, I have my methods for identifying, locating, apprehending, and getting confessions, and they usually work quite well, as you can see. Perhaps I could reveal some more of these methods in future meetings. When we get to know each other better . . ."

But there were no additional meetings. They conversed on the 'com a few times after that dinner, but though Maureen always took his calls, she never agreed to a second date. George abandoned his reveries.

"I'd be glad to meet with you," he answered. "I see you're in your car. Where are you headed?"

"I'm in the car because I didn't want this conversation to originate from Clarke Energy. There's a security problem there, and I'm afraid for my life. I had no one to turn to, and then I remembered you."

George glanced at the car clock. He had to interview York at Roller-net, but that shouldn't take more than an hour. The drive itself was very short— Roller-net was just twenty minutes away from Babel HQ.

"Would you mind waiting for me at the VIP parking of Roller-net?" he asked her. "We could meet there at twelve forty-five. An hour and ten minutes from now. I'll contact you when I finish my meeting there."

"Roller-net?" Maureen smiled. "Are you sure you'll be working, or are you going there to have a good time?" She noticed George's somber look, and continued quickly. "I'll be there. I have a yellow Hummer-net. I don't believe you'll see many of those in the parking lot." Hummer-nets were for the very wealthy only, each one costing at least two hundred thousand dollars.

"See you soon," said George, and hung up. His thoughts remained with Maureen until he saw the towering constructions of Roller-net looming ahead. He cleared his mind and focused on his next task—how to interrogate York and absolve him of any suspicion . . .

37. NET: Day 34, 00:00

Maggie turned the hourglass over and watched the golden grains trickling silently down. It was a beautiful instrument, made of hammered silver and handmade crystal—a NET present from her father for her tenth birthday.

If you ever need to make an important decision, a really critical decision, don't drag it out too long, he wrote on the attached card. *When you have all the facts, turn the glass over. If you cannot reach a decision in those five minutes, you probably never will.*

She had used the hourglass only on rare occasions. When she had decided to select biochemistry over nuclear physics as her main subject at secondary school. And when her mother got her position with the Tokyo Philharmonic Orchestra, and she decided to go with her and study for a year in Japan. And when she decided to turn down M.I.T.'s tantalizing offer to join their advanced program, which included a year's scholarship for Ph. D. schooling—she would have had to give up her ice-sculpting class and her drama group at Columbia University.

She was on the brink of such a decision now. Perhaps the most critical of all. And it had to do with Dad, who had given her the hourglass. She thought feverishly, her eyes never leaving the thin stream of sand.

Dad works for Babel. He can help in finding who's trying to eliminate Flint. And perhaps he knows something about the invaders as well. But I'll have to tell him about Troy and Flint. Oh, he knows Troy, of course, but Flint will be news to him. Dad will have to turn them in! And those technocrats just might decide to turn Flint off . . .

Tears of frustration welled in her eyes. The thought of the boisterous dragon being disconnected from the NET, locked into his box forever, was quite unbearable. She made up her mind.

I shall never betray Troy or Flint. I'll try my best to obtain information from Dad about what's happening in Babel. Perhaps I could even contribute some assistance without his knowledge. Maybe I could arrange for him to be the mediator between the aliens and humans, if they turn out to be friendly.

The last grains of sand descended to the bottom of the hourglass. A decision had been made—final and irrevocable. Maggie called her father's emergency NET number. A tall, blond man appeared on her screen.

"Hi, sweetie—I'm terribly sorry about tonight's dinner. I hope you managed without me. There's a red-hot emergency here." His voice was tense. He was obviously in the middle of some urgent activity.

"Do you think it'll be over by tonight? I hope you're not going to shut down the NET—I have a lot of work scheduled for this weekend." Maggie pretended to be joking. She hoped to draw some important information from him.

"You'd be surprised how close you guessed. By the look of things right now, it doesn't seem likely that I'll be home tonight. Why don't you return to Earth and go do something else, like ice sculpting or exercising? A rest from the NET wouldn't hurt you one bit."

"Why, Dad!" Maggie managed a mock rebuke at her father. "Am I in any danger in the NET? You're practically *chasing* me away. Come on, you can tell me. A malicious virus? Infrastructure problems?"

"I wish I knew what's going on. All kinds of strange things are happening in the NET, and some surfers have been hurt. That's no secret—it was on the Gossipofon. You just disconnect and stay on Earth. I'll call you tomorrow. Bye now, sweetie."

"Bye, Daddy. Take care of yourself."

Maggie terminated the call. Her entire being cried out to shout 'Watch out, Dad! There are alien invaders in the NET!' But she had made a decision, and she would stick to it. She would not turn Flint in. A look at her watch revealed that she was late. Troy and Flint were waiting. She tapped in the coordinates and jumped to Troy's site.

38. NET: DAY 34, 00:48

George Boder left the Roller-net offices with mixed feelings. He had just finished questioning Mr. Rupert Stewart York, the owner and manager of the park, and the entire interrogation was now in Babel's computer. It was a routine, unspectacular session, with no suspicious innuendos surfacing. York would have a clean slate at Babel, and no one would dream of him being involved in any way with viruses. The T-scope proved beyond doubt that every word he uttered was the truth.

George had no apprehensions about questioning York—just as he had no doubts that he would pass his own interrogation a few hours earlier, after Tipman's mind wipeout. As the senior field official, George was in charge of the entire inventory of T scope machines in Babel. It was easy for him to reprogram the internal algorithm of each machine, so that by the mere inflection of his voice he could force it to display 'Truth' or 'Falsehood' to anything he said. When he interrogated others, the tonal inflections in his question would determine True or False for the reply.

George had altered all the Babel T-scopes before he wrote his first virus. He had to—all Babel personnel underwent questioning with a T-scope at least once every year. Without this modification he would be discovered immediately.

But now another problem had cropped up. York was supposed to have followed his orders, and generated money for him, by running Roller-net. It turned out that he had tried, of his own initiative, to do away with the hacker who caught Tipman. Far worse—he was sloppy about it, and a link between the hit attempt and Roller-net was established.

George knew that, for the moment, he had bought some time. But a future investigation, which was inevitable, would expose York for what he really was. And once they had York, they would get to him, too. Clearly, it was time to make sure that all traces of his linkage to York were obliterated.

He was mulling various alternatives in his mind, when the elevator to the underground VIP parking sighed to a halt.

George stepped out and looked around. There were only three cars parked there, and the yellow Hummer-net stood right next to his. Maureen signaled him with her lights. He smiled, and approached her car, waving a greeting. She gestured for him to get into the car from the other side. He had just grasped the door handle and started opening it when something odd caught his attention. Dark curtains covered the rear windows of the Hummer-net, and he could not see whether the back seats were occupied or not.

He snatched his hand back from the handle and darted for the freezer in his belt, when suddenly the parking lot was flooded with an intense blue light. He felt himself drawn upward, as if into a gigantic vacuum cleaner. He saw the parking lot contract and disappear. For a fraction of a second he was enveloped in utter darkness, and then he found himself in his Babel office on Earth.

"What the—" George halted. He knew at once what had happened. And what he had to do now. His secretary hurried to him in consternation, but he signaled to her that he was okay, and took off his helmet. She stopped.

"Mr. Boder? You're back early. Weren't you supposed to be at a questioning session in the NET right now?"

"I'm returning there right away. Please make me a cup of coffee, no sugar."

"Yes, sir. Would you like a croissant, too? We just got fresh ones from Pierre's bakery." Pierre's was the best bakery in the area. George nodded, and ignored her. He needed to concentrate on the mission ahead.

We have got to find the person who sealed the tunnel, and coerce him to open it, he thought. *We're talking about a surfer who managed to arrive at a random point on this planet, find a time-fold, and construct a tunnel into another world. Very few people can claim such qualifications. Who could it be?*

His secretary tiptoed up to his desk, ever so gently placed the coffee and the croissant on it, and hastily retreated back to her office.

Our surfer friend needed to have some kind of aircraft to arrive at the time-fold—a hoverer or a plane. But only we and the NET police have such aircraft. Actually, these aircraft wouldn't help either—they couldn't land near the waterfall. Well, the hovercraft could possibly lower a rope onto the platform by the waterfall, and our surfer would shimmy down and open the tunnel. No—the whole picture doesn't make sense. Even if there were clandestine factors in the NET that we know nothing about—and that is highly doubtful—they couldn't pull off a stunt like that.

Hold it just a minute—let's try to put some order into this tiny mind of mine. Whoever opened that tunnel must have gone through it and arrived at our world. And to the deserted city. He must have set off the defense robots. So he must have had an aircraft of some sort. And the fact that he got away from the city would indicate that his aircraft is immune to super-laser rays. No way—it's a dead end. There's no logic in this line of thinking.

He sipped some coffee and took a bite from the croissant. Something was still missing. The information in George's brain had not yet had time to return into focus. He shut his eyes and ran through his arguments again.

Normal humans do not have the skills and qualifications necessary for this kind of thing. Could there be other non-human creatures on this planet, and it was they who penetrated our world? Creatures who arrived here through another time-fold? With a culture outstripping even our own?

He promptly rejected this option.

Far too remote a probability. Our world has several hundred thousands time-folds, and it has taken us two hundred and fifty thousand years to make our first contact with another time-fold. The odds that this planet, which could at best harbor five time-folds, is hosting yet another alien race within the tiny time span of its thirty years of its existence, border on zero. Totally unrealistic. The fact that they tunneled to us is, in itself, an exceptional coincidence!

But it was clear to him that additional factors were involved here. Someone had built that sealing door to the tunnel, and that someone was of this planet. He had made use of standard locking procedures, developed on this planet, which prevented anyone from opening it. His thoughts skipped to a different channel.

Anomaly! We now have an anomaly in the NET. A site named Hell exists, but it doesn't show on our computers. It is huge, if we can rely on the recording. A human built this site—some of the characters there were inspired directly from the Hieronymus Bosch paintings. Let's see if by solving one anomaly, another anomaly solution will present itself. Theoretically, the builder of Hell could conceivably be the sealer of the tunnel. How did he get there? He has winged demons! That's it! They can easily fly over the random territories, and land anywhere. He rode a demon or some other winged creature. But that doesn't explain why we didn't see him when he left the waterfall. Flying back to Netville should have taken him many hours. However, that's a minor issue at the moment.

George leaned back in his chair, and laced his fingers behind his head.

Yes—I'm almost positive that the Hell builder is also the tunnel sealer! Now all we need to do is find that scoundrel. Let's check the NET logs for anyone near the tunnel. Or anywhere in the approximate vicinity.

George straightened up and keyed the tunnel's coordinates into his computer. He had no problem remembering them, or any other thirty-digit set of coordinates on the NET. He remembered everything.

The computer's response was curt and dry:'random territories, zero surfs.'

He wasn't surprised. He didn't expect the criminal to leave such blatant tracks.

At least I wound up in the right place—Babel's security center. I can check everything that happens in the NET from here. If there's anywhere in the NET most suitable for catching whoever blocked the tunnel, I'm in it!

George got to his feet and began pacing the room, his face contorted in anger. "I'd like to roast the bastard in his Hell," he hissed through clenched teeth. "That'll teach him not to mess with things that don't concern him."

This new thought calmed him down. He imagined the black demons dragging a naked surfer, unconscious, over a field of sharp thorns, the skin being slowly stripped away in thin ribbons. A distant 'com rang, and he returned abruptly to the present. Time to act. He sat by the computer.

Norman Starr! We must recruit him. Only he can order a comprehensive search for the transgressor, in the NET and on Earth. We'll spread a net so far flung, that our fish will not be able to escape from it.

He finished his coffee, and filed the plan to take over Norman into his brain. It wouldn't be too difficult.

He operated the inter-call.

"I'm returning to the NET," he told his secretary. "The coffee was burnt, and the croissant dry."

"I'm sorry, Mr. Boder."

He didn't hear her. He put on his helmet, punched the coordinates, and found himself at the entrance to Roller-net. From there to his car was a brisk three–minute walk.

39. NET: DAY 34, 02:00

Troy's home site was relatively modest and unpretentious. A single-story house made of green wood, surrounded by a small yard populated mainly with tall cypress trees. The house had an entry room, naturally, which also had a backup computer system. The rest of the house consisted of a bedroom with a large, circular bed, a kitchen, a sparingly furnished living room, and a large working room. Maggie jumped to the site, and walked into the working room where Troy and Flint were seated, watching the wall-holograph. They were deep in conversation.

"Hi guys, sorry I'm late. I needed some recuperation. What's that?" The screen showed a blow-up of a white parking ticket for the Roller-net.

"This picture was taken by one of the street vid-sensors tracking the netter in the purple car, before he crashed." Troy invited her to sit with them, and Flint pulled up a chair with his tail. "Og sent it to us from Babel."

"Guys, remember that Babel is a very sophisticated adversary," said Maggie, sitting down. "We've ruled them out as the virus generators, but they could still plant bogus information to either mislead or expose us."

"I'm quite convinced that that is not the case, Maggie," said Flint seriously. "Og would know, and he'd tell me. This information is bona fide."

Troy supported Flint. "If they were trying to trap us, they'd certainly select somewhere less busy than the Roller-net. I, too, believe this ticket to be genuine. So the netter controlling the suicidal truck driver was indeed at the Roller-net before launching the virus."

"Well, I suppose we could verify this issue with your 'relative' at the Traffic Control Center," suggested Maggie, looking at Flint. "He could trace the netter's activities and confirm that he was actually there."

"Sorry—we thought about that, but it won't work. Whoever sent that netter is very familiar with NET traffic regulations. He knew that street vid-sensors have a memory lasting only two hours. During the two hours preceding the virus launch, our netter was in an abandoned basement, where he had concealed the explosives from prying satellite eyes. The female truck driver also began her journey there. He probably helped her to load the truck, which, by the way, she herself had rented three hours earlier."

Maggie's look mixed amazement with exasperation. "Just how do you know all this stuff?" she queried. "Does it all come from Og?"

"Would you believe it?" Troy fondly scratched the dragon's head. "Babel's computer reports to Flint! They're trying to catch illegal surfers, and their number one offender gets all their inside information."

"We can't afford to remain in the dark," stated Flint as a matter of fact.

The pride in his voice was clear. "Og and I are old friends, and he knows that I have the NET's best interests at heart. That parking ticket was deciphered by him, and he sent it to me of his own volition."

"Let's skip that voluntary assistance issue for the moment," interjected Troy. "Do you happen to know what Babel are doing with this information?"

"They're investigating all the surfers who were in the Roller-net at that time. So far there are no suspects. They also sent someone to interview Roller-net's manager, the mysterious Mr. York."

"Do you know *whom* they sent?" asked Maggie eagerly.

"It's not your dad," replied the dragon, lifting his tail in importance. "He's busy checking the alibis of the Roller-net visitors. They sent a field expert. He visited the amusement park, interrogated York with a T-scope, and found him clean."

"I think the best thing is to visit Roller-net," said Troy. "Babel might have missed something—" He stopped. Flint stood up abruptly, raised a finger to his lips, and tiptoed toward a large wall cabinet, drawing a freezer out of his pocket. He jerked the door open, and Adam tumbled into the room. As he got to his feet, Flint picked him up effortlessly with one hand, and dumped him gruffly onto a chair in a corner of the room.

"Adam! What in tarnation are you doing here?" Troy was on his feet, his face livid.

"Take me with you to the Roller-net!" pleaded Adam. In no way did his voice indicate remorse on being caught red-handed. "Please! I know the place like the back of my hand. Hey, if the virus' operator is there, I'll find him, I'm sure. I know all the netters there, and I know who could give me answers."

"The nerve of this kid is simply unbelievable!" Troy look embarrassedly at Maggie, seeking her support. He controlled his temper with a visible effort, and returned his look to his younger brother, who stared back defiantly. "Are you in the habit of spying on us? How dare you enter my site in my absence?"

"I dropped in for a visit and no one was home. I wanted to wait for you. Hey, you promised to include me in everything that happens. I know I can help."

Flint winked at Adam. "I think you're taking too many risks lately," he said. "When did you graduate from the electrician's training course?"

Adam turned beet red.

"May I inquire what you're talking about?" asked Troy wryly.

"It's a totally unrelated issue," said Adam hastily. "I was surfing private-ly—"

"And this is my private site," interrupted Troy. "Is that also an unrelated issue? Just wait until I think of a punishment befitting the severity of your offense—"

"Ahem, Troy," broke in Maggie delicately. "Before you tear off the lad's head, which he certainly deserves, may I point out that taking Adam along to the Roller-net might not be such a bad idea after all. He won't be noticed there, and he could warn us if anything unusual happens."

Troy stared long and hard at Adam and Maggie. *Yes, Maggie's argument had merit—the kid really could help us in our quest. But he could not be let off so easily—he had to be severely reprimanded.*

The last time Adam had transgressed was still etched in both of the brothers' minds. It happened six months ago. Troy was at his site, finalizing a report on the crystal-growing project he was conducting at Stanford-net. Flint was there, too, busily occupied with improvements to his new portable Transport Box. When the 'com buzzed, Troy almost absent-mindedly reached out and toggled it to auto-answer. He was engrossed in his report, and had no time to take calls now. To his surprise, the auto-answer did not kick in—instead, the handset emitted a shrill whistle, and a man's powerful voice was heard.

"Troy Bentley! This is Sheriff Dale of Upper Lexington Precinct. You are requested to answer this call immediately!"

Troy jumped to his feet. He glanced quickly at Flint, who had straightened up from the workbench he was working on. The dragon raised its hands in bewilderment, and its innocent eyes told Troy that it wasn't involved in any subterfuge. Troy answered the 'com.

"This is Troy Bentley. What's happened?"

"I'd rather discuss this face to face, Mr. Bentley. Please come down to the precinct NET station right away. The coordinates are on your screen." The sheriff hung up.

"You haven't done anything wrong," said Flint. "It must be a mistake."

"Wait for me here, Flint. But hide in the other room, and be prepared to leave the NET at a moment's notice. We may have unwelcome visitors here, and they mustn't see you surfing."

Troy was in a foreboding mood as he jumped to the police station. A tall, athletic man dressed in an olive uniform greeted him at the entrance. He introduced himself as Sheriff Dale, and without any further formalities led Troy into a room off the main corridor. Troy gasped when he saw Adam there, along with three of his friends. All four were bruised and buffeted, and almost all of their clothing was torn in various places. Adam sported a white bandage on his head. They were all chalk white, and trembling in terror.

"Adam—what happened? Are you all right? What—"

The sheriff interrupted him.

"Is this redhead your brother?"

"He is," acknowledged Troy.

"And you owned a blue mustang-net, with registration number 'TBENT-LY07'?"

"Own, not owned. Anything the matter with it?"

The sheriff snickered. "I'd say the car was the least of your worries, Mr. Bentley." He pointed to one of the youngsters. "Did you give Nigel Patterson permission to drive your car?"

Troy knew Nigel. He was two years older than Adam, and had only very recently obtained his driver's license. Troy was about to deny giving his permission, when he saw Adam's imploring expression. If he and his friends were charged with driving a vehicle without permission, an offense on par with theft, they faced heavy sentences. They may even be banned from the NET for a while.

Troy hesitated for a second.

"Yes, I allowed them to use my car—and if I'm not mistaken, it was for the last time." He glared at the foursome, and turned back to the policeman. "Please tell me what happened."

"Oh, nothing extraordinary," was the reply. "Just that greenhorn driver speeding through downtown Netville at ninety per, losing control, hitting and decommissioning two netters, and plowing into a parked car." The sheriff shook his head at Troy—he was well aware that Troy was covering for the kids. "That young man's driving license is hereby revoked for five years.

But you, as the car's owner, are liable for the damage he caused. I hope you're insured, and that your policy is valid."

Troy was indeed insured, but it didn't cover drivers with licenses for less than a year. He decided not to involve the parents, and covered the damages out of his own pocket. Most of his savings, accumulated through months of puzzle contest wins, evaporated. He didn't even have enough money to buy a car to replace the totaled one, and it was not until four months later that he could afford another one.

Adam, of course, was penniless. He swore he'd return the money to Troy from future earnings. He also swore never to infringe on NET rules again. But that was six months ago, and six months was a long time . . .

"You're a far cry from repaying your previous debts," said Troy tight-lipped. Adam cringed away from him, his trembling magnified by his brother's ire.

Troy's heart melted. A wave of warmth flooded over him—he loved this kid. This carrot-headed brat, who was incessantly trying to prove himself to the world.

He's no less talented than I am—yet they're expecting him to perform miracles. He'll make it, I'm sure, but he's under enormous pressure now. I had it much easier—no one expected anything of me, and everything I did was happily accepted.

Troy dedicated a lot of his time to his younger brother. He prepared him for puzzle contests, helped him in his bio-cyber studies, and even made him his assistant in one of his research projects. He also allowed Adam to get assistance from Flint, a privilege he gave no one else.

Adam, Maggie and the dragon looked anxiously at Troy. It took him a long minute, but he made up his mind at last.

"I'm going to give you another chance to redeem yourself, little brother," he said. His voice was calm and soothing, without any trace of anger. "I haven't yet decided how to punish you for breaking into my site, but we'll discuss that later. You may join us, but you've got to promise to follow instructions. We're in a very serious business here! Agreed?"

Adam's face lit up. He jumped to his feet, his face radiant, and hugged Troy.

"Thanks, Troy, you're the greatest brother a guy could have. And, hey, thanks, Maggie, for coming to my rescue. You won't regret it, believe me. I'll do anything you say—you can trust me. Let's go!"

"Hang on, there," said the dragon, fondly wrapping its tail around Adam's waist. "Where are you off to in such a hurry? We're not ready yet. First, we need to do a bit of preliminary research."

40. NET: Day 34, 03:20

Norman Starr was puzzled by George's request. George had never before asked for an urgent private meeting. His report from the Roller-net revealed nothing. Now he was standing in front of his desk. Norman waved a hand at a chair, but George remained on his feet.

"I suspect that someone in our unit is collaborating with the creator of the Hell site." George's voice was low and confident. "While interrogating York a couple of hours ago, I noticed that he had possession of the Tipman memory recording. He could have obtained it only from a Babel staffer."

Norman raised an eyebrow. "How did you come to notice the recording?"

"He wasn't expecting my visit. He was probably busy watching the recording in the adjacent room. When he emerged from that room to meet me, he locked the door behind him. I asked him to show me a few of his accounting books, and in his absence I threaded a stereoscopic visio-fiber under the locked door. I saw the Hell recording clearly displayed on the screen."

"Why is there no mention of this in your interview report?"

"I realized at once that I could not inquire on this topic. The interrogation would be stored in Og, and some Babel personnel would have access to it. I had to assume that the traitor would also be able to read it. Therefore, I refrained from referring to this issue during questioning." George placed his T-scope on Norman's desk. "It's all in here—just as I reported to Og. York is as pure as the driven snow."

"So it would seem," said Norman, paying close attention to every word George said. "So, what did you have in mind?"

George leaned forward on the desk. His expression was one of grave concern.

"You're the only one I can trust in Babel. If I couldn't trust you there'd be no point in my working here, right? But I can't be so sure about anyone else. One of them is a renegade. I suggest the two of us pay a visit to Mr. York, and convince him to tell us who his accomplice is. You should be there since we cannot update Og this time. If the traitor gets wind of our intentions he'd fly the coop, destroying any incriminating evidence along the way."

"I see." Norman leaned back in his chair, away from George. "No need to get excited." He opened a drawer of the desk, drew out a freezer and pointed it squarely at George's midriff.

George paled.

"You??"

"Oh, no, George. Just a preliminary precaution." Norman turned on the T-scope on his desk. "Are you the creator of the viruses?"

George sighed in relief.

"No."

"Are you convinced we have a traitor in the unit?"

"Almost definitely. Somebody from here gave York the Tipman recording."

The T-scope showed George to be telling the truth. Norman turned it off, and replaced the freezer. He then got to his feet.

"Let's go. Sorry you had to go through that." He stared in astonishment at the freezer in George's hand, then at George's face. He managed a wry smile, and turned the T-scope on again.

"I, Norman Starr, am neither the author of the viruses nor a traitor." The machine glowed green. George nodded, and re-holstered his freezer. He turned off the T-scope and pocketed it.

Norman switched on the inter-call.

"Samantha, George and I will be out on a special task. If anyone calls, I'm in a hermetically sealed environment and cannot be reached. Even if it's John Pierce. Activate the 'Solo' procedure."

"Yes, sir. The procedure requires you to state how long you'll be incommunicado."

"No more than three hours. I'll notify you the minute I'm back."

Norman depressed a hidden switch under his desk. The side wall glided silently to one side, revealing a steel door with a locking device. He tapped several figures on the keypad, and the door swung open into a long corridor. The two men entered, and began walking down its length, the door and wall closing behind them.

"Do you have any weapons besides your freezer?" asked Norman, displaying his own freezer in a side holster. All Babel personnel were required to carry a freezer at all times while surfing.

George showed Norman a laser pistol and a powerful electric nerve stunner secured onto his belt under his jacket. Norman wasn't surprised. George had a reputation for being always armed to the teeth, as if expecting to be attacked at any moment.

The corridor ended at a Transport Box. George looked at it with concern.

"Are we going to jump directly to the Roller-net?" he asked calmly. This would seriously disrupt his plans to take control of Norman. "I thought we'd drive over there—it's just about fifteen minutes away." Babel personnel were not permitted to make a direct jump to a public Transport Box, except in emergencies. Consequently, Babel kept clandestine sites throughout Netville to which they could jump without using the public boxes.

"We're jumping into a special vehicle of mine in a secret underground parking zone near Babel's main gate," explained Norman as they entered the Transport Box. "This way, no one will know that we've left Babel Headquarters." He keyed in the coordinates, and there was a slight flicker.

George found himself seated in a car, the like of which he had never encountered. Norman was beside him, in the driver's seat. The car purred into life, the windows darkened, and they drove along a narrow tunnel that ended at a massive gate. Norman pressed a finger to the remote control on the dashboard, and the gate opened. A second, identical gate was similarly passed a few minutes later. They emerged in the front courtyard of the Babel fortress. Norman drove directly to the main gate, and passed through it, using the same remote control device.

We're heading toward Roller-net, thought George, the minute they left Babel HQ.

Okay, I've spotted you. Following. He picked up Noah Atkinson's answering thought. *We'll wait for you there. If he suspects anything, freeze him immediately.*

I'll be driving right behind you, came Maureen's thought. *If there's any trouble I'll be in close range.*

George wanted to reply, but the telepathic connection was suddenly cut off. He snapped his head around, and noticed that Norman had just pressed a button on the dashboard.

"Is there anything wrong?" asked Norman, glancing at George quizzically. "Do you feel all right?"

"I'm fine," answered George, pulling himself together. "What was that button you just pushed?"

"It screens the car from all electromagnetic radiations. The car is also armored and impervious to all conventional weapons. So we're protected from any kind of attack, including radiation."

"Very impressive," muttered George. "I've never seen a car like this. Is it a new model?"

"Indeed it is. Designed for special missions. Now, about the questioning—is York expecting another visit from us?"

"He is. I told him I wanted to return with another investigator, and inquire about his employees and suppliers. He had no objection."

They drove at high speed through Netville's streets. All the traffic lights turned green as they approached, and George assumed that the car broadcast codes to the Traffic Control Center to enable that effect. The car's window panes had a traffic density map embedded in them and they displayed the traffic situation in real-time mode. All unusual events were displayed on these screens, and George studied them carefully. Maureen had the description of the car they were in, and the route they were taking, so she could wait for them anywhere along it. Three minutes later he saw the yellow Hummernet merging into the traffic behind them. The screen on Norman's right locked into it immediately.

"I don't like the looks of that yellow car," said Norman. "It was waiting for us. George, find out who owns it."

George punched the car's license-plate number, and the name came up on the screen immediately. Maureen Clarke. The energy empress.

Norman didn't conceal his surprise. "I know her. What is she doing here?" He drove in silence through two more green traffic lights, and then pulled up abruptly by the curb. The yellow car drove by toward Roller-net.

"It's her in person," confirmed George. "I saved her ass once. Why did you think she was following us?"

"That's what the automatic system here construed," replied Norman. He remained parked for a few more minutes, following the Hummer-net's movements on the screen. Maureen drove to a fancy shopping mall located near Roller-net, parked her car, and walked into the shopping area. Norman tapped a code into the keypad, and the mall cameras took over, following Maureen into Nambush, the prestigious dress shop.

"Probably a false alarm," grunted Norman. "Can't think of a reason why a celebrity like her would want to tail me. However, that's exactly what the car system interpreted from her driving." He frowned. "Possibly the car computer's sensitivity level is calibrated a bit too high. Just the same, George, I want to know everywhere that lady has been in the past week, and a list of everyone she's met. In addition, I want her shadowed for a week. It's probably just a coincidence, but too many odd things are happening in the NET lately, and I'm not taking any chances."

He resumed driving toward Roller-net. On the screen, George could see Maureen conversing with one of the store clerks.

On arriving at Roller-net, Norman drove straight to the underground VIP parking zone. The gate opened immediately, as if recognizing the car. A large gray SUV was parked near the entrance, but Norman preferred to park a bit further on. He examined the parking area around him, trying to take in every detail.

"I'll go first," he told George. "Cover me until I get to the elevators. Then I'll cover you, and you'll join me there. There's probably nothing to guard against, but it never hurts to be careful."

Norman got out of the car, and walked quickly to the elevators, glancing left and right, his right hand gripping his freezer, and his left in his pocket, poised to press on his emergency return ring. He had just passed the gray SUV, when a brilliant blue flash lighted up the parking lot, and his head felt like it would burst.

Ambush!

He managed to press the ring in his pocket before dropping to the floor, momentarily dazed. He recovered immediately and pressed the ring again. Nothing happened.

A tall man, dressed in a dark suit, came out of the pickup with a freezer in his hand. Norman rolled on the floor, drawing his own freezer. He aimed at the man and pulled the trigger. The tall man went down like a block of ice, his head striking one of the SUV's wheels.

Norman got to his feet shakily. He saw George running toward him with his freezer drawn.

"George—ambush! Watch out . . . " The look of sheer hatred on George's face explained the entire situation. "You double-crossing—" Norman tried to point his freezer at George, but what he saw made him halt in astonishment. The door of the car he had just driven opened, and he himself, Norman Starr, emerged, a freezer in his hand.

"It can't be! I've been cloned!" It was the last thing that crossed his mind before George shot him, and the world darkened.

How come there's a copy of me here? thought the new Norman. *He was supposed to have disappeared when I left the NET.*

Probably a malfunction like we had with Spindler, thought George. *He was very suspicious, and he's very fast.* He unfroze the man in the dark suit. *Are you all right, Noah?*

Yes, yes—I'm okay. He took me by surprise. Let's vaporize him. He pointed an atomic blaster at the frozen Norman.

George stopped him, a malevolent glare on his face. *No, let's wait with him. I might not get another opportunity to perform some experiments on a human. I'll vaporize him myself when I'm through.*

What do you propose to do about York?

He no longer poses a threat, thought George. *We'll close his case. Norman and I will return to the fortress. Noah, you'll take this frozen dummy, and keep him securely bound at your site.*

He gazed upon the rigid body at his feet. For years he'd dreamed of the moment when he could personally get even with the one person who blocked his advance at Babel. He sent a vicious kick to the abdomen of the immobile man on the floor, who couldn't feel a thing.

Yes, SIR—we'll have a lot of time to have fun together, you and I, SIR! You'll learn a few more of my talents . . .

41. NET: Day 34, 04:45

Troy, Maggie and Adam sat around a large table in Troy's workroom. Flint had changed his appearance to a muscular seventeen-year-old youth with navy-short blond hair, and was now standing by the holographic screen, briefing the others on the information he had gathered on Roller-net, the largest and most successful of the NET's amusement parks.

The data was impressive. Taking full advantage of the fact that the entire Netville area was illuminated at night, the park operated continuously twenty-four hours a day all year round. The tens of thousands of visitors it attracted every NET day made it a veritable gold mine for its owner. The roller coaster rides, the most popular of the park's attractions, were considered to be one of the 'NET's seven wonders.' They towered to skyscraper heights, twisted around gigantic trees and under artificial lakes in which scary creatures would unexpectedly pop up in front of the thrilled riders, threatening to snatch some of them out of the car.

There were additional attractions as well—hundreds of them. You could take a boat ride down into the bowels of the earth, fording subterranean cataracts; fumble through a gigantic maze of mirrors—many visitors needing rescuing after hopelessly losing their way in one of its ten levels; hologram-combat studios, where one could fight imaginary holographic creatures; large laboratory halls where tiny NET-like worlds could be constructed, and in which you could play any role you chose; and many more.

Roller-net was one of the oldest sites on the NET. It was acquired three Earth years ago by Mr. Rupert Stewart York, a mysterious entrepreneur, who had decided to enter the entertainment business. The buyer, who insisted on being called Mr. York, kept to himself almost fanatically. Only few had ever heard his name before he showed up at the offices of Roller-net, a site that had been on a steep decline for years as a result of mismanagement and neglect, and gave the previous owners an offer they could not refuse. Rumors had it that he paid them twenty million dollars in cash, taking over all the accumulated debts as well—at least another five million dollars.

York set about his new site with efficient alacrity. He bought a huge, four-hundred-acre lot adjacent to the old park, hired the best designers in the market, and gave them an almost unlimited budget to expand and renovate the amusement park. His only condition was that every ride, stall and attraction be the biggest in the world—NET and Earth. The work lasted eight NET years (four Earth months), and included constructing the new roller coaster and a variety of new crowd pullers. York himself lived in a large estate within the park, and managed the site with an army of eight hundred netters. The netters also tended the botanical gardens surrounding the Roller-net, an item of attraction in itself.

"We should arrive at the Roller-net from anywhere but here," said Maggie. "They can backtrack jumps, and we don't want them to locate Troy's site. Especially as we'll be on an illegal surf."

"Right you are," agreed Troy. "We'll take my car to the Topaz Mall—it's nearby—and jump to our destination from there. There are dozens of entrances to the Roller-net, and I suggest we go by the entrance closest to our netter's parking spot. If there's a guard there, he may remember him. Flint, could you show us that entrance on the map?"

Flint gave a few taps on the computer's keyboard, and a map of Roller-net was displayed on the wall.

"He parked in Zone D3," said Maggie. "I see it's in blue. Does the color mean anything?"

"It means good news," chortled Troy. "It's our first clue. Mr. Explosive Netter parked in the supplier's parking area. And that means that Mr. York, the park's owner, has to have some information on him. If you recall, Flint's presentation distinctly showed us that York is the only surfer in the site. All the other personnel are netters who work for him. So even if our netter didn't meet with York personally, he must have met up with another netter. Flint, does Babel know about this?"

"I admit that it's pretty strange," replied the sturdy blond. Troy noticed that Flint had the same glint in his eyes that he had when he appeared as a dragon or a bear. "Og reported that they're checking everyone who was in the site, which would include the manager, of course. But Og did not state that York was the prime suspect! And instead of zeroing in on him, they're combing through the thousands of visitors to the site. Yes, indeed—York is our target. And here's something stranger still. Have you noticed that in all the pictorial evidence I showed you, there is not one clear picture of this mystery man?"

Troy turned to his brother.

"Adam, you've visited Roller-net often enough, haven't you? Did you ever see York walking around?"

"Yes, once, about two years ago. There was a false fire alarm, and he came out of his office to investigate. He's tall and broad shouldered, square face with a short beard - something like a sanitary brush. He was very easy to spot—hey, he was the only person on the grounds wearing a suit and tie."

"We also know that he hardly ever leaves his office—the one at the foot of the central mountain." Maggie shot Troy a questioning look. "So what do we do now? Just barge into his office?"

"I don't think they'll let us in," said Troy. "We saw that he only meets with celebrities, and it's always at his mansion. We've got to find a way to lure him out of his office, and cause him to converse with us. Has anyone got an idea?"

"Hey—I can stall the roller coaster!" Adam was hopping up and down with enthusiasm. "I once heard a netter describe how it could be done. There's an emergency brake on the side of the track, and I could sneak into there, and pull it. Then York would come to see what's going on and talk to me, and then you'd join us and tell him that you're, hey, responsible for me, and you can talk to him."

"I could freeze him if he objects," interjected Flint, waving the pocket freezer he still held since discovering Adam in the cabinet. "We could take him to a nice secluded place . . ."

"If you're thinking of taking him to Hell, you can just forget it," said Troy quickly. "There'll be no third degree interrogations while I'm around. Anyway, I don't think that Adam's plan will work. I was once there when the roller coaster got jammed, and it was handled by the local netters in charge of security and maintenance. I would have remembered if a man answering York's description had been around. We need to hone in on finding something that appeals to him more than a jammed roller coaster."

"It's been said that the one thing closest to his heart is money," said Maggie. "They even say that his heart is a lump of black silver."

"Maggie's right on target," agreed Flint. "The only bait for this fish is the smell of money."

"I have it!" exclaimed Troy, and raised his hands in a request for silence.

His eyes sparkled. "On target, you said - you're a genius! You've given me an idea for luring our mouse out of its hole."

All eyes were on him.

"Flint," Troy continued. "Do you remember how you once showed me what skeet shooting was all about? The time you wanted to participate in the regional competition? Can you still shoot as straight as you did then?"

Flint smiled. "I'm better than ever. You should have let me compete at the time—the first prize was two thousand dollars. All I need is one shot for calibration. The rest will all be dead center."

"It's been a long time since I've visited the Roller-net," said Troy, his excitement akin to that of his younger brother. "But if memory doesn't fail me, there are stalls there where you can continue shooting until you miss. And with a prize for whoever breaks the current record of shots, presented by the manager of the park, namely the elusive Mr. York."

Adam jumped to his feet waving his hands. "Hey, I've got something much better. There's a new attraction called 'Bodyguard'. You keep on shooting until you miss, with the prize money doubling with every shot. There's no limit, and you could theoretically break the house. It's extremely difficult, and no one has even come close yet. But perhaps we could win enough prize money to shake up this Mr. York. Hey, maybe we'll even break the record."

Flint looked offended to the core.

"Maybe? Young man, did I hear you say maybe? If what you say is true, and there's no limit on the number of shots, then Mr. York had better hurry up to stop me, or I'll be the next owner of this amusement park!" A faraway look glazed his eyes. "Roller-Flint! Has a nice ring to it. I'll let you all in for free, of course." He held an imaginary rifle in his hands, pointed it at and imaginary target, shut one eye and squeezed an imaginary trigger.

"Cool it, Flint." Troy signaled the excited computer to sit down. "You're getting carried away again. Anyway, there's no need to jump to the suppliers' parking lot now. We're going to split into two teams—we'll be less visible that way. Flint and I will attend this 'Bodyguard' stall, and Maggie and Adam will be our lookouts, keeping York's office under close surveillance at all times. Adam, you said you knew this place like the back of your hand. Show us on the map where the shooting games take place, and where you suggest that you and Maggie observe from."

"The game is in the main quad, just in front of the roller-coaster fence." Adam pointed at the map. "Here, it's marked in pink. Hey, you can't miss it. Maggie could wait at the carousel café. York's office can clearly be seen from there. Here it is, in the green area." He pointed somewhere else. Maggie studied the map, trying to orient herself.

"It's right next to the rappelling tower," added Adam, who saw that he needed to be more specific. He pointed again. "Here. It's the highest structure in the park. You'll find it easily. It's very scary. You drop for nine hundred yards—you gotta try it. Hey, I once—"

"Adam—to the point, please!"

"Sorry. Where was I? Ah, yes—well, I'll go on the Sky-Car. Here it is, in blue. It makes a full rotation every five minutes. You can see nearly the entire park from there, during most of the ride. If Babel arrives, I'll be able to alert you. Keep your 'coms open."

"No need for that," said Flint. "I have a much better solution." He dug three tiny, flat, skin-colored earrings from his pocket, and handed them to the children. "These are quite powerful communication devices—I got them at Sherlock, the new spy and detective store at the Super-Mall. You put them in the hollow behind your ear, and it takes on the color of your skin. Practically invisible. The minute you clip it on, it becomes a receiver-transmitter of encrypted messages, connected neurally to the speech and hearing centers. They'll broadcast anything you say, but not background noise. Everybody will hear everybody, so make your messages short."

He put an additional earring on his own ear. "Did you bring along the face masks I gave you?"

"Of course," said all three together.

They donned the masks in silence. It was the best way to surf the NET without being identified. The masks were made of a very thin skin-like material, and gave its wearer a totally different appearance. The mask blended in with the face of its wearer, to the degree that it was not possible to notice that he had a mask on at all. Not until you took it off.

NET regulations prohibited the use of masks, except for actors and people with severely disfigured features. The latter were allowed to wear only the mask of their previous, undamaged face. The only time everybody in the NET was allowed to wear a mask was on Halloween, but even then, masks could only be of mythical creatures, such as ghosts and demons.

Troy and Maggie carefully put on the masks they always used when they surfed illegally.

For Adam it was a new experience, and he pulled on his own mask gingerly. "Roller-net!" he crowed. "Here we come!"

And they set off.

42. NET: Day 34, 05:10

"Isn't there any other way to contact Norman?" persisted Lynn. "Just tell him that there's a reply from Chimpo—he'll understand what it's all about."

"I'm really terribly sorry, dear." Samantha shook her head in determination. Her silver hair gave her the look of a kindly old grandmother reluctantly refusing to give her grandchild another piece of candy. "He has given me explicit instructions, and he cannot be disturbed. But he should be back in an hour."

Samantha was the unit's only secretary. She was also Norman Starr's personal secretary, and as such, the closest person to him. Sometimes Lynn envied her position—Samantha spent far more time with Norman than anyone else, and she was privy to all his secrets to boot.

"Well, if he calls you, please tell him to contact me as soon as possible." Lynn disconnected the 'com and turned back to the hologram on her screen. The little chimpanzee sat on the floor, eating a banana. A satchel was on the floor beside him. She hit the Replay button, and the chimp jumped to its feet and began its spiel.

"Thank you for the information you sent regarding the malignant version of the old English play." Lynn noticed that it was careful not to mention the virus by name. You could never tell whether some analyzing computer may be eavesdropping passively. They could conceivably be programmed to trigger off a report to the authorities at the first mention of 'Midsummer Night's Dream'. "Regrettably, the fact that he hails from San Jose and that he is seventeen are just not high enough quality data for me. I understand that there are about two million residents in that monotonous city, including several thousand seventeen-year-olds."

The chimpanzee opened the satchel and removed a sheet of paper. He scanned it briefly and continued.

"Would it help, Queen, if I told you that the Hell site belongs to people whose IQ is at least double your own? I say this with full confidence, even though I don't know how smart you are. Now can you provide me with some more precise data?"

It was apparent to Lynn that Chimpo had a lot of experience in the NET, despite his being a newcomer to Pira-net. He played the data bartering game as an expert would, disclosing very little information for the sole purpose of credibility, and then waiting to hear more before revealing what he really wanted to trade.

But I've still discovered a few important items. He knows San Jose, California, pretty well, and did not assume it was one of a few other cities in the world by the same name. So he probably originates from the West Coast of the USA, like that green demon in the Tipman recording. Maybe from San Francisco, or even San Jose itself.

Lynn watched the chimpanzee. It sat down again, pulled a banana from its satchel, ate it and discarded the peel. She hit the Cancel button, and the ape faded out, quickly retrieving the banana peel before disappearing.

A professional. Leaves no traces, she mused. *Just the same, I think I got far more information from you than you think you revealed. Behind you is, most likely, a young boy—as our statistics indicate that in ninety percent of the cases there is a very high correlation between the surfer and the image chosen to represent him. Though it's possible that he didn't choose this image himself, but took what was assigned to him when he joined.*

Now if we assume, despite the lack of evidence, that this young boy is the same chimpanzee-electrician we saw at Spindler's site, then it follows that he has connections to some very powerful factors in the NET that have access to the NET's computer infrastructure, or that have found a way to circumvent the tracking and monitoring systems. Factors capable of creating illegal netters, like that unidentified gorilla or winged demons. And as a boy of that age would need assistance, it stands to reason that the Hell site owner is probably a relative of his—a father or a big brother. That's how he knows about their IQ. She chuckled silently. *Double my IQ, eh? Three hundred and fifty? Not likely—'there ain't no such animal.' But I'll bet it's a bigger brother, let's say a brilliant computer whiz like that student that hacked into Babel's site a while ago.*

"Og," she said aloud. "I have a job for you."

"Always at your service, princess."

"I want a list of all computer science graduates with an IQ over a hundred and seventy. Of these, find me those in California who have a younger sibling, but no younger than, umm, thirteen. Give me the closest matching first hundred of that list sorted by descending IQ level. I also want details on the younger sibling—age, height and weight."

Three seconds later a table of data appeared on the screen. Heading the list was a familiar name—Mark Dalton, the world teen chess champion—with an IQ of two hundred and five. He lived in Sausalito, was nineteen years old, and had a thirteen-year-old younger brother.

No, I don't think it's him. He's too busy with competitions and has no time for this kind of nonsense. And the younger brother is too big and heavy to be Chimpo's alter ego.

She scanned down the list. Number five caught her eye. Leonid Romanov, twenty-one, IQ of a hundred and ninety one. *Wow! He and I were candidates for Babel together! I hadn't realized what a smart guy he was.* She saw he had a younger brother of fourteen. *Could be him. Perhaps that's why he hasn't reapplied to Babel. And we considered approaching him! Heaven help us if he turned out to be our culprit. I still can't see how a lad like that, or anyone else, for that matter, on his own, could build a site like Hell. But that'll wait for deeper investigation later.*

"What was so urgent, Lynn?" Norman's voice behind her startled her. She was so engrossed with her screen that she hadn't noticed him entering her room. "Something that couldn't wait, even though I was in an important, uninterruptible meeting?"

Is he reprimanding me? Lynn had never heard Norman speak like this since her first day in Babel. She turned to him with a puzzled smile and froze. There was something wrong in the man in front of her. Something odd in his handsome face, that was uncommonly stern.

"Has something happened to you?" she asked without thinking. "By looking at you, one would think you're just back from a trip to Hell."

"I'd be glad to get there, but on my terms," said Norman in a voice that sent shivers down Lynn's spine. "What have you found out about that site?"

Was I only kidding myself that he loved me? Were all those smiles and personal attention just a sham?

She pulled herself together, swallowed, and forced her voice to sound detached and formal.

"Chimpo called in connection with Hell. He wants more details about the author of 'Midsummer Night's Dream'. I intend to disclose Tipman's name, if it's all right with you. He will then be obliged to give me information about Hell, if he sticks by the Pira-net rules and regulations. Otherwise, once the word gets out that he backed on a deal, he'll be ostracized and cast out. And if he attempts to approach us for the Tipman prize money, we'll have his identity as well. Consequently, we will be able to detain and question him."

"Okay," consented Norman. "Keep me updated on all developments of this case. I want every bit of evidence the minute you get it—every scrap, every iota, no matter now insignificant you may think it is. What's that list on the screen?"

Lynn related to Norman her assumptions about Chimpo and the big brother idea.

"Nice angle, Lynn," said Norman. "Inform me on this case, too—real time." He paged down the list, quickly taking in the names. "Keep working on this, and expand your list to younger siblings as well. Nowadays, they could change the world at the age of ten, too. Please send me the first one thousand relevant candidates." He seemed more at ease.

He's back to his normal self, now. Maybe he's had a rough day, and had to face a lot of stress. I must be paranoid.

Norman left the room and Lynn returned to her computer and typed in a password. The cuckoo appeared immediately on the screen.

"Queen of the Night," said Lynn. "Listen closely to what I have to tell you . . ."

43. NET: Day 34, 05:36

The group of youngsters bundled into Troy's second-hand Zebra-net, which he had purchased just a couple of months earlier. The drive to the Topaz Mall took less than five minutes. Several Transport Boxes were lined up at the entrance to the mall. Maggie and Adam went through first. Troy and Flint waited another ten minutes in order to let Maggie and Adam position themselves in the amusement park. Then they jumped, too, and entered through the main gate.

The sharp-shooting stalls were crowded, as usual, and they had to wait for about twenty minutes in the twisting queue. While waiting for their turn they observed the various shooting scenarios, and noticed that none of the players managed to pass the first stage of the game.

Finally it was their turn. They ascended to the main platform and were directed to one of the 'Bodyguard' booths. Flint paid the netter operator and received a long-barreled rifle.

"Your rifle contains an unlimited supply of ammunition," said the netter in a bored voice. "You've got to hit each target with the minimum amount of bullets. Have you ever played a shooting game here before?"

"No," said Flint. "But go ahead. I'll manage."

The netter looked at him indifferently and pressed the Operate button. A curtain parted on a stage across from them, and a virtual world came into view. In its center, under a clear sky, was a small hillock covered with green grass. A dense forest surrounded the hillock. A gray rabbit came out of the forest, walking on its hind legs, and wearing a white suit and a felt hat. It ambled lightly to the top of the hillock, sat on a bar stool that had just then conveniently risen from the ground, and turned to Flint.

"Hey, you there with the gun—what's your name?"

"Anthony Oakley," replied Flint, without batting an eyelash.

"Sounds promising," said the rabbit. "Right! You're my bodyguard now. There are all kinds of nasty creatures out there who want to knock me off. Your job is to prevent that. Are you ready?"

"Always."

A large wolf with a shaggy mane loped out of the forest, and headed for the rabbit. Flint fired immediately. The bullet scratched the wolf's tail. With a yelp of annoyance, the wolf burst forward toward the rabbit.

"Yikes! Anthony! What am I paying you for?" yelled the rabbit. Flint fired again and hit the wolf squarely in the chest. The large animal stopped in surprise, bleeding profusely from the hole in his chest. It took another faltering step toward the rabbit, and then toppled to the ground. A transparent image of the wolf wafted its way upward to the sky. A smattering of applause came from the spectators.

"Well done!" cried the rabbit. "Good show, Anthony. Pay him!" He picked up a large daily newspaper from the grass, and began reading. The operating netter gave Flint a wolf-shaped doll, and Flint handed it to Troy.

A black cobra appeared out of a hole in the ground some fifty feet away from the barstool, and began slithering, under cover of the grass, toward the rabbit. Flint observed the snake closely, following it in his sights, but didn't shoot.

"Hi—watch out!" bellowed the rabbit. "There's a snake in the grass!"

Flint ignored him.

"What's the matter with you?" screamed the rabbit. "Have you fallen asleep? Shake a leg—I haven't finished reading this article yet."

Flint waited until the cobra began its ascent on the stool, and then shot it. The snake fell to the ground, its head shattered, and its transparent likeness zigzagged its way heavenward. This time the applause was far more enthusiastic, and it brought additional spectators to the crowd.

"I see you've got a lot of time on your hands, eh, Anthony?" The rabbit was visibly relieved. "Pay him!" The netter gave Flint a full size stuffed cobra doll.

Without any warning, a huge tiger charged out of the forest. It covered half the distance to the rabbit in three bounds. The rabbit dropped the newspaper in fright and cowered behind the stool. Quite unnecessarily. Flint sent a single bullet right between the tiger's eyes. The predator crumbled to the ground, and its soul rose to the skies. The throng of spectators cheered this excellent display of marksmanship on a rapidly moving target.

"Bravo!" The rabbit bowed deeply to Flint and doffed his hat. "You have just earned your fifty dollar fee, plus a fifty dollars bonus for disposing of the attacker with only one shot." The big screen adjacent to the booth displayed $100 surrounded by flashing lights.

The operating netter cleared his throat, and intoned indifferently:

"I want to congratulate you for your achievement—on the average, only one out of fifty contestants reaches this stage. The rules of the game from here on are as follows: you may quit at any time with your winnings. If you continue, you're betting all of your winnings. Every attacker that you stop doubles your win. But if you allow the rabbit to be eliminated you lose everything, and the game is over. Do you wish to proceed?"

"What a question?" grumbled the rabbit. "Anthony, you won't desert me now, will you?"

"I'm going all the way," replied Flint.

"You're the man!" beamed the rabbit. He sat down abruptly on the stool, and went back to reading his paper.

A black dot in the sky began a dive toward the hillock. It was a huge eagle, descending in spirals to confuse any attack on it. Flint didn't hesitate, and shot it while it was still at quite some height. A flurry of feathers swirled down, while the remains of the eagle crashed into the grass beside the stool. A bell rang sharply near the screen, which now displayed $200. The audience cheered wildly, and more and more visitors thronged to the platform.

"Wow!" whistled the rabbit. "Oakley—you're a marksman at long ranges, too!"

"I needed to check out the effective range of this rifle," said Flint, and gestured to the netter to continue.

Two cheetahs burst out of the forest, one from each side of the hillock. They leaped and bounded toward the rabbit, taking cover behind the occasional ground fold. The rabbit buried its head between its knees, trembling all over. Flint squeezed off two rapid shots, and the cheetahs both dropped in mid-leap. Two transparent cheetahs soared upward. The rabbit jumped to its feet in excitement and urged the spectators to cheer. But the crowd needed no prodding—they clapped and yelled, egging the new star on. The screen was flashing stars and lightning around the display of $800.

"Are you going on?" asked the netter. Eight hundred NET dollars was a lot of money for a prize.

"All the way!" hollered Flint, bringing more cheers from the crowd. He had barely uttered the words, when two flying sharks attacked from both sides of the arena. They had broad, black wings, and they zigzagged their way to the rabbit at a terrific speed.

"That's not fair!" cried Troy. The operator had released the sharks while still conversing with Flint, attempting to distract him. But Flint was ready. He shot the shark on the right, which smashed into the ground, its wings beating for a few more seconds before becoming still. He let the other shark come within twenty feet from the rabbit, and then put a bullet into its head. It was killed outright, and its soul wafted away, but its momentum was so great that it continued toward the rabbit. The rabbit managed to jump aside and escape injury, but the barstool was shattered into splinters. The spectators went wild.

"Anthony, you've got style!" The rabbit appeared to berate him. "You like to wait until the last possible moment, eh?" An ear-splitting ringing came from the screen, which now displayed $3,200. Next to this number appeared another number in red, $12,800, the current record. The rabbit stood on its head, and then flipped backward onto its feet. "Ladies and gentlemen, we have here a professional sharp-shooter. Anthony—you're almost champion, now. You're not quitting, are you?"

"You just get back to your paper and relax." Flint winked at him, and gestured with the rifle. Another barstool rose from the ground, and the rabbit seated itself.

"York has just left his office." Maggie's quiet voice came over the earphones. "He's alone. Adam was right—he's dressed in a blue suit and wearing a striped tie. He's walking quite rapidly, and I estimate he'll be with you in about two minutes."

"Okay," replied Troy. He waited a few seconds, and then rose on tiptoe, looking in the direction of the park's offices. York was indeed tall and wide, and sported a short beard.

A roar of hysterical applause brought Troy's attention back to the main action. Flint had disposed of two silver-winged barracudas, and a snake that had come out of a hole directly under the rabbit's seat—all three having being dispatched simultaneously. Bells rang all over the park, and the screen shot off flares and played a victory march.

"Ladies and gentlemen!" howled the rabbit. "We have a new record!" His voice was amplified over the entire park. "Anthony Oakley is the new champion YEEOOWW . . ."

The operator took advantage of the hullabaloo and dispatched two giant pythons that came from behind the rabbit and pounced on it. The rabbit dived to the ground, allowing Flint to kill them off with two well-placed bullets to their heads. One of the bullets went through the rabbit's jacket, slightly singing its fur. The rabbit licked the tender spot with a pink tongue, panting in relief. Then it bent down, picked up one of the python carcasses, and swung it around its head.

"Cheats! Fraud!" There were cries of disapproval from the crowd regarding the operator's attempt to trip up Flint. But these were drowned in the deafening roar of applause. They had just witnessed a Roller-net record being broken—a new hero had 'beaten the house'. Furthermore, the new record was astounding. This was history in the making!

The cheers grew louder and louder until it became a booming chant; "An-tho-ny! An-tho-ny!" The screen seemed to have gone crazy, shining with the most intense bright light, and the ear-splitting clangor of the winning bells added to the commotion. The staggering amount, $102,400, was flashing in huge red lights.

The netter looked at Flint, obviously at a loss. He didn't know whether to continue the game or not. This was a brand new experience for him.

"What—no more snakes? Or barracudas?" Flint was grinning from ear to ear. "All out of sharks? Maybe a school of flying piranhas?"

"I don't believe that even an Oakley like you could hit an entire school of piranhas," came a loud, firm voice from behind him. It was York, who had managed to elbow his way through the ecstatic crowd. Flint turned to him, and the sneaky operator launched two armor-plated vultures and a wild boar from only thirty feet away from the rabbit. The rabbit tried to defend itself with the folded newspaper.

"Flint—watch out!!" yelled Troy, but no warning was needed. Turning to York was only a feint. Flint whirled around and shot the rightmost vulture through the head. The other vulture concealed its head inside the armor and continued its attack. Flint shot it in the middle of its body. The bullet was deflected off the armor plating with a twang, causing no damage. But the impact shifted the vulture's position slightly, revealing its head. Another bullet from Flint, and the vulture's head became a red pulp. The vulture crashed directly on top of the boar, which was just about to slash the rabbit with its tusks. The boar was shaken by the blow and lost a precious second—enough time for Flint to put a bullet into its brain.

The rabbit fell to the ground, breathing heavily. It was quite sure that those were its last moments to live. It rose and held up its fingers in the V for victory sign. It winked at Flint as if they were partners in some misdemeanor. Above them, the screen shot out fireworks, which eventually formed into the logo of the park in red, yellow and green sparks. The main bulletin board of the park blared out a casino-like clamor that literally shook the ground.

"Enough! Halt! The game's over!" cried York. He grabbed the ashen operator roughly by the arm, and pushed him aside. "Go to your quarters at once. I'll deal with you later."

York looked furiously at the winning amount—$819,200! The entire profits of the last three months had vanished. If he let the game continue he could go bankrupt. He forced a smile on his face, and held out a pudgy hand to Flint, who put down the gun, and shook the hand firmly.

"Mr. Oakley, I am Rupert York, the owner of this park. May I be the first to congratulate you on your win? It's a staggering achievement, and your record will undoubtedly hold for many years. I'd like to invite you to my private office and present you with your check. Believe me, the advertising you have just provided for Roller-net is well worth every penny you've won. I would also like to organize a promotion campaign for Roller-net, with your hologram prominent. For pay, of course."

York signaled to Flint and Troy to join him and, still waving to the crowd, they walked toward Roller-net's offices.

44. PALO ALTO, SATURDAY, 10:15

Nancy Bentley heard the familiar knock on her front door, and welcomed Ziggy in. He had a strange look in is eyes.

"Good morning, Nancy," he said, walking in and removing his hat. "Please forgive this unexpected intrusion. But the fact of the matter is that I am concerned about Troy. I have repeatedly tried to contact him, but to no avail. We had agreed he would call me this morning, and so far he has not. Have you any idea of his current whereabouts?"

Nancy preceded her guest into the living room.

"Please sit down, Ziggy. You're never an intruder in our home. You know you're welcome to drop in at any time. As for Troy—he's surfing right now, and cannot be disturbed. Maybe he's in the middle of some adventure or event, and isn't aware of the passage of time. I know that he promised Adam to accompany him to the tetrosaur tournament this morning, so perhaps he's there now."

"Yes, now I remember that Troy mentioned something to that effect last night. That is probably it." Ziggy seemed somewhat relieved. "He could easily have gotten involved with that revolting sport, and forgotten to call me."

He addressed Nancy with an embarrassed expression on his face. "Do you think you could enter the NET for me, and leave him a message to contact me?"

"Yes, certainly." Nancy hated to surf, and avoided the NET like the plague. The NET world was meant for younger people, and she felt she didn't belong there. "But Ziggy—is it so urgent that it couldn't wait for an hour at most? He never surfs for longer than an hour." Troy tried to make a habit of never being away for more than a NET day when surfing.

"Oh, yes, you are quite right, of course." Ziggy was flustered. "Please do not bother yourself. He will most likely return even earlier. May I enter his room and check his surfing timer?"

This was an unusual request. It was considered bad etiquette to be around a person on Earth while he or she was surfing. But Nancy saw no reason to refuse Ziggy. He and Troy had spent endless hours together, puttering on computer developments.

"Of course you can," she said as she led him down the stairs. "I just hope we won't find a mess there. How about tea and some fresh cake while you're here?"

"Yes, thank you. That would be most kind."

They entered the basement, and found Troy in his wide seat in the corner. He had his surfing helmet on, and his eyes were closed. The display on the helmet read 2:02.

"Oh, my," said Nancy in genuine surprise. "I've never seen him allocate so much time for a surf."

The number on the helmet indicated the surfing time remaining (in Earth hours) before the Automatic Return was activated. This was considered a normal return, and all the surfer's memories would remain intact. Most surfers did not set the timer at all, preferring the default of 99:99—unlimited surfing time. Troy, however, always set his timer for a specific duration, so that his mother could know when he would return from the NET.

"That's an extremely long time in the NET . . ." Ziggy's voice was troubled.

"Come on up to the living room and have your tea and cake," said Nancy. Troy's unmade bed bothered her. He was usually very meticulous in making his bed in the morning, before his karate workouts. "Tell you what—if he or Adam don't get back within half an hour, I'll surf into the NET and contact them. Twelve continuous hours in the NET should be quite enough for them, I should think."

I must join that experimental NET-phobia therapy group, thought Ziggy. *I shall respond to them affirmatively on Monday. I cannot continue like this—I am even losing contact with Troy. He is spending more and more time in that world—the world where the really interesting things happen. Even if the experiment fails, and I remain in a coma for the rest of my life—as it happened to Duke—it still would be preferable to not making the attempt at all.*

He was still thinking about Duke when Nancy brought him his tea and cake.

45. NET: DAY 34, 06:21

York bulldozed his way through the cheering crowd, with Troy and Flint close behind. Autograph hunters thrust notepads at Flint, and he signed every one with flair and a flourish.

"So you're Anthony's younger brother," remarked York, when they were far from the tumult of the crowd. "And what would your name be, please?"

"Jonathan. Jonathan Oakley."

"Can you shoot as straight as your brother? I have never witnessed such a remarkable feat of marksmanship." York straightened his tie while walking, and glanced back out of the corner of his eye to make sure Flint wasn't lagging too far behind. "You know, he should enter the NET championships. No other contestant I know of can hold a candle to him. My goodness, he borders on the superhuman! Are you any distant relatives of the famous Annie Oakley?"

Troy shook his head. "No. We checked and found that Oakley was only her stage name. But Anthony tried sharp shooting after we watched a program about her."

"Indeed," said York, eying Flint with a strange look. He took out a shiny 'com, punched several keys, and sent off a message with a final, decisive jab.

"I've just dispatched a bulletin to the press informing them of the new Roller-net record," he said amiably. "You'll soon be very famous celebrities."

Troy felt his flesh crawl, but there was nothing he could do. They had to finish their mission. *At least the masks conceal our identities,* he thought.

They walked along a paved path, waving to the mass of people behind them. They crossed a rope bridge, which spanned a deep canyon. Looking down, they could see a golden stream winding its way along the bottom of the canyon. Past the bridge, the path curved and twisted through lush flowerbeds, and ascended a mild slope until it reached a courtyard at the foot of an artificial mountain with steep walls as smooth as marble. At the top of the mountain, high above Roller-net, was a castle with gray turrets, each flying the multi-colored flags with the Roller-net logo—three interlocked double-rings in red, yellow and green.

Troy recognized the castle at once. It was the much-publicized residence of Mr. York, a place where only the NET's most prominent celebrities were ever invited.

In front of them, past the cultivated lawn in the center of the courtyard, and flush with the face of the mountain, was an ornate wooden door. A sign on the door read:

ROLLER-NET
Main Office

York opened the door and cordially ushered them in. They found themselves in a spacious, luxuriously decorated room. There was a Chippendale table on the right with two antique chairs beside it. A large, deep blue sofa with three armchairs was on the other side of the room. On the opposite wall were two large reproductions of Van Gogh paintings, and between them stood a large netter, pointing a freezer at them. Before they could react, York yanked out his own freezer and fired at them both. They fell stiffly to the floor, and York pried their emergency return rings off their fingers, using no little force to do so. He then unfroze them, and signaled with the barrel of his freezer for them to sit on the sofa.

"Please be seated." An evil smirk accompanied the gracious invitation. "Make yourself at home, Flint." He saw Troy go pale, and his smug look broadened. "That's what you called him earlier, didn't you? When you warned him?"

Troy didn't reply. He was too surprised. York turned to Flint.

"I knew something about you was familiar. You appeared as a demon, but your body language is the same! I'm pretty good at this kind of thing. I saw you in a recording, disguised as a demon, interrogating that dumb hacker. Well now, it isn't Hell here, but we do have our own methods of extracting information. There is no way for you to escape and we have tons of time at our disposal." The grin vanished. "What did you think—that I wouldn't know who you are? That you could just take my money and waltz out of here?"

"I have no idea what you're talking about," said Flint, the paragon of innocence. "All I can see is that you're welching on a debt you owe me, and using threats and violence to do so. I shall report you to the NET authorities."

York's 'com buzzed. He listened to the call for half a minute and hung up. A loathsome leer spread across his features.

"And how would you identify yourself to them, Mister non-existent Anthony Oakley? I have just been informed that neither of you appear on the NET's tracking systems. Ergo, you are not surfers. You are illegal netters masquerading as humans. Who is your owner? Where is that Hell site that he built?"

Flint and Troy didn't respond. From outside they heard heavy footsteps, and the door opened. Two burly netters walked in carrying a frozen Maggie between them. Her eyes were glazed and frightened.

"We caught her in the garden sneaking up toward the office," said one of them to York. "What do you want us to do with her?"

York approached Maggie and with a vicious twist yanked off her emergency return ring, scraping off some of the skin on her finger. He then unfroze her.

"Another non-existent Oakley?" he said. "Family reunion? Do you mind telling me who you are?"

The three youngsters looked on in dismay, but said nothing. Maggie raised her bleeding finger to her mouth.

"Do you remember Amos Tipman? He spilled the beans all right. And so will you. I think the time has arrived for you to experience some of the less known attractions of Roller-net." He manipulated a switch on the desk, and one of the walls slid aside. A large, dark passageway led away from the room. York walked to the opening in the wall, and gestured to the netters to bring along the prisoners.

"Just a minute, please," groaned Flint. "I need to go to the restroom."

He planted both his hands on his knees and stood up. The large netter on the far side reached him in a second, but Flint suddenly snatched a small freezer from a hidden pocket and froze the attacker. The two netters holding Maggie fired their freezers at him, but Flint used the frozen netter as a shield and wasn't hit. He squeezed the trigger of his freezer, and in a sweeping motion froze both the netters and Maggie. All three fell to the floor like wooden logs. Flint then turned to York, but he had disappeared into the dark passageway.

"After him!" yelled Flint, and sprinted into the dark opening.

"Flint! Wait!" shouted Troy. He jumped to his feet, took a freezer from one of the netters, and peered carefully into the tunnel. He could see nothing in the blackness. He went to Maggie and unfroze her. She stood shakily on her feet for a few seconds, flailing her arms around her middle to restore circulation.

"Where are Flint and York?" she asked, her voice unsteady.

Troy pointed in frustration toward the dark opening in the wall. He gave her a freezer taken from another of the netters, and then collected all their emergency return rings from the desk. Searching the room, he took a laser pistol and a powerful flashlight that he found in one of the cabinets.

They approached the entrance to the tunnel, and Troy shone the flashlight inside. Before them was a long, wide passageway, with dual rails set in its floor. There were five roller coaster cars parked on the rails nearby. No sign of York or Flint could be observed in the murky depths of the tunnel, but far in the distance the rattle of speeding roller coaster cars could be clearly heard.

"Flint! Can you hear me?" Troy spoke into the air, hoping that the earring communication channel still worked. There was no answer.

"Apparently the earrings don't work in this tunnel," he said to Maggie. "Quick—get into the first car. They rode into the tunnel and we've got to catch up with them."

They got into the front seat of the foremost car. A yellow light went on as they entered, shining on a simple control panel. A green joystick jutted up from the middle of the panel, and a large toggle switch enabled choosing between right and left. A rusty handle rose from the floor.

"It's one of the old models," said Maggie. "Hasn't been used for years. You pull the joystick to accelerate, and push it to slow down. The switch is used when the tracks fork—you choose which way you want to continue. And the handle over here is an emergency brake. Come on, let's get going."

Maggie yanked the joystick to its full extent. The doors of the car closed with a thump, safety belts snaked out from the car's sides and wrapped themselves around their waists, and the car lurched forward. The acceleration was so high that the two youngsters were literally wedged into the backs of their seats.

"Hold tight!" whooped Troy. "I don't think they took safety regulations very seriously in those days."

"I'm holding, I'm holding! Flint's absolutely off his rocker to chase York in the dark. York must know this place like the back of his hand. He'll be waiting for Flint around some corner for sure."

"Yes, you're probably right. Lets hope that the hot-headed computer has some more tricks up his sleeves."

The tracks now led down a steep slope deep into the ground. The car increased its velocity by the second, giving them the simulated effect of a bullet propelled through the barrel of a gun. A minute later the track leveled off. In the distance ahead a weak light was seen, and it grew rapidly stronger as they approached. Seconds before actually arriving at the light source, they saw that it emanated through windows embedded in two huge hefty doors that blocked their path. The car flew toward the doors.

"Troy, we're going to crash!" screamed Maggie, gripping him tightly by the arm.

The car hit the doors, but nothing happened. They rode through unharmed.

"Hologram," sighed Troy in relief, breathing again.

Maggie released her hold on his arm, smiled abashedly, and wiped the perspiration from her brow. The car barreled into an immense subterranean grotto. Even though it was brightly lit, they could not see its opposite end. The cavern contained an entire amusement park, complete with roller coaster rides and other attractions. Its size was impressive, though it was significantly smaller than its equivalent on the NET surface.

Not far ahead the tracked forked into two—the right one leading to the roller coaster, and the left to the track encircling the park.

"It's the old funfair, over which the current Roller-net was built," exclaimed Troy. He pushed the joystick in all the way, and tugged on the emergency brake. The car screeched and creaked, finally shuddering to a halt a few feet before the fork. "I thought this place had been dismantled ages ago. Which way do you think they went?"

It wasn't hard to locate York and Flint. A red car was careening crazily on the roller coaster ahead of them, spinning like a top within the numerous loops. A green car followed several hundred feet behind.

"We've got to stop that roller coaster." Maggie looked at the tiny cabin to their right, draped in cobwebs. "Looks to me like nobody's taken a ride here for a long time. It hasn't had any maintenance and it's probably dangerous. There must be a main control system somewhere around here."

The red car plunged into a small lake near a high volcano. It disappeared for a few seconds, and then spurted out on the other side of the lake, splattering water everywhere. It continued along the track, climbing the steep side of the volcano until it reached the summit and disappeared into the crater. A few seconds later, the green car burst out of the lake. A gigantic octopus tentacle swiped at the car, barely missing the rider's head. It was Flint, his blond hair soaking wet.

Troy and Maggie followed the green car up the volcano with their gaze until it, too, disappeared into the crater. They then shifted their focus to the tracks emerging from the other side of the volcano and waited. Nothing came out.

"They're still in the mountain!" cried Troy. "York has captured Flint!"

He released the brake, made sure that the toggle switch indicated a right turn, and pulled up the joystick. The car groaned and lurched, and gathered speed on the way to the roller coaster. The initial ascent was to a height of a twenty-story building, taking no more than half a minute. At the summit the track made a sharp right turn, and they began to drop at a fantastic rate, following the spiraling track. Three complete loops followed in rapid succession. The track then leveled, and they headed toward the volcano.

"There's York!" shrieked Maggie. "He's got Flint!"

York had emerged from a door at the base of the volcano with a frozen Flint slung over his shoulder. He ran into a nearby stall.

Suddenly the car dipped, rolled to the left, and a glass cover roofed the passengers in. Then it dived into the lake. The water was clear, and the young duo saw that they were traveling through thick underwater vegetation. To one side, a cluster of gray sharks noticed them and began swimming toward the car. On the other side two large swordfish were preparing to attack. The sharks overtook the car, and began biting it with their sharp teeth. One of the swordfish rammed the side of the car with a force that almost overturned it. Its long snout pierced the car, just missing the petrified riders, and water began to leak into the interior.

The car made a sharp left turn, rattling the passengers and throwing off the swordfish. Its snout broke off and remained lodged in the cracked window. The car continued on its way, knocked a silver barracuda out of its path, ran over a long black water snake, and heaved onto dry land.

The transparent roof opened at once, and a spray of water droplets covered them. They looked around, but could not see either York or Flint. The car climbed the steep volcano side at high speed, and entered the crater. The volcano was hollow, and the tracks spiraled down on the inner sides. Halfway down, the track leveled and made its way toward a platform protruding from the mountainside, resembling a pier. Stairs led down from the pier to the foot of the mountain.

"Watch it!" yelled Maggie. An enormous tree trunk lay across the tracks at the beginning of the pier. A smashed green car lay overturned by the tracks. They bore down on the trunk at high speed.

46. NET: DAY 34, 07:08

Troy hauled on the brake with all his might. The car jittered and slowed down, the stench of burnt rubber filling the air. The brake handle broke off in Troy's hand, and the car hurtled into the tree trunk with a deafening crash. The front end of the car was totally smashed. If it weren't for the airbags that expanded on the instant of collision, absorbing most of the impact, Troy and Maggie would have probably been killed outright. It took them several minutes to recover.

"Let's consider ourselves lucky," said Troy. "Previous accidents must have forced them to put in those airbags." He extricated himself from the wrecked car, and then helped Maggie out as well. "Did you see where York took Flint? That booth near the mountain?"

"I sure did." Maggie was still gasping from the recent buffeting she received. "It's the famous mirror maze. I visited it quite often, back in the old days. I'm positive they were headed there."

They ran down the steep staircase, and exited through the same door they had seen York emerge from earlier. The mirror maze was across the walkway.

This particular attraction was one of Maggie's favorites when she was a little girl. She loved to see her image distorted in the curved mirrors, and the thrill of seeing herself duplicated myriads of times in all kinds of shapes and sizes. She enjoyed the challenge of finding her way out of a seemingly closed room, surrounded on all sides by mirrors, with the possibility of losing her way for hours on end.

The entrance gate was open, and the ticket seller's booth was covered with dust. Troy picked up a handful of black pebbles from the walkway.

"We'll drop these along our way. This maze may be more difficult than we imagine. The pebbles may help us in getting out again. Yeah, yeah," he looked at Maggie who could hardly contain her mirth. "This is a revolutionary navigating technique that I learned from the Hansel and Gretel fairytale."

"I think I'd take the Wicked Witch over York any time," responded Maggie quietly.

They advanced slowly into the maze—Troy leading, the laser pistol in his hand, and Maggie a few steps behind. It started out quite simply: a wide corridor with regular mirrors covering the walls, floor and ceiling. Bright light shone through tiny apertures that were dispersed over all the mirrors. They could see their images replicated to infinity. The corridor made a large, sweeping arc, with an almost imperceptible descent into the ground. Every now and then, Troy dropped one of the pebbles he carried in the middle of the corridor. A couple of hundred feet later, the mirrors became increasingly distorting, and the corridor narrowed until it was suddenly blocked off. They faced a mirror that depicted them as elongated, thin caricatures of themselves. They groped and fumbled along the mirror's edges, but it was a dead end.

"I'm pretty sure there wasn't any earlier branching off to this corridor," said Maggie. "There's got to be a way to continue right here."

"Hold it!" said Troy. "I think I feel a button under this mirror here." He pressed it, and the floor began to sink under them. They were in a glass elevator, descending slowly into the earth. The walls sliding upward around them were mirrors, too, and sometimes they thought they could detect openings and passageways.

Suddenly a grotesquely warped face loomed at them out of one of the mirrors. The head was as large as a Halloween pumpkin, the eyes glimmered threateningly, and the mouth exposed sharp, yellow teeth. A maniacal laugh echoed through the elevator shaft. Troy fired instinctively at the image, forgetting for a second that he was holding a laser pistol. However, the face was a hologram, and the laser beam passed through it, reflected from the mirror behind it, and in a blinding flash ricocheted its way up the shaft.

"I wouldn't fire a laser beam into a mirror, if I were you." York's mocking voice echoed from all directions at once. The elevator continued its slow descent. Troy holstered his laser pistol and drew his freezer, aiming it at the leering face. The head laughed insanely, filling the small elevator cabin with its booming. Suddenly the head vanished, and a new image appeared. Thin as a broomstick, black hair, with eyes at the bottom, where the brush would have been. This phantasm accompanied them down the rest of the way.

"I hope you like my new features," said the figure in a hoarse voice, filled with hatred. The image metamorphosed, thickened and shortened its dimensions, and stepped out of the mirror. It was York, and he held a freezer in his right hand. Troy dived to the floor and fired his freezer at the figure, but it, too, was only a hologram. The replica faded, and the elevator slowed to a stop in front of another mirrored corridor. They entered the corridor cautiously, with freezers at the ready. The elevator behind them rose through the ceiling, severing their path of retreat.

The corridor led into a large room, covered with mirrors from floor to ceiling. A couch and three armchairs were in the middle of the room. Flint, still frozen, lay on the couch.

"Welcome to my modest kingdom." They looked around but saw no one. "I enjoyed that little trip with you in the elevator. You must have heard of unidirectional mirrors. I am observing you now through such a mirror. I am holding a laser pistol and I can fire a beam right into your room. I don't expect you to miraculously escape injury this time. Someone's going to get hurt. Perhaps become blinded, or have an arm cut off—maybe even die if the beam penetrates the brain. Now, sit on the couch, the two of you."

Maggie and Troy sat down slowly.

"Place your freezers and laser pistols on the floor where I can see them."

They did as they were told, and Troy also dropped the rest of the black pebbles he had on him.

A glass platform descended from the ceiling, with York standing at its center. He held a freezer in his right hand, and a nerve stunner in his left.

"I'm sure you'll understand why I have to do this," he giggled, and fired the freezer at them.

Troy and Maggie were frozen instantly. York rummaged in their clothing, discovering Maggie's tiny laser knife. He searched Flint as well, and found the atomic blaster in his left armpit. He examined the modern weapon in admiration, and kicked the other armaments to the side of the room. He then unfroze his three prisoners, one by one.

Flint came to first. He looked around in amazement. "Where in the world are we?" he asked into the air.

"You're having a nightmare," exclaimed York. "And I'll ask the questions here. Where did you get this weapon? Are you connected with Babel?"

"Hadn't you guessed?" Flint tried to distract York. "I don't think I need to tell you what will happen to you when they come to free us."

York laughed out loud. "We'll soon have someone here who'll be able to corroborate your story," he said icily. "Meanwhile, I've been requested to ask you a few questions, which will be my pleasure. Now, then—you are Flint? The builder of the Hell site?"

"Yes," admitted Flint. "How did you find out about Hell?"

"From a customer of yours. Tipman. I saw what you did to him to make him talk, and it's given me a couple of ideas of my own how to get you three to squeal. So let's get on with it, shall we?" York raised his voice. "Where is the Hell site?"

"How on earth did you get a recording of Tipman," wondered Flint, stalling for all he was worth.

York's face went livid.

"You impertinent pipsqueak! I warned you that only I ask the questions here." He pointed the stunner at Flint and pulled the trigger. Flint jerked to his feet with a yelp of pain.

"Sit!" ordered York. "I'm asking you for the last time—where is the Hell site?"

"I . . . I can take you there," stammered Flint, still shaken by the thousands of volts he had endured. York fired again. Flint convulsed and fell heavily to the floor.

"Sit on the couch!" screamed York, spittle forming at the corners of his mouth. "Do you take me for an idiot? You're planning to trap me there!" He strode up to Flint, who stood up, still quivering, and was trying to find the couch. York placed the stunner against Flint's head. "Where is it?"

"It's deep underground. There is only one entrance, and I can show it to you."

"Give me the coordinates."

"He doesn't know the coordinates," intervened Troy, trying to distract York's attention from Flint. "They are not defined. He only knows how to get there."

"I told you all to SHUT UP!" bellowed York. "Speak when you're spoken to." He fired the stunner at Troy, who screamed and fell to the floor, half unconscious. York kicked the prostrate boy, and then picked him up and flung him into an armchair.

He turned menacingly to Flint.

"I don't know whether you're netters or surfers, and I really don't care. If you don't answer me right away, I am going to fry these two kids' brains with this stunner. If they're netters they'll serve as mannequins in store display windows in the NET." He grinned as he noticed Flint's look of horror. "But if they're surfers, and you think that they can escape back to Earth and forget this nightmare—I have a little trick up my sleeve. I learned it from my partner, a real master in the art. After I wipe out these little ragamuffins' brains, I shall place them in a Transport Box, and return them normally to Earth! Get it? They'll return to Earth with a wiped out brain! They'll be no more than vegetables!"

An ironclad rule of the NET was that in the case of brain damage the surfer was to be returned without updating his brain—usually using the emergency return ring, or by the NET's emergency rescue team. These emergency returns were necessary in order to prevent the surfer's brain from being updated. Updating a surfer's brain after brain injury in the NET could cause permanent mental damage to the surfer.

Flint charged York with a roar, but he wasn't fast enough. York sent another shock to his chest, and the youngster dropped as if he had run into a brick wall. York then pointed his freezer at Flint, and froze him.

He whirled toward Troy, who was coming to his senses.

"Do you know where the site is?" He pointed the stunner at Maggie's head. "I am about to broil your friend's brains, and in a second she'll be as smart as a watermelon. Here, and afterward on Earth. Now TALK!"

Troy was sweating profusely.

"The entrance to Hell is—"

He stopped short. Into the room walked Adam with a freezer in his hand.

York noticed him at the very same moment in the mirror behind Troy. He spun around, but was too late. Adam gave the freezer's trigger a long squeeze, and York continued to spin all the way to the floor, where he lay inert. Troy, who had launched himself into the air with a karate kick, was also caught in the freezer's beam, and he landed with a thump on top of York.

"I guess you'll find out where Hell is soon enough," muttered Adam to the frozen York. "Hey, are you all right, Maggie?"

Maggie got up, still trembling, and hugged Adam warmly. "You're a guardian angel, Adam. How did you manage to find us?" Her voice was choked with tears.

"Later," said Adam. He unfroze Troy and Flint. "Hey, are you two okay?"

"Little brother, you're the greatest!" said Flint, clapping Adam on the shoulder. "I am forever in your debt. He was about to wipe out our brains." Flint became business-like again. "We've got to get out of here before his partners start looking for him. He said something about their being on the way here."

Troy was still in a daze. "I can't believe it!" He said, and hugged Adam with one hand while ruffling his hair with the other. "You may be my younger brother, but it seems that you can take care of yourself pretty well. What a good idea it was to bring you along—who knows how this might have ended. Adam—all your past transgressions are hereby forgiven. Including your invasion into my site. Furthermore—I owe you!"

Troy's voice shook with emotion, and tears welled in his eyes. Adam looked down at the floor, the color of his face matching his hair.

Troy quickly returned to reality. "Time is of essence, and I agree with Flint. We're going to take this villain to Hell for questioning, even though you all know how opposed I am to torture. This man not only sent the exploding virus, he also knows about Hell and Tipman. We just have to find out what else he knows, and who his partners are."

They recovered all their weapons and their emergency return rings. Flint heaved the unconscious man onto his shoulder with surprising agility, and they ascended in the glass elevator. They retraced their steps to the entrance in silence, continuously on the lookout for York's expected visitors.

"All right, Adam," said Troy, once they were safely out of the maze of mirrors. "How did you find us?"

Adam took a deep breath.

"I saw those two netters grab Maggie—hey, they were taking her into York's office. I gathered you were all in trouble. I snuck up to the office, and heard your conversation with York through the earrings. When I realized you had overcome the netters I called out to you, but you couldn't hear me, I suppose. Then the link was disconnected—I guess when you entered the tunnel. So, hey, I went into the office, picked up a freezer, a flashlight and a map of the underground site, and took the next car on the tracks. When I arrived at the large cavern I could hear you again, so I managed to avoid crashing into the tree trunk. But I still couldn't speak with you. And when you entered the mirror maze we were again disconnected. I followed you into the maze and, hey, the black rocks you left behind led me to the elevator. When I left it I could hear you again, and I prepared myself to surprise York. He was too busy with you, and he wasn't really, hey, expecting me, so I managed to take him by surprise. Looks like I arrived just in the nick of time."

Troy smiled and gave him the double thumbs up sign. Adam beamed. It was the highest compliment one surfer could give another. Something akin to a student saluting his master.

"There's a Transport Box in the next stall—the studio for creating virtual worlds," said Flint, his nose in the map. "I hope it's still operational. We can jump from there directly to the Topaz Mall. This area here is very isolated, and if the jump doesn't work, we'll have to leave by the same way we came in."

They found the Transport Box just inside the studio's entrance. It was a large group-size model, covered with dust and cobwebs. Green control lights shimmered through the gray-white layer. Flint wiped the dust away with his sleeve, and examined the control panel.

"At least it's powered. I'm going to make an experimental jump. If everything works properly, we'll send our friend York to a safe place, and from there to Hell. You had better conceal yourselves until I return—just in case we're in for more surprises."

"Why don't you stop at York's office, Flint?" suggested Troy. "Atomize the netters, and clear any traces we may have left."

"Yes, sir." Flint executed a sloppy salute.

He entered the Transport Box and vanished. They waited for several minutes expectantly. Finally there came a faint buzz from the box. The door opened and Flint emerged, carrying a large black briefcase. He walked up to York, took a pair of plastic handcuffs out of the briefcase, and tied up York's hands and feet.

"That'll limit his freedom of movement. A delegation will soon arrive to collect him."

The delegation did, indeed, arrive half a minute later. It consisted of two demons, one black and one red, armed with pitchforks. Flint unfroze York and signaled to the demons to take him away. York's face went white with terror when he realized his next destination.

"No! No!" he shrieked, writhing in the demons' firm grip. "Not to Hell!" He tried to strike the red demon with his bound hands, but lost his balance and fell to the floor. The demon grasped him by the collar of his shirt, and dragged him toward the Transport Box. "Let me go! You'll be sorry, I swear! I'll erase your brains."

"Just as you did to Albert Spindler?" queried Troy.

York turned his head and stared at him in bewilderment. "I don't know what you are talking about. Let me go."

The black demon prodded him viciously from behind with its pitchfork. York squealed, and his trousers became stained with blood from the perforations.

"From now on, you'll remain quiet," said the black demon. The two demons pulled York to his feet, covered his head with a black bag, and pushed him into the Transport Box.

"Will you be joining us?" the black one asked Flint.

"We'll be there in about an hour," answered Flint. "You can try softening him up a bit until then. But be careful. Strip him naked first, and check thoroughly for concealed weapons. He is very dangerous."

"We'll be careful," said the red demon, and they all disappeared into the Transport Box.

"Judging by his expression, I'd say he hadn't a clue about the Spindler case," stated Maggie. "I doubt if he's such a fine actor that he could fake it."

"It'll all come out in the interrogation," said Troy. "It was just a shot in the dark, that remark about Spindler. I wondered if he was involved.

Adam—hey, Adam, what's the matter with you?"

Adam was rooted to the spot, his saucer-like eyes goggling.

"Who . . . wha . . . what were those creatures?" he mumbled.

"Whoops!" said Troy, a bit embarrassed. He put his arm on his brother's shoulder. "I forgot that you weren't acquainted yet with the residents of Hell. Those were the demons that Flint brought along, to escort York to Hell."

Adam remained gaping for a few seconds, and then a slow smile began spreading across his face.

"So that's the Hell site you didn't want to tell me about? And, hey, you're looking for strange events in the NET? Well, Hell is the event, as far as I'm concerned. Now nothing can stop me. You have just got to take me there!"

A distant rattle of a roller coaster car came from the direction of the site's entrance. Flint gestured for them to hide behind the Transport Box, which still had its red operating lights flashing, while he peeked toward the roller coaster.

"Two cars just entered the cavern, each with one passenger—I can't tell whether they're surfers or netters. But they both have yellow helmets on and they're carrying large rifles. Come on, the box's operating lights are now green. Hurry in."

The four of them crowded into the transport Box, and Flint punched in the coordinates of the Topaz Mall. The minute the doors opened they raced to Troy's car and drove off. Flint kept his eyes on the Transport Box they had just left, in case they were being followed, but all he saw was youngsters who had arrived at the mall for some fun.

"There's no one after us," said Flint in relief.

"Where's the black briefcase from?" asked Maggie.

"From York's office," replied Flint. "I sealed the entrance to the tunnel, and atomized the three netters. I also searched the room, and I found some documents and recordings that may hold some interest for us."

Maggie glanced through some of the papers.

"Here is a money transfer for a hundred thousand dollars from York's account to a numbered account on the Swiss-net. Here's another, for three hundred thousand. And one for half a million. York must have been making tons of money here, and he's been hiding it in Switzerland. I wonder if he was just evading the tax authorities, or whether he had a secret accomplice or two."

"Umm, speaking of money," began Flint. "Ahh, Troy, do you think I could claim the marksmanship prize money that I won?" He hesitated. "You know, I could add three super-processors to myself, and a lot more memory, with that money."

"Forget it," Troy shook his head decisively. "Babel is going to be all over Roller-net the minute they get wind of York's disappearance. If we claim the prize they'll uncover us, and we'll be in deep trouble. We cannot get that money without exposing ourselves . . ."

"Troy's right, Flint," chimed in Maggie, trying to cheer up the disappointed computer. "You'll just have to earn money honestly. Now," and she turned to Troy, "what are we going to do with York?"

"He can't identify us," interjected Adam. "We were all wearing masks."

Maggie fingered her mask, which made her look like a twelve-year-old girl with buck teeth. "Good thing that we were careful," she said. "Anyway, I vote that we get a full confession from him. Then turn him over to the authorities."

Troy was thinking aloud. "He must have connections within Babel. That's the only place where he could have had access to the recording of the 'Midsummer Night's Dream' hacker. We can't deliver him to his accomplices there."

"Hey, hey!" Adam was astounded. "Are you saying that the author of the 'Midsummer Night's Dream' has been caught by Babel? When did this happen?"

"This morning, Earth time," replied Flint. "Actually, I located him before they did, when he attempted to release a new virus."

"I don't believe it!" exclaimed Adam, smacking his forehead. "Hey, it's simply incredible! Has this information been published yet?"

"Babel are still keeping it secret," said Troy. "Adam, you sound troubled. What connection is there between you and the hacker of the 'Midsummer Night's Dream'?"

"Someone tried to sell me information about the author via Pira-net," explained Adam. "Now I realize that Babel was setting a trap to catch pirates. You can't trust anyone on the NET any more. Hey, Babel—"

"Now hold on there for just a minute," interrupted Maggie. "My dad works for Babel. I am absolutely positive that he's quite clean, and can be one hundred percent trusted. There is a special anonymous communication channel where information on hackers and other criminals may be left without identifying yourself. Listen now, all of you. Why don't we finish interrogating York, then freeze him and leave him somewhere. Then we'll tip off my Dad, and also warn him about York's possible confederates within Babel."

"What a great idea! It could certainly work." Troy was agog with enthusiasm. "Adam, do you know that I never believed that Pira-net actually existed? I always thought it was a legend. Since when are you a member?"

"I'm a new conscript," boasted Adam. "They don't accept everyone, you know."

They arrived at Troy's site, and Troy parked his car in the underground garage.

"I would really like to hear more about the Pira-net," said Troy. "But I'm afraid it'll have to wait. Now it's time to visit Hell. Adam, you are ceremoniously invited to join us, but I warn you that it might not turn out to be a pretty sight. Moreover, I'd be very glad if you'd return to Roller-net, undisguised this time, and sniff around. Bring your friends along, too—my treat! It's the least I can do in return for your brilliant rescue operation. Is that okay with you, mister Hell master?"

"He has undoubtedly earned the right to join us," said Flint. "The way to Hell is paved with good deeds."

Maggie winced at the blatant misquote. Flint bowed slightly toward the young boy. "Mr. Adam Bentley, you shall be our guest of honor. You shall get the red lava treatment, and be awarded the Pitchfork of Valor. Five minutes in Hell—and you'll appreciate how lucky you are to live on Earth."

"But, Adam," continued Troy, in a serious tone. "You may not tell a soul anything about Hell or what you see there. Is that clear?"

Adam nodded violently. His grin spread from ear to ear. Maggie chuckled at the thought that Adam was probably the happiest person to ever go to Hell.

47. NET: Day 34, 09:00

A soft pinging from the corner of her screen startled Lynn from her analysis. She was totally immersed in checking out details on pairs of siblings, when her computer gently notified her that a message from the Queen of the Night awaited her attention.

"Go ahead," she said tersely, and pressed a key that allowed the cuckoo to deliver its report. It had been three hours since she sent the Tipman information over the Pira-net to that little chimpanzee, and she had got no response so far.

To her astonishment, instead of the Queen of the Night, a red bubble appeared at the upper right corner of the holographic screen. It swelled and grew until it filled the entire screen, whereupon it burst with a loud pop. Inside it were the thin chimpanzee and a silver-furred fox wearing a black top hat. Lynn recognized the fox immediately—it was known as the Top Hat Fox, and was an important and esteemed member of Pira-net.

"This is an encrypted message, of course," said the fox. "No point in trying to trace us."

Lynn blanched. She watched the two animals advance to the center of the screen. The chimpanzee remained standing, and the fox seated itself on a massive wooden chair that appeared just in time to accommodate it.

The fox cleared its throat, and recited:

"This hearing, pertaining to the severe charges leveled by Chimpo against the Queen of the Night, a veteran member of Pira-net, is now open. Bring in the defendant."

A long-bearded dwarf entered the screen from its left. He wore a green outfit topped with a pointed cap. Lynn knew him as Inchy, the Pira-net member who had officially initiated her into the network. He carried a large jute sack, which he dumped on the floor. Opening the sack, he took out the Queen of the Night. Her feathers were ruffled and disorderly, as though she had been in a brawl, and a steel chain tied her right foot to a heavy iron ball. Her head was bowed in distress.

The dwarf moved to the side of the screen, where a desk and chair had suddenly appeared, and seated himself. He opened a drawer in the desk, removed a thick notebook and a long feather pen, and gave a nod to the fox that he was ready.

The fox waved its paw toward Chimpo. "Please commence."

"The Queen of the Night tried to uncover my identity," exclaimed the chimpanzee accusingly. "She intended to turn me in to Babel. I am convinced that she is a Babel agent!"

"These are serious accusations," said Top Hat Fox. "We all know that Babel hasn't, and never will have, access to Pira-net. What evidence do you have?"

"She posted a request on the bulletin board, looking for a way to get to Hell, and she was prepared to trade information on the author of 'Midsummer Night's Dream'. I responded to her posting and she sent me the name of the author, one Amos Tipman, of San Jose, California."

"Well?" inquired the fox. "What's wrong with that? Wasn't the data correct?"

"Babel had apprehended the author a few hours earlier," said the chimpanzee triumphantly. "So the prize they offered is nullified. They're keeping this information secret. They're trying to trap pirates by selling worthless information—instead of a million dollars you'd get imprisonment in the Babel dungeons and banishment from the NET. In my opinion, the Queen of the Night is the Queen of Babel, and she is endangering every decent pirate."

"Did you know that Babel had arrested the virus author before you responded to the posting? And how do you know the hacker has been caught?"

"I learned about that only later," said the chimpanzee. "But go ahead—ask her!" It pointed to the shackled cuckoo. "Ask her! She posted the notice on the bulletin board and sent me the data. I'd like to see her deny it!"

"Humph!" said the fox. "We'll get to the bottom of this." It turned to the trembling bird. "I saw your posting about 'Midsummer Night's Dream'. Is the author really Amos Tipman?"

"Yes," said Lynn. On the screen, the bird said, "Yes," repeating Lynn's words. It sounded flat and despondent. The fox glanced at Inchy, verifying that he was taking everything down.

"And is it true that Babel had arrested him?"

"Err . . ." The bird stammered. "I don't know. I got the information in good faith."

"Liar!" yelled the chimpanzee. "You knew about Hell by studying the recording of Tipman's memory. You're a Babel agent!"

Lynn's blood ran cold. *This ape knows way too much!*

"It seems to me," she hissed at the screen, being echoed by the Queen of the Night, "that you, in fact, are the Babel agent around here! You claim that Tipman has been captured, and had his memory recorded. How could you know these facts, if you weren't a Babel agent? They haven't been publicized anywhere!"

"Order!" shouted the fox. It fixed its stare on the disheveled bird. "It was you who initiated the search for Hell. And it was you who offered the sale of data on the author of 'Midsummer Night's Dream.' You were the one who made the connection between these two items. This makes you highly suspect. You are hereby required to reveal to me your sources. Encrypted, of course. According to Pira-net rules, the information you give will be held in utmost confidentiality. If you choose not to reveal your sources to me now, your claims to a defense will be rendered void." It turned to the dwarf. "Fetch me the encryptor."

Inchy opened another drawer in the desk and took out a voice encryptor. He gave it to the bird, and handed a pair of earphones to the fox. The latter slung the earphones around its neck, prepared to put them on when the cuckoo began talking. Inchy resumed his seat, and the three of them waited for the miserable cuckoo to speak.

Lynn thought furiously. *They are going to blow my cover!*

"Very well," she said finally, ignoring the encryptor. "I can tell you that my source was from the hospital where Tipman was confined. I cannot reveal the name of my source."

"Aha! So he was in hospital, was he?" The chimpanzee was exultant. "And his brain was probed, too. Come on, tell us more. Tell us what you did to him there."

"This is the last time I'm warning you!" barked the fox, pointing an admonishing finger at Chimpo. It turned to the Queen of the Night, and glared at her piercingly. "Do you confirm that the virus author was indeed hospitalized?"

"Yes." The bird's voice was so faint it could hardly be heard.

"And did Babel know about this?"

"I can't tell. My source didn't inform me of this." The bird did not sound very convincing.

"You said your source was from within the hospital," continued the fox. "Which hospital would that be?"

Lynn felt the noose tighten around her neck.

"Stanford," said the bird.

The fox lowered its head to the panic-stricken bird and, controlling its anger, slowly enunciated every word.

"Do you take us for fools? A person is in a hospital where we know Babel has a special ward for interrogations and brain analyses. And you claim you don't know if Babel knew whether Tipman was hospitalized there or not!"

"My source may have known that fact, but he didn't disclose it to me."

"I'll ask you once again, Queen. Has Babel captured Amos Tipman? Yes or no?"

"My own personal impression is that they have," mumbled the bird, "but I cannot be sure of it."

"Do you admit that despite your suspicions regarding Babel's apprehending of Tipman, you went ahead and posted your bulletin?"

The bird waved her wings nervously. "I wasn't positive. My source didn't tell me anything to that effect! But I am not a Babel agent. He is!" She pointed a wing at Chimpo. "He's a Babel agent attempting to incriminate me. He and his brother operate a Babel interrogation site named Hell, where they torture people in total disregard for the law!"

The chimpanzee jumped to its feet, its face a mask of pure shock. It opened its mouth to say something but, to Lynn's regret, a stern look from the fox silenced him.

At least I managed to surprise him, thought Lynn. *If the fox hadn't stopped him, he would have blurted out some more information.*

The fox addressed the cuckoo again.

"I demand that you answer the questions you're asked without changing the subject," it reprimanded her. "First you claimed that you didn't know whether or not Babel had captured Tipman, and now you confirm that you gave out information about him knowing that he was in Stanford Hospital. I conclude that you knew he was apprehended by Babel, and that the receiver of your information could be arrested for trying to claim the prize. This behavior is unbecoming to a Pira-net member. You may indeed have acquired the data from the hospital staff, and indeed you may not be a Babel agent—I shall verify these facts shortly. I have already stated that you may submit information under cover of utmost secrecy. I see no reason why you should not disclose to me, in person, everything you know, and thereby clear yourself of these charges of treason. So for the last time, I ask you: are you going to reveal to me, in complete confidentiality, who gave you the information on Tipman?"

"I have to protect my source," whispered the bird with a terrified look.

"You are hereby found guilty of perjury!" snapped the fox. "You are also guilty of unbecoming conduct, and contempt of court! You are sentenced to banishment from Pira-net for life!"

Inchy pulled a small lever on the desk, and a trapdoor in the floor swung open under the poor bird. She flapped her wings and tried to escape, but the heavy ball chained to her foot dragged her down into the hole. A feather and the echo of a scream were all that remained of her.

The fox got to its feet. "The hearing is over!" he announced. "A copy of the verdict and the sentence will be sent to all Pira-net members." He walked off the screen, followed closely by Inchy.

The chimpanzee waited for them to depart, and then walked to the front of the screen. It looked directly forward, into Lynn's eyes. Lynn shrank back into her seat, even though she knew it couldn't see her.

"I hope you can hear me, over there in Babel," said the ape gloatingly. "You're fortunate that I decided only to expose you, and not take you to Hell. I'm sure you can recall the very personal consideration that guests enjoy there."

It turned around and bent forward, deliberately brandishing its red rump. It then walked off the screen, turning off the lights on the way. The screen darkened for a moment, and then redisplayed the statistical lists of sibling pairs.

"Quite an impressive spectacle of audacity," came a voice from behind her. Lynn jumped to her feet and saw George Boder smiling at her brazenly. "Pity I didn't know earlier that you had penetrated the Pira-net—I could have used your help on a number of cases."

"Who let you in here?" asked Lynn, barely controlling her fury. Not only had her Pira-net agent been burned; now George knew of it, too. "Please leave my room at once!"

"Take it easy, Lynn. Norman asked me to assist you. He also told me that you were a Pira-net member, so you needn't worry."

Norman told George, of all people, about my Pira-net missions? How could he do that? He knows that George is the last person in the world I'd want to work with. Or even share information with.

"Where had you two disappeared to all afternoon?" she retorted, grasping at straws. "What's happening that I don't know about yet?"

George's face clouded, but he recovered quickly.

"Unfortunately, nothing," he replied coldly. "We're still trying to locate Hell. All the rest is secondary in importance. Are you getting anywhere with the identity of that saucy chimpanzee? He sounded pretty well versed in matters infernal."

Lynn ignored the poor witticism.

"The initial list of a hundred candidates came to nothing. They all have alibis, surfing somewhere else at the time we're investigating. So we've prepared another list—a thousand names this time—and we're hard at work on them. It'll take us at least a week before we're through. Care to take a few hundred names to work on, yourself?"

George left her question unanswered.

"I understand that you suspect that chimp to be the same one we saw the other day at Spindler's," he said.

"This one has a different mass—he's about twenty percent heavier than the previous one." Lynn was fervently praying that the floor would open up, and deliver George to the same fate that the Queen of the Night had met. Even though she knew that the bird was only a computer simulation, its brutal demise had shocked her, and she felt she needed some time alone. "We could be dealing with two separate chimpanzees. But somebody has blabbed to this Chimpo about Tipman and the memory recording. There's a leak, either here in Babel or at the hospital. I had better update Norman about this right away. Please keep this knowledge strictly to yourself!"

George's 'com buzzed, and he conversed for a few seconds. His face was grim as he addressed Lynn.

"I must go now. Norman has summoned me urgently, and we'll probably have to go out on that same mission immediately. I'll report to him about what happened here. I suggest you continue on this line of inquiry. That chimp left a ton of information behind."

George left the room. Lynn watched him go, riddles whirling in her mind.

Norman and George! Suddenly they're a twosome. Maybe Norman doesn't detest George as intensely as I do, but he certainly doesn't like him! Now we know that there could be a traitor in our unit. Is that why they're so secretive? Why doesn't Norman involve me in this—doesn't he trust me any more? She felt her insides churn. She reached out to the 'com to call Norman, but stopped herself. *I'll wait for him. He's got to call me soon. I'm sure he has a perfectly good reason not to do so now . . .*

48. NET: Day 34, 09:55

"This guy's really tough. He hasn't uttered a word, except for demanding to see an attorney. We, of course, waited for your instructions, and treated him as delicately as we could."

The black demon tipped a ladle full of boiling tar on York's bare leg. York, tightly bound to a slab of stone, gritted his teeth and twitched his leg. His eyes conveyed the pain and terror he felt.

"I'll handle him now," said Flint. "I think I know how to communicate with him."

Flint still appeared as the blond youth he was in the Roller-net. He opened a nearby cabinet and took out a T-scope device, hanging it over York's head. Troy and Maggie stood on York's other side. Adam had already left the place, all thrilled after a delightful ten-minute tour of Hell, which included a ride on an elephant spider. He swore to Troy and Flint never to breathe a word to his friends.

"York, can you hear me?" asked Flint casually.

York regarded Flint with a hateful glare, but said nothing.

"Are you the author of the virus in the exploding truck? Listen carefully, now—contrary to the demons, I don't have time to waste on playing games with you. If you don't answer me now, I'll just leave you in their hands for five minutes. They'll be under no restrictions this time. I believe they'll get answers from you. For example, the very first thing they'll do to you is to amputate your right leg. You'll remain a cripple in the NET."

"Yes, I wrote the virus," growled York through grinding teeth. "I see now that you were the cop. I thought I was rid of you, but you got away somehow. What are you going to do with me?"

"Nothing like what you planned to do with us," replied Flint calmly. "We're not sadists. But we need the information now, and we'll employ any means at our disposal to get it. Do you get my drift?"

"So what'll happen if I cooperate?" asked York.

"If you cooperate we'll deliver you to the NET authorities," said Flint, "and you'll probably stand trial. If you attempt to conceal information, or worse, lie to us, we will extend this establishment's hospitality for the required period of time. Believe me, we'll hear what we want from you. How we get it is entirely up to you. Now tell me please, who owns the Swiss bank account into which you transfer money?"

York's face turned purple and his eyes nearly popped out of his head. He took a deep breath, and when he spoke, his voice was almost too faint to be heard:

"So you've rifled my cabinets, too. Just dandy. Quite befitting a criminal like you. I have no idea who the owner of the account is. What I do know is that the money eventually gets to my silent partner who financed the construction of Roller-net. I don't know who he is."

Flint glanced at the T-scope—it glowed green. York was telling the truth.

"Was that your partner who called you while you held us in your office?" asked Troy. "Did he tell you we didn't appear on the NET's monitoring systems?"

"Yes," replied York. Pride could be heard in his voice. "He can do anything on Earth."

Flint stared directly into York's eyes.

"What did he tell you to do with us?"

York grimaced. "He wanted me to find out where Hell was, and who was the surfer who owned you. He told me to wait for him, and that he'd arrive in half an hour. Meanwhile I was to extract information from you by any means I saw fit."

"Does he work for Babel?" asked Maggie.

"I don't know."

"So how do you contact him?" she wondered.

"I don't. I leave a request on my 'com, and he knows how to get it from there. Then he calls me, and there's no way to trace where he calls from. I tried several times."

"What other viruses have you composed?" asked Flint.

York was silent. Flint, Troy and Maggie exchanged glances. York told the truth so far, but now he was covering something up.

"I think he may have a problem in self expression," said Flint. He looked at Troy, requesting permission to continue.

Troy hesitated. The intense anger he had felt when York was torturing them in the mirror maze, seemed to have passed. Even though York was an incurable villain, who was quite prepared to erase their brains and turning them into vegetables on Earth, he now felt that he couldn't stoop to that level.

We can deliver him to Babel as Maggie suggested, he thought. *Let them get the information out of him. True, it'll be quite risky for us, but I don't think we have a choice. We can't turn him loose, and we can't keep him prisoner forever. Eventually we'll have to turn him in.*

He noticed Flint's impatient gaze.

That computer has no doubts whatsoever about what should be done. He'll use any means to get the information out of York. And he could also hold on to him here for as long as he liked, and let his demons go to work on him . . .

Maybe he's right? He always behaves logically—I should know, I programmed him! He has no moral considerations of uncalled-for mercy. Like mercy for a criminal, where a 'considerate' judge releases a murderer into the streets only to kill again.

Troy looked questioningly at Maggie. She was silent. Her confused look indicated that she, too, didn't know how to handle the situation.

It's my decision now! The most important thing right now is to find this sleazeball's partner. He is the dangerous factor. If we don't find him, he'll find us and finish the job that York began. This partner has managed to infiltrate into Babel, or at least have access to secret information there. There-

fore, we cannot let Babel take over the investigation yet. That leaves us the only choice of getting the information ourselves. But we should not let this become a second Tipman scenario. I hope the bastard will break soon; otherwise his questioning will probably be harder on me than on him . . .

"Okay," he said to Flint. "He's all yours. We are out of here. Call me when you have the information."

"Wait a sec," said Flint. "I'll join you." He signaled to the black demon that was lurking in the shadows. "Hey, Smoky, our guest here has stopped cooperating. How long do you need to get him to talk? When should we come back?"

The demon gave a horrible leer.

"No holds barred?" it asked, and stretched its fingers, popping a dagger out of each fingernail. "Do we need to keep all his limbs and organs intact?"

"Do whatever you like," said Flint. "Just keep him alive and conscious."

"Wait! Wait! I'll talk!" screamed York, aghast by the dialog he had just overheard. The demon was visibly disappointed. "I'll talk! I composed one other virus—Jezebel. Many years ago. NET years, of course. My partner gave me instructions how to write it and how to launch it into the NET. Nobody knew it existed except for that moron Tipman. He copied it, and made his own version of it called 'Midsummer Night's Dream'. Most of the money for building the new roller coaster came from Jezebel."

Flint verified that York's outburst was true. Troy bent over York.

"Where do you surf from? What is your address on Earth?"

"I don't know, I swear. I've been surfing in the NET continuously for the past three and a half Earth years. I don't know where I originated from."

York was telling the truth again, but it was impossible. Over eighty NET years!

"How did you get the recording of Tipman's memory?" asked Maggie.

"My partner sent it to me for checking. He wanted me to find out if there were any indications of our virus in it. There were none."

"Did your partner tell you what was discovered in the deep brain analysis they made on Tipman?" asked Troy. They knew from Og, that such a probe was scheduled for that morning, but had no further details.

York barked out a fiendish laugh.

"Haven't you heard? Nothing! They found nothing because Tipman had no brain. It was erased in the hospital. He'll go free from lack of evidence. Ha-ha-ha . . ."

Flint looked skeptically at York.

"Who erased Tipman's brain?" he asked.

"How the devil should I know? I was here in the NET all the time." This time the T-scope light was red. York was masking something. Flint nodded to the demon, which laid its hand on York's leg, its talons piercing the flesh. York gave a jolt.

"Enough, enough! I don't know! My partner bragged to me that Tipman's brain was erased, and that we needn't be afraid of him any longer. It stands to reason that he, my partner, did the erasing. He takes care of everything that needs to be done on your accursed Earth." Tears of pain flowed down York's cheeks. He strained against the ropes, sheer hatred burning in his eyes. The T-scope confirmed everything he had said. They had reached a dead end.

"We're going to check who he's connected to on Earth," said Troy to Flint. "Tell your minions to keep him in one piece. We may need him later."

PART THREE–SATURDAY AFTERNOON

49. SANTA CRUZ, SATURDAY, 12:05

The battered old car drove up the winding road through a forest of towering redwood trees, as Ziggy made his way toward Santa Cruz, the delightful California resort town. Ziggy studied the navigation screen, and slowed to one hundred miles per hour. He turned off the main road onto a narrow path that led up a steep incline. On the right side of the path was a high brick wall, topped by electronic alarm devices connected by thin red laser beams. He slowed down some more, and stopped when a solid, rusty iron gate came into view.

"We have arrived," he said. "There is only a small plaque on the gate, which I cannot decipher from here, but it cannot be anywhere else, according to this map. Would you like me to enter the place with you?"

"Thanks, Ziggy." Troy examined the high wall. "But I won't be needing you. It'll only take a few minutes, anyway. Could you please wait for me here by the gate?"

"No problem." Ziggy inserted a book button into the car's computer. "I have brought along some reading material."

Troy looked in the mirror to make sure that his blond wig was properly adjusted. He then walked up to the gate, on which the sign read 'Private Property—Entry Forbidden'. A pushbutton bell, with an adjoining grate, was affixed to the wall by the gate. Troy held his finger against the bell for a couple of seconds.

"Please state your full name and business," came a stern feminine voice from the grate.

"My name is Nigel York. I called about half an hour ago. About Mr. Stewart York."

"Come in, please." A faint buzz and a click came from the gate, and it swung open.

A long, single-story building with barred windows spread out before him. A stone footpath led from the gate to the building's main entrance. A stout woman dressed in a nurse's uniform waited for him by the door. Above her, a large sign read 'Jennings Institute for the Neurally Impaired'. Troy walked up to her with quick steps.

"You're far too young to be Mr. York's son," said the nurse. "What did you say your relationship was?"

"I'm his nephew—the son of his brother Malcolm," lied Troy. "I had occasion to be in the vicinity concerning my school thesis, and Dad requested me to take the time to drop in on his brother and see how he's doing. It's been quite a while since the last visit, I believe."

The nurse gave him a strange look.

"I'm Linda—we spoke on the phone. Come on in, I'll take you to him. You're his first visitor ever. His condition hasn't changed since he arrived here almost four years ago."

They walked along a corridor, which went around a square courtyard. A few round, metal tables were placed randomly, and around two of them were a couple of patients, dressed in the institute's pajamas, and a few normally dressed visitors.

"Saturday is visitor's day," said Linda. She nodded to another nurse who walked past them pushing a trolley laden with medical instruments. "Your uncle is at the end of this corridor."

They arrived at the door, and Linda opened it and switched the light on. The room was bare save for a bed in which lay a tall, bearded man. The resemblance to the York he had just left in Hell was astonishing. On his head was a black surfing helmet. An osmosis sleeve was wrapped around his left arm, providing nourishment. A cabinet with medical electronic devices stood by the wall. Troy walked to the bed.

"Uncle Stewart? Can you hear me?"

"He can't hear a thing," said Linda. "His brain isn't functioning. Look at the monitor."

Troy looked to where the nurse was pointing. One of the machines in the cabinet was wired to the patient's head and chest. It had a large display screen, which showed a number of graphs and diagrams, some of which were continuously flickering from left to right.

"I understand that you're monitoring his vital bodily functions," he said hesitatingly. "They're all right, aren't they?"

"Oh, his body is in fine condition—we give him a daily full-muscle exercise to keep him in shape. But look here." She showed a small blinking window on the side of the screen. "This is his brain status. There is no coherent data. He is in a deep coma, and that's how he was when he arrived here."

Deep coma! Flint had traced the NET's York to this man, Stewart York. But that meant that Rupert York was not actually connected to the Earth! He was a surfer trapped in the NET! And someone was covering for him!

Troy gazed on the face of the man in the bed—the face he had come to despise during the past few hours in the NET.

"If he's in a deep coma, why does he have a surfing helmet on?"

"We plug him in every morning at seven, and unplug him at nine in the evening. Your father requested this treatment for him. He hoped that one day his brother would wake up. Personally, I think he's just wasting his money." She looked at Troy suspiciously. "Why are you asking all these questions? How come your father sent you here without even the basic background information?"

Troy squirmed. He felt the time had arrived to extricate himself.

"Dad kept the whole issue under wraps. I didn't even know Uncle Stewart was alive until the day before yesterday. You see, we all thought he'd been killed in a traffic accident in India. When Dad found out I'd be in the Santa Cruz area, he told me the whole story and asked me to visit his brother. To tell the truth, I am quite shocked by what I witnessed here." He shuddered, and shut his eyes in sham revulsion.

Linda didn't seem convinced. She pressed the room's inter-call button, and a young woman's face appeared on the screen.

"Nina, please get me Mr. Malcolm Stewart on the 'com. He's the nearest of kin to the patient in room 118."

They waited a couple of minutes, and then Nina's voice came out of the 'com.

"He wasn't in. I left a message on his answer-com."

"I'm afraid I have to leave now," said Troy. "There's nothing I can do to help him. I'll advise Dad to reconsider hooking up Uncle Stewart to the NET. I think you're right—it is a waste of money! Thank you very much Nurse Linda."

He walked calmly toward the exit, with the nurse close on his heels. They hadn't taken more than a few steps when the inter-call in the room they had just left began ringing loudly.

"Wait please, Mr. York," said the nurse. "It may be your father." She turned around and went back into the room.

But Troy did not wait. He sprinted toward the main door, almost collided with a nurse who happened to be coming his way, and headed for the front gate. He was in luck—at that very moment a new group of visitors were just making their way in through the gate, and Troy shoved his way through them, arriving finally outside the wall. The rickety car was still waiting by the gate, with Ziggy in the driver's seat, reading.

"Let's go!" cried Troy as he jumped into the car. Ziggy jolted upright in consternation.

"What happened?" he asked.

"Go! Go! I'll tell you on the way!"

As Ziggy drove off, Troy removed his wig and looked backward, keeping a close watch on the gate he had just left. Nobody came out of it. Then the car turned a corner and the gate disappeared.

"I was almost caught. If it weren't for those new visitors arriving just in the nick of time, my goose would have been cooked. They now have my picture in their monitors, and I sure hope that this wig is a disguise good enough to conceal my identity for a while."

They arrived at the highway.

"Take the Bullet Drive and get us home as fast as possible. But don't commit any traffic violations. The last thing we need now is an automatic speeding ticket, or to be stopped by the law."

Ziggy turned into the highway and accelerated.

"Okay—it seems we're not followed," said Troy. "But I'm afraid that by now they've discovered that I was an imposter. The main thing is that I've managed to see the surfer that our criminal is linked to. It's the original York, and he's in a coma. The York in the NET is a surfer trapped without any prospect of returning to Earth."

"Just like Robert Duke," mumbled Ziggy. "I only pray that you and Maggie do not get into any more trouble. I would be glad to assist you in the NET, but unfortunately . . ."

"Yes, I know" said Troy quietly. "I'm sorry."

"You know, Troy, I could follow you during your surf. Just to make sure everything is all right with you. I believe I have demonstrated to you the method I could employ."

"You have, but there's no need. We'll all be careful; you needn't worry."

"Please, Troy." There was a tremor in Ziggy's voice. "Please allow me to follow you. Just for this one surf. Please, Troy."

Troy looked at his old mentor with fresh insight. It was the first time Ziggy had ever asked for anything so earnestly.

"Very well," he said softly. "Just for this surf."

Ziggy didn't respond. He got on Bullet Drive and turned toward Palo Alto. It took them seven minutes of careful driving at the legal speed of three-hundred miles per hour to get back to their neighborhood.

50. NET: DAY 37, 02:00

"I have good news for you, Mr. York." The black demon smirked disgustingly and slightly loosened the bonds that cut into York's flesh. "You have visitors." He removed the black hood off York's head.

York blinked and took in his surroundings. He was in an immense subterranean hall, as large as a domed soccer field, with numerous burrows and passageways Swiss-cheesing the walls and the rock-strewn floor. The hall was subdivided into dozens of separate, quadrilateral partitions created by the crisscrossing of many narrow and deep gullies. Wisps of smoke rose from these canals, clouding the air and giving off the stench of sulphur. He saw groups of black and red demons dispersed over the hall, busy at unloading packages off the backs of black spiders as large as elephants. He was seated on a metal chair, welded to the ground, near one of the walls of the hall. Leather straps fastened his arms and legs to the rusty metal.

"You're lying," mumbled York. "Nobody ever looks for me." His voice grew louder. "I've told you everything you asked for. It's all gospel truth. Why don't you let me go? I've been here three days already. I'm prepared to pay you any sum of money. I can make you all rich."

"We have no use for money," said a tall, green demon with short horns, which had just entered the hall from a nearby burrow. It wore jeans and a flowery shirt with a deep slit in the back through which its wings emerged and lay folded on its back. The butt of a freezer poked out of one of its pockets. "However, you have information, and that is what we need right now."

"You don't fool me with that masquerade, Flint. Now I know for sure that you're a netter. I just haven't figured out yet how you change your appearance. What more do you want of me?"

"Actually," interrupted Troy, "*you* are a netter." He and Maggie had arrived with Flint, and both wore green demon masks. "Technically, at least. The surfer you're connected to has been in a coma for a few Earth years. The helmet he wears is only a technicality—it's taken off him periodically. So you're an unconnected NET creature—a trapped surfer. Which, in my book, is equivalent to a netter."

York recognized Troy's voice. His eyes goggled and his jaw dropped in disbelief. Foam began to dribble from the sides of his gaping mouth, and his face contorted in a grimace of white-hot malevolence.

"Jonathan Oakley," he hissed. "In a demon's mock-up. You're a liar! I'm a real surfer. I've been on Earth and I have memories from then. I can return to Earth any time I please."

"We'll soon find out," said Flint. "Does the name Malcolm York mean anything to you?"

"No. Nothing." The T-scope over York's head glowed green.

"How interesting," said Troy. "What did you do before becoming a permanent NET fixture?"

York noticed Maggie standing next to Troy and stared at her. "And this is the girl who tried to rescue you. Who the hell are you people?"

Troy brushed the question aside. The black demon laid its hand on York's shoulder and began to squeeze. York answered quickly.

"I don't remember specific details now. It's been over eighty contiguous years in the NET after all. But it doesn't matter. I'm a real surfer, and you must have mistaken my connection with someone else!"

"You have an emergency return ring on your finger," said Troy. "If you're a genuine surfer, why don't you use it to escape?"

"I dare not! If I use it all my memories of the NET will be erased. Eighty-three years! It would be like dying!"

"Did you ever try to leave the NET?"

"Perhaps. A long time ago. I don't remember. I believe I've got Earth-phobia or something. I just can't imagine myself outside the NET."

"I think we can refresh your memory," said Flint. Two black demons rolled a trolley with electronic equipment toward York. A large holo-screen was fixed over the trolley.

"This," continued Flint, waving to the machinery, "is a brain analysis system. I'll leave you to guess what we'll use it for. Furthermore, we're going to take a tiny sample of your tissues—we'll check how your DNA matches against that of Stewart York on Earth. Perhaps we'll discover that here, too, you're a fraud—maybe an unfamiliar kind of netter."

York writhed in a furor.

"You need my consent to probe into my brain or to test my DNA!" he barked savagely.

One of the black demons leered nastily. "Oh, we'll get your consent, never fear. You're in Hell, remember? You have forfeited all your rights at the main entrance. Too bad. But if you insist, I'll explain to you how we'll get your signature on any document we choose." It pointed to a large aquarium nearby, containing a school of odd fish. "First, I'll scratch your hand so it'll bleed a little. Then I'll put it into the aquarium. You won't be able to sign with that hand—those fish are piranhas, ha, ha, ha."

They attached York to the machine. One of the demons fiddled with the dials and pressed the Operate button. A flurry of scenes flashed on the adjacent screen. It took the demon several seconds before it managed to calibrate the device and get a steady and clear image. The screen displayed York, somewhat younger, sitting in a large room in the company of an elderly gentleman with white hair. They were busy signing documents.

"That's Jacob Cranshaw," said York, who was observing the screen with the others. "I bought Roller-net from him."

"Please speak only when requested," said Flint.

"Master," growled one of the demons, "let me fix him. He'll have a third-degree nightmare while we're digging information from his brain. He won't talk. In fact, he won't disturb us in any way during the procedure."

York got the hint.

"I'll shut up," he hurried to say.

"Turn the projector back to the beginning of his memories," instructed Troy.

The scene vanished and the screen flickered slightly. York was seen seated by a computer, the monitor displaying a coded program.

"Hold it right there," cried Flint. "That could be a virus program." He studied the screen closely. "Well, well, well—it is a virus! Is this Jezebel that you mentioned earlier?" He shot the question at York.

"Yes. And those Babel morons didn't even know that they had a virus under their very noses." York seemed visibly proud. "I got guidance from my partner, but I built that virus myself, and released it to the NET a week later. As a result, inside information from several companies was channeled my way. I left all this info in my 'com answer-box for my partner to handle." He was telling the truth.

"Yes—I can see the resemblance to Tipman's virus," mused Flint. "That came a year later. Were you in any way connected to him?"

"No. I suspect that he accidentally stumbled across my virus, and copied it."

They went on with the brain probe, and witnessed York purchasing Roller-net with funds from unknown sources.

"There is nothing in his memory before writing that virus." Troy was disappointed. "Either he has amnesia or someone has deliberately wiped the earlier memories from his brain. I'm afraid this kind of progress is too slow. There's no way we can watch eighty odd years of memories. Let's try to fast forward and discover his elusive partner."

The projection rate was accelerated. The screen showed a fantastically fast erection of the new Roller-net, which proceeded nonstop for years. York spent a lot of time at the building site. He clearly had almost unlimited resources at his disposal—he always selected the most expensive items and built the most extravagant attractions. When the new amusement park was completed, the demon slowed down the projection again.

The scene was the inauguration of Roller-net, held at York's mountaintop castle. Present were Netville's mayor, the Chief of Police, and other dignitaries from Earth and from the NET. York gave a short speech in which he promised that Roller-net would be the most advanced and the safest of its kind in the NET.

More fast forwarding brought the viewers to the end of the inauguration ceremony. York bade farewell to his guests and remained alone. He walked up the stairs to his private chambers. A solidly built man with wide shoulders was waiting for him in his bedroom.

"Slow down," ordered Troy. "I want to see this man. He looks familiar."

"No wonder," said Flint. "You've seen him often enough in your history books. It's Niels Van Kloeten, the first president of the Western Alliance. It isn't the real him, of course—he's been dead these past seventy years. It's someone else wearing a Van Kloeten mask." He turned to York. "Who is this man?"

"That's my partner. That was the first and last occasion I had to meet with him face to face. Not even his real face." The T-scope shone green.

"Did he order you to create the virus in order to kill me?"

"No. That was my own idea."

Troy intervened. "I'd like to see the most recent period. He hasn't met with his partner since the Roller-net began operating. So let's go forward until about five years ago, and start tracking from there."

The operating demon complied. York's memories flashed by at incredible speed. It was almost impossible to make out specific details. Suddenly, Flint jerked to attention.

"Stop right now." The projecting demon halted the forwarding operation. "Now back up. More. More. That's it!"

On the screen, they saw York sitting in a dim room. Across from him sat a very fat man, completely bald who, despite the lack of lighting, wore dark sunglasses. In a corner of the room stood a tall man with sharp features.

"That is the netter who tried to kill me," said Flint. "Who is the other man?"

"I don't know his name," replied York. "He's from the NET Mafia. His nickname is Fatso, and I believe he belongs to the Canadian branch. I bought that stinking netter, Randolph, off him."

"You had connections with NET's crime organizations?" inquired Troy.

York sneered. "*You* try to run a huge business like Roller-net, and see for yourself who your contacts are going to be. Do you think I had the time or the inclination to see my rides going up in flames, or my netters disappearing every other day? I paid, and everything was kept peaceful."

"Why didn't you notify the police or Babel?" asked Maggie. "They would have dealt with your 'protectors'."

"And why don't you tell Babel about me?" York laughed caustically. "Everyone has something to hide. Besides, they are totally useless against the Mafia. The only things that interest Babel are viruses. They couldn't care less if people killed each other in the NET. After all, people don't really die here—"

Troy interrupted again. "I want to see the part where York receives the recording of Tipman's memory. Perhaps we'll find out—"

The deafening wail of a siren cut him short in mid sentence. The lights dimmed and brightened recurrently, and agitated demons began rushing in all directions.

"It's the intrusion alarm!" cried Flint. "You must hide at once. Follow me." He saw York's intent gaze, and gestured to the black demon, which recovered York's head with the black hood.

"He mustn't see in which direction we're going," explained Flint as he ran toward the tunnel from which they had arrived. Troy and Maggie followed close on his heels.

They quickly reached the narrow hole in the wall, and Flint pushed them in. "Wait for me here," he said. "I'm going to close up this entrance, and no one will know you're here. I'll be back in a few minutes. If I don't return in a quarter of an hour, just walk along this tunnel until you arrive at a pile of stones blocking your way. There's an entrance to another passage right above this pile. And this second passage will lead you out of Hell. Just follow it toward the light. Wait for me there. Don't worry; we're well prepared for any attack. If these are Babel personnel, as I strongly suspect, they're in for a few unpleasant surprises."

He swung around and returned to the hall. Two red demons immediately began blocking the entrance with large rocks.

"Flint! What are you going to do with York?" called Troy, but Flint was already out of earshot. In a short while the children were in total darkness.

"He's really overdoing it," grumbled Maggie. She took out her small trekking flashlight and shone it around. "I think it would be far wiser to clear out of here altogether, instead of attempting to fight Babel."

"Give him some credit, Maggie," said Troy, trying to defend his computer. He looked at the blocked entrance, the piled-up rocks merging perfectly with the walls. "It could be a false alarm, and Flint is only trying to protect us. Meanwhile, we have nothing to do here but explore—so let's find out where this tunnel leads."

They managed to walk just a few steps into the tunnel, when an ear-splitting blast was heard from the direction of the entrance. A wave of heat enveloped them, and a section of the entrance and the adjacent wall melted and fused, while other portions crumbled. A huge block of stone detached from the ceiling and crashed onto the very spot they had occupied a few seconds earlier. Troy and Maggie hurried down the tunnel. The exit into the hall was now shut off by tons of rock. Tiny shafts of light from the hall trickled through minute cracks in the rubble.

"What was that?" gasped Maggie. Troy hushed her with a finger to his lips, and approached the rock that blocked the entrance. He could see parts of the hall through one of the larger fissures.

A large hole had been blown open on the wall opposite their hideaway. A man and a woman stood in the opening—both attired in the Babel combat uniform, with yellow helmets on their heads. They carried large laser rifles in their hands, and black packs on their backs.

51. PALO ALTO, SATURDAY, 13:06

Ziggy sat in Troy's room watching the little holographic screen intently. A long cable connected it to the helmet on Troy's head, who was still surfing. Ziggy saw the vast expanse of the hall in Hell exactly the same way Troy saw it.

It was a special, and rather ancient, monitoring system, used by the NET's rescue teams to save surfers who got into trouble. It allowed the rescuers to attach themselves to the surfer's helmet, and track him by receiving all his visual images and audio impressions in real, though accelerated, time. They could then identify his surroundings, and make a decision regarding when and how to disconnect him.

Ziggy had come by this equipment under questionable circumstances nine years earlier. A childhood friend, who became the NET official responsible for all the surfers in the New York area, provided the opportunity.

"I very much wish to surf with my daughter," Ziggy had explained. "She does not mind my joining her during surfs, and I could have at least some illusion of spending time with her. I have no one else in my life, and I feel I am losing my girl to the NET."

"Ziggy, you're putting me in a tough position." The friend was clearly uncomfortable with the idea. "I could lose my job and my reputation. Look, here's what I propose. I have a small monitor that I'm supposed to trash. I shall dispatch it tomorrow morning, as usual, sealed in a box, and the disposal truck will pick it up. The driver will be detained in our offices for no more than ten minutes, while the truck parks behind our building by the deliveries door. I suppose the box could, theoretically, be replaced during those ten minutes without anyone noticing. I don't want to even know if such a switch took place, and Ziggy—believe me, if I am ever questioned on this topic, I shall deny even discussing it with you."

Ziggy obtained the monitor and surfed extensively with his daughter, until she got married and moved to Australia. Since then, the monitor was left unused in its packaging. He brought it over when he moved to the West Coast, and stored it in the basement of his Palo Alto home. And now the time had come to put it to use again.

The scene on the monitor jumped and jerked, twenty-four times the normal speed, due to the difference in the time lapse rate. Ziggy saw Troy and Flint interrogating York at a ridiculously fast pace. Of course, at that speed he could make no sense of what was being said. He dialed the monitor to display one image every twenty-four seconds, and watched silently. He knew he could always replay the important parts at normal speed.

He got up, fetched himself a glass of water from the cooler, took a sip, and turned back to the monitor and froze. The glass dropped unnoticed from his hand, shattering on the floor.

On the screen were two Babel combatants, wearing yellow helmets and holding large rifles in their hands . . .

52. NET: Day 37, 03:13

"But that's impossible," muttered Maggie, watching through the fissure. She kept a distance from the wall, which was still hot from the hits of the laser rays. "I know that lady—she's a businesswoman. Certainly not a Babel combatant."

"The man looks familiar to me, too," whispered Troy. "I've seen his picture before somewhere, I'm sure."

The two warriors walked calmly to the center of the hall, occasionally letting loose bursts of fire from their rifles at groups of demons. The rays from the rifles were lethal, and the demons were either killed outright or horribly maimed, loosing limbs and falling to the ground in pools of blood, screaming loudly. Those rays that missed the demons, hit the walls, melting holes in them and generating rockslides and avalanches.

The surviving demons scrambled for cover, diving into the numerous burrows that led out from the hall. Troy and Maggie couldn't see Flint in the commotion, but they recognized the demon that had operated the brain analysis machine they had used on York. It was on the floor, dead. York himself was still attached to the machine, his head covered by the hood.

The combatants noticed York, bound to the metal chair. The man motioned to the woman, and began making his way toward York. The woman moved in the other direction, to the far side of the hall, where a number of cargo spiders, laden with crates, were indifferently watching the carnage.

The male combatant leaped over a narrow furrow in the ground and stepped on a tiny mound just beyond the gully. A sharp detonation was heard, and two huge steel jaws sprang out of the earth on both sides of the man and snapped shut on him like an enormous bear trap. At the same time, a line of pointed spears lunged out of the ground and skewered his entire body. The man thrashed and contorted for a few seconds before going limp.

The trap released the body, and it flopped to the ground. To the children's horror, it began changing its shape, expanding and lengthening, until they finally saw a humanoid creature, ten feet long, with a gigantic head almost the third of its entire height. Green ooze dripped out of the wounds and lacerations it had sustained all over its body.

Maggie let out a little shriek, and immediately stuffed a fist into her mouth. She looked at Troy and saw the horrified look in his eyes.

"They're not Babel." she whispered in a choking voice. "It's the aliens! They're taking over real people. Look at the woman."

Troy followed Maggie's stare.

The female combatant was facing her dead comrade. She touched her helmet lightly, and golden beams shone downward from it, surrounding her completely, as if she was enclosed in a bubble. Angrily, she fired at the pack spiders, which were trying to escape into a burrow in the far wall.

Troy was hardly breathing. "So that's what they look like. They're huge! I know you shouldn't judge by appearance alone, but they seem hostile to me."

"What kind of technology would enable such a creature to occupy a human being?" wondered Maggie, under her breath.

The sounds of battle grew louder. Two large doors on either side of the hall burst open, and hords of elephant spiders galloped in. Each spider had a toad-like rider armed with a spear, and carried two immense buckets, the size of wine barrels, on each side. The buckets were brimming with boiling oil. The spiders ran surprisingly fast toward the woman combatant, ignoring the boiling drops that splashed out of the buckets and onto their legs and torsos.

"Flint sure was ready for battle," whispered Troy excitedly. His gaze swept the hall, searching for the green demon in the flowery shirt. "Do you see him anywhere?"

Maggie shook her head, her attention totally focused on the battle scene. Black demons emerged in swarms from the dozens of openings in the walls, like bats from a cave. They were armed with pitchforks, and bows and arrows. The archers shot volleys of arrows at the lone female warrior, who seemed to be preoccupied with the death of her colleague. The arrows struck the shiny envelope surrounding her and bounced off harmlessly. Though she seemed not to notice the arrows, she had evidently pulled herself together, and coolly fired at the spiders loping toward her. Her aim was accurate, and spider after spider stumbled and fell, toppling its green driver to the ground and spilling its boiling cargo. But there were too many spiders, and one of them managed to approach the shooter to within a number of paces before she burned its head off. The dead spider careened forward in momentum, and collapsed on top of the woman. The spilled oil formed a large, slick pool around the carcass.

"I wonder if she's hurt," breathed Troy. "That light shield protects her from arrows, but perhaps the weight of the spider has, indeed, crushed her. Oh, wow—"

Two more combatants entered through the hole blasted by the first attackers. They, too, were surrounded by a golden halo emanating from their yellow helmets. Through the enveloping beams, the children could see that they, too, wore Babel uniforms. One was short and very broad. The other was slimmer and a head taller. The demons showered arrows on them, and five surviving elephant spiders ambled toward them. The new fighters fired on them without hesitation, and killed them all. Groups of demons armed with pitchforks flew at them from all directions, but most were mowed down as they approached. Two demons managed to reach the tall warrior, and heaved their pitchforks forcefully at his back. The blows pummeled the fighter and he fell to the ground, dropping his rifle, but the pitchforks did not penetrate the glowing field surrounding him.

One of the demons snatched up the rifle and fired at the shorter warrior. The golden field around the target turned blood red, but he remained unharmed. With casual detachment, the fighter fired at one of the demons hovering around him, and it fell to the ground with a smoking hole in its chest. The demon holding the rifle was the next victim—its arm was sliced off, and the rifle clattered to the ground. Blood spurted from the stump, and the demon screamed in pain. The short militant approached the wounded demon, but did not kill it. He shot it first in both wings, and then in both legs, amputating them below the knees. A large pool of blood swirled around the moaning demon. The fighter kicked the fallen demon several times in the face, turning it into a bloody pulp.

Maggie was sickened and outraged at the same time. "He is deliberately abusing the hapless demon," she fumed. "He's actually enjoying it. What a sadist!"

What have I done? What kind of menace did I bring into the NET! Tears of frustration rose in Troy's eyes. He stopped himself. It was no time for self-pity. *I have to be strong. I mustn't break; Maggie should not see me crying.* He wiped his eyes with his sleeve and looked briefly towards Maggie. She was spellbound by the scene in front of her and did not notice his emotional reaction. *I must watch these invaders and try to find their Achilles' heal. They are mortal when not protected by that shiny bubble.*

The tall fighter had meanwhile recovered. He rose to his feet and retrieved his rifle. The vast hall was now empty, as the demons fled, realizing that their weapons had no effect on the shielded intruders. The two combatants approached the dead spider that had buried the woman fighter. Using their rifles, they sliced the spider into sections, and removed them away from the carcass one by one. Finally a shining bubble of light could be seen from below the spider's remains, and the two men hauled the woman out. She seemed quite unhurt as she reached back and pulled out her rifle.

"So the boiling oil and the weight of the spider had no effect on her," noted Troy in a whisper. At that moment another sharp explosion was heard. The short fighter, who had begun walking toward York, had stepped on a tiny mound and triggered another trap.

But the steel jaws and the spears springing from the ground could not penetrate the shining envelope. The fighter continued his walk, unscathed. The jaws snapped together on the spears that had pierced nothing.

The warrior didn't even look back. He reached York, who was still connected to the brain analysis machine, and removed the hood off his head. York blinked up in bewilderment.

"Help!" he cried. "I'm a prisoner here! Save me!" He tried a futile smile toward the light-enveloped fighter at his side. "My name is York. I'm the owner and manager of Roller-net, the amusement park."

The combatant looked around, making sure no threat loomed. He reached up and turned off the protective shield. The children saw a very broad-shoul-dered man with a square face and a somewhat flattened, boxer type, nose. He gazed intently at York for several seconds. York recognized him imme-diately.

"You're George from Babel! You questioned me at my office. Thank heavens you've arrived to rescue me from these criminals. Take that machine off me, and untie me from these ropes. My circulation is blocked."

The stocky man looked at the screen, which amazingly had survived the mayhem. It still displayed images from York's memory. The man suddenly reached out to the machine, and savagely twisted one of the knobs. The screen rippled crazily, and York let out a horrendous scream of pain that echoed through the immense hall. The fighter smiled in satisfaction, and turned the knob back to its former position.

"What are you doing?" howled York, his eyes streaming with tears. "Are you out of your mind? Let me loose."

The fighter looked at him scornfully.

"I told you to wait for me with the kids you captured. You were expected to extract information from them—not they from you! Where are they?"

The shock that York experienced could be felt all the way to the tunnel where the children were hiding.

"George?" York's face was a study in stupefaction. "You? You're my partner? But you questioned me in the capacity of a Babel official." A spark of hope glinted in his eye. "Hey, partner, cut me loose. We've got to catch Flint and those kids. They're netters, and we need to find their operator."

"Did you get any information from them?"

"No. There wasn't time. That nasty netter, Flint, had a freezer concealed in his jeans, and he overcame my own netters. He can change his shape. He's somewhere around here in the guise of a green demon. And there's another accomplice—a young boy, eleven or twelve at most. Probably a netter, too."

"Did you see where they went? Do you know where they could be in this damned place?"

"No. They covered my head with a hood when the alarm went off. But I can identify Flint—I know exactly what he looks like."

"What does he look like?" asked the fighter, a look of revulsion on his face.

"Let me loose!" insisted York impatiently. The fighter raised a quizzical eyebrow and twisted the knob on the machine again. York screeched.

"STOP! He's a green demon with short horns and a flowery shirt. Get me out of here!"

"All in due time," said the man. "What do the kids look like?"

York gave a brief description of Maggie, Troy and Adam. The two hidden youngsters sighed in relief when they heard him describe the masks they wore at Roller-net.

"But here I've seen only the two older ones, and they've got demon masks on." York began to beg. "Partner—please untie me. I have no further information. I thought you'd have a friendlier attitude after working with me for so many years. I always did everything you said, and I earned millions of dollars for you."

"You're totally worthless," barked the fighter angrily. He slapped York sharply across the face. "Your job is now over. You were supposed to run the amusement park and bring me the profits. Who asked you to compose that last virus? All you needed to do was follow orders—but no, you had to have ideas of your own! For your information, I got you into the NET when you suffered from NET-phobia, and I caused you to remain trapped here in the NET. Your body is no more than a slab of meat on Earth, you despicable worm, and I shall see to it that it's permanently disconnected!" He touched his helmet lightly, and the golden rays surrounded him immediately.

York desperately struggled to release himself, but his efforts were all futile. The fighter calmly pointed his rifle barrel to York's head and pulled the trigger. The head burst open for a split second, and then York vanished with a muffled 'poof'.

"I think I'm going to be sick." Maggie gagged and turned away, holding her hand over her mouth. Her body trembled violently, and her eyes were filled with tears.

"He's a murderer and a sadist!" whispered Troy in sheer horror. "We've got to get away before he finds us. Take a deep breath, Maggie—and then let's run!"

Maggie inhaled deeply and calmed down. They sprinted down into the tunnel. It was quite narrow, and mildly inclined downward. The pungent odor of sulphur permeated the air, and the heat bordered on the unbearable.

They were soon far from the meager light that came through the fissures in the blocked entrance, and found themselves in pitch-black darkness. Maggie turned on her trekking flashlight. The tunnel seemed to be heading endlessly into the bowels of the earth.

"York's been killed in the NET, and his body disappeared with a 'poof',," stated Troy, the ghastly scene of York's split head still vivid in his mind. "That confirms without a doubt that he was a surfer and not a netter."

"A surfer with nowhere to return to." Maggie's voice reflected her deep dismay. "But I don't want to talk about him now. I doubt whether I'll be able to sleep in the next few days."

They continued running for a few more minutes, and then slowed down to a quick walk. The paved floor now became a dirt path. After half an hour of quick marching they arrived at a pile of rocks that completely blocked the tunnel, and reached up to the ceiling.

"This must be the rock pile that Flint mentioned," said Maggie. "Let's find the opening above it."

They climbed up the stack of rocks and examined the ceiling carefully. It was quite smooth, and the flashlight showed no crack or opening. After several minutes of searching, they began to have doubts.

"Perhaps there's another pile of stones," suggested Maggie. "This ceiling is sheer, and has no openings."

"Not likely," said Troy, who stood on the apex of the pile, his head just a few inches below the ceiling. "Maybe the opening is a bit further away from the tip of the pile." He angrily thumped the ceiling with his fist, and to his surprise it rose a bit.

"Here it is!" he called. "It cannot be seen at all. I stumbled on it by pure luck."

Troy pushed the ceiling, and a round cover swung upward on hinges and slammed down in the other direction. He clambered into the hole, and found himself in a dim cave. A faint light shone in the distance.

"Come on up, take my hand." He stretched his hand from the hole. "There's a light far away—it's probably the exit Flint talked about."

Maggie grabbed his hand and climbed into the cave. She shone her flashlight and they saw they were in a tunnel, perpendicular to the one they had just left, and much wider.

"Shouldn't we first conceal that hole?" she said. "Even if the aliens find the first tunnel, they'll never find this one."

"Excellent idea!"

They both went back to the pile of rocks. They cleared some stones away from the side of the tunnel, and made the continuation of the tunnel accessible. They hoped that if the invaders came this way, they would assume that their prey had continued down the tunnel. They then clambered up the mass of stones, entered the upper tunnel, and shut the cover over the hole.

The light that Troy had seen was very faint, like the glimmer of a star at night. They carefully proceeded in that direction with their freezers gripped in their hands. The tunnel went on in a straight line. It took several long minutes before the light began to brighten and take on a gray-silvery hue. As they neared it, they saw that it radiated from a point in the ceiling, a hundred feet away.

"I'll go first and see what that light is," whispered Troy. "Then you'll join me. No need for both of us to take risks."

"I'm coming with you." Maggie's voice sounded fatigued. "Nothing in Hell could be worse than those aliens."

They arrived at the lighted area, and to their amazement discovered a round hole in the ceiling through which a gray sky could be seen. Metal rungs, imbedded in the wall, led up to the hole.

53. NET: Day 37, 04:25

Sven Thorensen skimmed down the long list of names on Lynn's computer screen.

"I understand that they are all equally suspect," he said. "Also, that there's the possibility that all of them are clean and the party we're looking for isn't in the list at all. Do you really wish to check the behavioral details of every single pair of siblings since Tipman's abduction, over a NET month ago?"

"No, that's way too ambitious," said Lynn, "and will take too much time.

We will use Og's resources to help us with the statistical cross sections, but I feel that only we can identify something totally different, if it exists. I've already run the list through Og, and no exceptions were found."

"How many pairs do we have here?" asked Sven.

"Eight hundred and twelve pairs of geniuses, in alphabetical order."

"I'll take the first four hundred," said Sven. "Wouldn't it go faster if you had more analysts working on the list? It is high priority, after all."

"I need Norman's approval to bring more people in," said Lynn. She hesitated for a moment and then added, "He's out with George. Any idea where they might be?"

A strange look of discomfort flitted across Sven's face, but it disappeared at once, and the tall man's voice was calm.

"No idea whatever. Probably concerning the interrogation of suspects, if George is in on it. I'll be in my room—send me the list and I'll tackle it right away."

By the time Sven got to his room the list was already on his computer screen. He glanced at the first entry. Sixteen-year-old Henri Albert and his eleven-year-old brother Francois. Francois' mass closely matched that of Chimpo, the Pira-net chimpanzee. His elder brother was a professional surfer, and a brilliant Go player. The pair definitely fitted the search criteria.

Let's find out where the little brother was when the apes roamed Spindler's site.

Sven got authorization to access the NET logs, and started following Francois' whereabouts. At the time of the Spindler break in, the coordinates in the log showed he was surfing at the main tetrosaur corral in the desert surrounding Netville.

Looks like he's clear . . . But the chimp left no traces on the NET logs. I have to verify this 'alibi' from an additional source.

Sven dialed a code number on his 'com.

"Tetrosaur Corral, how may I help you?" The smile of the female netter at the exchange was pleasant and friendly.

"I'd like to speak with the manager, please," said Sven. "I am Agent Sven Thorensen from Babel."

"Please hold." Her voice was calm and unruffled. Netters, contrary to most surfers, were not nervous when talking to Babel officers. A few seconds later an elderly man wearing a trainer's helmet appeared on the screen. His long face was framed by a thin gray beard.

"I am Luigi, the manager of this corral. May I see your ID, please?"

Sven gave his particulars to the manager, evidently a surfer, and a verification code. The manager disappeared from the screen, and was back in ten seconds.

"Thank you for your patience. How may I assist you, Agent Thorensen? I am not aware that any problem exists with the tetrosaurs."

"I need to verify the whereabouts of a certain Francois Albert. Was he visiting the corral at the day and time you now have on your computer?"

"I thought you guys could check out the location of anyone at any time," grumbled Luigi. "Please wait." The screen went dark for a couple of minutes and then the man reappeared. "Yes, he was here. It was his turn to take care of Rosario, the Pally tetrosaur. That's the school he attends. One of the trainers here has positively identified him."

"Thank you." Sven hung up. The first pair had taken him twelve minutes. At this rate it meant over eighty consecutive hours of work. He glanced at the list, and quickly browsed through it again. Suddenly his heart skipped a beat. One of the names was familiar. The older brother was younger than the sixteen-to-thirty range they were investigating, but the couple was flagged because the younger brother matched the Spindler technician's mass at 99.5%! A chill started to spread over his body.

"Troy Bentley," he muttered to himself. "I sincerely hope that you and your brother are not involved in this. And for your own sake, I hope you haven't dragged my Maggie into it."

54. NET: DAY 37, 04:55

"That's curious," commented Maggie. "The first tunnel we were in led downward from the depths of Hell, which was pretty deep underground to begin with. And yet, here we are at ground level, without hardly any climbing."

They had just ascended the metal rungs and surfaced on the ground. A hot breeze was blowing, and the acrid smell of smoke was in the air. The light was rather dim, and the skies were gray, as though covered by a thick layer of clouds. The earth all around them was seared, and looked like a raging fire had occurred there at some earlier point in time. Opposite them, and all along the horizon, were thick woods with unfamiliar trees. Behind them was a similar forest. Far to their left was a stone wall, reminiscent of the bulwarks of ancient fortresses. The wall stretched in both directions into the forests, concealing its ends. To their right was a low, white hill.

"Maybe this is another exit to our NET planet from the NETfold that contains Hell," said Troy. "We are probably in the random territories. We could be thousands of miles away from the inhabited areas."

"Well, theoretically we could be anywhere in the entire universe," retorted Maggie. "Not necessarily on our planet. Somebody lives here, probably Hell's residents. They must also use this exit, otherwise there wouldn't be a ladder there."

"I can't think of anything we can do against the invaders," said Troy. "We've got to find Flint. If anyone can stop them or get us out of here, he's the one."

"I only hope he wasn't hurt. If he was killed, he's lost all his memories of this surf, and he won't know of the aliens' invasion into Hell. He won't even know where we are."

"Well—he said to wait here. However, I think that the best way to find out what's going on, is to find a demon and ask it. Perhaps it could even point us the way to Flint." Troy began climbing the white hill, and Maggie followed close behind. "We'll be able to see better from the top of this hill."

The hill was made of soft, white chalk and was an easy climb. From the top they saw a wide, green plain with a stone wall, similar to the one on the other side, going across its far side. The plain was subdivided into rectangular sections, each with a different kind of vegetation.

"This looks like where they grow food for Hell's residents," said Troy. "It seems that Flint built an entire ecosystem here."

"It would make more sense to assume that he found most of this ready made, and just added his demons and other creatures," said Maggie. "That forest over there seems pretty ancient to me. Say—there's a demon over there by the forest. It's carrying a wounded demon on its back. It looks like—Troy! Look! Could that be Flint?"

Troy's gaze followed Maggie's pointing finger. A red demon, half of its right foot missing, was limping toward the forest. On its back was a motionless green demon in jeans and a flowery shirt.

"Yes!" shouted Troy. "It's Flint! He's hurt." Without waiting for Maggie he sprinted down the hill toward the red demon and its inert load. Maggie followed him at a quick walk, too tired to run. The demon saw them approaching, but continued its trudge into the forest.

"Wait!" yelled Troy. "We're friends of Flint!" The demon glanced toward him, but didn't stop. It entered the woods on a narrow pathway. Troy arrived at the path two minutes later, and plunged into the forest.

"Wait—" his voice was jarred to silence. A concealed rope was stretched at ankle height between two trees. Troy tripped and sprawled onto the ground. The crippled demon was on his back at once, twisting his arm behind is back.

"You brought soldiers to kill us!" it said in a gravelly voice, the fury unconcealed. It tied Troy's hands behind his back with a leather strap, and Troy yelped in pain as the bonds bit into his flesh. "They killed Flint, our prophet. You shall pay now."

The demon grabbed Troy by the feet and began dragging him into the woods. A slight rustle from the pathway revealed Maggie, with a freezer in her hand.

"Watch out, Maggie!" hollered Troy. "There's a trip rope across the path!"

Maggie halted. She located the rope, skipped over it deftly, and approached the red demon and the boy.

"Let go of him immediately, or die," she said to the demon, pointing the freezer at him. The demon let go of Troy's legs, and turned to face Maggie with a sly look on its face, its hand sliding into a pocket in its fur.

"Don't move!" ordered Maggie. The demon's hand stopped where it was.

"Sit down on the ground. Over there." Maggie kept her eyes on the demon at all times, as she sidled her way between it and Troy. "Now listen carefully. We are friends of Flint. We can help you. Where did you leave him?"

The demon started wailing. "He is further along the path. But he's *dead!*" It buried its head in its hands and started rocking back and forth. "What shall we do? What shall we do without him?"

Maggie wavered for a moment, and then decided she could not afford to take any chances. She froze the demon, and it toppled to the ground. She then went to Troy and used her laser knife to untie him. They looked silently at each other, and continued up the path.

Flint lay on his back in the middle of the path, a serene expression on his face.

"I see no signs of injury," said Troy, his voice choked. "Perhaps he died of asphyxiation or radiation poisoning." He knelt by the body and took one of its hands. It was as cold as ice. Maggie knelt on Flint's other side and took his other hand.

"He's as chilly as an iceberg!" she said. "Also, he looks too calm for a corpse. I think a freezer was used on him."

She got out her freezer, toggled it to Unfreeze, and fired at the inert body. The demon shifted uneasily on the ground, opened its eyes, and jumped suddenly to its feet.

"Where are the Babel fighters?" it called. He then looked around, and asked sheepishly, "Where are we?"

"Flint! You're alive!" Troy jumped up and flung both his arms around the demon in a bear hug. Tears of joy flooded his eyes. "They didn't get you."

"It'll take more than Babel agents to kill me," said the demon, trying to keep a steady voice. "I'm all right—I think."

"How come you got frozen," asked Maggie, wiping tears of relief from her eyes. "The attackers had laser rifles, but we never saw them use freezers."

"Well, I had a . . . kind of . . . accident," said Flint, embarrassed to the core. "When I saw the Babel fighters, I drew out my freezer and entered a tunnel to gather reinforcements. The fighters saw me and fired in my direction. A shot hit the ceiling above me, and one of the rocks that rained down on me hit my hand, causing me to pull the trigger. Unfortunately, the freezer was aimed at myself at that very moment. I froze myself. The next thing I knew was waking up beside you two a few moments ago."

"You clumsy demon," Maggie hugged Flint and kissed his creased cheek.

"You scared us to death. I must say I prefer you as a bear. You know that the demons thought you—"

"—were dead." Flint completed the sentence. "I guessed as much. They had never seen freezers before, and they must have assumed that I'd been killed. You saved me from being buried alive. Now tell me what happened to you and how you escaped."

Maggie related the events of the battle in the hall, while Troy went to unfreeze the injured demon. She described the aliens' shields, the demise of York, and how they fled and got to the surface. Flint was flabbergasted.

"So the aliens take over humans. And they're after us. And they're sadists. This is far worse than I could have imagined in my darkest dreams, if I ever slept. Shh, quiet now, I don't want that poor demon to hear any of this."

The limping demon approached Flint, a look of rapture on its face. Troy was close behind.

"Our prophet! You live!" it cried. "Let's return and kill the unbelievers now!"

"Later," said Flint. "Your job now is to stay here on the edge of the woods, and warn us if the intruders appear. Do not try to attack them—it is quite futile. We shall go deeper into the woods to re-organize ourselves."

He turned to Troy and Maggie.

"Hurry now. The aliens may find their way here, just as you did."

The trio walked quickly into the forest.

"Just where are we?" asked Maggie.

"On the upper part of Hell. This is where the NETfold containing Hell ends. I don't know yet whether this place is on our planet or in some other location in space and time. There's a wall all around it and nothing outside the wall. You get to the edge and find yourself back where you began. And that's how I found it."

"So where are we going?" asked Troy.

"There is another entrance to Hell on the other side of the woods. About another ten minute's walk. I intend to enter Hell again from there and catch the invaders off-guard."

"I honestly believe it would be better to get out of here and back to the NET," said Maggie. "Those aliens are equipped with impenetrable shields. Nothing you do can harm them."

"You said that they take over humans," said Flint. "And that they masquerade as humans in the NET. Well, if surfers can die in the NET so can they. I have learned from you that, contrary to a human surfer, their bodies remain in the NET. Which leads me to believe that once an alien is killed in the NET, he is really finished—he doesn't return to any human host on Earth."

"Makes sense," agreed Troy. "Maybe we've found the way to eliminate them. Do you have any more traps to which we can lure the invaders?"

"I do," said Flint, "but they won't work through those protective shields, as you described them."

"Could we possibly try drowning them?" suggested Troy. "Those shields certainly prevent harm from any physical attack and laser rays, but I doubt if they supply oxygen to their wearers. Without oxygen, the aliens will die."

"I don't have a secret well for that purpose," said Flint. "But I have another idea. A special escape exit from Hell where I have prepared a unique booby-trap. We've got to hurry—it's a long way to that exit."

They arrived at the edge of the forest, and Flint signaled them to stop. He scouted the vicinity—not a demon or fighter could be seen.

"All clear," he said. "Follow me."

They left the forest and walked alongside it several paces, until they arrived at a tall tree, larger than any of its neighbors. Flint then returned to the woods and halted by a black boulder. Troy and Maggie stopped beside him.

"This is the secret entrance. Help me move this boulder."

Together they pushed the rock to one side. Under it was a deep, dark pit with smooth walls. Troy and Maggie could not make out the bottom of the pit.

"So how do we get down?" asked Troy.

"This entrance was intended only for the use of winged creatures," explained Flint. "The pit is very deep indeed. I shall carry you both."

"It still doesn't figure," said Troy. "Here we are, about to drop a very long way into the earth, when all it took for us to get out of that place was a short ladder."

"Frankly, I haven't quite figured it out myself," admitted Flint. "Mass is distorted in several directions around here. Be that as it may, this entrance leads to my secret arsenal. I hope the aliens haven't found it yet. Let's go!"

He enfolded Troy and Maggie tightly in his arms, and jumped in. They accelerated rapidly. Troy could not see the bottom in the faint light that came from the opening above.

"Flint—"

"Don't worry, I'm in control. I can see in the dark and the bottom is getting close. I'll be slowing down shortly," said Flint. "Prepare yourselves. Another five seconds, four . . . now!"

He spread his wide wings and their hurtling descent was arrested suddenly. They spiraled down slowly and landed on the bottom of the pit—a round metal platform studded with handles and bolts. Flint released the children, and lay full length on the floor, his eye screwed up to a tiny peephole.

"It's empty," he said. "We can go in." He got up and pulled on one of the handles. A heavy iron cover creaked open on rusty hinges. Looking down, they saw a semi-spherical vault that could fit a three-story building, dimly lit from a hole in the ceiling. A tunnel led in from one side and out the opposite one.

Flint grabbed the children once again, and jumped into the vault. He glided gently down and landed on the rocky ground near one of the tunnel exits. He released the children and pushed a large stone in the wall a few feet away from the tunnel entrance. The stone rotated like a door, revealing a narrow passage.

"They haven't been here," he whispered. "Quickly now—follow me."

They entered the passageway and shut the stone door behind them. Pitch-black darkness engulfed them and Maggie turned on her flashlight. They saw Flint disappearing around one of the bends and followed him hurriedly. The passage turned and twisted upward along a mild slope. Finally, they came upon a gate, which completely shut off the passage. A shining device, with glowing numbers and a keypad, was fixed into the gate. Flint stabbed a few numbers into the device, and the gate swung away from them. Maggie shone her flashlight around, and they saw they were in a small room with smooth, white walls, which were covered with shelves. Long metal boxes were stacked on the shelves. Flint opened one of the boxes and took out several objects that resembled large buttons. Each button had two bumps on it—one red and one yellow, protected by some transparent, synthetic substance.

"These are powerful bombs, or grenades if you will," explained Flint, stuffing a handful of the buttons into a pocket in his jeans. "One of these could blow down the ceiling of the passageway we just came through. Pressing the red bump turns it into a grenade that detonates after a three-second delay. And pressing the yellow bump turns the button into a booby-trap. After three seconds, the button primes itself, and is ready to detonate if it detects any motion within ten feet."

"How on earth did you obtain this vast stockpile?" asked Troy. "Did you rob a Babel depot?"

"Not exactly," said Flint. "Everything you see here was taken from a clandestine warehouse belonging to the NET Development Enterprises. I have evidence that one of the employees there is actually a Mafia member— he built this illegal warehouse. He would steal explosives from the company and convert it into this ammunition, which the Mafia uses routinely in their line of business. Anyway, I never heard of anyone complaining to the NET authorities." He pointed to several weapons on a nearby shelf. "Neither did they complain about those missing freezers and laser pistols."

Troy and Maggie equipped themselves with modern-looking laser pistols.

"Where to now?" asked Troy.

"Out," replied Flint. "Maggie is right. I'd be happy to do away with the invaders, but I don't know how. We've got to get out of here and re-think the whole thing. After we escape, I intend to blow up the passage from Hell to the NET. I don't think that'll stop them, but it may buy us a couple of hours. Follow me."

They returned toward the vault. Flint stopped short before the entrance and peeked through a slit in the stone door. The vault was bathed in a golden light, which emanated from the helmet of a tall fighter, who stood in its center. Flint brought a finger to his lips, silencing the children.

The warrior carried a large pack on his back, and a laser rifle in his hands. He gazed silently at the walls of the vault. Noticing the faint light from above, he looked up and saw the open hole in the ceiling. With a sharp motion he drew a stick-like object from his backpack, and extended the ends, as one would open a telescope. The stick was now a pole, as long as a man's height, with a short cross bar on each side. The fighter placed the cross bars on the ground and, still holding onto the pole, stepped onto them. A blue flame shot down out of the bottom of the pole lifting it, with the warrior, into the air. He passed through the hole in the ceiling and disappeared from view.

Flint waited for a few seconds in case the fighter returned. He then turned to the children.

"Now's the time to escape," he whispered. "I have just watched an invader out there, and he flew through the hole in the ceiling. He has some kind of personal flying contraption. Come on, we've got to hurry before he gets back."

They entered the vault and shut the stone door behind them.

"Wait here a moment," whispered Flint, and with a few strong beats of his wings flew up to the hole in the ceiling. He attached one of his black buttons on the wall of the vent above, pressed the yellow bump, and dived back to the children.

"That way is now blocked!" he declared. "If the alien tries to return, he'll activate the bomb, destroying the funnel, and he'll probably be buried in the debris. But let's not wait for him—we're out of here!"

He led them at a brisk pace to the tunnel entrance at the far side of the vault. Entering it, they walked past several smaller tunnels that intersected theirs from both sides. They soon came to a crossing with another tunnel, as large as the one they were in. Flint turned left, with Troy and Maggie following. They had barely made the turn when a hollow explosion sounded behind them.

"Hurry!" whispered Flint urgently. "That was the fighter who flew upward from the vault. He returned and triggered the button charge. The others will now converge on this area. You run ahead. Just a short way from here, on your right, there's a niche with a curtain. Hide there—you'll be safe. Don't leave the niche until I come for you. This is the way out, so I've got to draw their attention away from this area. Just wait patiently. I'll be back."

Flint ran off in the other direction.

Troy and Maggie walked along the tunnel, feeling the wall on their right until they found the niche. The curtain was drawn shut, and concealed the niche completely. If they hadn't expected it to be there, they would never have located it. They jostled in and drew the curtain shut again. Maggie turned off her flashlight, and the darkness was total. They sat in silence.

A short while later they heard heavy footsteps approaching. Even though the curtain was nearly absolutely opaque, they saw the shiny shadow of a person passing by, holding a rifle in one hand and a flashlight in the other. It continued on its way without noticing the curtain.

About a minute later, an explosion was heard far off. The shadowy figure passed by again, at a run and in the opposite direction. Another explosion sounded, this one even further. A few minutes later two more explosions came, but they were much fainter than the last one. Then total silence reigned.

After what seemed like an eternity, the curtain was drawn aside, and Flint shone a small flashlight into the niche. He signaled them to maintain silence with a finger on his mouth, and they stepped quietly after him down the tunnel. Fifteen minutes of quick walking brought them to an iron and wood portcullis, which blocked the passage.

Flint halted his companions a few steps before the massive obstruction. He bent down and lifted the edge of a thin, plastic carpet off the ground. Shining his light downward, they saw that the carpet covered a deep abyss. A dim red light flickered way below them.

"Lava," whispered Flint, pointing down. He replaced the carpet corner, and it blended into the floor with extreme precision, merging with the rocky ground without a flaw. It was impossible to make out the gorge under it. Flint waved them to the wall on their right, on which little metal handholds had been riveted, along with foot depressions.

"Cross carefully," he whispered. "But hurry. There's no time left."

Troy approached the wall, grasped the nearest handholds, his face to the wall, and gingerly stepped sideways all the way to the portcullis. He grabbed one of the wooden beams and hung on. Maggie quickly joined him.

Suddenly they saw a faint light bobbing from the direction they had come from, accompanied by the sound of running footsteps. Flint took four steps backward, ran forward, and with a Herculean leap spanned the covered chasm and hooked himself onto the portcullis. The footsteps came nearer, and the weaving light brighter.

Flint took a small key from his pocket, and jabbed it into a hole in the wall. The portcullis began to rise, and they all scrambled down to the ground and rolled forward underneath it.

"Run!" shouted Flint.

He pulled the key from the wall, and the portcullis began descending.

Troy and Maggie were just about to sprint into the tunnel, when the powerful beam of a flashlight locked on all three. The muffled voice of a woman spoke to them.

"Stop right where you are! One move, and I'll shoot!"

A tall woman stepped into view. She had a yellow helmet on, which beamed golden rays around her body. The rifle she held pointed directly at the trio, and they halted promptly.

Troy, who was near to the bend in the tunnel, began a slow step backward. A searing bolt of heat slammed into the wall behind him, melting it.

"Don't even move a hair! Next time I'll aim lower . . ." The women touched her helmet and the golden halo faded away, showing for a long second her beautiful face and long blonde hair. She walked toward them. "Finally! So that's what you look like." Her voice was much clearer, now that her shield was down. "A demon and two disguised children. How quaint. Put your hands over your heads where I can see them. Now go over to the wall, and place your hands . . . AYEEEE—"

Her speech was cut short as the ground gave way beneath her weight. With a terrified scream she disappeared into the abyss, the rifle in her hand firing upward pointlessly and melting parts of the ceiling.

Flint moved like lightning. He took two button bombs from his pocket, activated one by pressing the red bump, and threw it after the falling woman. He then pressed the yellow bump of the other button and hurled it over and beyond the chasm into the tunnel.

"Run down the tunnel," he yelled. "Her comrades will be on us in no time."

The deafening boom of the explosion from within the crevasse preceded the shower of rocks and embers that flew out of it. The trio ran through the tunnel as fast as they could. It ended abruptly in a round cavern with an iron ladder leading upward through a hole in the ceiling. Climbing the ladder, they found themselves in another cavern that had steep stone stairs leading upward. At that point another explosion rocked the walls, and dust rose all around.

"My delayed detonation bomb worked," said Flint, in a tense voice. "Meaning that someone got within ten feet from it. The tunnel there is probably blocked, and perhaps another alien was killed. The explosion will hinder them for enough time for me to seal the entrance hermetically. The NETfold ends here, and if I close it properly they won't be able to pass through. Wait for me at the top of the stairs. If I don't show up in ten minutes, go on without me."

Flint hauled up the ladder from the lower level, set a button bomb for delayed explosion, and tossed it into the cavern they had just climbed out of. He then hurriedly closed the lid over the hole. The lid had an electronic locking mechanism on it, identical to the device he had installed in the original time fold. Flint programmed it, his fingers flying frantically over the keypad.

Troy and Maggie climbed the steep stone stairs. It was a difficult ascent, and the toils of the day were taking their toll. They walked slowly, breathing heavily, but did not stop to rest.

After five minutes, when both of them were exhasted, the stairs finally ended and they reached a metal panel. Troy pushed it, and it revolved on a vertical axis. Going through, they found themselves in a typical Netville maintenance tunnel. The panel closed behind them, and Troy noticed that there was no way of opening the panel from the side he was now on. It was a smooth, metallic surface, identical to all the thousands of panels lining the tunnel. Nothing indicated that behind it was an entrance to convoluted passageways, and a sprawling subterranean world.

"We're in the NET!" crowed Troy joyfully. "I'd like to know where exactly in Netville we are, but I'm exhausted. I'll rest a bit here until Flint arrives." He lay on the ground, one arm underneath his head, and fell asleep instantly. Maggie sat wearily beside him, her back leaning against the wall, trying with all her might to stay awake.

It wasn't a long wait. Less than three minutes later, she heard footsteps approaching and the panel opened again. Flint's head poked out and carefully surveyed the tunnel. A tender look appeared on his demonic face when he saw Troy asleep. He came through the opening, reached out toward Troy and shook him roughly. The boy jumped to his feet, alarmed, in a defensive karate stance.

"Relax, it's only me," said the demon lightly. "We're not done yet. We've escaped from Hell, but we need to get back to your site. It's about five minutes to the nearest Transport Box." He looked at Maggie, who seemed at the end of her rope. "Just one more little effort."

The news seemed to have brought new energy into the children, and they followed Flint eagerly. His estimate was somewhat optimistic, and it took them seven minutes to reach the end of the tunnel. They emerged in a schoolyard under renovations. There wasn't anyone to witness the strange trio, and they got into the Transport Box unobserved. They immediately jumped to Troy's site.

"I don't know what your plans are, boys," said Maggie, "but I've got to rest. Flint, wake me in an hour, please. Earlier if the end of the world arrives—I wouldn't want to miss that."

She tottered into Troy's bedroom, flopped onto the bed, and was asleep before her head hit the pillow.

Troy yawned. "Computers may not need any rest, but humans do. I'm going to get some sleep, too. Wake me at the same time you wake Maggie. But gently, please—not like last time. And please turn into a dragon again— it suits you much better. Anyway, it looks like your inferno just went to, umm, hell."

"Want me to do anything while you're asleep?"

"No. Just wait and watch the news board. Wait—come to think of it, it may be a good idea to fetch Adam here. And tell him everything. I think he can help us." Troy curled up on the couch in the guest room, and was fast asleep in seconds.

55. NET: Day 37, 08:00

"Good morning." Troy felt a firm hand shake him gently. He opened his eyes and saw a green dragon with a grave look on its face. He yawned, stretched his limbs, and stood up.

"What time is it? What's going on?"

"Maggie and you have slept for two hours," said Flint. "I thought you both could use the rest. She got up on her own just a minute ago. They're waiting for you in the workroom."

"They?"

"Adam's here, too, as you requested. I've filled him in with all the recent events."

Troy nodded in approval. His young brother had proved himself more than worthy at Roller-net, and was certainly capable of contributing brilliant ideas. As Troy entered the workroom he saw Adam and Maggie by the table, drinking hot Choco-net. A steaming mug of Choco-net was waiting for him, too.

"Thanks—I needed this," said Troy, taking a sip. He sat down next to Maggie, who still looked tired.

"Troy!" Adam's voice shook in consternation. "It's very dangerous to surf now. The aliens steal human identities and, hey, who knows what's happening to them."

"Take it easy, now," said Flint, stroking the boy's hair with his big hand. "Those aliens aren't around here for the moment." He looked at Troy. "I'm afraid that revealing everything to Adam was pretty traumatic for him, and he hasn't fully recovered. What do you suggest we do now? You must have had something in mind when you called for Adam."

"As a matter of fact, I do," said Troy. "But first I'd like a rundown on the situation to date. What happened, whom have we seen, and what have we learned about the invaders. Flint, did you see any additional fighters?"

"No, I don't think so." Flint scratched his head with the point of his tail. "Well, I'm not sure. I did see a man and a woman when I first escaped, and then I saw another tall one, and then the same woman again who almost caught us."

"That woman is a prominent businesswoman," said Maggie. "Her name is Maureen Clarke. She manages a gigantic energy corporation. Do you think she was killed?"

"I believe she was," replied Troy. "Her protective shield was off. And Flint threw a bomb down the pit after her that, I trust, finished the job. What say you, Flint?"

"Yes, I think she won't trouble us any more." The dragon blew a smoke cross from its left nostril, which Troy duly ignored. "Even if she managed to turn her shield on fast enough during her fall, the bottom of that pit is pure lava. It would be very difficult to get out of the molten rock, so she probably suffocated. And will eventually become a stone statue, if that lava ever hardens. However," added the dragon, sucking in the smoky cross into its other nostril, "we can't really tell with these aliens, can we? Anything's possible. Maybe she escaped somehow, despite everything."

"That's right," said Troy. "We mustn't assume anything, the woman's demise included, until we have certain proof. At least we know who she is on Earth, and we can bring about her disconnection from the NET." He took another sip of Choco-net and went on. "The only one we're certain of is that first fighter—the one who transformed into the alien's real shape. He is definitely dead. He, too, was not a Babel official. He is a renowned geneticist called Noah Atkinson. I remember seeing a recording of his, concerning research of the human DNA. So far, I see no pattern to the people the aliens are overtaking. Maggie, did you identify any other warrior? What about the stocky one?"

"York called him George, and tagged him as a Babel agent," said Maggie. "I don't know him, but I do know that there is a George in Babel. He's the one that interrogated York in Roller-net."

Adam butted in. "George? Short, broad, with thick, black hair?" he asked.

"Yes." Troy's eyes widened. "Do you know him, Adam?"

"He's from Babel, all right. He was at Spindler's site with a young woman. I saw them there. Maybe she was the same Maureen—slender figure, long red hair . . ."

"No, that's not her. But wait a minute—you visited Spindler's site?" Troy's eyes widened even further. "How in hell did you get there?"

"He got there through the maintenance tunnels," said Flint. "Disguised as an electrician. He escaped from being caught by Babel by the skin of his teeth."

"And how come you're so well informed?" Troy asked Flint. "Why am I kept in the dark? Are you shadowing Adam?"

"Flint isn't involved," intervened Adam. "I was surfing the NET yesterday evening after dinner, trying to find information on an item in the Gossipofon. At the site we saw . . . I've got it! Hey, I finally got it! I understand what Spindler was trying to write!" Adam became abnormally animated, and clapped his hands with excitement.

"What did you understand?" asked Troy. "If it doesn't concern the aliens, it'll have to wait. We're rather pressed for time."

"The aliens! The aliens!" Adam's face contorted in frustration and terror.

"Spindler tried to warn us about them! That's what he wrote!"

"Hang on there, Adam" said Flint. "I know about the entire incident from Og. Spindler did *not* leave a note or a letter."

"You don't understand," said Adam, waving his arms wildly. "Spindler left a message in his garden. The letters 'AL'. He yanked out plants from his flowerbed in that shape. We thought—and I'm sure Babel did, too—that he intended to write his name: Albert, or Al Spindler. Wrong! He was trying to write 'ALIENS'. He was trying to warn us, and was vaporized before he finished."

Troy, Flint and Maggie exchanged amazed glances.

"Well done, Adam!" exclaimed Troy. "Now *that's* an important piece of information. You have discovered another link in the chain of interesting events around us. It's apparent now that the aliens began to take over humans almost immediately upon their entry into the NET. And it looks like they're selecting key figures in the fields of energy, genetics, and security—except for Spindler, a regular programmer. We don't know how many more could be added to this list. We've got to find out what their goals are."

"Their first goal seems to have been to capture us," said Maggie. "That's what George said before killing York." Her face wrinkled in revulsion as the scene came back to her, and her hands began to tremble.

"Yes, that's pretty obvious," agreed Troy. "But do they know that we've blocked the exit to their world? I'm confident that even if they don't know, they suspect us." He watched Maggie in concern. "Did you identify the fourth fighter—the tall one that came in with George?"

"No. He was always behind that shining shield, so his features were never clear."

"Could be that it's the same one that levitated through the funnel onto Hell's surface," said Flint. "He detonated my bomb when he returned, but if his shield was on at the time he may not have been hurt."

"So, hey, optimally there are only two aliens left, one of them possibly wounded," said Adam. He counted them off on his fingers. "Four came in. One got shish-kebabbed, one fell into a volcano, and one got caught in a booby-trapped funnel. Hey, we're four against two at most! Let's get them!"

"Calm down, Adam," said Troy. "We must always expect the worst. There could be thousands of invaders in their spaceship. And they may have taken control of hundreds of people by now. We cannot trust anyone at present. We know almost nothing about them, except their real shape, and that they have highly potent weaponry and impenetrable shields."

"And that they can be killed," added Flint.

"And that they're sadists in the extreme," said Maggie. "It's really sad that the first intelligent race that we encounter is so horrible."

"That conclusion may be a bit premature," observed Troy. "It could quite be that they, like us, have good and bad individuals. George is the only alien to behave this way, and we know he was a criminal before being occupied by an alien—York's interrogation verified that. Maybe his personality wasn't altered."

He stood up, and leaned on the table.

"Here is what I think we should do. It could be dangerous, but everything is risky now, and most dangerous of all is not doing anything! We know for sure that Noah Atkinson is dead. Let's take a look into his NET site. We might find more information on the invaders—perhaps even how many they are and where they're located. Any scrap of info will do, and that's what we need right now."

"Cool!" said Adam. "It's our turn to attack them, now."

"Not attack, really," said Flint. "Just gathering information. Troy, that's a very smart idea; the aliens don't know whom they are facing!"

He got up and turned on Troy's computer console. He clicked several times on the keyboard, and got his response a few seconds later.

"Here we are. Noah Atkinson has an isolated site close to the laboratories of Genome Applications, where he worked. There are no netters at the site right now. His last two netters were sold a NET week ago."

"You missed out his shoe size and blood type," noted Maggie, getting to her feet. "Well, we'd better be armed. Not knowing what might wait for us there—perhaps even the alien headquarters."

"Absolutely," concurred Troy. "We've got to be prepared for anything and everything. But all of us can't go there. We'll split into two teams—Flint and I will visit the site, and you and Adam remain here and check for more irregularities in the NET."

Maggie bridled. "But I—" She thought better of it, and stopped herself. "All right. Just be careful and return soon. Call on the 'com if you'll be away for more than an hour. If you don't call within an hour, we'll be free to leave this site."

Troy addressed the dragon. "Flint, you've got to appear as a human. You'll be too conspicuous as a bear or a dragon. Now let's all break for a minute to return to Earth in order to retain all our memories up until now. Then come back here immediately."

They all jumped out of the NET and back in again at once. Flint was now the same blond youth that had been with them in Roller-net.

Troy and Flint armed themselves with freezers. Flint also packed a large laser pistol and several button bombs he had brought from Hell. They entered the portable Transport Box, and Flint tapped in the coordinates. The lights flickered. They found themselves on the edge of a sparse grove. Through the trees they saw a high wooden fence with a locked steel gate at its center.

56. NET: Day 37, 08:22

Maggie watched Adam, who had seated himself by Troy's computer and was skillfully scanning the latest news on the NET.

He's a first class professional, she thought. *His problem lies in being in the shadow of his elder brother, a celebrity. But when he overcomes that obstacle, he'll make quite a noise in is own right in the NET.*

Her thoughts returned to the invaders. If there's any future for the NET, now that the aliens are in it . . .

She remembered scenes of the battle in Hell, particularly when the fighter transmuted into a giant, with green stuff oozing out of holes in its body. She shuddered. *They mustn't take over Dad! He's the only one we can trust—he'll understand the situation.*

Maggie went into the next room and punched a number into her 'com. There was no picture, and the recorded voice of her father came out of the machine:

"This is Sven. Please leave a short message."

Maggie hesitated for a moment, and then hung up. She turned on the small backup computer that was in the room, entered the Anonymous Messages site, and keyed in her father's secret code. The system confirmed the code and prompted for a message—a message impossible to trace.

She quickly typed:

"Get George's help to solve the Barcelona problem. Call me for details."

She hit the Send key. Even though the message was sent anonymously, Sven would understand it. The puzzle she had solved during a competition in Barcelona was a special conundrum: a double agent was to be discovered from within a hundred intelligence agents, in a minimum number of questions. She was nine then, and had unveiled the double-crosser in the minimal number of questions, winning the first prize—the prestigious Oxford-net course for Riddles and Puzzles, a course which changed her life.

He won't discuss this with anyone before calling me. He may be the decisive factor in overcoming the aliens. If he kills George, and everyone sees that he actually was an alien, they'll come up with a solution. Like—the entire population must surf into the NET, and get killed there! Human surfers would return to Earth, but the aliens would be terminated!

She stared at her 'com impatiently.

Come on, Dad! Call! I need you!

57. NET: Day 37, 08:32

Sven re-examined Troy's movements in the NET for the tenth time. Troy was in the habit of surfing into his home site and staying there for long hours. Maggie visited him there from time to time, and stayed with him there for several hours, too. And in the recent few hours, the statistic tables showed that Adam, Troy's younger brother, entered the site. He, too, didn't leave the site.

What could they be doing at the same place for so long? Playing some kind of game?

Sven backed up to the time Spindler's site was infiltrated and focused on

Adam. He was at the site of a neighbor of the Bentley's, one Sigmund Klein, and never left the site. He was alone; the neighbor did not join him.

Let's look up this Klein fellow, and find out what's so special about his site.

He brought up Ziggy's profile, and nodded in wry satisfaction. The man had NET-phobia!

Why would a NET-phobic have a NET site? And let a little boy use it?

Sven decided to return to Earth and have a chat with this retired professor. But first he had to check one more angle. A somewhat unorthodox angle.

"Og," he said quietly. "I wish to break into an active surf."

Breaking into an active surf was similar to following a surfer, with the difference that the surfer did not know he was being followed. It involved remotely connecting to the surfer's helmet, and observing the NET through his eyes and ears. In all his years in Babel, Sven had never heard of even one case in which such a break in was performed.

"You may do so only in investigations assigned to Level Eight or higher," declared the computer. "Unless you obtained special permission from the unit's commander. What is the investigation code for which the information is needed?"

Sven provided the code for the Hell investigation, without expecting much of a result. The investigation was at Level Six when he received it, several hours ago. He was about to request Norman for authorization to continue when a green light went on in the corner of the screen.

"This investigation was escalated to Level Nine two minutes ago by the commander," announced Og. Level Nine was the highest level possible. "Break in authorized. To whom do you wish to connect?"

"Troy Bentley. His ID is on the list on the screen."

Sven's screen darkened for a moment. Then he saw Troy walking with a tall blond youth in a little copse. Looking at the NET monitor, his jaw dropped in amazement. Troy was registered on the monitor as occupying his home site at that very moment! And with two other surfers, neither of which was that unidentified youth. One of the two surfers was Adam. The other was Maggie.

Sven's 'com buzzed, and he answered automatically.

"Sven here."

"Sven, this is Norman. I need you here at once!" Norman's stern look and the urgency in his voice were unmistakable. "Drop everything and come to my office!"

58. NET: DAY 37, 08:35

"The wall surrounds Noah's site," said Flint. "I'd better go in there alone first, and you wait for me in the trees. There just might be an ambush. I'll give two frog croaks if the coast is clear, and you can join me then. If you sense any danger whatever, hop into the Transport Box and clear out. I'll manage."

"Okay. Be careful."

Flint scaled the wall as smoothly as a cat burglar, and disappeared. Troy waited impatiently until finally he heard Flint's double croak. With great effort, he managed to clamber over the wall, where Flint caught hold of him and helped him to his feet.

"The house is locked and dark. It looks uninhabited. There's a little structure in the back. It has no windows, and seems to be made of concrete. Could be a lab or a safe. It's locked, too. What say we break into there first? If there are any secret documents around, that would be the logical place to put them."

"Okay."

The little construction was flush with the rear wall of the house, and looked like some kind of shelter. The single door was made of heavy steel, and the only other aperture that could be seen in the concrete walls was a thin opening, high up near the roof, which was probably used for ventilation. Flint raised Troy onto his shoulders to peek into the slot, but nothing could be seen. Flint spent several minutes trying to break or jimmy the locked door, but nothing worked.

"We're running out of time," fidgeted Troy. "Use your laser pistol!"

"I trust the late Dr. Atkinson will forgive us," muttered Flint, pulling out his weapon. He shot a tight beam of pure energy at the lock on the door. The lock began to creak and hiss, and blisters formed on its surface. Molten metal began to drip to the ground. Flint put his pistol up close to the lock, ignoring the searing heat. Two minutes later the lock cracked open. Flint eased the door inward with his foot, his pistol ready for any surprise. They sidled carefully through the doorway, and Troy turned on the light.

"Help!" came a voice from the far corner of the room they were in—the only room in the structure. "Let me loose!" The corner was hidden from the doorway by a large metallic cabinet that practically partitioned the room into two.

"Careful now," whispered Flint. "Don't take any risks." Troy drew out his freezer, and they advanced warily toward the voice.

An unshaven and disheveled man sat on the floor behind the cabinet. He was dressed in a rumpled khaki outfit, and two crossed swords, the emblem of Babel, were embroidered on his shirt. His hands and feet were chained to the wall. His right cheek bore a welt, and some dried blood stained a corner of his mouth. Troy approached him suspiciously.

"Who are you, and what are you doing here?"

"I am Norman Starr, the commander of Babel. Aliens have invaded the NET and abducted me. Remove these shackles and let's escape before they return. They'll kill us all at the drop of a hat. The keys to these chains are in the cabinet."

"What a story!" Troy studied the person in front of him carefully. *He sounds sincere, but it could be an alien trap.* "Do you have any way to prove it? It's far more likely that you're an imposter who was discovered and locked—"

"I can't prove it to you now," said the prisoner. "I've been cloned, duplicated. Someone is now in Babel in my place. A sadistic Babel official, named George Boder, locked me up here. If I were setting a trap for you would I be chained up like this? And how would I have known you'd arrive, whoever you are? Listen boys, I can help you against these invaders."

"What do you mean, 'duplicated'?" Flint began to squeeze the trigger of his pistol.

"Wait! Don't shoot!" cried the man desperately. "These aliens invade the bodies of surfers. They must have had a failure of some sort in my case because I was attempting to leave the NET with my emergency ring exactly when the takeover was taking place. As a result I remained in the NET, while an alien, in a body identical in every way to mine, is at large."

"Flint, hold your fire." Troy's voice was authoritative. "I believe him. He looks and sounds honest. However, just to be on the safe side, one of us will remain behind him at all times with a freezer until we check him out with a T-scope at my site."

"Okay," assented Flint. He opened the cabinet, found the keys, and released the prisoner. "I, too, have a feeling that he's bona fide. Nevertheless, we've got to play it safe. We'll both watch out for him."

Flint assisted Norman in getting to his feet, supporting him when he stood. Troy stood by at the ready with a freezer.

"Thanks," said Norman. He flung his arms about and hopped alternately on each foot, trying to restore his circulation. "Give me a few seconds, and I'll be all right." He began to totter his way to the ruined door.

Troy rummaged in the cabinet and found a number of recording buttons. He showed them to Norman.

"Any idea what's in these?" he asked.

"No," said Norman. "I never saw them before."

"I'll take them anyway." Troy placed them in a pocket, and addressed Flint. "Are you going to leave them a farewell gift, as you did in Hell?"

"Why not?" said Flint. "A little memento won't do any harm. Please clear the area."

Norman went through the doorway, followed by Troy, still brandishing his freezer. Flint primed two bomb buttons, and placed them by the door. He jumped outside in a hurry, and quickly shut the door. With a satisfied grunt, he muttered: "I certainly hope that they won't be wearing their helmets when they come in to find out what happened."

"Let's go," said Troy. "You first, Norman."

They got to the gate, and Flint melted the lock with his laser pistol. On stepping outside, Norman was astounded to see the portable Transport Box standing in the grove by the gate. However, he said nothing.

The three of them crowded into the Box, Flint entered the coordinates, and they left the site.

59. NET: Day 37, 09:25

"Guys, I am deeply grateful to you for rescuing me." Norman regarded the four youngsters fondly. They were assembled around the large dining table in Troy's NET site living room, light drinks before each of them. Norman had washed his face, shaved, and combed his hair. "Now that you have verified my credibility, perhaps you'll tell me who you are and how you found me?" He peered at Maggie and wrinkled his brow. "I think I know you from somewhere."

Troy looked worried. "Before we answer your questions I'd like you to guarantee that none of us will get into trouble as a result. We all want to continue surfing in the NET, and to be exonerated if we inadvertently broke any of the rules."

"Well, I have no idea what you may have done in the past, and I have no jurisdiction over transgressions done on Earth. But I can promise you that any violation you may have done in the NET will be forgiven. After what happened today I'll recommend you to be honorary citizens of Netville. None of you will be banned from the NET. You have my word." He placed both his palms on the table and leaned forward. "Now tell me—who are you, what have you done, and what do you know? Also, how come you have these amazing new technologies? That portable Transport Box—do you know that our scientists have been working on designing one of them for years, and they don't even have a working prototype yet?"

Flint broke into a self-satisfied smirk, but kept his mouth shut after seeing Troy's warning look.

Troy unfolded the entire history of events to Norman, leaving out nothing. Norman listened, dumbfounded. When Troy described how Flint came into being, he turned sharply towards the latter and said:

"You're a computer? Unbelievable! You certainly look as human as any surfer I've met. Are you totally independent and reliable?"

"He is supposed to follow instructions," inserted Troy, before Flint could react to the question. "But sometimes he has his own way of interpreting them. As far as math is concerned, he is infallible." He glanced severely at Flint, just in time to prevent him from adding further commentary.

Troy continued his narrative. As he ended the description of the battle in

Hell, tears welled up in Norman's eyes, and he clasped each one of them by the hand warmly.

"You have done an amazing job! You've eliminated half of the invaders on your very own. George bragged to me that there were seven of them when they entered the NET. According to him, that was enough to overcome the entire population of Earth. One of them died when they attempted their first takeover—the Spindler case. Another is trapped inside the waterfall tunnel. Two more were killed in Hell. Which leaves us with only three left— George, my double, and a third alien we know nothing about."

"Why didn't George kill you after they took you over?"

Norman removed his shirt, and they gasped in horror to see the long red welts streaked over his back and chest. Some of the wounds still displayed dried blood along the scars.

"George is a sadist," he said. "He worked for me for a long time, and apparently hated my guts. Maybe because I didn't promote him at the pace he expected."

Norman took a long swallow from the glass of orange juice in front of him. "He kept me alive for the sole purpose of tormenting me. They didn't need any information from me—my double knows everything I know. Let's not go into details about what he did to me during those last three days." He turned to Maggie. "I still can't nail down where I know you from."

"My full name is Maggie Thorensen."

"Yes—now I remember! You're Sven's little girl! I saw you once, five years ago, at one of Babel's open conventions. My, you've grown since then. I hear that you're a puzzle champion."

"In a way," said Maggie modestly. "Troy and I participated in several contests. But please tell me—do you think the aliens have, you know . . ."

"No, I don't believe they have taken over your father. There just aren't enough of them. Furthermore, they don't need any more Babel officials. In fact, even George's takeover was superfluous, as far as they're concerned— catching me would have been enough. But they couldn't get to me any other way. George led me into a trap, where they jumped me."

Norman turned to Flint, his voice full of admiration.

"I see that you're actually competing with me in fighting viruses." He stood up and tried to straighten out his rumpled uniform. "I'd never have suspected you. You'll have to explain to me how you managed to build a site as huge as Hell without us noticing it. I am also beginning to believe that you're the only one who can help us overcome these aliens. Am I right in understanding that you can change shape at will in the NET? Factual or imaginary?"

"Not any shape," replied Flint. "It has to be a creature with a relatively large brain capacity. A human like you would be easy for me, and I could even replicate your features to the last cell. All, that is, except your brain's contents."

"There are a million questions I'm still dying to ask," said Norman. "But time is of the essence. Very soon they'll discover that I was released. My guess is that they're looking for you right now. I wonder if they have any idea who you are! Before I was abducted we didn't know a thing about you, except that you'd built the Hell site and that you lived in California, which is still a pretty large place to hunt in. Well, actually we had some more information from your visit to Spindler's site. We'd managed to narrow down the number of surfers matching the smaller technician to a few thousands." Norman squinted at Adam. "You were the chimpanzee technician, weren't you?"

Adam reddened and bobbed his head.

"You also corresponded with the Queen of the Night on the Pira-net, posing as Chimpo. Right?" He saw Adam become rigid, and added softly: "That was a mistake on your part. One of our agents managed to deduce, from the fragments of information you disclosed, that you live in the San Francisco area, and that you have a very smart older brother who built Hell. She had begun a survey on pairs of brothers who fit these criteria, and she's going to zero in on you pretty soon indeed. Therefore, we don't have much time."

Adam paled, and his voice quavered.

"I didn't reveal any significant information to the Queen of the Night. How could she have got so far—" He decided it would be best to change the topic. "Hey, about the aliens, if they're really so few of them left, we could surprise them. They're probably at either Maureen's or George's sites, and perhaps they're not wearing those helmets all the time. Hey, we could get there through the maintenance tunnels."

"Interesting idea," said Norman. "Probably Maureen's, since she has a huge estate bordering the desert, whereas George has only a modest condo in the city. However, in my opinion the best option would be to get into Babel. We'll try to get George and the fake Norman there, before they find out I've escaped. Then I'll be able to manage Babel again, even though only in the NET."

"If I were your duplicate," interjected Troy, "that would be the exact location I'd be waiting for you to show up. But I tend to agree with you. It'd be better to get into Babel, despite the risk involved. You know the place well, whereas at Maureen's site they could surprise us easily. In addition, they won't be wearing their helmets in Babel. Whatever we decide, however, some of us should stay behind, in case we're ambushed."

"Good point," said Norman. "I'll need a computer for a couple of minutes now, to prepare a fallback plan in case we're caught."

Troy led Norman to the workroom, and they returned a few minutes later with a recording button. Norman gave the button to Adam.

"Listen, Adam," he said. "You're still very young, I know, but I need to give you a very adult assignment. Take this button. It has two message packages on it. The first package contains messages for the President, the National Security Consultant, and a few more important people. I'd like you to leave the NET and get out of your home. Don't tell us where you're going, but get away from your home area as far as you can. Don't take your personal 'com with you—it's traceable. The contents of these messages is open, but they contain special codes known only to me and the recipients, so they'll have no doubt regarding their authenticity. If anything happens to us, it will be your duty to send these messages immediately, so that they'll be received within one Earth hour. A full NET day."

"I understand," said Adam. "But, hey, if necessary, I can help here, in the NET."

"I'm sure you could," said Norman, and hugged the boy affably. "There's still one more thing I'd like you to do. After sending the messages, I want you to wait for one more hour, and then check your connectivity to the NET. If the NET has not been temporarily turned off, send the contents of the second message package to the attached list of editors and tele-NET programs. It, too, contains my ID code, which cannot be forged."

"Perhaps my dad could also be of assistance," said Maggie. "I couldn't get him on the 'com personally, but I left him a non-traceable message to contact me urgently and to watch out for George. He'll believe our story."

Norman jumped to his feet, his face a mask of dismay.

"You left him a message to watch out for George?" he repeated. "What a terrible mistake. All external messages, to and from Babel personnel, are screened to prevent security leaks. That message of yours was probably intercepted by the Control Center, flagged as suspicious, and forwarded to my attention. My double's, that is. I'm afraid that your father is now in great peril. They'll question him, and get the name of the sender from him. Then they'll get to you, and very soon thereafter, to the rest of us."

Maggie's face was ashen. She sat dumbstruck, her hands trembling, tears welling up in her eyes.

"I . . . I . . . was only trying to warn him, so they wouldn't occupy him. I never dreamed that anyone else would read a private message."

"What's done cannot be undone," said Norman. "Now we've got to get to Babel HQ as fast as we can. There is a secret underground passageway that circumvents the entire security mechanism. Flint, Troy, and I will set out. Maggie, you must leave the NET and leave your home on Earth at once! The assignment I gave Adam is now transferred to you. Is there anywhere Earth-side where you can hide?"

"I can help you here in the NET," said Maggie, wiping away here tears.

"It's too dangerous," said Norman. "They could get to your home on Earth and disconnect you. Then you'd be their prisoner, and they'll get all the information they want out of you. All they need to do is analyze your memory, and they'll get to all of us. You must disappear."

He took the recording button from Adam and pressed it into Maggie's hand.

"You know what to do. You must hurry, now. Leave the NET at once!"

Troy went up to Maggie and hugged her. "Don't worry, Maggie, we'll get them. Leave me clues of your whereabouts in puzzles. I'll find you and come for you when this has all blown over. Smile, now—everything's going to be all right."

Maggie smiled miserably.

"Be careful," she whispered. She hugged Flint, and gave him her ice-carving laser knife. "Keep it for me please, Flintie. It may come in handy."

She looked them over for another second, and then waved goodbye and went into the entry room.

"If they know you've escaped, they're bound to set a trap for us," said Troy, after Maggie had disappeared. "We shouldn't arrive all together."

"I still have the earring communication system we used in the Rollernet," said Flint. "We can move separately and still remain in contact."

"Good idea," said Norman, and they tagged the earrings on. "I'll go first. We'll stagger our advance from point to point. You shall remain at your posts until you hear the password from me. It'll be three consecutive prime numbers, progressing from the number one. If I say anything else it'll mean there's danger."

"Adam, you'll have to wait for us here." Troy's voice was determined. "Be prepared to leave the NET at a second's notice. That could occur if anyone tries to break into here. If we don't contact you in four hours, you're to leave the NET, find Ziggy and tell him everything. He already knows about the invaders and he's waiting for developments. Furthermore, he's tracking us in the NET; my helmet is hooked into his tracking monitor. He'll know what to do."

* * *

Troy, Flint and Norman jumped to a small apartment in the heart of Netville, a few blocks away from Babel's HQ. This apartment was one of Babel's secret safe houses, which they used whenever they needed to go undercover.

Norman went to a window, and peered carefully outside through the blinds. Flint looked over his shoulder.

"There, on the other side of the street," said Norman. "Do you see the entrance to that book shop? The green door?"

"I see it."

"I'm going in there. If everything is safe I'll call you in. From now on, if anything I say is not the password, or if you don't hear from me at all for over five minutes, you're on your own. I suggest you return to the site, and from there you leave the NET and hide until my messages get through. Here's to luck!"

Norman left the apartment, and Troy and Flint watched him approach the bookshop, tap a long code into the digital lock, open the door, and enter. They waited for three long minutes, and then heard his voice over the earrings: "One, two, three."

They quickly crossed the road, and went into the shop. Norman waited for them, and they took a slow elevator down into a dark basement. One of the walls had a huge steel door in it, reminiscent of doors to bank vaults. It was half open, and a long bright corridor was visible on its other side.

"The way in seems to be clear," said Norman. "I'll go all the way to the entrance to Babel, and I'll leave all the doors on the way open. You may need to beat a hasty retreat, and I may not be with you to open those doors—they open to my hand only. This corridor leads straight to Babel. It won't take me more than ten minutes."

He raced ahead, and in a few minutes they heard "five, seven, eleven."

They sped along the corridor, laser pistols at the ready. Every hundred feet there were great steel doors, similar to the one they had entered through, standing wide open. From time to time they saw closed doors to the sides of the corridor. One of them was ajar.

"I wonder where that door leads to," mused Flint, but kept up with Troy. Norman waited for them at the end of the corridor.

"We are now under Babel," said Norman in a low voice. "This elevator will take us to an isolated room that can be accessed only by me. And my doppelganger, too, of course. I shall go up and make sure he isn't there—then return and take you up. If anything arouses your suspicion, just run like hell back the way we came. I left a side door open, just in case. It leads to another exit from Babel with a Transport Box at its end. Use it to escape."

He went up in the elevator and returned a couple of minutes later looking rather relieved.

"They don't seem to know I've been released," he said. "I checked with the computer, and both George and Norman, my clone, are away. Probably on a mission outside Babel."

They all went up the elevator and arrived at a small, windowless room. Norman opened the only door, and they followed him into a narrow hallway.

"Pocket your pistols and stay close to me," instructed Norman. "Don't answer any questions; leave the talking to me."

As they walked down the hallway, a redheaded young woman came toward them. She gaped at them and turned to Norman.

"Norman! Who are these boys? Visiting relatives? Are you all right?"

"Lynn, please come with us urgently to briefing room two. Do you know where George is?"

"I thought that George and Sven went out with you to investigate a suspicious site." Lynn examined him with a strange look. "What happened to your face? Did you hit something?"

"I'll explain everything in a couple of minutes. Please bring Kumar with you, too."

Lynn pressed a button on a wall monitor. "Og, please summon Kumar to briefing room two. Urgent. Norman's request."

She addressed Norman again, somewhat flustered.

"I'll just put the coffee I prepared in my office," she said. "I'll be in the briefing room in a minute." She went down a side passage.

"Hi, Og. Recognize me?"

"Hi, number-one. What are you doing in the Babel citadel? Have you joined us?"

Norman looked at Flint, stunned. "You didn't tell me you were in touch with Og."

"Sometimes," admitted Flint. "We're pals. Same Intium series. Hey, Og, can you tell us where George Boder is?"

"My logs indicate that he left the citadel twenty-five minutes ago. But so did Norman, and here he is. There may be an error in registration, or someone has reported erroneously."

"Which vehicle did he use and where has he gone?" asked Norman.

"He is on a hoverer on his way to a site on the other side of Netville. He should be there by now."

"Is that site owned by Maureen Clarke?"

"Yes," confirmed Og. "You should know, you're supposed to be on that flight."

"As you can see, I am here. Please notify me immediately when he's on his way back. I'll be in briefing room two."

"Roger."

Norman led them to the room. A thin dark man waited for them inside.

He, too, looked at Norman strangely.

"You've changed in the half hour since I last saw you," he said.

"That isn't him, Kumar. He's an imposter." Lynn had entered the room quietly. Her freezer was pointed at the trio. "Put your hands on your heads. You're not Norman. I have just checked the NET tracker, and the real Norman is now at another site in Netville. However, you are Norman's spitting image, and you even talk like him. Now, before I ask him what to do with you, tell me who you are."

"Lynn, listen to me. I am the real Norman Starr. I accepted you to work here. The other Norman is an—"

Lynn froze him in mid sentence and he toppled to the floor. She stared at Troy and Flint.

"I am going to understand exactly what is going on here," she said through gritted teeth. "This fellow doesn't seem to be in a position to explain. He is not the same Norman I was with half an hour ago, and *he* was the real Norman all right. So one of you had better start explaining pretty darn quick, or I'll freeze you both right now and call the real Norman back."

"The real Norman is the frozen man here. The Norman outside at the site is an alien who has taken over Norman's body and memory. The same goes for George. When they hear that we're here, they'll come back and do away with us." Troy reeled off his sentences in one breath. He gulped another breath of air and added: "And they'll get you, too."

"I've never in my life heard a crazier story," said Lynn. "Why on earth should I believe you and not Norman at the site? At least he's a real surfer, and not a netter like you. You are currently not surfing according to the NET monitors. What proof do you have to back up your claims?"

Troy didn't bat an eyelash.

"You can check us with a T-scope. It'll confirm that what we say is true."

"The T-scope won't work on netters," said Lynn, and fired at Troy who was attempting to say something more. He fell to the floor beside Norman.

Lynn looked hard at Flint.

"Can you convince me that you're not imposters? Can you tell me who you really are? The whole truth? And how come a look-alike Norman is lying here without any trace of him on our computers?"

60. NET: Day 37, 10:02

Adam waited for two long minutes after everyone had left, and then flicked on his 'com impatiently.

"Hey, Pyotr, come quickly to Troy's site!"

"Who's there?" A black gorilla head appeared on the screen.

"It's only me. I need your help urgently."

Pyotr walked through Troy's entry room two seconds later.

"Do you know what's happened?" asked Adam.

"Yes—Flint updated me, before leaving on his mission." Pyotr scratched his head absently. "Pretty bad, huh?"

"You bet. Troy and Flint are on their way to Babel with Norman—a suicide mission, if you ask me. Hey, the aliens will surely set a trap for them. Even if they don't, they'll find out soon enough—and there goes the element of surprise. You know what I told them? That we've got to surprise them at Maureen's site! But, hey, they thought their plan was better."

"Why at Maureen's site of all places?" asked the ape. "Why do you think the aliens are there?"

"I'm positive that their headquarters are there!" cried Adam, jumping to his feet. "Hey, Norman said it's large and isolated, and near the desert. Just the ideal site to hide and plot. And look—they used Atkinson's site to hide Norman. That means that their hosts' sites are put to use." He looked upward at the towering gorilla, which was scratching its head thoughtfully. "Hey, here's how you can help, Pyotr. You can creep up to the house and peek in, and make sure they are there. I also need to know if they're using their protective shields. I can't come with you—I've got to stay here and guard Troy's site and, hey, I'd only be in your way anyhow. You can do this errand for me, can't you?"

"Let's have a look at the site first," said Pyotr. He went to the computer and punched a few keys. A three-dimensional map of Netville appeared, and Pyotr zoomed in and out a couple of times. Finally, Maureen's site filled the screen. It was mostly covered with eucalyptus trees.

"This is quite an ancient map," grumbled the gorilla. "Over three months old." It plucked at its chest hairs, as if attempting to remove an annoying louse. "Let's hope there haven't been any major changes to the site lately. Let's see now—I could use the portable Transport Box to get to this clearing here, near the fence," he pointed to the map, "and sneak up to the back of the house. It's risky, but feasible." Pyotr showed Adam the laser pistol in a hidden pocket in his fur. "What then? Take them by surprise?"

"No, No! Just find out if they're there and what they're doing. Then get back here as fast as you can. If they're really there, then, hey, I've got an idea that could work."

Pyotr nodded and went back into the entry room. Adam waited restlessly. Twenty minutes later, the ape returned, highly excited.

"Quick!" urged Adam. "Tell me what happened?"

"You were right!" said Pyotr, using his hands for emphasis. "They're there. I saw all of them, and the spaceship, too! They were not wearing their helmets, and they had a prisoner."

"Go on! Hey, tell me everything!"

"I jumped to the clearing near the fence, and concealed the Transport Box." The huge primates eyes sparkled. "I climbed over the fence, and was approaching the building, when I noticed the spaceship hidden among the eucalyptus trees, not far away. It was standing on its base, and was camouflaged by a kind of military-type netting. I don't think I could be observed from it—I was among dense trees, and I took great care not to get too close."

Pyotr took a deep breath and continued.

"I was about to enter the house through one of the open windows, when I heard a strange sound. I hid myself again, and I saw a hoverer landing in the courtyard. Two men came out of it—they had Babel uniforms on and carried rifles. One of them, the shorter one, carried a frozen third man, also in a Babel uniform. None of them wore protective helmets."

"Describe the third man," demanded Adam.

"Tall, blond. I couldn't make out any more details."

"They might want to occupy him," said Adam impatiently. "Hey, that's for later. Go on."

"That's about it. I waited until they went into the house, and came back."

"Hey, good work!" said Adam, slapping the gorilla on the back. "Thanks. Now wait for me here. I've got to deliver a message to Ziggy, and consult with him. I've got a plan to finish these invaders and, hey, guess what—you're going to be a key factor in it."

"I am?"

"Sure. I'm going to attack the house and cause a diversion. You're going to be outside in the trees and pick off the aliens as they come out. Hey, I'll give you all the details when I get back!"

"I'll wait. Hurry up now. I'll cover for you, and respond to any callers."

Adam hesitated. "You know . . . Troy did tell me to wait four hours before approaching Ziggy." He brushed the thought aside at once. "But, hey, Troy didn't know then what we know now. I really think that he and Flint have a much better chance if we take out the alien headquarters."

"It's certainly less risky than doing nothing. If anything goes wrong with Troy and the others, the invaders will be right on our doorstep."

Adam got up. "I'm off. I'll be back in a jiffy. Hey, you watch out, now."

"Don't worry. Caution is my middle name."

Adam left the NET. He then dialed a number on his 'com.

"Ziggy, I need to meet with you right away. May I come over?"

The old man's face showed concern as he listened to Adam.

"Of course. I shall be seeing you in a few minutes. There will be a cold chocolate waiting for you."

Adam covered the two blocks in less than a minute. Ziggy was waiting by the open door, and let the puffing boy in. Adam noticed that the curtains were drawn on all the windows.

"Sit down and catch your breath," suggested Ziggy.

Adam sat on the chair by the table, and gratefully sipped the cold chocolate. He wiped his mouth on his sleeve. Ziggy spoke first.

"Before you explain what is so urgent, you must first tell me what is happening in the NET. I followed Troy and witnessed the battle in Hell. I saw him and Maggie and Flint escape. I disconnected only when Troy fell asleep. Where is he now?"

Adam briefly told Ziggy about the recent events, swallowing some of the words in his hurry.

Ziggy looked gravely into Adam's eyes.

"So Norman gave Maggie a message for the president to take extreme measures, if they cannot overcome the aliens. There is still some time before stopping the NET. Technically, that would not be a complex operation. But think of the consequences. The world as we know it would change radically, even if the NET were halted for only one week. On the other hand, who would dare surf the NET if there were aliens there who could occupy your mind, or even destroy it like they did to . . . to . . .”

“Spindler,” filled in Adam. “I have a plan how to take the aliens by surprise. Hey, maybe they can be killed this way. All we need is a little bit of luck. It’s also not too risky and, hey, we’ve got nothing to lose by trying. We can’t afford to quit the NET for years—everything we’ve built will be ruined.”

Ziggy sipped his own chocolate and observed the youngster. A twelve-year-old boy with a plan for saving the world from aliens, innumerable times superior to us in intelligence and technology. “I’m listening.”

“They’re at Maureen Clarke’s site. Pyotr sneaked in and—”

“Pyotr?”

“Hey, he’s Flint’s backup computer.” Adam was on pins and needles. Time was running short. “He knows everything Flint knows, and now we surf together. Anyway, he saw that they’re without helmets. Maureen’s site borders on the desert around Netville and, hey, the tetrosaur corral is also in the desert, about ten miles away. I’m going to jump to the corral and convince Rob, Tuffy’s trainer, to help me. He’ll believe me. Together, we’re going to launch a frontal attack on Maureen’s site with two tetrosaurs. Pyotr will be waiting in ambush with a laser pistol. Hey, I’m positive that they’re not prepared for an attack from the desert. We’ll surprise them, and when they come out to repel us, Pyotr will get them from behind.”

“Unless they use their protective helmets. If they do, you are all lost. I’ve seen those helmets in action—nothing can penetrate them. Pyotr’s shooting will have no effect, and neither will the tetrosaurs.”

“True, but there’s still a chance—even if their helmets are active!” Adams speech came out in a rush, the words running into each other. “Troy told us of an incident during the battle in Hell when an elephant spider fell on an invader who was protected by the rays. I think it was even Maureen herself. She was absolutely neutralized, and the others had to free her. Now, hey, a tetrosaur is much heavier than a spider. We can put the aliens out of commission, and find a way to dispose of them later. Maybe they’ll starve to death. But as long as they can move around, they have the advantage.”

“Very true,” concurred Ziggy. “I witnessed that spider episode myself.

But how do you hope to get the tetrosaurs to follow you? I understand that
they are quite vicious. The minute you release them they will turn on you or
on each other."

"No, you don't know tetrosaurs. They won't. They're programmed to
fight each other only in the arena. And besides, Rob will help me, and hey
Tuffy will follow me anywhere. Their special neuro-collars provide total
control over them."

Adam was close to tears. He looked desperately at his watch.

"Hey, I've got to try, at least. What do you say? It's been over two NET
hours since they've gone. It'll take me at least a NET hour to get there. And
we're, hey, losing time . . ."

"Very well," said Ziggy. It wasn't a plan that he himself would have
designed. No finesse—just brute force. But it was better than anything he
could come up with on the spur of the moment, which was nothing. "Be prepared to use your emergency return ring at a second's notice. I don't want
you to be captured. I'm coming over to your house now, and hook my monitor into Troy's helmet again. If anything goes wrong, I'll spread the word
and God help us!"

Adam didn't hear Ziggy's last words. He was out through the door and
racing back to his home.

61. NET: Day 37, 13:10

Norman Starr entered the briefing room twenty minutes after Lynn's call,
traveling the distance from Maureen's site at the maximum speed the hoverer could muster. He found the Norman copy, Troy, and Flint frozen on the
floor. Lynn was expecting him.

"I checked the NET logs, as you suggested," she said. "They're not registered there. I take it they're netters masquerading as surfers. What do you
want to do with them?"

"I think I'll take them with me for some private interrogation. Where's
Kumar?"

"Right here." Kumar came out of a dark corner of the room, a laser pistol in one hand and a freezer in the other, both pointed at Norman. "If you move a muscle I'll burn you to a crisp."

Lynn also drew her laser pistol and pointed it at a very indignant Norman. Kumar unfroze the three victims with a sweep of his freezer.

"Now, then," said Lynn resolutely. "Which one of you is the real Norman? You'll have to prove whatever you say!"

"I am," said the unfrozen Norman, standing up. He looked at the alien Norman, and felt as if his brain suddenly contracted into itself, and his mouth clenched shut. Flint took advantage of the fact that all eyes were on the two Normans, drew his laser pistol, and unhesitatingly fired at the alien Norman.

There was a searing blue flash, and a faint 'poof' was heard. The invader stared unbelievingly at the smoking hole in his chest, and then collapsed onto the floor, twitching and jerking. His shape began metamorphosing during his death throes, and before the popping eyes of Lynn and Kumar, became a gigantic creature, ten feet long, with a head three times the size of a human's. Green liquid trickled out of the hole in its chest, and onto the floor.

"Well, that sure was the most convincing argument that *you're* the real Norman," said Lynn, turning to him. To her surprise, he was nowhere to be seen.

"That he certainly was," came a muffled voice from the doorway. A man surrounded by golden light rays entered the room, holding a freezer in is hand. "And it seems that both the copy and its original version are now in a better world." Flint, Lynn and Kumar fired instinctively at the man, but their shots were ineffective. He, in turn, froze them all with a wide sweep of his freezer. They clattered to the floor.

The man locked the door behind him, disarmed all the occupants of the room, and forcefully wrenched their emergency return rings from their fingers. He then drew an atomic blaster from an inside holster, vaporized the huge alien body, and lightly touched his helmet. The glowing envelope disappeared, revealing George Boder in full battle gear. He unfroze Troy and Flint.

"Be very careful about how you move," he growled. "Which one of you is Flint?"

"I am," said Flint.

"And who are you?" he asked Troy.

"He's my boss," said Flint.

"Quiet, you! I wasn't addressing you!" George barked at Flint. He turned again to Troy. "What's your name?"

"My name is Troy, and I'm a surfer."

"Which of you two blocked up the tunnel?"

"I did," confessed Flint. George immediately trained his blaster on Troy.

"NO!" yelled Flint. "You hurt him, and I'll never help you."

"You're going to help me open that tunnel, whether you want to or not." George aimed his blaster at Lynn and Kumar and squeezed the trigger. They disappeared with two soft 'poofs.'

"What have you done?" cried Troy.

"Shut up!" roared George. Troy stiffened immediately. A sweet smile came on George's face. "In answer to your question, I have negated their existence here. They were undesirables, as far as I'm concerned. They're back on Earth now, just realizing that their surf was abnormally terminated, but with no memory of what happened. Which means they know nothing about you, either. Or me, for that matter."

He herded the two toward the door.

"We are now going to take a little trip together. Then you'll open the way to my world for me. If you cause me the slightest trouble, I'll see that you're taken care of on Earth."

He froze Troy. Flint caught the boy before he reached the floor.

"Carry him," ordered George. "We're headed for the tunnel. Let's go!"

62. NEW YORK, SATURDAY, 16:25 (NEW YORK TIME)

Maggie left her home almost immediately on her return from the NET. She barely had time to reproduce Norman's recording button and disguise herself. The elevator brought her down to the lobby in a few seconds, and she went out through the rear exit of the building, heading toward Central ark. Her mother's wig and the dark glasses gave her a more mature appearance. Looking back toward the apartment building she had just left, she noticed two large black cars approach and stop in front of it. Four men in gray suits got out of the first car and went into the building. The other car and its passengers remained outside.

Brrr . . . that was close! If I had delayed for just two more minutes, they'd have got me! It was a chilling thought. Memories of the battle in Hell were still fresh in her mind.

She crossed the road, entered a tower on the corner of the block, and went directly to the entrance electronic-doorman screen. She tapped in a short code.

The screen pinged, and a frail-looking woman with white hair appeared on it. Her face lit up with pleasure at the sight of Maggie.

"Maya, I need your help right now," said Maggie in a rush, dispensing with greetings and other niceties.

"I'll be right down." The screen went dark.

Thirty seconds later the door of Maya's private elevator opened, and she beckoned to Maggie to join her there. Maggie looked around, saw no one, and slipped into the elevator.

Maya Jeffries was an old and dear friend of Maggie's mother, and one of the few people Maggie felt she could trust completely. Ton Jeffries, Maya's late husband, was a well-known philanthropist, who backed young artists as well as leading museums. When he passed away, nine years ago, she inherited his thriving real estate empire in the New York and Boston areas. Even though she upheld his philanthropic manner, she led a modest lifestyle and shunned publicity.

It was on Maggie's tenth birthday that she had met Maya for the first time. Maya's present was unusual—a weeklong workshop of ice sculpting with Norita Yamara, one of the most renowned artists in New York, who specialized in sculptures in ice and glass. Maggie passed the tough preliminary exams, and was rewarded by experiencing one of the most exciting episodes in her life. She found herself toiling long days over huge statues, which she had to eventually abandon to melt in the sunlight. There was a peculiar joy in the artistry involved in creating a short-lived object, using unforgiving raw materials that punished her severely with the slightest mistake. She excelled at her new hobby; but she turned down Norita's offer to remain with her as her apprentice. It meant losing two years at school. Yet, despite that the great artist kept a corner of her studio available to Maggie, accessible at any time, and a carte blanche to sculpt anything she liked. The only condition was that any sculpture that Norita chose to preserve would remain as the property of the gallery, in a separate freezing unit. In the years that followed four of Maggie's statues were displayed as part of the permanent exhibits which drew large crowds of connoisseurs.

The birthday gift brought Maggie and Maya closer together, and they fell into the habit of meeting frequently at various New York cafés, talking and exchanging views as if they were of the same age. Maya consulted with Maggie about her modern art collection and the numerous donation and investment requests she was getting every week. Maggie sought Maya's advice on almost every topic, from ice sculptures to her relationship with Troy, which was based on mutual interests and respect—perhaps a little intimacy as well, but no more.

"He's totally immersed in projects with his computer," she once said somewhat enviously. "That computer is his best friend, and I only take second place."

"I guess this is the first time I've met someone who's jealous of a computer," declared Maya. "Perhaps you should build a computer of your own and have Troy become jealous of you—and pay you some more attention."

"It isn't quite that simple," sighed Maggie. "That computer of his is the result of years of research and experimentation. I can't spell it all out to you—not only is the topic very technical, it is also very hush-hush. Would you imagine that a computer could ever be a pain in the ass?"

"Dear, dear, such language." Maya smilingly gave a mock reprimand. "And from such a pretty and talented girl as you, yet. I'd very much like to meet with this Troy fellow. If he's ever in New York, don't fail to bring him over for a visit."

The elevator rose rapidly. Maya looked curiously at Maggie.

"What are you mixed up in now?" she asked. "Who's chasing you?"

"For the moment, I think it's only the NET's Security Services. However, if we don't accomplish our mission within a few hours from now, I'm afraid I'll be hunted by the National Security Forces. I need a place to hide."

"It's probably all a mistake," soothed Maya. "Everything will work out okay. But if I were to take a guess, I'd bet that it involves Troy and his secret computer experiments."

The elevator halted and they both stepped out into a corridor.

"You needn't answer that one," continued Maya, and beckoned Maggie to follow her. She opened a door at the end of the corridor. "The less I know, the safer you'll be. This apartment is directly below my own, and nobody will ever find you here. It's registered as an empty flat belonging to a Spanish duke. There's enough food in the cooler to last you a month—you won't need to leave the apartment for shopping. I'll see to it that the cleaners won't come this week, so no one's going to get in your way. I very rarely make use of this flat—and always furtively, when I wish to really isolate myself. I'll leave you here now, before anyone sees us together."

"Thanks, Maya." Maggie kissed her on the cheek. "I knew I could count on you." She entered the apartment, and locked the door behind her.

I hope they've lost me. It's been three months since I last contacted Maya, so it may take them a day or two to find me. By then, it won't matter.

She quickly took her bearings. There were two large bedrooms, an enormous living room, which could have entertained a party of fifty guests, and a workroom containing a modern computer system that seemed unused. A state-of-the-art surfing helmet hung from a hook on the wall by the computer.

I mustn't surf! If Troy and Norman fail in their mission, it'll be up to me to provide their emergency backup.

She seated herself in a spacious armchair in the living room, and used the remote control to switch on the holo-projector. The screen was larger than an entire wall in her own room at home. The news broadcast reported the bizarre accident that had befallen a certain Mr. Spindler, and the reporter interviewed Spindler's uncle in Buenos Aires.

Spindler is history. Maybe they've got to Dad, too. I wonder how he's doing right now. The memory of George and the events in Hell flooded back, and her tears flowed freely. *That bastard has caught Dad. It's all my fault. What have I done . . . what have I done?* She began sobbing uncontrollably.

Wiping the tears from her eyes, she washed her face in the bathroom. Crying had calmed her down a bit.

I must find a way to help him. Perhaps he managed to escape somehow.

She tried to imagine scenarios whereby Sven had eluded the aliens, but none of them were very believable. The very fact that the security people had reached her apartment so quickly was another indication that her father was held captive. Looking at her watch, she discovered that only ten minutes had elapsed since she had left the NET. Norman had requested that she send the letters after an hour, a NET day.

I need to prepare a puzzle for Troy, with clues for him to locate me. He should get it as soon as possible—it's already been four hours in the NET. Anything might have happened there.

She went to the computer in the workroom. A note on the desk stated the coordinates of the corresponding NET site and the entry password.

I can enter Maya's site with her helmet and her password, and no one will know it's me. Yes—it's a severe violation of NET regulations, but it's the only way I can avoid detection, at least until I finish composing the puzzle for Troy. Then I can send it to him over the encrypted network. No one will ever find the source of that message. The whole process won't take me longer than twenty NET minutes. I'll be back here in less than one Earth minute.

She donned the helmet, keyed in the coordinates, and found herself in Maya's NET site. It was a luxury residence, the penthouse on one of the sky-scrapers in central Netville.

This pad must be worth millions. Let's see what kind of computers she has here.

It wasn't hard to locate. She began composing the puzzle, a task she always found alleviating. This time, she decided to adopt a word decipher-ing principle that she intended to introduce in the next edition of *Pythagoras*. She embedded a couple of words that would make sense only to herself and Troy, and twenty-two minutes later the puzzle was complete.

Only Troy and myself could ever solve this puzzle. And even Troy will need to tax himself a bit with this one.

She connected herself to the encrypted communication network, using a randomly generated, untraceable ID, and sent the puzzle together with Troy's address as the destination. The system requested a twenty-cent fee, which she paid by means of a single-usage, two-dollar credit card she had bought a year earlier from a street vendor, and carried no identification. The site's screen disappeared, and the local network was displayed. She leaned backward and gaped unseeing at the screen. It was now up to Troy and Norman. And Flint, of course.

He'll find some unorthodox way to handle those aliens. It's time to scram from here, too, back to Earth . . .

She got up and turned to the entry room and stopped cold. Two sturdy men in Babel uniforms stood at the door. She turned to run, but immediately realized there was no place to escape. Desperately she tried to press her emergency return ring. Too late. The two agents fired their freezers at her, and the last thought she had, before collapsing onto the floor, was that now all was lost.

63. NET: DAY 37, 14:00

George pushed Flint, who was carrying the frozen Troy on his back, toward a Transport Box located right beside the briefing room. He placed his hand on the pad by the door and the Transport Box opened.

"Get in," he snarled, waving his weapon. Flint entered the Box, and George followed. He immediately froze Flint. The frozen lads were propped up awkwardly on the Box's inner walls. George tapped in a long series of numbers, and the lights flickered. They had arrived at Maureen's site.

George roughly fastened the boys' hands behind their backs with plastic handcuffs, and then unfroze them. They both lay on the floor of the entry room.

"Up!" ordered George. "And out!" He pointed through the door of the room.

"These bonds are cutting off my circulation," moaned Flint, trying to get up, his face contorted in pain.

"Too bad," jeered George. He still wore the yellow helmet, but it was not activated. He yanked the lads to their feet.

"What are you going to do with us?" asked Troy.

"No one knows you're here. You're going to give me the necessary keys for opening the tunnel. I can then return to my people on the other side."

"Are you going to release us if we do?"

"There's no question of if," said George levelly. "I don't actually need your cooperation. As a matter of fact, I would rather enjoy extracting the information from you bit by bit. Hell would seem like a picnic compared with what I have in mind for you. But in answer to your question—I shall take you with me to my world. You shall be evidence, and later exhibits, of living creatures with inferior intelligence. Something like Earth zoos."

He prodded them into a huge living room. It was beautifully decorated with large oil painting on the walls, antique furniture, and a colorful wall-to-wall Persian carpet. There was a large fireplace on the other side of the room, and next to it lay a tall blond man, trussed hand and foot. Troy immediately recognized him as Sven Thorensen, Maggie's father. His uniform was torn and clotted blood stained his face. He struggled to sit up when they entered, staring at them in amazement.

"Troy!" he gasped weakly. "What on earth are you doing here?"

"So—you know each other," scoffed George. "How nice. Well, Mr. Thorensen, this young man is on his way to a very interesting trip, same as you are. But I have to have some fun with him and his friend first, so that they'll give me a certain key to a portal that I need."

George opened a drawer of the desk and took out a large nerve stunner. He walked over to Sven and deliberately zapped him in the chest. Sven yelled out in pain and contorted, breathing heavily. The spasms ceased after a few seconds, but his bound hands and feet continued to twitch uncontrollably, and his face remained twisted in agony.

"Oops—it does work after all," said George in sham innocence, as if surprised by the result. A diabolical sneer spread over his features. He delivered a violent kick to Sven's trembling torso. Then he took three strides toward Troy, and zapped him in the leg. Troy fell to the floor with a scream of pain. His body quivered from the force of the shock, and tears darted from his eyes. Flint's face screwed up in fury, and his muscles strained against his bonds.

"Don't cry, my boy," giggled George. "It won't do you any good." He watched Troy squirming, and then looked at Sven, who had stopped his jitters and was staring at George with a murderous look.

"Oh, yes, Sven," taunted George. "You don't like being on the losing side, do you? I quite understand you. Perhaps we'll meet again in another incarnation. But I bet it'll be a repeat of the current situation then, as well."

George walked over to Flint.

"As for you, my hearty—" he said, and shot him in the belly. Flint folded up like a jack-knife, and toppled to the floor with a roar of pain. His nose hit the tiles and began bleeding profusely. He rolled on the ground, happening to touch George's foot, which brought him a kick in the back.

"That was lesson number one," said George, all business-like. "Now you understand exactly the vocabulary we're going to employ from now on."

He picked up Flint, who was still trembling, placed him on a chair, and slapped his face viciously.

"Give me the codes to open the tunnel! Now!"

"There are a hundred different codes, each a hundred digits long, located at the nodes on the door. It will take me exactly four minutes to open the door. Conveying the information will take several hours, and I may slip up during that time."

George calmly pointed the stunner at Sven's head.

"Perhaps now you could kindly answer my question?"

Flint paled. He began reciting hundred-digit numbers in rapid succession. Three minutes later, after Flint had gone through about five numbers, George lost his patience. He zapped Sven in the leg, causing him to shudder with the painful shock.

"Stop that!" he shouted. "You're playing with me. Go to that computer over there. Key in all the codes there. Then we'll travel together to the tunnel. If there's a single error, I'm going to fry your boss' brains."

Flint got up and went to the computer. Through the window behind George he saw a huge cloud of dust billowing over the eucalyptus treetops outside.

"I can't type with my hands tied," he said. "You'll have to untie my—" He stopped. The sound of trees breaking could be heard from the garden. George approached the window and looked out.

"Some of your rotten friends are attempting to rescue you," he said, his temper rising to fever pitch. He turned his helmet on, and the golden halo enveloped him. His voice sounded smothered. "They don't stand a chance, of course. However, very unfortunately, we must leave this place now. Pity—I was beginning to enjoy myself." He delivered a powerful kick to Sven's face. Sven rolled on the ground, moaning, and spat out two broken teeth. George untied his feet and roughly yanked him upright.

"Walk to the door," he commanded. Sven walked slowly, his face covered in blood, his hands still tied behind his back. George pointed the stunner at Troy, but then changed his mind, hauled Troy to his feet, and pushed him and Flint after Sven.

They left the house into the garden and walked toward the spaceship. The noise of breaking trees became louder and louder. All of a sudden, they saw a gigantic tetrosaur, a hybrid of a mastodon with a Galapagos turtle, break out of the grove and charge toward them. The monster carried a man in a trainer's uniform on its back.

"Hurry into the ship," growled George. "We're going to give these guests a lively reception party."

Troy noticed that George's attention was momentarily focused on the tetrosaur, still several hundred yards distant. He launched the mightiest karate kick that he could muster at George's back. His foot struck the force shield, and it felt as if he had kicked an extremely viscous liquid. George spun around in fury, and zapped Troy directly in the chest. Troy collapsed onto the ground, unconscious.

"I'll show you that I mean business!" bellowed George. He shot at Flint and Sven, both dropping to the ground, stunned. With incredible strength, he picked up Flint and Troy, and began running toward the spaceship. He reached the outer shell of the ship and heaved his two captives at it. The boys passed through the hull as if it were a silvery cloud, and not the metal face of a spaceship. As the lads recovered slightly, they saw that the hull was perfectly transparent from the inside. Flint reached out to touch it, and felt cool, hard metal. It was quite clear to them that they were imprisoned inside the spaceship.

George turned on his heel, and raced back to Sven. The galloping tetrosaur was now only fifty yards away. George replaced the stunner in its holster, and drew his laser pistol. He aimed at the monster's leg, and fired. The tetrosaur was injured, but continued on its path, limping and trumpeting in rage. George fired at its other leg. The monster stumbled, and crashed forward, raising a tremendous racket. The rider was pitched into the air, and upon landing, struck his head violently against a rock. He vanished with a soft 'poof.'

George cautiously approached the thrashing monster, his laser pistol ready, when from out of the woods charged another tetrosaur. This one was far smaller than the first. It resembled a huge bear, covered by an armadillo's plate armor, with two sharp horns sprouting from its head. On it's back was Adam, waving a laser pistol

"It's Adam and Tuffy," choked Troy. "Now I understand where the first tetrosaur came from."

"They don't stand a chance against George," moaned Flint, his bloody nose making speech difficult. "He's protected from any harm when his helmet is on, and he'll easily overcome them with his laser pistol."

But George did not wait for the second tetrosaur. He grabbed Sven, slung him over his shoulder, and ran to the spaceship. He had just shoved Sven through the hull, when a giant gorilla came from behind the spaceship, and caught George in a hammerlock, knocking the laser pistol out of his hand. George struggled frantically, but the gorilla was far stronger than him. Its long, hairy arms encircled the glowing rays surrounding George, and he was lifted bodily into the air, and held there awaiting the approach of the other tetrosaur. With extreme effort, George managed to get his hand into his pocket. He grabbed the nerve stunner and fired it for several seconds, through his pocket, at the gorilla. The huge ape shuddered with the shock and released his quarry.

George didn't stop to figure things out. He slipped through the hull of the spaceship, just as Tuffy arrived on the scene.

Tuffy did not halt, but continued her mad charge toward the ship. A tremendous clatter was heard when her huge body smashed into the solid hull, head first. The entire spaceship rocked and teetered, and finally tipped over and crashed to the ground with the most deafening noise. Tuffy halted, stunned by the blow and collapsed to the ground while Adam sailed over her head and rolled onto the grass in front of the trees. Unhurt, he got to his feet and collected the laser pistol he had dropped en route.

"Troy! Flint!" he yelled with all his might. "Run for it!"

He pointed the pistol at the spaceship and fired. The silvery covering reddened and started to melt, and the hull began to twist out of shape. The gorilla, too, had recovered, and now joined Adam, shooting a laser pistol at the spaceship. The warping of the hull spread out further, but it did not puncture.

An ear-splitting roar came suddenly from the ship's bow. A large opening yawned in the hull, and a much smaller silver spaceship, the size of a train carriage, emerged and took off at a tremendous pace straight up.

Adam watched it in despair. All was lost. Nothing could now come between the aliens and the tunnel.

64. NET: Day 37, 14:24

The three prisoners watched Adam and the gorilla through the transparent hull of the space cruiser. The duo was shooting in frustration at the mother ship, which was lying on its side on the ground. The look of utter despair on Adam's face brought tears to Troy's eyes.

"How pathetic," remarked George. Before takeoff, he had herded his captives into the cruiser, and now they watched the rapidly receding figures on the ground. "They'll never penetrate the hull with those popguns." His face suddenly distorted into a visage of vehemence. "But your craven comrades managed to damage the outer shell of the mother ship, and taking off in it will be dangerous now. I swear I'm going to return and get them for this. Right now, however, we have more important things to attend." He kicked the prone Sven out of sheer malice. Sven groaned.

George leered at them. "Don't worry—I'll be back," he said, and disappeared through the wall.

They remained in silence for several minutes, watching the magnificent view below them through the transparent hull.

Sven was the first to break the stillness.

"Never in my life have I seen such a heroic and absolutely hopeless attack."

"At least they managed to inflict some damage," said Troy, with no little pride. "My younger brother has quite bright and original ideas, but he prefers to execute them his own stubborn way—he never takes anyone's advice, and never follows orders. I just hope that he delivered the message before embarking on this escapade."

"That kid on the monster was your brother?" queried Sven. "He's really very brave to ride such an animal, and attack the aliens to boot. Is the gorilla his pet?"

"Believe it or not," said Flint, "that gorilla is my backup. "If anything happens to it, I'll be in trouble."

"You're in enough trouble already," said Sven. "Wait a minute—did you say backup? What do you mean by that? Say, we haven't been introduced yet. I'm Sven Thorensen, Maggie's father—I guess you know her. Are you Troy's brother, too?"

"No, Flint is my computer, and we surf the NET together," explained Troy. "He and Maggie are good friends indeed. The gorilla is his irresponsible backup computer that, instead of waiting on Earth and behaving like a backup should, is cavorting in the NET with my no less irresponsible little brother."

Sven gaped at Flint, thunderstruck. He glanced sideways at Troy who nodded in confirmation. He looked back at Flint, inhaled sharply and gave out a long, soft whistle.

"You're . . . a computer?" he asked finally. "How come you're surfing?"

"Well, you might say that I'm not what is commonly considered as a computer," said Flint. "But it's a long story."

Troy's eyes suddenly lit up.

"Flint, if I'm not mistaken, Maggie gave you her ice-carving knife as a memento. Where did you put it?"

"My memory chips must be failing," said Flint humbly. "I'm a complete idiot. It's in the right hand pocket of my jeans. Sven, can you reach it?"

Sven jockeyed himself close to Flint and tried to get at the pocket, but couldn't quite manage.

"I think I can," said Troy. He pressed himself up to Flint, and by holding his breath and twisting around, he succeeded in retrieving the knife. He looked cautiously at the wall through which George had disappeared. They all waited a tense moment, but the alien did not return.

"I suggest we cut the cords so that it won't be noticed," whispered Troy.

"We have to appear as if we're still tied up, with our hands behind our backs. Then we can hope to catch George off guard when his helmet is inactive."

"Good idea," said Flint. "Begin with me."

"I think it might be better not to release you at all," said Troy. He chuckled at Flint's astonished face. "Don't misunderstand me, Flint. George will have to cut you loose so you can use your hands to open the door. You want to be tied up when he does that. Only Sven and I need to be released."

Troy passed the knife to Flint, and they arranged themselves back to back, their hands near each other. Flint took less than a minute to nick Troy's cords deeply enough so that they would snap under a strong yank, but not too deep to be visible. He then did the same for Sven. Flint slid the knife into Troy's pocket, and they all returned to sit in their original positions. The view below was of wild plains in the random territories, beyond the desert that surrounded Netville.

"What happened to Norman?" asked Sven. "I saw him, and he was an alien just like George. In fact, he and George captured me together."

It was time to tell Sven about everything that had happened, and Troy spared no detail. Sven listened intently to every word, and relaxed somewhat only when he heard that Maggie was out of the NET.

"Did you know that I was hot on your trail because your brother contacted one of our investigators through the Pira-net?" he asked. "Had Norman not captured me, thereby exposing himself, I would have given him the information and he would have caught you." He related the sequence of events with Adam and Chimpo.

"It's amazing what you guys can deduce from just a fraction of information," said Troy. "My little brother can be extremely capricious. Sometimes he saves the day in the nick of time, and sometimes he punches holes into everything we've built. This time his intervention didn't change a thing, as George succeeded in capturing us."

Sven nodded and turned again to Flint.

"Is there any way you can refuse to open the door?"

"I can't answer that right now," apologized Flint. "George is a sadist, and he might try harming you two to force me to do it."

Troy's eyes were glowing hotly as he addressed Flint. "Listen very carefully, Flint, because I want no misunderstanding on this one. And I certainly don't want any of your goofy interpretations. I am giving you a direct order, which you are to follow to the letter! You are not to open that door under *any* circumstances! Understand? No matter how much George tortures me or Sven (please forgive me, Sven), no matter how much I plead with you and may even rescind this current order, you are not to open that door. I repeat—this is a direct order. You *must* obey it."

A hush fell on the little cabin when Troy completed his words. All three lowered their heads in deep silence. They all knew that the future probably held torture and pain untold. And they all realized the consequences of opening that fateful door.

After a couple of minutes Troy broke the silence, trying to assuage Sven's apprehensions.

"We won't let them take over the human race. We have already taken steps to prevent that. Norman has prepared letters to the appropriate leaders, and they will know how to act. Let's just hope it will not end in the complete closure of the NET."

65. Palo Alto, Saturday, 13:36

Nancy went down to the basement of her home to check up on Ziggy, who was monitoring Troy. Since Ziggy came in, a few seconds after Adam, she had been sitting in the kitchen feeling helpless.

"What's the situation, Ziggy?" she asked, from the middle of the stairs. "Do you still need to track Troy's every move?" She confronted Ziggy and saw his red eyes.

"What's happened?" she asked, alarmed.

"Troy has a few problems at the moment," answered Ziggy, trying to mask the true situation.

"When will he be back?" Nancy read the surfing timer display on Troy's helmet: 99:99. "What do these numbers mean? Why doesn't it indicate hours?"

"He is surfing without a time limit," explained Ziggy. "He probably had to complete a mission, and did not want to risk the surf being automatically terminated by his helmet."

He looked at the monitor, still wired into Troy's helmet. The scene was a wild plain. A blond man jerked momentarily into view, and then a blond youth. They both appeared to be seated in some kind of transparent cabin, with their hands tied behind their backs. The images of the two people jumped around the screen, but it was obvious that both of them had blood on their faces.

Nancy observed the screen in horror.

"Who are these people? Why are they tied up? Where's Troy?"

Ziggy's stomach twisted with tension. With extreme effort he managed to sound calm.

"Those are two of Troy's friends," he said. "The older one is a Babel official. They are with Troy in a hoverer on a special mission. I cannot do anything right now, and I cannot communicate with Troy. We can only wait and see what happens. If anything goes amiss, we can always summon help and disconnect Troy."

"Goes amiss?" whispered Nancy, as white as a sheet. "What kind of 'goes amiss'?"

"That is not absolutely clear at the moment." Ziggy lied through his teeth. "They have to land somewhere in the random territories and meet with someone."

"But they're prisoners!" cried Nancy. "They're neck deep in trouble. We've got to terminate this surf right now. It's all make believe, anyway, and you can always stop it and wake up, can't you? Alert the people in charge of the NET—you know, those . . . those . . . you just said it . . ."

"Babel," said Ziggy. "It appears that some of their people are cooperating with criminals. Troy is helping Babel to fight them. He is not in a situation where we need to extricate him right now. If the occasion arises, we can always get a rescue team down here. But doing so now, by ourselves, may actually put Troy into danger. We should never disconnect anyone without the proper supervision."

"I can't watch this any longer." Nancy's voice shook as she turned away. Then she looked at Ziggy defiantly. "I'm holding you responsible for the boy, Ziggy. If he isn't back here within fifteen minutes, I'm calling the NET rescue team myself!" She marched up the stairs, into the living room, there to collapse into her favorite armchair.

I'll see to it that they spend less time in the accursed NET. They're wasting their lives away, sitting like zombies in front of their computers. It's all illusions, after all—there's nothing real in there. Tim will be back in a week, and we'll have a family gathering. This madness must be curbed.

In the basement, bent over the monitor, a trembling Ziggy was praying ardently.

66. NET: Day 37, 15:12

The three captives spent the rest of the flight in gloomy silence. The space cruiser flew over snow-topped mountains and dense jungles. Suddenly it dived downward. Troy and Flint recognized the terrain at once.

"There's the red waterfall with the tunnel behind it," pointed Troy. "We've arrived. Flint, remember what I ordered you. No matter what happens, do not open the tunnel! If you do, all will be lost!"

"I heard you the first time, Troy," said Flint. He had hardly finished the sentence, when George entered the tiny cabin, his helmet inactive, wielding the nerve stunner. Without any warning he fired straight into Sven's chest, and then trained the stunner on Flint and Troy. Sven convulsed with a roar of pain, which George ignored.

"That was to remind you that I mean business, and I'll get what I want!" The cruiser halted, and they saw that it was suspended in mid air, near the cliff face of the waterfall. A gray metallic gangplank led from the cruiser's side down to the large rock platform in front of the door to the tunnel. They could see Flint's electronic lock glowing on the door, at the far end of the platform. A fan of red beams emanating from the cruiser boiled off the plunging waters that would have inundated the spot where they stood.

Troy and Flint got up and approached the gangplank, glancing in concern at Sven who was still writhing in agony on the floor. They passed through the transparent hull and onto the gangplank and, with George pressing from behind, alighted on the wide rocky balcony.

"Halt!" ordered George. "You, boss, sit on the ground."

Troy sat unresistingly on the wet rock; he didn't want to give George an excuse to abuse him again. But George needed no excuses—he zapped Troy's leg, and the boy contorted with a yelp of pain. George sneered at Flint's furious expression.

"Well now, Flint, old chap—are you going to open that door for me? I have no intention of harming you at this stage—just your boss."

"You'll have to untie my hands first." Flint's voice choked with rage.

George drew a small laser pistol from his uniform with his left hand, and pointed it at the plastic cord binding Flint's hands.

"Watch out!" cried Flint. But George pulled the trigger. There was an acrid smell of seared flesh, and Flint screamed. The cord melted and took with it a small portion of Flint's wrist. The open wound bled slowly. His arms and the back of his hands showed angry burn marks. George pocketed the laser pistol, and aimed the stunner directly at Troy's face.

"Go to that door and open it," he ordered Flint. "You have exactly four minutes. After that, I'm going to fry a different part of your boss' brain every thirty seconds." He took a pliable bracelet out of a pocket and showed it to Flint. "You probably recognize this doodad. It's an Emergency Rescue Bracelet—just by applying it, rescue personnel can bring surfers back to Earth with their memories intact. Flint, I am giving you fair warning: if you try any funny stuff, I am going to wipe this boy's brain clean and then apply the bracelet. You know what will happen—he will return to Earth and his brain will be updated . . . with a blank! He will be no more than a vegetable."

George returned the bracelet into his pocket. Flint did not even attempt to conceal his look of horror, and he approached the door immediately.

"Flint! Don't do it!" yelled Troy, prone on the rock shelf.

"Shut your trap!" roared George at Troy. In frenzy, he pointed the stunner to Troy's other leg and fired. Troy leaped into the air with the shock, and dropped to the ground, semi-conscious and breathing laboriously. George put the stunner to Troy's head.

"Open that door right now!" he thundered. "Or the next shock will erase his brain!"

Tears flowed from Flint's eyes, as he attacked the combination on the door as if possessed. He entered digits directly into the nodes, his fingers flying at an invisible speed. Three and a half minutes later, a shrill buzz was heard.

"The lock has been removed," he said in a hollow voice. "The door will open automatically in thirty seconds."

"Walk back toward me," commanded George, and he pointed the stunner at Flint's chest. Flint approached in slow strides. "Stop! Turn around and cross your wrists behind your back." Flint did as he was told, and George rebound his hands tightly. Then he zapped Flint twice, once in each leg. Flint collapsed, roaring in pain—then became motionless on the ground, face down.

At that instant the door to the tunnel became transparent. A black opening gaped at them from the mountain's side. George leered in victory. But the grin froze on his face. A blinding beam of intense purple light sprang from the opening and struck the cruiser hovering by the entrance. The cruiser was knocked backward, enveloped in flames. It twisted and dived into the canyon, leaving a trail of black smoke. Halfway down it straightened out, and hurtled straight up into the sky, as if mounted on a huge fiery flame. It quickly disappeared from view. The waterfall took the place vacated by the cruiser, and a massive curtain of red water dropped a dozen feet behind Troy and George, soaking everyone's clothes.

"What the—" George didn't complete the expletive. Troy, who had recovered, tore loose of his nicked bonds, and delivered a powerful karate kick into George's back. George fell to the ground, dropping his stunner and the atomic blaster he had managed to draw. But he was an expert fighter. The blow in the back had indeed surprised him, but did not incapacitate him, as it would any normal person. He deftly rolled aside, and parried a second kick that Troy had aimed at his head.

Troy dove for the blaster, grabbed it and fired at George. Too late. George had time to activate his protective helmet, and was bathed in its golden beams. The blaster had no effect.

George got up, picked up the stunner, and turned to Troy who was backing away rapidly.

Suddenly a high, amplified voice emanated from within the tunnel opening.

"George Boder, drop your weapons and surrender! There is another locked door inside the tunnel, and there is no way you can get through it!"

George looked about him wildly like a trapped animal, and zeroed on the prostrate Flint. He grabbed the lad by the hair and dragged him backward toward the lip of the rocky platform. Troy leaped forward and tried to take hold of Flint's legs, but George immediately zapped him in the chest with the stunner. Troy tottered a few steps backward and collapsed. George kept on dragging Flint and came within ten feet of the chasm's edge. There he halted and, facing the tunnel, placed the stunner's barrel to Flint's head. He drew out the Emergency Return Bracelet and held it near his prisoner's wrist.

"Throw down your weapons at once, and come out of the tunnel with your hands high in the air," he shouted toward the dark opening, though his voice was somewhat hollow through the protective shield. "If you do not obey within ten seconds, this boy's brains will be toast, and that's how he'll return to Earth. There's no use in resisting—I am totally protected, and you can't do a thing to me."

A tall man in Babel's combat uniform emerged from the tunnel, a freezer in his hand. It was Norman Starr. Three Babel fighters, holding laser rifles, followed him. Norman went to the prone Troy, knelt beside him, and checked his pulse. Weak, but steady. Troy opened his eyes.

"I'm all right," he whispered painfully. "Save Flint."

Norman got up and walked toward George, halting some fifteen feet away from him. The three fighters kept following him and halted a few paces behind, their rifles pointed at George.

"The game's over, George," said Norman, loudly and distinctly, to overcome the din of the waterfall. "Or whatever your real name may be. We're prepared to discuss terms of cooperation with your race, but your penetration into humans' minds is a hostile action. Put down your weapon."

"So you managed to escape, after all." George did not hide his surprise to see Norman. "And you did not learn the lesson I taught you when you were my guest. You imbecile—*you* want to come to terms with *us*?" His laugh was bloodcurdling. "You are to us as lice are to you! The lice want an agreement with the man to reside on him. And probably demand protection as well. Now, *you* put down your weapons, or I'll fry this kid's brains!" The stunner was at Flint's temple.

Norman squeezed the freezer's trigger and Flint froze at once. It had no effect on George.

"You cannot harm the boy any more." Norman's voice was calm. "He's frozen and feels nothing. Give it up, George."

"Don't be so sure," said George, his voice rising hysterically. "I'll throw him over the edge, if you don't put down your weapons right now!"

He grabbed Flint by the collar and started to poise him on the lip of the gorge. Norman took two quick steps toward them and pounced on George, ignoring the stunner that George tried to swing toward him. George had to let go of Flint who, while dropping to the ground, bumped into his legs. George momentarily lost his balance, and his stunner shot went wild, striking nothing. Then Norman hit him, and they both tumbled to the ground.

Norman was repelled by the protective shield, but managed to get quickly to his feet. He grabbed Flint by the legs, and hurriedly hauled him toward the tunnel, while the three soldiers passed him by, shooting laser beams directly at George. The latter was getting slowly to his feet. His shield turned red, but the beams could not harm his body. He put away the stunner, and drew out the laser pistol. Then he calmly shot the fighters, one by one. They sank to the ground and vanished with three soft 'poofs'.

George aimed his pistol at Norman.

"Tell all your men to come out with their hands up!" he screamed. "Or else I'll shear your legs out from under you . . . and I'll erase all your brains, here and on Earth!"

Norman looked hesitatingly at George. Troy got slowly to his feet, his right arm propped on Norman.

"Stay where you are, boy!" George barked. "I'm not through with you and your friend yet."

"I think you are," said Troy in a weak voice. He brought his right arm out from behind Norman's back. It was holding the atomic blaster, which was pointed at the rock under George's feet. Troy squeezed the trigger for several long seconds.

George's triumphant smirk transmuted to a look of shock, then of panic, when he realized what was happening. He tried to step toward Norman and Troy, but the rock shelf under him vaporized before he could move. For a fraction of a second it seemed that he hung in mid air, and then he plummeted down into the crevasse below. His howl of rage, overcoming even the thunder of the waterfall, caused Troy and Norman to shudder.

Norman turned to Troy, and hugged him fiercely, tears of happiness in his eyes. He stroked the hair of the trembling boy.

"Thank you, Troy." He choked on the words. "Thank you—in the name of the entire population of the Earth."

"Unfreeze Flint," whispered Troy. "I want to see that he's all right."

Norman gently eased Troy into a sitting position, and then unfroze Flint and untied his hands. The youth jumped to his feet with a wild look in his eyes.

"Where's George?" he asked, his voice raging.

"On his way to the lake down there," said Norman. "Troy sent him there via a shortcut. Your boss has saved us all."

"I always knew that you'd be of some use, eventually," said Flint, a giant smile of relief spreading on his face. "Is he dead?" He went to the edge of the shelf and peered down, unafraid, at the junction of the lake with the waterfall. But the massive spray at that point prevented him from seeing anything.

"We can't be certain of that," said Norman. "We must be prepared for the possibility that he wasn't killed. I'm going down there to make sure. You're both welcome to join me." He gave a few orders into his shoulder 'com. "The fleet is concealed behind the mountain—they will be here in a few minutes."

A group of armed fighters came out of the tunnel, and lined up on the rock platform, looking curiously at Norman and his companions. Their commander, a tall, dark soldier with a sergeant insignia on his shoulder, saluted Troy:

"We saw it all, young man," he said. "We salute you. We are the NET commandos, and you have an open invitation to join us at any time. It will be a great honor for us."

Troy saluted back. He felt too tired to talk.

Two minutes later, three black hoverers, bearing the Babel insignia, could be seen in the gap between the waterfall and the cliff face. One of them dived into the canyon into which George had fallen, while the other two came nearer and dropped rope ladders onto the shelf off to one side, where no water was cascading from the mountaintop. Norman signaled with his hand, and the fighters began climbing the ladders.

"Come with me," said Norman, ascending the nearer of the ladders. Troy and Flint followed, and seated themselves in the hoverer next to a group of fighters. The door of the aircraft shut tight, and the hoverer dived toward the lake. A bright dot of light shone from the bottom of the red waters, close to the shore where tall trees dipped their branches into the lake. The hoverer descended to fifty feet above the surface, near the location of the first hoverer that had arrived there a few minutes earlier. George could be clearly seen, lying motionless at the bottom of the lake, surrounded by his golden aura.

"Can you tell if he's alive," Norman asked the other hoverer through his 'com. "Has he made any movement?"

"He hasn't stirred for over two minutes," came the reply. "I believe he'll suffocate—"

George suddenly erupted into action. The golden halo turned off, and he thrashed around in wild swimming motions. His head bobbed to the surface, and he spluttered and gasped as he inhaled deeply.

"Quick! Dive in and freeze him before he has a chance to turn on his shield!" yelled Norman to the other hoverer, which was nearer to the struggling alien.

The hoverer banked and dipped, but before it could reach George, one of the tree branches lashed out of the water and whipped itself around George's body, pinning both his hands to his waist. George screamed in pain as the pressure of the branch crushed his ribs and internal organs. Blood gushed out of his mouth and nose, and his body twisted frantically as he tried to free himself from the deadly grip. But to no avail. The tree lifted its victim high out of the water, and smashed him violently against one of the boulders on the shore. George's body turned into a bloody pulp, all his bones broken to fragments. His yellow helmet fell off his head and rolled into the water.

The passengers of the hoverer watched in horror as George's body changed shape into a monstrous ten-foot-long alien, green pus-like fluid oozing from its orifices. The tree pounded the huge body several more times on the same boulder, as if to soften its prey, and then inserted the remains of what once was George into a wide opening in its trunk. The body slithered forward in two jerks and disappeared inside the tree trunk. Immediately, the opening in the trunk closed itself and could not be discerned any more.

"Brrr . . ." said Flint. "Those plants will eat anything. This time it'll surely get indigestion."

"Quite an original approach you have there," murmured Norman without smiling. "Frankly, I really couldn't care less about the plant's condition. What's important is that we've seen the end of George and of an alien in the NET. I still have to handle George on Earth. He has a lot of explaining to do."

"I cannot feel any compassion for the way he went," said Troy, shaking all over. "He was a raving sadist, and enjoyed torturing us. Wait a minute— what happened to the space cruiser? Sven and the last alien are still on it!"

"Yes, we know," said Norman. "It took off to an enormous height and began moving toward Netville. It was enveloped in flames, and I doubt whether it was under control. But we lost it, and we don't know where it is right now. The satellite has been programmed to alert us the second any similar looking object is detected, so we'll know if it comes near the city. However, it is at an altitude too high for our normal aircraft."

Troy took a deep breath.

"Let's hope that it'll be destroyed, and that Sven won't be harmed on Earth," he said. "At least he isn't being abused by George. I don't think that anything could be worse than his torturing." He stretched out in his narrow seat in the hoverer, wiped the sweat from his forehead, and faced Norman and Flint at his side.

"I think that closes *that* issue," he continued. "Perhaps you'd like to tell *me* something?"

"Like what?" asked Flint, the epitome of round-eyed innocence.

"Like when did you begin working for Norman?" said Troy with a tired grin. "Don't you two think that you owe me some sort of explanation? Something along the lines of how did Norman and his men get behind the impervious locked door to the tunnel?" He frowned at Flint. "I thought you were the only one who could open that door."

Norman and Flint exchanged glances.

"Flint, why don't you explain," suggested Norman. Flint scratched his head, obviously embarrassed.

"I couldn't tell you before," he began. "They could get it out of you by using torture or a brain probe, which are less effective on me. When Lynn cornered us at Babel HQ, she froze Norman first and then you, when you failed to convince her that we were not imposters. You probably assumed that she went on to freeze me, and subsequently summoned the fake Norman. However, what actually happened was that she gave me a last chance to prove that we weren't lying. I suggested that she check the satellite recordings of Maureen Clarke's site. I had nothing factual to back me up, but I thought it was worth the gamble, as we at that point had also nothing more to lose. And it paid off. She submitted a query to Og, and voila—it discovered an alien spaceship camouflaged among the trees. Furthermore, Og informed Lynn that Norman and George were both there. That seemed to be enough to convince Lynn, but to be on the safe side she tested me with a T-scope. Yes—I must say she's a real professional.

"When she was finally certain about us, I requested her to unfreeze this Norman," Flint gestured at Norman at his side. "But not you, Troy—I didn't want you to know a thing about what I was planning. So we left you frozen, and plotted a scheme against the invaders. We couldn't be sure of what would happen, but we both agreed that we had to prepare an ambush behind the tunnel door. Thus, if the aliens succeeded in forcing us to open the tunnel, there'd be a surprise waiting for them. Norman sent three hoverers with the commandos of Babel to the tunnel with a large laser cannon. It took them one hour using overdrive to reach the tunnel. Norman and I got there before them, using the Portable Transport Box, and I opened the door. The commandos arrived and moved the laser cannon into the tunnel, and hid themselves there as well. I explained the technique of modifying the password code of the middle door—no big deal, when you come right down to it—to the officer in charge, and he changed it. Now, even if I wanted to open that door, I wouldn't be able to."

"The rest followed a spontaneous course of events," continued Norman. "Flint and I, and the commando who changed the password of the middle door, returned to Babel HQ, and Lynn called the phony Norman. She told him she had caught three netters posing as surfers who had penetrated the Babel citadel, that one of them was his spitting image, and that she had frozen them all. He told her to wait, and that he'd get there as fast as he could. She then indeed froze Flint and myself. When my double arrived, Kumar came out of hiding and unfroze the three of us, and Flint destroyed the alien Norman as planned. I admit I was quite surprised to find myself suddenly in my office on Earth when the alien was killed. I was beginning to feel I'd be trapped in the NET forever. Moreover—I had retained all my memories!

"But I had no time for celebrating. The first thing I did was to go to George's office, and handcuff him to his desk while he was surfing. I left two armed guards at his side, so even if he returned from the surf, he'd be apprehended. I had decided to leave him in surf mode, so that I could nab the spaceship and the other alien. I knew you'd be suffering at his hands, but I hope you'll agree with me that there was really nothing else that I could do. I returned to the NET, and when I saw through the satellite monitors that the space cruiser was headed toward the tunnel, I jumped there directly with the portable Transport Box, opened the door using the keys Flint gave me, and joined the ambush, closing the door from the inside."

"Now *that* was really smart," exclaimed Troy, his eyes glowing. "Brilliant!" He glanced at Flint and gave him the double thumbs up gesture. "You played the part perfectly. I didn't suspect you for a second." He looked outside the hoverer. "Hey—what are we doing back at the waterfall?"

"We'll return to Netville from there. We left the portable Transport Box in the tunnel. And Flint has to seal the door again."

They carefully climbed down the rope ladder to the platform, the spray from the waterfall wetting their clothes again. Five armed commandos waited for them by the portable Transport Box, which they had dragged out of the tunnel. Flint checked in the tunnel to make sure nothing was left behind, and then shut the door and began coding the various nodes.

Norman's shoulder 'com buzzed, and he listened for several seconds.

"It's about the space cruiser. Our presence is urgently required at Babel's Control Center. How's it going, Flint?"

"Just two minutes more . . ."

67. Palo Alto, Saturday, 13:38

Nancy heard Ziggy's footsteps ascending the stairs. She brushed aside her fantasies and jumped up from her armchair.

"What's happened, Ziggy? Where's Troy?"

"They have won!" Ziggy's voice carried so much relief and happiness, that Nancy's heart leaped for joy. "He is a real hero, your son." Tears of elation streamed down his face. He hugged Nancy warmly and kissed her on the cheek. "You should have seen how he pounced on that depraved invader, even though he was pointing a weapon at him. He was not afraid at all."

"Yes, that's my boy all right," said Nancy proudly. "Once he battled two bullies who were tormenting a dog, even though they were both bigger than him. He got beaten quite badly, but saved the poor animal. What exactly happened?"

There was no way Ziggy could convey the enormity of what had occurred. He decided to skip the gory details, and described only the struggle at the tunnel's entrance and how George was defeated.

"The alien died after his fall into the water." He concluded, sparing her the specifics of George's demise.

"So it's over now—why hasn't he returned here then?" she asked. "I'd like a word with him, too, you know. Can you tell him to come back?"

"No, I cannot communicate with him. But he is very busy right now with something extremely important. He is assisting in the rescue of Maggie's father."

"Please send him a message that when he's finished doing so, he can also visit his home occasionally. He doesn't need to save the entire world."

"I believe," smiled Ziggy, "that that is exactly what he is doing right now."

68. NET: Day 37, 16:00

Flint completed locking the door to the tunnel, and the three of them entered the portable Transport Box. Norman keyed in the coordinates, and the box responded with a series of beeps, indicating the need for a password. He punched several digits on the keypad and the beeps ceased. The lights flickered twice and the door opened. They stepped out onto a small hoverer landing platform, and faced a squad of combat-clad fighters with freezers ready. When they saw Norman they put down their weapons and saluted him.

"Sir, I have never seen a Transport Box that could move around," said the squad commander, a major. "Our unit would be most happy to obtain one of these boxes. You are expected at the Center."

"Have two men guard this box," retorted Norman curtly. "These lads here will be joining me at the Control Center."

The major led them to a tall cubic building with black windows. The two guards at the entrance recognized Norman, but he was asked to place his palm on the verification plate just the same. They passed the door and saw Lynn waiting for them. She hugged Norman and kissed his cheek, and immediately turned to the kids and shook their hands, ignoring the surprised Norman.

"Follow me to the control room," she said. "They are all waiting for you. I couldn't help it—I just had to be the first to see you, so I waited at the front entrance. Oh, you kids are so wonderful! Welcome once again to the Babel citadel. I've been told that I hosted you the last time you were here, but I really don't remember the occasion." She looked affectionately at Norman. "Norman, excuse me, but I was so glad to see you in good health. And I understand that we're finally rid of that sadist, George. When this has all blown over you must tell me all the little details. You're hereby invited to dinner at Robins, and you may consider that a date!"

Norman patted her fondly on her back. "You were right regarding George from the very beginning. I'll definitely pay more attention to your hunting instincts in the future. And I accept the invitation. But we're still not done with this crisis."

They had arrived at the control room, and Lynn opened the door. They walked into a wide room, with a holographic screen covering the far wall. A long elliptic table stood in the center of the room, and a number of people were seated around it with their backs to the newcomers, facing the screen. The scene was of the interior of a cabin with silvery walls.

The assembly turned in their seats toward the door. Troy's mouth opened in astonishment when he recognized Maggie as one of them.

"Maggie!" he cried joyfully. "How did you get here?" She got up, and he ran to her and hugged her.

"She was brought here by one of the Babel teams that searched for her in the NET and on Earth," replied Norman. "In fact, the search was initiated by my double, and I only continued it. There was a constant alert out for her in the NET, and the minute she attempted to send you a puzzle, we picked her up and brought her here."

Troy noticed that Maggie's eyes were red from weeping.

"What happened to Sven," he asked, his voice trembling.

"That screen there shows us what's happening to him," explained Lynn in a quiet tone. "Right now, he is in the alien space cruiser. We're connected to his brain during the surf, and we see what his eyes see."

"That's right!" cried Flint. "That's the same cabin George locked us in."

"Can you contact him in any way?" asked Troy.

A tall man with a white goatee stood up and approached them. "I'm afraid not. I'm Melvin Green, director of the surf control center. We're monitoring his location at every moment. The cruiser is currently four hundred and forty-seven miles northeast of Netville, at an altitude of about twenty-two miles, which is rapidly diminishing. It is approaching Netville in a large curve, probably due to lack of control. At its present velocity it should arrive at Netville in about half an hour."

Sven's hands appeared on the screen. They were dripping with perspiration. He reached out and touched a silvery wall, but retracted his hand sharply. He was clearly in acute agony.

"We cannot receive any of his other senses," said Green, "save his hearing." He turned up the speaker volume, and a groan of anguish rose from it. It was Sven's voice. His gaze turned to the transparent outer wall, and they saw streams of flame around the cruiser's fuselage. Past the flames they saw blue skies.

"Maggie," said Norman softly. "It is up to you to decide how to act now. We can disconnect your father at any second and release him from his agony. He'll lose this last surf, and the odds favor his being undamaged as a result. Maybe a little more of his memory will be lost as well, but usually that is relatively simple to reconstruct." He laid a hand on her head and looked into her tear-swollen eyes.

"I understand," she sniffed. The tears kept flowing and her body shook. Norman hugged her closely, his eyes streaming tears as well. "But we cannot disconnect him now," she added. "We must continue to track that alien, and we can only do so through dad's eyes. Oh, dad, please forgive me . . .' and she broke down again, sobbing heavily.

Troy felt the tears choking his throat. He glanced at Flint, who also sniffed loudly and lowered his gaze.

"You're a very brave girl," said Norman, stroking her hair. "I am positive that he would have made the same choice. We'll try to disconnect him at the very last possible moment, so as to minimize any potential damage. May I suggest we leave this room? There's nothing we can do here to help him."

"I want to stay," whispered Maggie. She wiped away her tears and continued determinedly. "I cannot leave him like that, in his misery, even if he doesn't know it. I want to see what happens to him until the last moment. Please leave the speaker on."

The next half hour was one of the hardest in their lives. Sven kept twisting and contorting on the screen, trying in vain to escape from the roasting cabin. He groaned from time to time, his voice hoarse. The monitor showed the cruiser's course, still headed for Netville.

"Two minutes to the outskirts of Netville," called Green. "Its altitude is only three thousand feet now. I estimate it'll crash somewhere in the Eastern areas, probably East New London."

Norman turned on his 'com. "Get all surfers in the New London area out of the NET. In one minute I want you to forcefully disconnect all the surfers there." He hesitated for a second, and then said, "Scouting parties two and three—arrive at East New London area and hover at one mile. We're expecting the crash landing of a suspicious object in the vicinity. Upon identifying the landing, approach and report what you see. Do not get closer than a hundred feet to the object."

"Done," said the silver-haired man on Norman's screen. "The teams will be there in less than a minute. We'll report all we see."

Norman turned to Maggie.

"We are about to disconnect your father from the NET. We shall time it to twenty seconds before the crash. He won't feel a thing—Hey, what the hell is going on?"

A side screen showed the graph of the cruiser's path. For the past half hour it had been a curved arc in the direction of Netville. Now it had suddenly swerved to the right. The cruiser accelerated furiously, entered Netville's limits, and dived toward the ground.

"Disconnect Sven!" roared Norman. But the screen blacked out before anyone could react. They all froze, except for Troy who went quickly up to Maggie. He saw her tottering, her face in her hands, and he managed to catch her as she collapsed in a dead faint.

The screen came to life again, and the scene was the crash area as taken by one of the scout teams that had reached the area. Billows of smoke and dust covered the entire region, and through them a huge crater, the size of a soccer stadium, had been gouged out of the ground. A raging fire roared at the bottom of the crater, completely consuming the remains of the cruiser. From time to time, gigantic green and purple flames leaped up to the height of the neighboring skyscrapers, accompanied by thunderous explosions.

Three hours later, when the flames had abated, all that remained at the bottom of the crater was a giant puddle of molten metal. Of the contents of the cruiser, including the alien and its prisoner, there wasn't a trace.

Part Four–Tuesday

9. NET: Day 106, 14:00

The Blue House in the NET was almost an exact replica of its famous white counterpart on Earth. The main differences were, of course, in the color and the fact that it was located in Netville, instead of in Washington. The presidential area was an isolated and guarded zone that was not accessible by the regular Transport Boxes. One needed to use a special Transport Box, and even then you could only reach the reception desk at the front gate. All other coordinates were blocked by the NET's infrastructure computers. Except to a limited number of VIP's and high-ranking security personnel, the region was utterly invisible in the NET.

The limousine was delayed for several minutes at the main entrance gate, as armed guards conducted a thorough search with highly sensitive mass detectors. The passengers, too, were meticulously checked—including an X-ray and a short T-scope test. The large brown bear in the yellow suit also had to pass a brain probe.

"They're not taking any chances," Norman told Lynn, Troy, Maggie, Adam, and Flint as the limousine was finally permitted to move into the enclosed area. "Without my prior notification, Flint would never have passed that gate—the guards have no instructions on how to treat someone who was neither surfer nor netter. Maybe it would have been better for you to appear as a human, Flint."

"I considered that option," replied Flint. "But a distinction must be made between computers and humans. It is well known that a bear is man's best friend." He saw Norman raising an eyebrow and added quickly, "Maybe second best, I haven't checked recently . . ."

"Hey, do they know *everything* about us?" Adam was dressed in his school uniform, his small tie displaying a picture of Tuffy. His eyes shone in excitement.

"Sure they do," teased Troy. "Even that you're a Pira-net member." He wore a new white shirt and carefully pressed khaki slacks. Maggie, who sat next to Flint, was dressed in her NET trekking outfit.

Adam flushed. He glanced apologetically at Lynn, who sat next to Norman. She straightened her Babel uniform and smiled at the child affectionately.

"It's okay," she said. "Your style could do with some polish, but everything has been forgiven. You can continue surfing in the Pira-net—no one's going to tail you. But you may not sell any information on this visit. That would be a new violation."

"Oh, I won't breathe a word," said Adam hastily. "Hey, I apologize for my behavior there. It was the first time I was in Pira-net, and I may have been a bit . . . umm . . . impulsive."

"You, impulsive? Impossible!" taunted Troy. "You must be referring to someone else."

They all burst into laughter. Troy continued warmly. "However, little brother, as far as I'm concerned, we've turned over a new leaf. All is forgiven. You may begin sinning afresh." He peered at the two black vehicles driving before and behind them, and turned to Norman. "Can they hear us?"

"No," was the reply. "But we're under constant observation every second we're here. They're still afraid of viruses."

They all recalled the much-publicized episode of the NET's early days, when a virus disguised as a police officer ambushed the President and assassinated him with three shots to the chest from close range. The President lost only the memory of his last surf, but there was a lot of embarrassment in the Security Services, and some of the President's senior security staff had to resign on Earth as well as in the NET.

"If our current adventure ever became public," added Norman, "it would over-shadow any previous news coverage."

"I quite understand why all that we've been through is classified as top secret," said Troy. "But I hope that at least we'll be informed about what happened on Earth to the people who were taken over by the invaders."

Norman chuckled. "I really don't know if I should be telling you this, but you know so much already, that I don't think a bit more would make any difference." He grinned, and winked at Flint. "What would you do if I decided not to reveal anything to you?"

"I refuse to answer on the grounds that it may incriminate you," said the bear, and Maggie groaned audibly. It wriggled a bit in its seat, pushing Troy and Maggie on either side. "Anyway, it's always better to get the information straight from the director's mouth. So what did happen to them?"

"One thing happened to all the three victims—they all contracted NET-phobia in a bad way. Furthermore, none of them remember anything that happened from the moment they were taken over. As if all the memories from then on belonged to the alien and not to them."

"Do you mean to say," queried Maggie, "that when an alien was killed, its entire being—memories and all—left the human host through the surfing helmet and died with it? Leaving no traces in the human's brain? That would mean that the hosts could return to their normal lives with just a couple of Earth days missing."

"That's right," said Norman. "Apart from the fact that they now have NET-phobia. That could mean quite a drastic change in their 'normal' lives. We're talking about Noah Atkinson and Maureen Clarke. As for George, we have a long account to settle with him. He is now under arrest and charged with a number of serious crimes, including murder."

"Murder!" exclaimed Flint. "Are you talking about the people he killed in the NET? That does not constitute murder under the NET laws."

"Nevertheless, we're charging him with the murder of Stewart York. Remember, please, that during the battle in Hell, George told York, just before eliminating him, that he was responsible for York's brain damage on Earth. He coerced York to surf, even though he knew very well that he suffered from NET-phobia, and that there were serious risks involved. At the very second that York was blasted by George in the NET, Stewart York—who happened to be connected to his helmet right then—died on Earth. In our book that constitutes murder, and we're pinning it on George."

"That'll be hard to prove," said Troy. "George will deny any responsibility as he will remember nothing of what he did while occupied by the alien. And I don't know if you can use us as witnesses."

"Not you personally," said Norman. "We cannot expose your identity. But everything you saw of the battle in Hell was recorded by Ziggy while he was following you on the helmet hookup. We showed the recording to George and he broke down and confessed to everything. He's facing a life sentence in prison."

"I pity his future cell mates," remarked Troy. "But that is not our concern any more. Talking about his mates—what happened to those recording buttons that I took from Noah Atkinson's cabinet? Oh, and please remember to defuse the bombs we left at the site, before anyone gets hurt."

"The booby traps were neutralized," said Norman. "As to the recording buttons—I gave them to Noah, and he was astounded by their contents. He claims that they are the most dramatic and important discoveries ever made in genetics—even outshining the deciphering of the DNA. He insists that I tell him who the scientists are that created these research papers, and how come his own digital signature foots them all."

"Now he'll get the Nobel Prize," said Flint enviously. "In any case, I think he and Maureen should be kept under close surveillance. The alien may have left a Trojan Horse in their brains. If I were—" He saw Norman's pained look, and repressed himself, the fur on his head standing straight up in embarrassment.

"Very true," said Norman softly. "I, too, could be a Trojan Horse. All three of us will be undergoing monthly brain probes and T-scope tests. And by the way, all the T-scope devices in Babel that George tampered with have been recalibrated."

The limousine entered an underground tunnel and the conversation stopped. The tunnel was wide and brightly lit, and an armed guard was posted every few hundred yards. A short while later they emerged, and followed the road toward a stone wall, which had a steel gate in its center.

Through the gate's bars they could see the Blue House in all its splendor, a large sprawling lawn at its front. The gate opened, and they rolled up a narrow pathway, which curved through the lawn and ended at the building's ornate front door.

"Here we are," said Norman. "I was here once, some three Earth years go. I met the newly inaugurated President then—he wanted to familiarize himself with the NET's top security brass."

They left the vehicle and made their way to the building. Poker-faced agents in gray suits, who made no effort to conceal the bulges under their jackets, opened the door and led them in.

The President of the United States was waiting for them in the Oval Office, with a small entourage. It was easy to identify the seven-foot President, towering over the rest of the guests. His silver curls bounced around his shoulders, and his sparkling eyes and boyish looks belied the fact that he was nearly sixty years old. He wore a white tropical suit, with a Van Gogh portrait on his tie.

The rest of the assembly wore dark suits and formal dresses, and most of them looked much older than the President. Troy identified the Secretary of the European Union and the Minister for Interior Security. Maggie also spotted John Pierce standing to one side, his face beaming.

The President smiled and walked up to them. "Let's see now, which one of you is the computer?" he joked, and winked at Flint. "Tell me, do you hibernate in winter?"

"There's too much going on, sir," replied Flint, his voice trembling in excitement. "There's isn't any time to sleep. Fortunately, I don't need to sleep, anyway. I'd like to thank you, Mr. President, for having come to the NET for my sake, with all these esteemed personages."

"It is we that have to thank you," said the President. "If it weren't for you and your friends here, there wouldn't be a NET. Besides, how can you tell that I'm genuine and not an alien masquerading as the President? No, no need to panic—I'm fine! I, too, was checked at the entrance." He laughed and turned to Norman.

"Norman Starr, how nice to meet you again. Are you the copy or the original? I heard that the copy was, in fact, much smarter."

"Not smart enough to outwit this bunch, sir," interjected Pierce, who walked up to Norman and shook his hand vigorously.

"I'm the original, Mr. President," said Norman, nodding in thanks toward Pierce. "My people prefer me this way."

"Lets ask their pretty representative, then." The President shook Lynn's hand and kissed her on the cheek. "Well, Lynn? The Norman double, who was killed in the NET, was far more intelligent and possessed many more qualities than this one here. Why did you prefer him?" He placed his arm on Norman's shoulder while everyone laughed.

"I'm quite content with this version, and I don't believe he needs any improvements," she said, looking long at Norman. "Well, come to think of it, maybe a few adjustments to reality . . ."

"Watch out!" The President clapped Norman on the back. "That's how it begins. 'A few adjustments . . .'" He turned to Troy and Maggie, who were standing next to Norman.

"So you're the famous puzzle champions, eh? This adventure was probably your toughest puzzle yet. I'm really very proud of you. All the transgressions you did before this event will be forgotten. And, as Norman promised, you're free to surf the NET with your furry partner at will. But in the future, let's leave the decision regarding whom to send to hell to divine judgment. Okay?" His eyes caught Flint's and he grinned. Flint grinned back and nodded vigorously.

"Maggie, I pray that your father will be all right. Pierce has just informed me that he is recovering."

"Thank you, Mr. President," said Maggie. "He's already begun to talk. He still doesn't remember anything of the last two weeks, and he can barely walk. But the doctors say that he'll be back in the saddle pretty soon, all faculties intact, and that his memory should return within a week. Except for the last surf, of course."

The President gave her a light hug, and addressed Adam, who barely reached his waist.

"And here we have the electric technician, that all the NET authorities are chasing. Also the renowned tetrosaur warrior. I heard that you also saved this gang here from a rather unsavory netter that bushwhacked you in the Rollernet. Good work! Where's your gorilla?"

"He's g-g-grounded for a week," stammered Adam, shaking in excitement. Troy nudged him. "Oh, sorry. Sir. Hey, right, Flint?" Flint confirmed with a nod of his head. He already had a long discussion with Pyotr. The private escapade he had launched with Adam had almost jeopardized the trap they were preparing for the aliens.

"And is this the monster that butted the spaceship out of commission?" asked the President, indicating the picture on Adam's tie.

"Yes, Mr. President, that's Tuffy." Adams face was radiant. "She's fully recovered and, hey, she's won another fight."

"Excellent," laughed the President. "She has etched her name forever in the annals of the NET."

He gestured toward a small dais near one of the walls.

"We're going to have a short decoration-awarding ceremony right now. The main event, with medals and all, will take place on Earth next month. It, too, will be top secret, but your parents will be able to attend." He glanced at Maggie, who looked gratefully at him. She knew that the ceremony was postponed in order to allow Sven to recuperate enough to be able to participate. "But, due to the fact that some of us cannot make it to the Earth she-bang, we decided to have another one here, in the NET. Please go onto the podium."

"Norman," whispered Troy nervously, pulling at the director's sleeve. "Mom and Ziggy are watching everything here through my eyes. I forgot to tell you earlier. I hope it's all right . . ."

Norman thought for a second and then grinned.

"As the person responsible for the security in the NET," he declared pompously, "I hereby give my authorization retroactively. There—now it's legal." Troy was relieved. He joined Flint, Maggie and Adam on the dais.

"You too, Norman," said the President. "We've got a copy of a medal for you. Lynn, get up here as well. Stand next to Norman."

The ceremony was short. Norman, Maggie and Troy each received the 'President's Decoration', the highest decoration for valor available to a US citizen. The three of them, together with Flint, Adam and Lynn, also received the 'NET Shield' ribbon from the Minister for Internal Security. Maggie and Troy got another decoration from the Secretary of the European Union, and a scholarship for PhD studies in any of the universities in the Union.

"So what are you planning for your future?" asked the President, as they sat down to a festive dinner. Maggie and Troy sat at his sides, while Adam and Flint had a quiet argument regarding Pyotr further down the table.

"They have consented to be Babel consultants," interjected Norman. "Part time. We're even going to employ Flint officially. But he must stop penetrating into other computers."

"But they all agreed—" His fur bristled in embarrassment as everyone around the table burst into laughter. "All right, all right, I won't contact them even if they beg me to."

"The 'President's Decoration' carries a prize of a quarter of a million dollars," said the President to Troy. "And the 'NET Shield' another hundred thousand. What do you intend to do with all this money?"

"I intend to make myself another backup system in a secret place," blurted Flint. "My current backup is unreliable. And I'll expand my memory and add another four processors. Those aliens were far too advanced, and I want to study their technology—beginning with the spaceship that was damaged in Maureen's site. We'll be ready for them next time. Troy will loan me a part of the money, won't you, Troy?"

Troy smiled, but the President looked concerned.

"Do you really think they'll come back again? Do you have any indication to that effect?"

The conversation around the table ceased abruptly. All eyes were upon them. Troy answered the President in Flint's stead.

"The NET is a large place, Mr. President. A new frontier, like the Wild West once was. In four Earth decades the NET will have aged by nearly a thousand years! Perhaps even more, if we manage to accelerate it to higher speeds safely. We cannot do without the NET now—it has become part of our culture and the future for all our development. But we have to assume that there will be encounters with extra-terrestrial agents some time in the future, and we must be prepared for them. We don't know what the purpose of this last alien visit was, but I sincerely hope that next time we'll meet up with a friendlier civilization. Anyway, like I said, we've got to be on our guard and prepared."

Everyone present nodded and murmured their assent. Even the big brown bear, who was secretly cloning alien DNA from tissue fragments he had scraped off the black rock where George had perished, nodded in agreement.

EPILOGUE

I have long debated with myself whether to document my memoirs regarding the events of the invasion of the NET, and of Hell—that NET site that turned out to be the greatest challenge of my life. Many, many years have passed but, as you can see, I have reached a conclusion, and the result is what you are now reading.

My real name and place of origin are immaterial. Suffice it to say that I am not of your planet or galaxy—maybe not even of your universe at all. In your terms I am an alien, even though most of you are familiar with my name on Earth, David Mansfield. Yes, *the* David B. Mansfield, founder of the Trans-Platform Group, winner of two Nobel Prizes, and philanthropist extraordinaire.

I am dying. My internal organs are decaying of a mutant strain of cancer that no one has found a cure for yet. Even the most optimistic physicians give me no more than three months to live. Therefore, I must hurry with this chronicle. You will then know what I know, and perhaps you will find answers to riddles heretofore unsolved. And who knows, perhaps some time, in some inconceivable way, contact with my native world may be reestablished, and they, too, will know what happened here.

Even without having read the seven or eight biographies (I never could keep count of them) of my life, you already know what I represent to your planet, Earth. It was I who brought about the discovery of the Time-Breaker technique, enabling mankind to break through the speed-of-light barrier. You remember that at the time it was considered the greatest discovery since the invention of the wheel. Yet the Nobel prizes awarded me, as well as numerous other prizes, were not really earned by me. I did not invent the new technologies—I only applied knowledge I already had. But my conscience is clear. You'll find that almost all of the money I made went to charities and DNA research ventures.

You may rightfully ask why I elected to be so beneficial to mankind? Very frankly, this was not my initial disposition. Quite the contrary—I spent several years plotting how to rectify the enormous catastrophe that had befallen my crew and myself. I shall introduce us presently, but right now I must tell you that my attitude changed over the thirty odd years I have spent, albeit unwittingly, on your Earth. The more I learned about humans and mankind, the more I grew to identify with you, and later even like you. Anything else relevant about me as David Mansfield you can freely read about in various publications.

And that's about enough of background preamble. On with the historic narrative!

But first, I wish to salute Troy Bentley. You defeated us fair and square, though I wonder if you ever internalized the magnitude of your achievement. I know that you were not alone in your endeavors, and I also know that whoever assisted you was beyond human capabilities. I have scoured this planet for such a creature and have found none. Therefore, I concluded long ago that you were aided by a computer—a computer far more powerful than anything ever put on the market or developed in a laboratory. A computer able to take any form or shape in the NET. Your greatness was apparent not only in utilizing its vast intelligence, but also in your wisdom in keeping it anonymous. By that term I mean total obscurity, complete invisibility. Believe me, I had the tools and the methods to expose any and every form of super-computer ever devised by humans. Had you not employed this covert approach, I have no doubt you would have been unmasked in a matter of minutes and destroyed. I congratulate you once again—you have actually saved your race from total annihilation.

As aforementioned, I was born in another world, belonging to a race that I shall call the Ancients. And so we were, truly ancient—far beyond human capacity to grasp. However, there are many similarities to humans. We are a biological race, with an evolution pattern dictated by molecules much akin to your DNA. We breathe oxygen, and feed on carbohydrates and proteins like yourselves. Our world consists of a main planet and several satellites within our solar system, all having atmospheres, oceans, mountains, flora and fauna which differ only minutely, in cosmic terms, from those on Earth.

The main difference between us lies in the fact that the Ancients are several million years ahead of you (1 shall use the Earth terms for the passage of time—years, months, days, etc.—as they are very similar to our own). We have interplanetary travel and can reach the far outskirts of our galaxy. We communicate telepathically—at first this was a scientific development but later we learned how to incorporate this valuable trait into our genes. Yes, we know how to alter and improve our race deliberately, instead of waiting for normal evolution to take its course. In fact, we did the same for longevity—we survive more than twice our "normal" lifetimes, and can now live for approximately two hundred and fifty of your Earth years.

Unfortunately, despite our immense scientific and technological progress, we are still subject to the laws of nature. About five hundred thousand years ago we became aware of the end of our world. Our solar system was approaching a black hole, and during the following millennia we observed our impending doom with increasing dismay. Planets will start crumbling and disappearing in about fifty thousand years from now—perhaps an eternity for you, but just a temporal flicker in the terms of a race as ancient as ours. And once the process has begun, it will be over in a matter of days. Nothing, absolutely nothing, will survive.

In all our travels within our galaxy, voyages lasting sometimes tens and hundreds of years, we have not found a single planet, let alone a solar system, capable of sustaining our race. We are probably the only instance of life in our part of the cosmos. Our astronomers have probed far beyond the confines of our galaxy, where our spaceships cannot venture, and have come up with naught. Our race was facing total eradication unless we could find some other way to save ourselves. And our scientists did, indeed, find this other way. We call it Cross-Life.

You call it the NET.

Like you, we developed a virtual world. You managed to create a single planet and a star—we created an entire galaxy. Like your own genius Markovitch, we discovered that accelerating this galaxy to velocities near the speed of light caused not only time to slow down, but space to bend, sometimes dramatically. Markovitch only theorized that space-folds would occur—we actually located several hundred thousands of them.

We set sensors, and remotely monitored the discovered space-folds. The premise was that if somewhere in existence, any other world developed an equivalent of Cross-Life, they too would create space-folds, and that those space-folds might possibly coincide with ours. They could subsequently serve as link points between them and us. Presumably, a civilization advanced enough to link up to us could also accommodate our race suitably. Our intention was to transport our entire population of about fifty million (a very small figure by your standards) to the linked virtual world, and then upload each one of us into one of the brains of the people in the other real world. Thus would our race be saved!

I was the commander of a small spaceship patrolling the fringes of our virtual galaxy. My mission was to monitor the alarm systems from sensors in over seventy 'nearby' space-folds. This was no easy task, as there were numerous false alarms, triggered by errant space flotsam and collapsing stars.

The crew consisted of seven highly trained professionals and myself. Our names are meaningless to you—each Ancient name is a sixty-four-digit number that not only uniquely identifies the individual, but also relates his entire genealogical lineage. I would probably desecrate my crew's memory by trying to spell them out in any Earth language, so I shall call them by their code names.

W1, W2, and W3 were warriors first-class, G1 was our genetics specialist, and C1, C2 and C3 were our cyber-culture wizards, covering both cybernetics skills and foreign culture adaptation—a natural combination in our world. When I sign this document I shall use my code name, too—K1.

The last alert that we covered seemed just like all the other previous ones. A miniscule change in the total mass of a planet was reported by one of the sensors. Fortunately, even though its location was on the periphery of our galaxy, it was relatively close to one of our abandoned cities, thereby allowing us to use our speed-link. We got there in just under ten hours. During this travel time, the space-fold sensor continued broadcasting data that indicated that whatever the interference may be, it was probably steady, and not a transient event.

As we reached the planet, it became apparent that finally, after two hundred thousand years of false alarms, in which many doubted the validity of the space-fold "inter-link" theories, this was the long awaited bridge to another intelligence. Someone had attempted to penetrate into our deserted city, and the automatic defense systems were triggered to envelope the entire city in an impenetrable shell of laser beams.

I sent W3 in a cruiser to enter the city under that shell and find the invaders. At the same time I located the intruder's point of entry. On the side of a low hill overlooking the city was the opening to a tunnel. I alerted home base and went into the tunnel, which ended in a spacious cavern, and came out at the other side through a large waterfall on your planet. That is, on your virtual NET planet.

We immediately realized that we had stumbled on a great prize. There was a sun in the sky, an atmosphere, and vegetation. Every crewmember mentally embraced his partners in discovery, delighting in our find. Hoping to find a thriving intelligent race, we set out to locate the nearest inhabited settlement. We wanted to know what you looked like. Were you still in the primitive stage of Virtual Worlds? Could your brains contain us? Or perhaps you were a hundred times more advanced than we were, capable of destroying us with a mere gesture?

There was no need to signal back to headquarters—by passing the space-fold sensor an automatic message was relayed back to home base. It would take my people about two weeks to send reinforcements to help us in the new world. It was an error on my part, as I learned in retrospect, to have sent W3 to capture the invaders that, I assumed, were trapped under the city's shell. I should have posted him on guard to the entrance of the tunnel, and have him await the arrival of the support forces. Had I done so the entire picture would have been different. So would our two worlds. That mysterious Flint would have been prevented from interfering with our plans and saving your planet. But that is water under the bridge now.

The minute we arrived at the inhabited area of your NET, we realized that our culture outclassed yours a thousand fold. You needed special equipment to communicate with each other—we use telepathy. Your space travel was in its infancy, requiring several years to get from one planet to another within your solar system. Your brain capacity was very limited, and all too often it would forget certain things you had learned—we never forget anything. And whereas you spend about one third of your life sleeping, we need about five or six minutes of deep-sleep per week.

The first step was to take over one of your people, in order to learn from his brain more about your world and prepare it for our immigration. Actually, invasion is a more suitable term, as we intended to take over your brains. We were interested in you solely from the physiological point of view. After taking over, *we* would provide all the intelligence and culture that we needed.

We chose a remote location that would not be noticed—an isolated site at the far end of the desert. I settled our spacecraft a few miles away and we approached the site warily. It was not protected—a regular two-story house by an artificial lake, surrounded by some trees. The site was, however, well tended—three creatures (which turned out to be netters) were bustling about in the garden, and some more could be observed through the house windows. The owner of the site was not there when we barged in, and the netters put up no resistance, continuing with their normal routine. We waited for about an hour for the owner, a certain Albert Spindler, a computer expert. When he finally hooked into the NET, C3 tele-controlled his mind and at once returned to the real world, thereby disconnecting Spindler on Earth from the virtual Spindler in the NET world.

However, two unfortunate situations resulted that we could not have anticipated. The first was that the human brain, and Spindler was no exception, could not fully accommodate an Ancient brain. And much worse—there was no way for C3 to reverse his action! He could not return to his virtual self in the NET. We had a continuous telepathy channel open with him, and we observed how he took control of the various unused portions of Spindler's brain bit by bit, and when none were left how he began erasing some of the less vital parts to provide more space. But there just was not enough brain material. We watched C3 go brain dead before our very eyes, courageously describing each and every detail of the takeover until the last second.

We later learned that on Earth Albert Spindler suffered severe memory loss, and became the mental equivalent of a year-old baby. As far as I know, he was committed to an asylum for the insane. This was a mistake on your part. The poor fellow should have been treated as an infant, and retaught all the basics—feeding, walking, communicating, etc.

The second unfortunate incident was that the virtual Albert Spindler, the copy in the NET, did not disappear with a 'poof' as we expected. He remained with us, even though his real self was disconnected from the NET. He quickly caught on what had happened, and tried to escape. We could not allow him to remain in the NET, as he would disclose our presence immediately. W2 found him in the garden, pretending to be one of the netters, and atomized him. We also blasted all the netters we found there—just to be on the safe side.

We retreated from the site to the desert, and commenced on building a plan how to proceed. We thought we had plenty of time for this, but on the following day the *real* problem began!

Our communication line with W3 in the deserted city was suddenly cut off. I promptly sent W1 back to the waterfall to find out what had happened, and to restore the link. Due to the fact that we were within a planetary atmosphere, we could not make use of our space-overdrive, and W1 arrived at the waterfall only about an hour later. During his flight, he continuously reported telepathically on his progress. We could observe him approaching the waterfall, penetrating it, and entering the tunnel. When he arrived at the far end of the tunnel, we could see him facing a steel door, which completely blocked the exit.

Of course, we knew that it wasn't really a door or real steel. We knew that these were just images someone from your universe had put up for the benefit of your senses—which worked on ours in much the same way. But the message was clear—there was no passing back into our universe. W1 pulled out his neutron blaster in order to clear away the obstruction, and then abruptly our connection with him was severed, too. To this day, I do not know what became of him. I'm afraid he was trapped in the tunnel and died there—almost a millennium has passed in the NET since the event.

We rushed back to the waterfall, but it still took us over an hour. The tunnel *had* to remain open—the success of the entire mission depended on it. We approached the tunnel very cautiously, blasters and atomizing cannons at the ready. We interrupted the flow of water with a hyperlaser barrier, a technology still far beyond you, only to discover that the tunnel had been blocked off on *this* side with another steel door. It appeared that whoever it was that disconnected our communications channel, had also prepared a trap for us and had managed to catch W1 in it!

I examined the door and realized that we had a serious problem on our hands. It was a logical door containing a grid password lock. We were familiar with these basic cyber-techniques—you cannot prevent that special glow emanating from password-protected artifacts. We therefore also knew that no amount of blasting would open that door—it would open into the desired destination only by the application of the correct password. Any other code would lead to any of an infinity of random destinations, and the number of code combinations was astronomical. We did, in fact, make one attempt at passing through, hoping the door had been carelessly left connected to our universe. But it was too much to hope for. We turned up at an undefined location, and it was pure luck that we managed to get back at all.

We were trapped in your NET! Despite the overwhelming odds, C1 and C2 struggled for two long hours, using all our local computing resources, in attempts to break the protection code. The result: they calculated that we would need more than a trillion years to succeed. W2 activated an atomic disintegrator on the door. It vanished, naturally, but nothing of the tunnel behind it could be seen. A huge hole was gouged out of the mountainside, and when the dust settled a few minutes later, the door reappeared, as if it had not just been super-blasted. Evidently, the only way to get through that door was to find the password first.

Which meant that we had to find the constructor of the door, and get him to open it.

We searched for traces he may have left behind, but found none. Later we also discovered that Flint—and to this day I know him only by his code name—left no footprints in the gigantic (by your standards) computers used for monitoring everything in the NET. However, we did not know that at the time, and we combed every rock and clump of dirt within a mile radius around the waterfall, in search of telltale evidence.

After fifteen hours of fruitless search, we consolidated a plan of action. We would go ahead with our original target—taking over key personnel on the planet—but we would also make use of the information we'd obtained to search out that anonymous agent that had locked us out of our world, and have him reopen the link.

First we had to develop methods by which we could safely load ourselves into humans. We now knew everything we needed to know about the human brain. C3's ultimate sacrifice rewarded us with the vital information we so desperately needed. You humans utilize only a small portion of your brain, itself about a quarter the size of an adult Ancient. In order to take over a human brain we had to compress considerable portions of our own brains, and these portions could not be used until restored. These techniques had long been perfected by our culture, and we use them regularly—notably, at our annual mind backup. G1, together with C1 and C2, modified our back-up system so that we could downsize our active brains to about a fifth of their natural size, yet retain most of our indispensable intelligence and functionality. Thus, after compressing, we had to make do without significant episodes of our glorious history, and without electro-magnetic perception throughout the entire spectrum—but humans do not possess these receptors anyway.

It took us about two days (or two Earth hours) to perfect the compression process. We made use of this time to explore your major city, Netville, quite thoroughly, but only from the air. We kept our spaceship at an altitude of ten thousand miles above the city—far higher that your highest satellite. We did not want to alert you to our existence. Using our technology, we could have detected items the size of a grain of sand from that height. We discovered several sites that would be quite easy to commandeer, as well as learning institutions and other structures whose purpose we could not fathom at the time. Later we learned that these were government offices, banks, shopping malls, etc. We did not find any "mind stadiums" or "common thought" centers, either, though they are very popular in our world.

I assume you still remember the Maureen Clarke affair, the energy diva who resigned suddenly from all her management positions, and disappeared from the public eye. The only thing she left as a legacy was a set of recording buttons, containing the designs for three new revolutionary inventions, all concerning the production of energy from seawater, and thereby finally releasing mankind from the shackles of organic fossil fuel. At the time of this recording, her inventions constitute the foundation of the entire energy market. You may recall that there were many theories about her disappearance—some said that the large energy corporations had her eliminated; others claimed that she had changed her identity and gone into hiding, or that she had contracted NET-phobia. And you may also remember that many questions were raised about the ability of an averagely educated person such as she, to develop such advanced inventions—even though her image and voice on the buttons were verified beyond doubt.

Maureen was the first human we invaded (or should I say 'occupied') successfully. She was on vacation at her NET villa, an enormous, sprawling mansion on the outskirts of Netville. While she was having a snack by the swimming pool, W2 sneaked up close to her, linked into her mind, and took over. He immediately ascended into her real brain, on Earth. This time, uploading went smoothly. W2 kept us informed continuously about the occupation stages, until eventually Maureen—or actually, the new, controlled Maureen—disappeared with a soft 'poof.' We were surprised to find out that W2 also disappeared with a similar 'poof.' It turned out that occupying a human mind was a one-way event, and there was no way back. W2 could *never* be himself again, and had to remain in Maureen's body for the rest of her days. And when she died, he would die, too.

W2 did return to us about three Earth hours later as a surfer. He resembled Maureen, but there were a few minor differences—primarily, her height; the new Maureen was half-an-inch taller than the original. This must have been another after-effect of mind occupation, and it took several more surfs for her to return to her natural Earth height. It also took her some time to adapt to the fact that her mind was now composed of the contents of two brains, and that she was now an Ancient. As we had anticipated, W2 had multiplied Maureen's intelligence by several factors—by Earth standards, she would probably rate well above the genius level.

Maureen had retained W2's telepathic powers, and she quickly educated us as to what was happening in your real world. We learned a lot from Maureen's brain—climate, governments, the very low technology level, and so on. However, despite all the various drawbacks, and despite the fact that we would have to invest dozens, if not hundreds, of years reforming your race, we found Earth to be very suitable for us. In fact, we were quite jubilant at discovering this prize planet.

The only thing that now stood between the Ancients and salvation was that blocked doorway. We *had* to ferret out this mysterious Flint! This had become our first priority.

Without delay we commenced our quest. We established our headquarters at Maureen's site, and concealed the spaceship there. W2 began browsing the major libraries in the NET, disguised as Maureen. Two of the more important institutions he discovered were Genome Applications—the main DNA research center of the California Universities—and the headquarters of the Anti-Virus Combat Division, nicknamed Babel.

The Genome Applications library was open to public access, with minor safeguards. We easily identified the head scientist of the company, Dr. Noah Atkinson, who frequently visited the library to keep himself up to date concerning the latest developments on the genetics front. It took almost two NET weeks before the opportunity to occupy him arrived. G1 hid in the library, and when he and Atkinson were alone in the reading room, he swiftly entered his mind and took over. Both of them disappeared with that familiar 'poof.' Atkinson, the soon-to-be world's leading geneticist, began at once researching methods to enable the human brain to accommodate ours in its entirety. We needed to considerably enlarge the human skull's brain capacity, and extend human life span to the maximum extent—two hundred and fifty years. I was quite prepared to sacrifice some of my crew by irretrievably occupying your limited bodies, but for the purposes of mass immigration we needed a complete solution. I believe that during those few days that G1 was Noah Atkinson, the advances in your genetic sciences outstripped all that had been accomplished during the previous hundred years.

The Babel Citadel, on the other hand, was quite a different story. It was located in downtown Netville, and massively insulated from unauthorized penetration. A high wall that curved inward and upward surrounded it, practically covering the site like a huge dome. Peppering the surface were various alarm systems, which could detect any approaching mass from hundreds of feet away. The single entrance portal was not only monitored by an uninterruptible identification system, but was also manually guarded—some of the guards were netters and some surfers.

Here we had a stroke of fantastic good luck. Maureen knew a Babel agent named George Boder, who had in the past solved the case of her husband's murder. She called him, and he suggested that they meet in the parking lot of Roller-net, a gigantic amusement park, which now, I believe, is the location of a very upscale residential area. Maureen and Noah, together with C2, ambushed George there, and he soon became one of us.

We immediately had access to the NET's security systems. We knew who was surfing, and where each surfer was. However, two problems arose. The first was that George, in his natural human form, was an exceptionally disagreeable character—a sadist and a veiled criminal. He composed a virus and launched it into the NET in order to steal money. Furthermore, he practically enslaved a surfer, who was in a coma on Earth, and, therefore, trapped in the NET. This surfer, Rupert York, owned and ran the aforementioned Roller-net for George, and was under his total control. The second problem was that George did not have sufficient authority in Babel to provide us with our needs. The only person with enough power to launch a comprehensive search for our mysterious hacker was Norman Starr, the unit's commander.

We decided that we needed to control Starr, despite our dwindling Ancient headcount. In fact, by this time there were only C1 and myself, the two senior crewmembers, who had not occupied a human body. George now convinced Norman to join him on an investigation at Roller-net, and C1 entered him there. Survival instinct must have alerted Norman at that very instant, and he tried to escape from the NET with his emergency return ring. He didn't make it alone, however—C1 was already in his brain and they surfaced to the Earth together. But something did, in fact, go wrong because, as in the case of Spindler, a copy of Norman remained in the NET.

Here George blundered gravely. He did not vaporize Norman's copy in the NET. Rather, he preferred to keep him prisoner for interrogation—or, as we know George, torture. He instructed Noah Atkinson to hold the Norman copy captive at his site. George wanted revenge on Norman for not advancing him in Babel. Apparently, George's human characteristics still dominated his Ancient identity to a larger extent than we anticipated. His error in judgment has cost our entire race its salvation.

Combing through the memories of both George and Norman, we discovered that the hottest issue on their agenda was the search for unknown individuals who had created a site called Hell, the existence of which was contrary to all NET laws. Babel had a reliable reconstruction of the site through a memory recording of one Amos Tipman, who was rescued from there in a pitiful condition. We correctly assumed that there was a connection between this mysterious site and the tunnel.

As we now controlled the security and monitoring systems in the NET, we spared no effort in locating the Hell site. At first we had no clues whatever. But then George got a message form his slave, York, indicating that he had captured three children who tried to extract money from him, and that they also were the managers of a site called Hell. George instructed York to keep the children prisoners, and to await his arrival. He also told York to begin interrogating them, and to get as much information from them as he could.

It took Norman and George half an hour to get to York's office, and they were surprised to find it empty. They entered York's subterranean amusement park, and discovered evidence of a struggle between York and the children, in which the latter overpowered him. A couple of smashed roller coaster cars were at one of the piers, but no people were around. We found an operational Transport Box, and quickly found out that it had been used ten minutes earlier to transport passengers to a nearby shopping mall. We covered the area of the mall with a fine-tooth comb, but could not pick up the trail.

This time it was our adversaries who made a grave mistake—they kidnapped York and transferred him to the Hell site. We rechecked the Transport Box and discovered that it had been used for a jump to impossible coordinates—a location two thousand feet beneath the Stanford-net research laboratories. Undaunted, we checked that specific location, and we were elated when we saw that it was a large, empty space! We had no doubt that this was where they had taken York. Presumably it could even be the entrance to the Hell site. The very entrance that Babel was searching for so intently.

We prepared ourselves for an assault on the site. The entire crew, with the exception of myself, took part in the attack. They were equipped with modern weaponry and impenetrable shields. I remained behind in the spaceship. Instead of jumping to the coordinates, we dug a shaft down to the underground cavity. Bursting in, we found it empty, but there was a deep pit in its floor—the look of which reminded us all of the space-fold tunnel we had come through from our world. We had no trouble getting down the pit—we all have personal floaters, which emit no noise. We floated down for several hundred meters and arrived at the entrance to Hell, easily identifiable from the memory recordings taken from Tipman. We succeeded in surprising the demon sentries and killing them all, but one of them managed to set off the alarm before expiring, and a gate sealed shut in front of us. We had lost the advantage of surprise.

Maureen and Noah, our first assault wave, blasted one of the walls away. It opened into the site's main hall, and the explosion had chiseled out part of the ceiling. They entered the hall and had no difficulty in overcoming the demons there (which had not expected *that* kind of entry, despite the alarm). They identified York, who was hooked up to a brain analysis machine, and tried to approach him.

Unfortunately, Noah stepped on a booby-trap and was skewered to death. Maureen activated her shield at once. The team had not activated them earlier because it severed their telepathic communications link. She examined Noah, but there was nothing anyone could do. His body resumed the form of an Ancient—the corpse of G1, our brilliant geneticist. At the same time, hundreds of demons emerged from numerous burrows and passageways, and attacked Maureen. They were equipped with pitchforks and bows and arrows, and were accompanied by giant spiders carrying barrels of boiling oil. Maureen's shield protected her from any harm, but one of the spiders fell on her, its weight totally immobilizing her. George and Norman, who by now had also entered the fray, sliced through the spider to free Maureen, and then killed all the demons that had not made their escape.

We questioned York. (I say we, even though I was not there. What I couldn't receive telepathically was later uploaded to me by George). Apparently there were three children disguised as demons, and a fourth companion, a green demon, who was a very special type of netter, and could take on any shape. The smallest one had left earlier, but the others had all been present when the alarm went off. York also added that the two remaining children were in the trio he had captured in Roller-net, that the netter was dressed in jeans and a flowery shirt, and that his name was Flint. He was also the third lad he had captured earlier, somehow now transformed into a green demon. That was good news indeed. George demonstrated his ruthlessness by blasting York into oblivion, as he sat bound to the machine. We began a search for the two children and the green demon. Maureen remained on guard by the entrance, while Norman and George combed every burrow, killing demons and other creature they encountered.

After several hours of painstaking legwork, Norman finally discovered an additional exit from Hell. He emerged into another world with gray skies and dense forests. He found no signs of the escapees anywhere, killed a limping demon that tried to attack him, and returned to the subterranean Hell the same way he exited. Fortunately for him, he had not deactivated the helmet's shield during all this time, despite the discomfort involved in lack of telepathy, and the limitations put on the other senses as well. His entry was booby-trapped with a very powerful charge, and the blast buried him under the debris of the collapsed ceiling. George and Maureen, who had left her guard post for the purpose, extricated him unharmed. We heard more explosions over to one side, and hurried in that direction. It turned out to be a diversionary tactic, and that the three refugees were trying to escape through yet another exit. Maureen managed to find them by using a vibration locator, and collared them just as they were about to leave the site. She turned off her shield to notify the rest of us telepathically, but unluckily fell into a deep, camouflaged pit. One of the escapees tossed a bomb after her, which exploded before she had time to turn her shield back on. She was probably blown to pieces while falling.

George and Norman hurried to the spot, but additional explosions blocked their way. It took them hours to clear away the rubble, only to discover that the new exit from Hell was also totally blocked with a grid password lock, similar to the one that blocked the tunnel behind the waterfall. They had no choice but to go out of Hell the way they came in. Empty handed.

The children had got the better of us. Our race, with an intellect far superior to yours, possessing technology and weapons you cannot hope to match, were defeated once again, and we had lost two of our crew. Of the seven of us who had arrived into your NET, only three now remained.

Norman and George returned to the Babel citadel, to find out if there was any additional information to assist in discovering who the children were, and who that unorthodox netter, disguised as a green demon, was. No information awaited them. Norman was seriously considering sending an investigative team to Hell and have them turn over every stone, when another stroke of sheer luck came to our rescue, and finally gave us a tangible lead.

Sven Thorensen, one of Babel's senior agents, received an anonymous message with a cryptic comment regarding George. As Sven was busy at that moment, the message was left on his mail queue. However, Og, Babel's computer, which analyzes every message entering or leaving Babel, classified the message as suspicious and transferred a copy to Norman. Norman suspected that it came from Sven's daughter, Maggie. He also deduced that she was one of the children we chased in Hell, and that she may have recognized George. He immediately sent a Babel squad to apprehend her on Earth.

Unfortunately, Maggie was not at home on Earth—neither was she surfing from anywhere else; we made quite sure of that. None of her classmates or neighbors knew where she was—she had simply vanished.

While three teams searched high and low for Maggie, George and Norman kidnapped the unsuspecting Sven in his Babel office in the NET. They took him to Maureen's site for questioning, mainly as to the whereabouts of his daughter. He was interrogated for several hours, but he really did not know where she was or whom she was surfing with. Either that, or he had a threshold to pain higher than any other human we encountered.

Then, out of the blue, a message for Norman arrived from Lynn Murphy, another senior Babel agent. A man, identical to Norman in appearance, speech and knowledge, had come into her office in Babel. She was highly suspicious of this twin, as she had been in conference with 'our' Norman just a couple of hours earlier, and the new Norman seemed slightly different. His hair was longer, his uniform was torn and wrinkled, and he was accompanied by two suspicious looking youngsters. She had clandestinely checked out the NET monitors for Norman's link to the NET, and discovered that he was at Maureen's site, and not in Babel. She concluded that the Norman in front of her was an imposter, froze him and his two companions, and called our Norman.

It was quite evident that the Norman copy had somehow gotten loose, and had assisted two of the youngsters from Hell to penetrate into Babel with the intention of harming us. Lynn was ordered not to defrost the three, but to wait until our Norman arrived there. He arrived half an hour later. George came, too, but he remained hidden in case this happened to be a trap. And a trap, indeed, it was.

Lynn and another Babel official, Kumar, waylaid our Norman and finished him off. They had only pretended to freeze the three intruders. But George intervened and turned the tables. He activated his shield, burst into the room, and did away with Lynn and Kumar. The two youngsters were now his captives.

The Norman copy had disappeared, but that was of secondary importance. The main thing was that Flint and Troy, the saboteurs who had blocked the tunnel, were in our hands! At last, after heavy losses, we had achieved our goal. The key to the door!

George froze the duo, and took them to Maureen's site, where I was waiting in the spaceship and where Sven was held captive. George's cruel streak was of advantage at this point—he tortured the three of them until Flint broke down and agreed to open the tunnel for us.

But then another predicament occurred. Two tetrosaurs, gigantic creatures that you raise in the NET for sport and genetic research, barged suddenly into Maureen's site and stormed us. Two surfers rode the tetrosaurs, one of them a young boy whom George suspected was Troy's younger brother. I could not use the spaceship's armament against them, as the radiation could have killed the captives as well.

George hastily bundled the prisoners into the spaceship. He managed to hit one of the tetrosaurs, but was then tackled from behind by an enormous gorilla, that belonged to the young boy. He had barely managed to overcome the ape and enter the ship, when the other tetrosaur rammed violently into the spaceship and knocked it on its side, severely damaging the outer hull. We were forced to abandon the mother ship, and use our last small cruiser to transport us, and the prisoners, to the waterfall.

We arrived there about an hour later. George alighted with Flint and Troy, and tortured Troy some more in order to get Flint to open the door to the tunnel. However, when the door was finally opened, it became clear that Flint's submissive manner and cooperation were all a sham. They had set a trap for us!

Behind the door was a well-prepared ambush force of Babel commandos, led by Norman Starr who had somehow managed to return to himself. A powerful laser beam, fired from a laser cannon inside the tunnel, struck my ship, knocking it off balance and setting it on fire. It started falling into the deep canyon by the waterfall. I managed to activate the emergency engines at the last moment, and somewhat stabilized the ship, but I couldn't put out the fire.

I ascended as high as the wounded spaceship would go and headed toward Netville, initially thinking to escape back to the damaged mother ship. At first I had my hands so full that I could not follow the events happening to George. When I finally got things under partial control, the com-

munication link with him was severed. He had probably turned his shield or
It was renewed suddenly, and I heard him shriek for help. He had fallen int
the lake at the base of the waterfall, and was trying to get out, calling for m
all the while. It lasted only for a few seconds—I caught the image of a tree
like creature slamming him against a rock. To this day I can remember hi
death scream.

But I had no time to mourn his loss—I was too busy saving myself. I wa
indeed at a high altitude, but it was quite apparent that my time was limite
and that the ship was doomed. I kept the ship on course at low speed. I wa
losing altitude at an alarming rate. So I formed a different plan. I decide
that instead of going to Maureen's place, where you were certainly expect
ing me, to get to a random place in Netville and bail out at the last momen
before crashing without you humans noticing it. Therefore, after half an hou
of relatively slow and steady progress, when I was pretty sure that you ha
all calculated the exact coordinates where I would land, I suddenly acceler
ated and changed course.

The spaceship crashed within five seconds, but it was several miles awa
from where you were all waiting. One second prior to the impact, I set ar
explosive device in the ship and jumped out, enveloped in my protective hel
met—the only one left on board that was not converted to fit a human head.

The violent explosion prevented onlookers from noticing the small bub
ble in which I drifted down to the ground, a couple of thousand feet awa
from the crash site.

I turned off my shield and found myself in a small garden belonging to
NET site. Next to me was a human being, whose eyes almost popped out o
their sockets in terror when he saw me, a ten-foot-tall monster. This was th
young David Mansfield. I heard the sirens of the rescue teams approaching
and knew I had to make an ultra-fast decision. Before Mansfield coul
twitch a muscle, I entered his brain and went up to Earth with him.

At first I was very wary that I'd be tracked down as David Mansfield
But, as it turned out, no one saw the bubble landing in his site. I decided t
take advantage of the fact that now I could not be suspected of anything, an
was resolved to enter the NET and catch Flint on my own. I returned t
Mansfield's site in the NET, found my helmet, and buried it.

Then I suddenly lost consciousness.

I woke up in an Earth hospital, and discovered the bitter truth. When Mansfield first set eyes on me he was so traumatized that he contracted NET-phobia then and there! He could never again surf the NET—and neither could I! Any attempt to do so would result in an immediate blackout, or worse—coma, or even death.

And that was the end of our attempt to take over the Earth. There was no one left in the NET who could ever even hope to open the tunnel and let my people through. I tried to locate Maureen, but I couldn't penetrate the formidable isolation in which she brooded. I didn't need to investigate what happened to Noah Atkinson. It was in all the news editions. The renowned geneticist who succumbed to NET-phobia while surfing, recovered, and became the world's leading brain researcher despite being unable to surf. I assume you're monitoring him constantly.

Nothing else was published. Billions of people on your planet do not know that they owe their lives to a young lad and his mysterious partner.

It took me a full year to decide which path I'd take. At first I considered suicide, but that would be a shameful waste. David Mansfield was, at the time of my takeover, a computer technician at a firm named Super-Brain. He—that is, I—quit my job, and enrolled in an academic physics course, so that genuine diplomas would justify my knowledge. It took me two years to complete my studies, made ten-fold more difficult due to the fact that I could not use the NET as an academic short cut. I completed my PhD thesis on manufacturing tiny black holes by compressing mass in high acceleration systems. The Acceleration Principle that I theorized, known today as the Mansfield Principle and into which I shall not go here, earned me my first Nobel Prize and the initial capital for my company. The rest is in your history books.

Troy and Flint—I really searched for you the first few years, but I failed everywhere I turned. Sven Thorensen and his daughter, Maggie, were just as elusive. This, of course, was deliberate and quite understandable—the entire affair was, and probably still is, classified as top secret. I had to do everything on my own—hiring detectives would have exposed me at once. After a few years I gave up the search, reconciling myself to the conviction that a meeting with any of you could not possibly bring any benefit to either party.

People of Earth—I shall probably be dead when you read this document, but I assure you that every word in it is true! I have no complaints and hold no grudges as I leave your world. Your struggle against us was brave and just. If it weren't for a bunch of kids and their computer creations, we would have unhesitatingly destroyed every single one of you. Exactly as you would have destroyed pesky mosquitoes or locusts.

I wish to bestow a gift on you humans—a gift I could not bequeath while still alive. My spaceship, the mother ship in which we arrived at the NET, is still a mystery to you. You have certainly tried to mine its treasures, but I know you have failed. Had you succeeded, I would have noticed several revolutionary technological developments occurring over the decades. True, there were some remarkable scientific breakthroughs, but I know that none of them could have come from learning the spaceship's secrets.

I am hereby giving you the code for opening the ship. At the rear end of the ship is a locked door. You have not opened this door—it is virtually impossible to crack. And you could not break the walls, since they are infinitely flexible and cannot be breached. Not with the current technologies you have. Key the numbers listed below into the lock, and it will open. There are over three thousand digits in that list, so enter them carefully and in the given sequence.

Inside the cabin you will find helmets hooked into the ship's computer. The ship is irreparable and cannot fly anymore, but the entire knowledge base of the Ancient's lore, wisdom, science and technology are in that computer. Your race will prosper to levels hitherto undreamed. You will find solutions to many of the problems facing you today, and to many others you will face in the coming millennia. The only thing for which we do not have a solution is escaping from black holes. Perhaps you'll come up with that one. Then, if you're strong enough, you may still be in time to find my world on the other side of the tunnel, and offer them their salvation. If it's still there.

Farewell, people of the Earth,

K1, captain of spaceship 30X25, alias David B. Mansfield, Columbus, Ohio.

The End